Zoar

Book Two

Camella Wade

Contents

Part I

Chapter One ~ The Domain

A voice whispers my name from within the black abyss, "Althea."

The sound echoes like overlapping ripples in water. I listen hard, but I still cannot determine from which direction it came. It is a familiar voice.

As the echoes die away, I realize where I have heard the voice. The Spirits, it is the voices from the Domain.

This is it! I am finally leaving Neoinas! I have been stuck in this silent purgatory for what feels like an eternity.

I did my duty as the Dreamer and stopped the sodocs from destroying magic by destroying their lair, an inverted pyramid with strong magical protection. We were not sure how Zixus, the leader of the sodocs, created the Pyramid. We had a few pieces of information, but nowhere near the whole puzzle. The one thing we were sure of was that it had to be destroyed along with Zixus himself to stop him from destroying magic. That was the only way to save the world.

With the help of the pixies, the spirits from the Domain, and my friends, I carried out my task to stop the sodocs. The pixies gave me the key to accessing my powers: the mark of magic – a circle intertwined within a triangle to form a shield which protects me from outside magic and a funnel to strengthen and focus my own magic. I used my powers and the Pyramid crumbled along with everything and everyone in it, including me. That is why I am currently stuck in Neoinas watching the playback of my life over and over within my bodiless mind like a film reel.

After the echoes fade back into silence, the surrounding void fades with them. I am in the Domain.

I am back in my body!

I fall upon my knees, wrap my arms tight around my middle, and let the warm tears wash down my face.

I can cry!

I gasp and choke at the feeling of finally being able to cry again. Now that I have started, though, I am not sure I can stop.

I stay curled up on my knees inside the beautiful rainbow nebula known as the Domain until the voices once again whisper my name. This time it is louder than a whisper, but just barely.

I look up; no one is here.

"Althea," the voices of the spirits sound the same now as I remember them before, "your work is not finished. The Pyramid's destruction was not the end of this war. We were not aware. We are sorry. This war has gone far past the terror of Zixus and his sodocs."

The tears rolling down my face cease with dread. Their words repeat in my mind before I am able to stand on my feet and reply, "What do you mean?"

The voices of the Spirits reply without skipping a beat, their melodious echo fills every crevice within the Domain. "Malice causes damage. Malice and ignorance cause devastation."

I cannot help but laugh a little. That sounds like something Nedra or Pilate would say. Oh, how I miss them! I wonder if they are okay. I hope they are still alive.

The Spirits' words pull me out of my thoughts before I

drown in them, "Zixus caused damage with his plan to rule the world. We thought when you destroyed the Pyramid, that threat would be ended. That was not the end of it, however. Inside of the Pyramid, Zixus had trapped wild magic. We are still not sure how he managed to trap wild magic in the first place. Our only deductions are that your predecessors gave him the knowledge. Knowledge that cost them their lives. That magic is now loose, set free from the Pyramid, and taking over the world. If it is not stopped, nothing will survive."

What are they saying? This does not make any sense. "What? How does wild magic take over the world? I thought it was only found in secluded places untouched by man or fae."

"Imagine the world is a giant garden. If the garden is not maintained and grows wild, the weeds steal nutrients away from the produce. They grow taller and stronger covering everything in their path. Before long, all that remains are the weeds. Wild magic is like weeds. With nothing to control it, it will not take long to destroy everything on this planet until only it remains. That means no humans, no fae, no hegira, no human realm, no Reverie including Sengsourya and Ceres. Everything we know would be gone and replaced by the tangled growth of wild magic."

Wow. That is a lot to take in all at once.

You would think I would be used to this shock by now.

"So, lack of magic destroys the world, and too much magic destroys the world. What is it I am supposed to do? I am assuming you do want me to do something."

"You are still the Dreamer. Only you have the power necessary to save the world, and magic. You will return to Reverie, rejoin your friends and allies, and solve this problem."

Great, here we go again. "I do not suppose you would have any advice on how to do that would you?"

"You have grown so much on your journey already, more than you know, Althea. You will know what to do when the time is right. Now, go."

Chapter Two ~ Back from the Dead

I open my eyes to see Aspen leaning close to my face. She and some nearby companions gasp loudly.

I try to sit up so I can look around. Unfortunately, vertigo takes over, and I am forced to lie down and close my eyes again.

Nedra immediately checks on me through our link. I can tell by the sound of his voice that he has been crying. "Althea, you are alive! Wait, what is wrong? Are you okay?"

I hear him growl, and Aspen heatedly shouts back, "Do not blame me! I have done everything I can. Without me she would have died hours ago!"

I hear hurried footsteps rushing in our direction. Apuri's voice stands out among the shouting chaos like smooth honey. "He knows, Aspen. We all know. Nedra was just startled and worried."

He is closer now, right over me. I know without seeing that he is looking down at me. He speaks to Aspen in a soothing voice, "You go rest; I will sit with her. If she wakes again, I will send for you."

I hear a huff of stubbornness from Aspen and then her slowly retreating footsteps.

I try to open my eyes again, but they feel like solid lead. I realize my head is throbbing and the rest of my body feels like I was run over by stampeding elephants. I manage a small moan, and Apuri, sitting at my side, places his hand on mine. He whispers something, but it is too quiet for me to understand. He starts wiping my forehead with a cool wet cloth.

Before I drift off, I whisper to Nedra through our link, "I am alive!"

* * * * * * * * * *

I am not sure where I am. All I see is green. Green moss, grass, and leaves from trees, vines, and bushes are everywhere. It looks like a jungle.

It must be somewhere in Reverie though because they have that certain magical glow coming from within them. I follow a trail of thick braided vines beneath my feet.

I stumble no further than ten feet when my heart stops and slams into my throat.

This is definitely not Reverie.

The braided vines have coiled themselves around a highway speed limit sign. All that remains is the top half of the sign, from the top of the numbers up. There is no other sign of civilization.

I stand and watch, appalled, as the vine continues, sprouting flowers and other small greeneries until the sign is completely consumed. Now there is nothing left of it whatsoever!

This must be wild magic.

But what happened to the people? I turn in circles looking for any sign of human existence.

Nothing.

I feel the blood drain from my face. I think I may be sick. The Spirits were right.

How am I going to fix this?

* * * * * * * * * *

I feel eyes watching me; the hairs on my body stand on

end and a warm tingling sensation tickles at the base of my skull and the tips of my fingers. My eyes flash open; I quickly take in my surroundings looking for the threat. It takes my eyes a moment to adjust to the dim light provided by a nearby campfire. Muffled voices are all around me. I sit up as fast as I can and get into a defensive position. Something bad is happening; I can feel it.

"Althea, stay calm. Tell me what is wrong." Nedra's voice rings clear as a bell through our private link.

"Nedra?" I ask aloud.

"I am here," he replies softly through our link.

I close my eyes tight and open them again slowly. I focus on controlling my breathing and have another look around. Someone touches my hand; it is Apuri. The initial urge to withdraw my hand dissolves, and I smile up at him. It is so good to see his strong sand-textured face again, and those eyes, such warmth and comfort harbored in those eyes. I relax against him and look around again. It is still dark, but with the light from the campfire I am able to pick out faces amongst the crowd: Aspen, Tilda, Clementine, Saffi. Is everyone here?

Wait a minute; where are we? I search for a clue, but it is too dark.

"Some light," I mumble aloud thinking to myself what would aid in my search.

Before I even have time to blink, an enormous bright light appears high above the campsite setting everything within a hundred-foot radius aglow.

Everyone, including myself, gasps. I look around to find the source of the light. Whoever made it must be pretty powerful. The best I could ever muster with light was barely a few feet. Everywhere I look eyes are staring back at me.

"Althea," Nedra whispers to me privately, "this is *your* magic." He sounds just as amazed as everyone looks.

I look down at my hands, then back at the light.

I did *that?*

It is unbelievable. There is no way! It dims and quickly

blinks out, submerging us once more in that darkness lit only by the dim orange glow of the campfire. My heart races.

I brace myself and slowly turn to look at Apuri. His face reflects my own shock but with a hint of wonder. I shrug slightly to show him I have no answers.

Movement behind Apuri catches my eye. I turn slightly to see around him and find a figure lying on a bedroll further behind us away from the fire. I sit up to get a better look.

Apuri follows my gaze and answers before I can ask, "Tsar."

Something in his voice lingers like bitter lemon juice on an empty stomach.

"Tsar? But, but he - Stix; I saw him!" I fumble over the words. The last time I saw Tsar, his father, Zixus - also known as Stix by his adversaries - had pierced and shattered Tsar's branch woven chest with an iron hammer. He should be dead right now. I can see the delicate forms of Lady Nell and Noni on either side of him – the movement that caught my attention.

"I am good at what I do." Aspen speaks in a matter-of-fact tone. "It does not look good, but he is still here, for now."

Now aware of the presence of the rest of my companions, I realize I have not seen or heard Not.

"Notyal! Where is Not? Is he okay?" Panic sets in. What am I going to tell Mel?

"He is okay," both Nedra and Apuri say together. Nedra hums deeply and continues, "He went down to the lake to rehydrate and relax for a bit. I am sure he is already on his way back after seeing your bright light. Althea, what happened?"

For the first time since waking tonight, I turn to look at Nedra. I know I could share everything with him in an instant by removing that mental block. But a whisper of that dread from Neoinas slips into my thoughts and I keep the wall in place, for now. I can feel everyone's unasked questions, all their eyes watching me.

Aspen, the diligent healer, notices my stress and shoos everyone away. "That is enough excitement for now. The

Dreamer still has a lot of healing to do. Let her finish resting now. We will have time to talk more in the morning. Althea, I will send Not by before we all retire for the night."

Everyone heeds her instruction and goes back to bed.

I lie back down on my own bed roll and hold Apuri's hand. I can feel him and Nedra watching me. I know they have questions. Heck, I still have questions. I cannot answer theirs yet.

I know Nedra can feel my block in our link. I appreciate him not pushing me to talk.

I remember when we were reunited after Nedra was taken by the sodocs. He kept his block and would not share his horrors with me. It was something he needed to work through on his own first.

I glance up. I can see in his eyes that he is thinking of the same memories. I reach my free hand out and touch his leg.

I speak softly through our link, "I am sorry, my friend. I did not mean to make you go there again."

He shakes himself out of his thoughts and smiles down at me. "We will get through this together." I return the smile.

Apuri clears his throat to let us know Not is returning. I sit up just as he reaches us and meet him for a hug. We embrace tightly sharing love and emotions better communicated through contact than words. As we separate I laugh to shake the lump in my throat and wipe the tears from my face.

"Did you enjoy your swim?"

He smiles and replies, "Oh yes, and I was able to get a message to Mel. We should hear back from her in a couple of days. It is good to see you awake. But we can discuss this later; Aspen said you needed rest. I, too, could use a good sleep," he finishes with a yawn.

He retrieves his bedroll and retires for the night. Nedra and Apuri assure me they will stay by my side the whole time.

Morning finally comes after a restless night of haunted dreams. Unfortunately, being awake does not put them further from my mind as I had hoped. I hear Apuri snoring softly beside me and gently slide from under my blanket to keep from waking him.

I laugh to myself remembering a time when I was always the last one awake, savoring every minute of sleep. All of that has changed now. Everything has changed.

I stand up staring down at my empty side of blankets, wondering how things would be now if I had not quit my boring office job and gone to the park on that hectic day. What if I chose not to follow Pilate into the unknown Painted Forest?

No matter how the events of my life would have turned out in an alternate reality, I know one thing for sure, I am happy. Here and now I am happy. My dreams flash through my mind and my insides clench as if to challenge the thought.

Still, even with the threat of wild magic and the task to once again save the world, I feel I am truly myself living the life I was meant to live. And for that I am happy.

Nedra interrupts my thoughts, reminding me I am not alone. "Good morning, Althea! How are you feeling?" I can sense his excitement at me being up but also his hesitation on if I should be.

I laugh as I turn to him and reach out a hand to rub his smooth ivory head. His beautiful bone colored scales never cease to fascinate me. Their raw natural color is more beautiful than any gem around, and the deep red glow of his embers beneath only serve to highlight that beauty even more. I continue rubbing his head up one of his strong black horns and down to the other skipping just over the teardrop-shaped silver laced obsidian in his forehead.

It is an exact match to my amulet and the key to our private link. It is amazing how something so small and simple could hold such great power, allowing two people to communicate endlessly without another soul's interruption or knowing. It is a reminder just how special Nedra is, not just to me, but in his own right as well. Dragons, like pixies, are one of the last living creatures of old magic, powerful, raw, and pure.

It sounds kind of like wild magic.

That is it! That is where I start! The thought burns through me. I cannot contain my excitement. "That is it!" I shout again, aloud this time.

"What is 'It'?" Nedra asks.

"I will explain later," I reply through our link.

Apuri, Not, and a few others sleeping nearby jump up from their bed rolls ready to defend against an unseen attacker. Excited about my idea, I leave no time for them to understand or adjust. I simply kiss Apuri and run into the group of sleepers in search of help.

"Althea!" Apuri and Nedra yell together, though I am the only one to hear Nedra through our link. That being the easiest route, I quickly give him a synopsis of the events underway to destroy the world and my most recent revelation about wild magic being closely linked with dragons and pixies. I explain that I am now on my way to find Tilda, the water advisor.

Nedra says he will do his best to contact the Chobudda to help.

I find her not far away in a somewhat secluded spot with her family – Indri, her partner, and Idona, their daughter. I do not, however, see their pixie, Mitzi.

I wake Tilda as quietly as possible and gesture for her to follow me away from her sleeping family. She looks at Indri and Idona and nods before following silently behind me.

I never thought about her family when I saw her earlier. A pang of guilt shoots through me. I should not have woken her. She should be with her family. Really, none of them should even be here. That reminds me, I do not know where *here* is.

When we have walked far enough to talk comfortably without waking everyone, I stop fast and turn around. I make sure I speak first before she can ask any questions.

"I know you have questions, and I will try to answer them. But I have a few questions I need you to answer. First, where are we?" I look around again trying to get some clue, but nothing looks familiar. "And second, where is Mitzi?"

Tilda's mouth hangs open for a minute; then, she shuts it quickly causing a slight ripple throughout her face. Her beautiful skin is literally flowing water. Her magical, and still somewhat creepy, sand textured eyes stare at me in confusion. She answers slowly as if she is unsure of the answer herself, "We are in Reverie, and Mitzi is still with the other pixies in the Deep Dark Forest. Why? What is going on, Althea?"

I sigh in disappointment. I really need to speak to the pixies. I guess I will have to tell her eventually. Like with Nedra, I quickly sum up what has happened since the fall of the Pyramid and Zixus. Relieved she does not ask anything about Neoinas, I skip to my meeting with the Spirits inside the Domain and the trouble with wild magic being free. She looks confused at first, but then shrugs and nods to herself muttering.

I give her a minute to process everything.

While she is doing this, I let my thoughts drift back to the last time I saw the pixies and Louveri. Louveri! My heart almost stops at the thought of seeing her again. With all of my adventures of destroying the Pyramid, being trapped in Neoinas, and then coming back to life after going to the Domain, finding Louveri again felt like nothing more than another dream. I laugh at the thought, "Just another dream," for the Dreamer.

Pulling myself out of my own thoughts, I tell Nedra to keep searching for Mitzi. They need to know what is happening, and we need answers. While he tries to find her through the link again, I tell Tilda what we are doing.

She nods in understanding, but her face turns serious, business first. This is the Tilda I remember, the one I met in Inon. That feels like a lifetime ago. "We must tell the others about this. Now." She turns and starts walking back toward the camp.

She stops briefly by her family and kisses Indri on the forehead, his short gray fur ruffles softly at her breath. As she rejoins my side and continues walking to the middle of the camp she says, "He will know where I am when he wakes."

I steal another glance back at her family. Again, I wonder why they are here and not back home in Inon.

It does not take long for us to reach Clementine, the nature advisor, and another one of my dear friends.

Clementine is already awake and having a private little picnic. I smile at the yimi berry sandwich and sweet rose tea. It was a meal we shared together on our first day of meeting while we traveled for me to be paired with a dragon. I was filled with so many emotions that day: excitement, fear, doubt. I was so overwhelmed then, but I made it through.

Clementine and her magical tea were one of the first steps for me accepting this new wondrous path of being the Dreamer after following Pilate into Reverie and meeting him in his quaint little book shop, *Find It*.

I smile at the picture of him sitting in his oversized armchair surrounded by mountains of books. His bright light bobbed at the end of a single antenna just between his two rounded mouse ears allowing him to easily read his current choice of books for the day.

Pilate! I bet he can help. His help was more than priceless the last time. I ask Nedra to reach out to Nook, Pilate's dragon, as well and see if there is anything he knows. The thought of seeing Pilate again makes me smile. I honestly thought I would never see my little friend again. Pilate is the one who led me into Reverie and watched over me until I got here. I wonder what he is doing now. Is he snuggled up in his oversized chair reading a book in his cozy shop? Or is he out somewhere in the middle of all this mess?

I look around at the camp. In my haste for answers, I overlooked everyone here. Everyone who helped save me and the world. I see Tsar in his secluded sanctuary with Lady Nell and Noni. My heart aches for them. Again, I see Zixus smashing Tsar's chest with a large iron hammer. I clutch my own chest in response to the memory. I have not even talked to them yet. How could I be so rude? Lady Nell was there for me when she had no obligation to be. We developed a sisterly bond I thought I would never have with anyone again after Louveri died.

"Althea!" Clementine and Tilda are shouting. They share a look that says they are not sure I am well.

I wipe a tear from my eye and smile at them. "I am sorry, but there is someone I must see right now. I will be right back; I promise."

I leave them at Clementine's picnic and walk as fast as I can, without attracting too much attention, to see Lady Nell.

As I arrive by their secluded camp, I see they are still asleep. I sigh and turn to leave when Tsar lets out a rough cough. I turn back to check if he is okay and see his hand raise slightly off his chest. I proceed cautiously to not wake his protective duo.

Lady Nell lies less than a foot from Tsar wrapping herself and her blanket around her daughter. Noni's red curls peeking from under the edge of the blanket are the only evidence she is here.

I softly step over to Tsar's other side and crouch down on my knees. His chest is wrapped entirely in long bandages made of woven green blades. The quality of wrapping is evidence of Aspen's experience. I wonder how long she has been a healer. Tsar coughs again, trying to speak. I lean my ear right by his mouth so he does not have to strain as much.

"Thank you, Dreamer," he whispers before coughing again.

"I should let you rest," I say before shifting back on my feet to go. He catches my arm to stop me. I look at him. Our eyes only meet for a brief moment, but that look will haunt me for a lifetime. Within his icy blue eyes I see the haunting void of Neoinas. I never thought of him being there.

I shudder then look back at Tsar taking care not to look into his eyes.

He gestures for me to come closer to listen. I lean down. "You have changed," he whispers. "How?"

Not sure what he means or what to say, I mutter, "I am

sorry. I do not know. You really should rest, Tsar." The words echo in memory of Aspen's orders to myself, and a wave of guilt flushes to my cheeks. At least I am able to walk. I look again at Tsar. If I had just denied his request to kill Zixus he would be fine right now. I rest my right hand on his shoulder. I wish I had healing powers to go along with the rest. I close my eyes and picture Tsar's body being filled with magical healing light.

My hand feels warm and then I feel a tingle at the base of my skull. I feel a warmth travel from my core through my arm and out my hand into Tsar. He gasps, and my head instantly hurts, a splitting pain on the right side of my head just behind my ear. I quickly shut my eyes and grab my head to stop the pain.

"Althea!" I hear Nedra shout through our link.

"Nedra," I try to speak to him through our link, but I cannot complete the thought. I feel drained, and I cannot focus.

I hear footsteps approaching quickly, but I cannot open my eyes to see who it is. I feel myself being lifted off the ground before I black out again.

My heart is racing. I try to breathe, to calm down, but I cannot. I open my eyes slowly, afraid of what I will see.

I gulp, trying to swallow the lump in my throat. I knew what was coming; I do not know why I am so shocked. Trees. Trees everywhere. Some are saplings no bigger than my pinky. Some are huge. "Ancient," they whisper in my mind.

But I know they are not ancient. There is no way. The trees, all of them, are growing through houses and driveways. The little ones barely make an impression where they sprout, but the larger ones, the ancients, uproot entire structures.

This is a dream. I know I am dreaming, but the dread of what lies before me tells me this may not be a future occurrence.

I think this is happening now.

I have to wake up. I have to tell the others.

* * * * * * * * *

I wake up with a gasp. I open my eyes to see everyone standing over me again. The face that has my attention, though, is Aspen's.

"I told you to rest!" she breathes through clenched teeth.

I catch my breath and try to explain, "I know, but I had this dream. And then I remembered what the Spirits said. So, I talked to Nedra and that led to the pixies, which is why I went to see Tilda. But then I saw Tsar, and I felt so bad about what happened. And then, and then, I'm not really sure what happened next."

Aspen purses her lips, flares her nostrils, and closes her eyes. "Okay," she says and opens her eyes with a more understanding look on her face. "I know that we are still in trouble. The birds are talking, and it does not sound good. And," she continues, holding her hand up to stop me from butting in, "I know you are the Dreamer and this is your job. But!" She practically shouts to keep my attention, "We need to know what is going on. What happened to you after the Pyramid fell? Why have you changed?"

"Changed? Tsar said that too just before- What happened anyway?"

"Well, you healed Tsar by transferring light energy from within yourself to him. Not entirely healed him, but a good amount. He is now able to speak without pain. Now, why have you changed? What happened?"

"I am sorry, I really do not know what you are talking about."

Nedra chimes in through our link, "Althea, have you looked at the mark of magic since waking?"

I glance down at my left wrist where Mitzi, Tilda's pixie, marked me with a tattoo of sorts. The Mark of Magic, of Reverie, is a triangle intertwined with a circle. It enhances my own magic - magic that I am still learning about - while shielding me from harm. It was a simple, pale white mark like a scar. Now it is surrounded by a splash of colors, like the

Domain itself.

"Here, use this." Lady Nell hands me a small mirror. I did not see her sitting just behind me. I am surprised she left Tsar's side. Something has changed in her, too. Her spirit is broken. I take the mirror and flip it open, not sure what I am going to see.

"Whoa!" I say aloud. Now I see what everyone is hyped up about. The Mark is not the only thing that changed in the Domain. My eyes are now two swirling vortexes of rainbow clouded irises.

I take a deep breath and let it out slowly. Then I brace myself and look at the huddled crowd around me. "Okay," I say to them, "I think it is time I catch you all up on our current events." I recount my story starting from when I entered the Pyramid in South Carolina.

By the time I finish the story with me waking up at this camp, everybody is gaping at me silently. I cannot tell if their mouths or eyes are opened wider. The awkward silence makes me wonder if I should have left my experience in Neoinas out. Even Nedra is speechless. I take advantage of our private link.

"Nedra, why does someone not say something? I am not sure what else to say," I finish lamely.

He grunts - a deep, short rumbling that resembles a growl more than his comforting chortle. Everyone snaps out of their shock driven stupor, shutting their mouths and remembering to blink.

Nedra replies, "I understand why you did not, but you should have told me all of this sooner. Now that we know everything, perhaps we can help more." Not sure what to say in return, I simply shrug my shoulders and nod.

As I glance at the faces around me I see Tsar lying back on the ground. I cannot see his eyes now, but I know he is reliving his own experience in Neoinas. I know he heard my story. I wonder if he had a similar trip through the Domain before waking back in his body here. Lady Nell sees me watching Tsar and adjusts her position to close the gap that allowed me to see him. She whispers something to Noni who hops up off her mother's lap and runs to Tsar quietly, curls bouncing all the while.

I glance up at Lady Nell meeting her eyes for just a moment before Tilda breaks the silence. In that brief moment I am able to feel a swarm of emotions from the traveling gypsy: confusion, sadness, pity perhaps, but mostly anger.

She blames me for what happened to him. And why shouldn't she? I blame myself. My cheeks warm and I choke on my emotions coughing to clear my throat before turning my attention to Tilda.

Tilda is, as always, business first. Whether she saw the glance between Lady Nell and myself or not, she is not going to let it get in the way.

"I am sorry, Althea, that you had to endure that time in Neoinas. It is not something many look forward to in life. Still, we have a very pressing matter at hand. If your dreams of wild magic taking over are current happenings as opposed to premonitions, it is even more pressing. Nedra, please keep trying to reach Mitzi, and let us know as soon as you have. You were right in thinking the pixies would have the most answers about wild magic. We will go see them together as soon as possible and get our answers. Aspen, when will she be able to travel?"

Aspen looks at me with more understanding in her eyes, understanding and, if I am not mistaken, admiration. She softly stammers out a reply to Tilda – all the while keeping her eyes on me - as if still lost in thought. "Travel? Yes, she may, I mean, maybe tomorrow?" She reaches out a hand requesting to see the mark on my wrist. I extend my hand and she gingerly grasps the sides of my wrist between her thumb and forefinger. With her other hand hovering slightly over the mark, she turns my arm one way then the other.

With the studious look of a doctor examining her first mystery illness, she mutters, almost inaudibly, "Think of water. Do not conjure it, just think of it."

Not sure what else to do, I follow her instructions. I close my eyes and do my best to force everything out of my mind except the thought of water. The image of Tilda's magical staircase – a flowing spiral staircase that wraps around a giantess of a tree from the ground to the door at the base of the canopy. It flows like an escalator carrying its subject to their desired destination to or from the water advisor's home. I think of the tranquil sound of the water, that of a gentle stream, and the ever-changing translucent colors from blue to green to brown and all the tones in between.

I feel a slight tingle on my wrist and at the base of my skull, the same feeling just before I blacked out by Tsar. I open my eyes and see the colors around the mark have changed to those blues, browns, and greens of the water, and they are actively swirling upon my skin.

Aspen lowers her hovering hand but maintains her hold on my wrist. "Now fire," she says simply. I close my eyes again, clearing my mind. I picture the small flame I first controlled in Queen Melanomie's private quarters in the water realm, Ceres. I am careful not to conjure the small flame, simply admire the memory of it. The warm colors, the way it danced slowly at first, then jumped, and twisted with more energy.

"Look," Aspen commands gently. I once again open my eyes to see the colors have changed. The blues and greens have dissolved into bright warm yellows, reds, and oranges. The warm tingle on the mark and at the base of my skull increases slightly.

Aspen is smiling. "Such a gift," she breathes in a whisper.

"Okay," I say, slightly unsure. "So, it is directly connected with my magic, but what about earlier? What happened to me when I was with Tsar?"

Everyone looks at Aspen, hanging on her every word. She smiles and asks, "Did you see a color, like with these elements, when you were with Tsar?"

I try to remember exactly what happened. "Yes, I

remember thinking, 'This is all my fault.' And I desperately wished I could just make him better. I wished I could heal him. And then, I felt something within myself, something warm. It was a golden light, much like the warm rays in the sky when we travel by light. It grew here," I place my free hand over my middle, "and it spread up my body and into my arm like a channel. It was like I could see it going from inside me into Tsar. I knew whatever it was, it would help him. It grew brighter and warmer, and then, that was it."

Aspen is wearing a big grin now. I think her face might just split in two. She releases my wrist and claps her hands together in pure joy. I do not think I have ever seen Aspen this giddy. It is actually somewhat amusing. She presses her hands together against her mouth in an attempt to contain her excitement. The shriek of a hawk escapes her lips, and she quickly presses her hands tighter. She breathes to calm herself, lowers her hands to her lap, and, still smiling like an overly proud mother, says with too much excitement, "Do you not see? In addition to all your other amazing gifts, you also have the ability to heal!"

Everyone around me expresses their admiration at my powers. Even Lady Nell relaxes some, and something in her eyes changes. I can still see a struggle of emotions on her face, but we will have time later to talk. I am still not sure what to say, but it seems I do not have to. Aspen, unable to contain herself any longer shrieks, "I am not the only one anymore!"

Immediately embarrassed by her outburst, she lowers her voice back to its normal quietness and explains, "You will be able to help me heal everyone! I will train you, of course, much like Queen Melanomie did with the elements. It is just so exciting! I have been the only healer for a long time." Her excited tone drops slightly at the end, but she continues smiling to hide it.

Clementine, sounding almost as excited as Aspen, jumps into the conversation. "I wonder if you have even more abilities! What about powers like the hegira? What about truth like Ver-" She quickly stops herself. Verity was the truth advisor. She was one of the first to die in the recent battle against the sodocs. I saw it happen in one of my dreams. She was stabbed, from the back, through the stomach. Her pure white dress and skin was quickly stained crimson with her blood. She saw me, or perhaps only knew through her abilities that I would see her, and whispered her last plea for me to hurry. That one word haunted so many hours spent in Neoinas. "Hurry!"

"Althea."

I realize Apuri, Not, and Nedra are trying to return me to the current world. Their repeated echoes bring me back, and I quickly smile to hide my fear. I know they can see it, but it does not need to be addressed, not yet.

Aspen, seeing my distress, quickly changes the subject to more current matters. "You asked about traveling," she addresses Tilda. "If she agrees – I could talk her through it – with Althea's help we could all be ready by first light tomorrow."

They both look at me. It is my decision. They insinuate it is my decision, but really, just like this whole journey, it is not my decision. I have to help. It is my duty. We must do everything possible to hurry and save the world, again. I nod to say that I am in, and the crowd breaks apart. Everyone immediately returns to pack up their personal belongings and prepare for the journey tomorrow.

It is only now that I realize the other advisors are not present; Tilda and Clementine are the only ones here. They are more than Advisors, though: they are my friends, as are Aspen and Lady Nell. I must remember to make time to talk with Lady Nell one-on-one. We cannot have personal feelings getting in the way of this mission, and I need every person willing to help. There are a couple other small groups of fae I do not recognize. They must have been part of the battle and chose to stay behind with Tilda and Clementine.

I still have not figured out where we are either.

Nedra, helpful as ever, answers my question through our link, "We are in Reverie, Althea. Safely camping inside one of the Gateway Trees closest to the glamour border. When we left the Pyramid, we had to hurry to find cover and get you and Tsar help.

"Right. Thank you, Nedra." I reply through our link. "I guess I should go with Aspen to help heal. Better to start now so I can get some rest before tomorrow."

I tell Apuri and Not what I am doing, and they agree to pack up our site, leaving only our bedrolls and something to eat out for the night.

I hurry after Aspen to start my new training.

Chapter Three ~ Healing the Hurt

Our first patient is a young male faerie; I am guessing he is a nature faerie by the dark gray-brown tone of his skin and his mud clumped spiky hair. At first, I do not see anything wrong with him. Maybe Aspen is testing me.

He is sitting on a large rock, leaning forward, looking into the fire. His elbows rest on bended knees hiding his hands in front of his torso. As we step closer he straightens and turns to meet us. The pain and sadness in his large, almond-shaped eyes cause my chest to tighten. His irises are dark emerald green, edged with the tiny pointed teeth like the edge of a leaf. They are beautiful, but I would bet they really shine on one of his better days. The pain and sadness has muted his magic.

Just as I am about to ask what is wrong, I glance down and see his hands. They are completely burnt from the tips of his fingers to halfway up his forearms. As bad as they look – shriveled and flaking like the pages of a book swallowed by flames – the smell is even worse. I have always heard the smell of burning flesh is one of the worst smells; it would seem that is something faeries and humans have in common.

I try to control my breathing. I am glad I did not eat any of Clementine's picnic now. It would probably be on my shoes.

"Hi, Trevin," Aspen speaks softly, "I am Aspen, remember? I have brought someone with me today. This is Althea, the Dreamer."

At hearing this, he perks up a little, but his injuries still prevent any great change in his demeanor.

"Hi Trevin. We are going to help you now. Do you want to share with me how this happened?" He looks questioningly at Aspen. She smiles and nods that it is okay. Aspen and I sit side by side in front of him.

Aspen speaks to Trevin first and then to me. "Tell us your story, Trevin, for every story deserves to be told. We will listen while we heal. Althea, watch me and do as I do."

Trevin holds both hands out straight in front of him and begins his tale. "I was so excited to join the fight," he starts with a distant excitement as if recalling a dream. "I was tired of the same old boring schedule back home. Some friends and I eagerly gathered quick packs and marched off to Lauk."

Aspen holds her hands one above and one below Trevin's charred right hand. She is careful not to touch him. I watch her for a bit before doing anything. In an instant, I am able to feel her energy. That warm tingly feeling returns, only this time it is not mine. As I watch her hands move slowly from Trevin's forearms down to his wrists, I see a warm golden light flow from the palms of her hands into Trevin's arm. As the light flows, Aspen keeps her breathing calm and steady. She is focused, but it is obvious this is second nature for her.

The black charred skin is rejuvenated with new life and slowly returns to its earthy gray-brown tone. I follow Aspen's lead and place my hands above and below Trevin's arm, careful not to touch him. I glance up at his face. His eyes are closed as he continues to recall the events leading up to his wounding moment.

"We heard the Dreamer had come, but we did not see her or her warriors. We did not mind, though. We knew we would have our moment in glory once we won this battle." A tear escapes the inside corner of his eye and rolls gently down his cheek. I clear my mind, only half listening to Trevin's tale now. I control my breathing and focus on that healing energy.

"Pace yourself, and only give when the excess ebbs. Never use your own reserve, or you will be back on your own bedroll again," Aspen instructs softly so as not to interrupt Trevin's tale. Honestly, I am not sure he is even telling his tale for us anymore.

I let the energy grow within myself until it is able to flow effortlessly from my hands. I focus on healing Trevin while half listening to his continued tale in the background.

"In the beginning, it looked hopeful," he says with an attempted smile. "Everything worked according to plan. We were stopping sodocs left and right. We thought we were wearing them down, but really, it was the other way around. We were fools. They sent pawns out on their frontline. Once we stopped all of them, the real threat appeared. sodocs with iron. I have never seen iron before, only heard about it in the stories."

He stops talking, and I open my eyes fearing it is due to the pain. I check his arm between my hands, but it is healing nicely, if a little slower than Aspen's. His entire right arm is healed up to the wrist. She is now working on his hand. A little more work and I will make it to his wrist on his left arm.

Trevin takes a deep breath and continues his story. "One of my friends disappeared in the chaos, but the other was by my side the whole time. I heard him scream." He cringes at the memory. "When I turned to see what happened, it was as if the world had stopped around me. Nolin, my friend, was trapped under a large piece of iron gate. It was burning every inch of him. He would not stop screaming."

He swallows hard and takes another breath before going on in a quivering voice. "I did not know what else to do. I knew he could not handle it much longer; he was going to die. I had to help him. I could not let him lie there screaming and burning under that dreadful thing. Without hesitation, I reached down with both hands and grabbed the iron gate to pull it off of Nolin. It was so heavy, though. I decided to take a different approach: I crouched down to take hold of the gate from underneath. If I could not pull the iron, maybe I could push it. It worked, but it was still hard work. I could hear Nolin's flesh sizzle, and the smell of his burnt skin flooded my nose like a toxic gas. My eyes burned, but I was already crying so it really did not make a difference.

"I tried to hold my breath, but I had to breathe in order to push the iron gate. It burned terribly. Eventually my cries mixed with Nolin's and I was unable to tell them apart. His screams began to fade into whimpers. I successfully removed the gate from my friend and collapsed. Everything was quiet then. I did not feel anything anymore. I suppose I was in shock. I knew, though, lying there on the ground, that Nolin was dead. It did not matter; I can still hear him screaming."

I finished healing the last of his hand moments ago, Aspen moments before that. We let him finish his story though. As Aspen said, "Every story deserves to be told." I gently hold his newly healed hand between my own. I wish desperately that I could heal this pain, but grief is not something a healer can speed along.

Trevin opens his eyes and looks at us for a moment before realizing his hands are no longer burnt. We sit back as he raises them up in front of his face. He begins to laugh, and I fear he may be hysterical. The laughing is soon choked down by tears, though.

Without warning, he throws himself forward embracing the two of us in a hug. Not sure what to do, I look at Aspen. She smiles gently and pats him on the back. I do the same. Trevin takes a couple steps back, embarrassed, and thanks us through flowing emotions.

We say our goodbyes and head back to my camp spot where Apuri and Not are preparing lunch, or is it breakfast?

"You did a wonderful job!" Aspen says warmly as we walk side by side through the camp. "How do you feel?"

How do I feel? Wow, that is a loaded question. "Um, fine

I guess. I mean, the healing did not drain me like last time, but..."

"His story?"

"Yeah," I breathe, relieved she understands. "Does that happen all the time? How do you handle it?"

Aspen smiles, with the wisdom of years of experience. "You must learn to protect yourself, your own emotions and energy. You cannot get attached to patients and their emotions. But I do insist you let them tell their stories. Not only is it a great way to distract them from the healing, but what I said is true. Every story deserves to be told."

I nod and wonder, as we approach a delectable smell at my camp spot, what is Aspen's story?

Apuri and Not have combined their knowledge and love of all things food to create a savory and scrumptious soup with a side of herbal bread for dipping. I have no idea how they do it. We are out here living off the land and they are able to cook up a gourmet meal with nothing more than some flour and a bunch of weeds.

I may not understand how they do it, but I definitely appreciate it!

I greet Apuri with a hug which lasts a little too long creating an awkwardness amongst the group.

Thankfully, my stomach relieves the tension by releasing a rather loud complaint of hunger. We all laugh while Apuri quickly retrieves some bowls from his pack and begins filling one for each of us. Aspen declines her bowl saying she has already made plans to eat at her own site. As she turns to head back, I stop her.

This may not be the best solution, but I need to talk to Lady Nell, eat, and solve the problem of wild magic. I want to talk to Lady Nell one-on-one without her turning me away. Maybe if she has some advanced notice, and time to prepare herself emotionally, we can smooth everything over quickly.

"Can you ask Lady Nell to meet me tonight down by the stream after Noni falls asleep?"

Aspen hesitates like she wants to say no, but presses her lips together and nods, "Of course, Althea. Now, eat and get some rest. You will need your strength."

I take her advice and lie down after finishing my soup.

* * * * * * * * * *

I am inside the Advisor Tree.

Apuri is to my right, Louveri to my left. On the other side of Louveri, sit Lady Nell and Tsar.

The advisors are standing at the other side of the room.

All of the advisors are here, save Verity, of course. In her place is someone new. She has the same ethereal appearance as Verity. Similar haunting white eyes. A notable difference, however, is her hair. Instead of the shimmering white mane, this faerie's hair is blacker than night itself. The tips swing low, resting softly at the small of her back.

Ophidius is missing as well. I wonder where he could be. Did he die in the battle as well?

"The decision is made then," the new truth advisor says with an air of finality.

What decision? What is going on? I take a step forward to ask the very questions in my mind when I sense a figure behind me. I turn to see who it is and catch my breath.

I am standing face to face with myself.

I have seen things like this on TV before I found my new path, my destiny, in Reverie. Watching the characters acting out their fictional scenes I always shouted clever comments at the screen. Questions for them to ask, comical actions, snide jokes to play on oneself. Now, however, they all elude me.

I am as speechless as the characters that once entertained me. At least I am the only one here who is aware of the scene proceeding.

Distracted by my own strange musings, I realize I have missed the conversation.

What decision is made? Why does everyone seem so serious? As everyone begins to disperse, I hear Lady Nell tell the new truth advisor, "We should tell them the news as soon as possible."

Argh! What news? What is the point of magical dreams if I am going to miss all of the details?

Hey! That is it! I am dreaming. I know I can control myself, where I go, and what I see in my dreams, but I wonder...perhaps it is possible to control time in my dreams as well.

I try to speed things up.

It is hard to control, so I stop.

The good news is that it works!

Now, I need to see if I can slow down.

I take a breath and think, "Slow."

It works! It is easier than fast.

Okay, now, to see if I can go back in time. I take another breath and fight the urge to close my eyes. I need to see what is around me so I know when to stop.

Time to rewind this dream!

I let my breath out slowly and think, "Rewind."

My stomach lurches, and my head begins to spin. I cannot see what is happening.

Something went wrong!

Everything is jumbled and spinning.

I think I am going to be sick!

I need to stop now, but it is not working!

"Help!" I shout.

"Althea!" I hear Nedra's voice, and I am pulled out of the dream.

* * * * * * * * * *

I sit up with a cold shock and barely make it off of my bedroll before I vomit into the grass. I hear voices around me, but I am not sure who all is here. I crawl on my hands and knees back to my bedroll and lie down with my eyes shut.

The world is still spinning around me.

"Althea, what happened?" Apuri sounds concerned. "Just lie still. Aspen is on her way over."

"You should not have tried an experiment without

notifying someone first!" Nedra huffs heatedly. Even through our link he speaks a bit too loud for my liking. It is clear by "someone" he means himself.

I groan and, unable to focus my thoughts, reply aloud, "I am sorry, but time was running out. I had to get some answers."

Nedra huffs again and asks, "And did you get them?"

"No! There, I said it. Are you happy?"

"Umm, Althea?" Not's shy voice slips into the perceived one-sided conversation.

I slowly open my eyes but remain lying down. I realize, now, that nobody else was privy to Nedra's side of the argument, or even what my rambling is about.

I take a deep breath and let it out in a huff. Using my arms, I slowly push myself up into a sitting position. Just as Apuri said, I can see Aspen on her way over. She does not look happy either. From the looks of it, I was not the only one in the middle of dreaming.

Ugh, I may as well wait until everyone else gets here so I do not have to keep repeating myself.

"Nedra, can you get Lady Nell, Clementine, and Tilda? Tell them it is an emergency."

Nedra obliges, even though he is still upset that I did not alert him to my idea beforehand. I hate that it will use his energy, but I do not know what else to do.

"I did not know it was going to happen beforehand!" I snap silently to him. He simply lets out a low growl. Apuri and Not turn to look at him, then back at me.

I wave it off and nod behind them at our arriving guests. Aspen sits down beside Apuri and quietly checks my vitals. After checking me from head to toe, her concern eases some, but she still looks concerned.

"I really do not understand it," she says. "I thought at first it could be effects from the healing, but you seem perfectly fine. Even your wounds have healed existentially since the last time I checked them."

I sheepishly look up at her and say under my breath, "It was a dream."

"Oh," she says, and her color visibly pales.

I attempt a smile and gesture at the others walking over. Catching on, she nods and sits patiently with the rest of us until everyone is here.

With everyone seated and attentive, I relay my recent dream aloud. I catch a glance between Tilda and Clementine at the mention of the new truth advisor. I explain how I was able to speed up and slow down what was happening but had some trouble when I tried to go back in time.

This time it is Lady Nell who chimes in with some words of advice. "Time is not something to meddle with, Althea. If you wish to see the past, it is best to patiently meditate with that request in mind. When you are ready, you will see what you need."

That is right; I forgot about Lady Nell's psychic abilities and their similarities to my own. I nod and thank her for her advice. I will figure that part out later. I still need to talk to her tonight. If I remember, I will bring it up then. She may have more useful advice on the subject.

"What about the rest of it, though? What do you think the decision was?" I look at each of my companions for insight. Nobody has an answer.

Okay, well if nobody has any answers, I do not see the point in dwelling on what happened.

As everyone heads back to their own camps once more, I notice Tilda and Clementine walking together in a deep, hushed conversation.

I look at Apuri, "Think they know something?"

He shrugs and answers, "Well, I am not sure that they *know* something, but they do look concerned. It might be worth knowing, but why would they not have told you while they were here?"

"Yeah, I figured they would. Do you think it would be rude to ask?"

He shrugs again. "Probably, and they are your friends. Maybe do as Aspen recommended and rest for today. You will have another chance to ask them about it; I am sure."

I sigh with inner defeat, "You are right, I guess. It is probably better to focus on one problem at a time anyway. We should work on getting to the pixies and learning what we can about wild magic."

We just finished our last meal for the day. Everyone is getting ready for a good night's sleep to be in their best condition for tomorrow's journey to the pixies. I spent the rest of the afternoon helping Aspen heal anyone who needed it and resting during her mandatory breaks.

I tell Apuri, Not, and Nedra, "Goodnight," in case they are asleep by the time I get back. I ready my bedroll and make sure everything is packed for tomorrow, then I head down to the stream to meet with Lady Nell.

Walking to the stream under the light of the full moon is both relaxing and energizing at the same time. I feel a deep calm come over me as I walk between the trees, under the dappled moonlight.

With the camp behind me, it is easy to block out any distractions. I do not want to think about wild magic or pixies right now. I just want to enjoy this peace as I walk with the trees.

It feels like no time at all before I am standing on the bank of the sparkling stream. I look around, but I do not see Lady Nell anywhere. Maybe she decided not to come.

Disappointed, I sit down on the bank. I remove my shoes and let my bare feet bask in the cool water. I soak in the moon's glow, and my entire body fills with a tingle. Magic.

I do not pull away from it now, though. I know what it is; I know it is a part of me. I smile at the phrase and let the magic flow from the stream into myself, enjoying it, embracing it.

The water feels like it is intentionally sparkling extra bright tonight. I feel like it is trying to tell me something. That is silly, water talking. I am going to stop thinking, clear my mind, and enjoy the feeling of the water's magic.

As I feel the magic flow through me, I remember being inside the Pyramid. The image of Tsar's chest being smashed into splinters by Zixus flashes through my mind, reminding me why I am here at the stream. I hoped to clear the air between Lady Nell and myself over what happened. I do not want to lose her as an ally. More importantly, I do not want to lose her as a friend.

I hear someone approaching. As if summoned by thought, Lady Nell emerges from behind the trees. I pull my feet from the water and rise to greet her.

"No, please, do not get up. I will join you." She removes her sandals before sitting down beside me and places her feet into the cool stream.

"Ah," she lets out a soft sigh and closes her eyes.

I slide my feet back into the cool stream. I want to say something, but I honestly do not know what to say. Instead, I sit quietly and let her enjoy the water as I was able to moments before.

When the silence becomes too loud to bear, it is obvious neither of us knows what to say. We cannot sit here like this all night.

"Nell, I am sorry about what happened to Tsar." I let the words spill out on their own. They come out so fast, I worry she does not understand me. I look over at her. She is sitting with her feet still in the stream, her arms extended behind her as a prop in the cool grass. Her expression is contemplative.

Finally, she sighs and sits upright to look at me. "It is not your fault. I am the one who should be sorry for being such a jerk. Everything just fell apart all at once. I kept watching for him to come out of that place, and then it collapsed. The sodocs we were fighting turned to dust, and then the Pyramid crumbled into a thousand pieces right in front of us."

I pull my feet from the stream and cross them under my legs as I turn to face her to show I am listening. I barely feel the soft grass on my water numbed feet.

Nell continues without pause. "Everything stopped, even my heart. Chaz would not land with us, he was not concerned about Tsar, he did his job and was ready to return home. That is what Nedra said anyway."

I nod. Nedra, being a dragon, is the only one, aside from Ophidius, the animal faerie advisor, able to understand the Chobudda, an ancient majestic dragon covered in feathers. The Chobudda stay to themselves within their own tree inside Reverie. They were called for help before the battle ensued. Chaz agreed to help us on our mission to destroy the sodocs and The Pyramid. I guess, once that job was finished, his mission was complete.

"I am not sure what Nedra said to him," Nell continues, "but he finally convinced him to stay and help us search for any survivors. It was obvious Nedra and Apuri were not going anywhere without you, dead or alive. I left Noni on the sidewalk and went to help search through the rubble. It felt like an impossible task. Chaz ended up having to help Nedra lift the bigger blocks of rubble, while Apuri and I moved all the iron we could. Since Not could not touch the iron, he set to clearing all of the smaller debris. He also pointed us in the direction he last saw the two of you. That was when Aspen showed up. I was not sure from where, but I did not care. I had to find Tsar.

"When we found your bodies, there was no time for emotions. We quickly grabbed you both and, with the help of the dragons, flew to sanctuary inside Reverie."

Wow, I have not heard what happened after the fall of the Pyramid from anyone yet. I had no idea my friends went through so much, and they still did not leave us behind.

"When we landed," Nell continues even though her voice is getting choked with emotion as tears fall down her face. "Aspen immediately examined the both of you to see if there was anything she could do. You were both unconscious, and it did not look good. There was a bit of debate on whom she should save first. In the end, Nedra was adamant that you would want Tsar to live, and would be furious if you ever found out we saved you without even trying to save him. I am eternally thankful to him for that decision.

"Aspen patched up his wounds the best she could and healed his insides with magic until she exhausted her own energy, but he still would not wake up. The next day she apologized, saying there was nothing else she could do and she had to help you, too. I never left his side, even when you woke up. I was so afraid if I looked away for even a moment I would lose him. But you... I do not know what you did, Althea, but you brought him back to me."

She finally gives in to her emotions and throws herself on me in a sobbing hug. Still at a loss for words, I simply hug her back. I know too well the place I brought Tsar back from. Neoinas! That is why I saw it in his eyes. That empty feeling passes through me, and I shudder.

"It is going to take him some time to forget that place, Nell. Well, to recover from it, at least. Nobody could ever forget it. The best thing you can do is be there for him." I hold my arms out. "Friends?" She leans in and we embrace in another hug.

As we let go, Lady Nell wipes her face and turns back to the stream. She leans down and cups her hands together to gather some of the water. The reflection of the moon in her hands is breathtaking. As she splashes the water on her face, I swear I am able to see that light from the moon flow into her.

I lean over to look at the water flowing smoothly in the stream.

"You should try it," she says, gesturing to the water. I cup my hands together. As I lower them into the water, I am instantly filled with the tingling energy of its magic. I raise the water, and the reflection of the moon's bright shining face, up to my face and splash the water on my face and gasp to catch my breath. Not only is the water cold, but that surge of energy I felt in my hands went straight into my face, and I was not prepared for that.

Lady Nell laughs and offers me one of the scarves from around her waist to dry my face. I graciously accept it as she begins to laugh. I wipe my face and hand the scarf back to her. She dips it in the stream. We watch it flow, stretching with the current as Nell holds onto one end. She picks it up slowly, allowing the stream to pull and fill every fiber of it before carefully rolling it into a loose ball.

What is she doing? I think to myself.

As if reading my mind, she says with a smile, "I am going to surprise Noni. She has been asking for moon water for Tsar."

There is a brief silence before I decide to ask, "Nell, this might sound crazy, but do you ever see magic? Like vibrations, and light?" I keep my eyes on the stream, hoping the light of the moon is not revealing my flush of embarrassment.

I can hear the smile in her voice, "It is energy you see. Everything has energy; everything is made up of energy. That is how your magic works. I thought you had figured it out when you mastered your magic."

"Ha!" I laugh sarcastically, "I have not *mastered* anything. I rushed to figure out something I needed to do. Really, it has all been instinct or quick practice, but it still felt forced."

Nell unsuccessfully tries to hide a yawn. I realize we have been here for a while.

I push myself up and say, "We should get some sleep. We have a long day tomorrow."

Nell agrees and we walk back to camp together, still barefoot and laughing softly. Before we part to go to our own sites, Lady Nell says to me in a serious tone, "Practice with energy, with love, and with fun. And, Althea, be careful when you dream."

She gives me a hug and we part our separate ways. I wish we had longer to finish talking. Alas, time is ever moving. Nedra, Not, and Apuri are already asleep, so I quietly slip into my bedroll beside Apuri. By the sound of his snores, he is not waking anytime soon. I get as comfortable as possible and relax for the night. Before allowing myself to fully drift off, I reach out to Nedra.

"Nedra?" I whisper through our link. "Nedra?" I say it a bit louder this time. Thankfully, I do not have to worry about waking anyone else.

"Hmm? Yes, Althea?" He grumbles sleepily.

"I just wanted to let you know I am back and I am about to go to sleep. I will try it again, going back to see what the decision was at the Advisor Tree.

"Alright, Althea, I am here. If anything goes awry, I will wake you immediately."

"Thank you, Nedra. Goodnight." He lets out a low rumble in reply.

With Lady Nell's advice about meditating with intent, I think of going back to the dream, to the beginning.

Once I feel I have a grasp on the beginning, I allow myself to drift slowly into a quiet slumber. The word "beginning" floats at the edge of my mind as I fall into the dream realm.

* * * * * * * * *

"I am surrounded by darkness. My heart begins to race. Neoinas!

No... No, something is different here.

Suddenly, thoughts fill my mind like a narrative voice:

In the beginning there was love. From it was created something meaningful and powerful. The Creator made the earth and all nature and creatures in it. But He did not stop there. He created a caregiver to tend to His creations, love them, and enjoy them.

And thus, Man was created!

The Creator was pleased with Man and blessed him with many great things: beautiful scenery, fresh air, clean water, amazing animals, and most importantly, fellowship together. When the Creator would leave him, though, He noticed how lonely the man was. So, He decided to create a companion for him.

And thus, Woman was created!

Life was grand for the Creator and His creations. After a while, however, something changed. Man and Woman were not content with their life with the Creator. They wanted to be more. They wanted to be creators, too.

Instead of going to the Creator with their desire, they took what the Creator already made and broke it to make it their own. They cut down a tree and used the wood to carve their creation.

They were disappointed when it did not breathe, move, or speak. The Creator called out to them, and they were afraid.

The Creator was heartbroken. If the Man and Woman had only come to Him, they could have created together. Instead, they tried to do it in their own understanding.

They did not realize when they cut the tree, they cut their bond with Him and nature itself.

Now, they would have to wait until death when they would enter the Creator's home, the Domain, to be at peace.

Chapter Four ~ Gateway Trees

"So, I think maybe I went a little too far back." I say with a laugh between bites of one of Apuri's biscuits.

We have all gathered around to share a quick breakfast before our big journey. Next, Aspen and I are going to do one last healing on Tsar. Thankfully, he was able to sit up and eat today. Still, there is no harm in doing one more healing before we hit the road. Yesterday, we made sure everyone was able to walk for our travels.

I have been telling everyone about my dream while we eat.

Noni, at hearing about the Creator, pipes in excitedly, "Did you see Him? Was He amazing? I know He was!" She bounces up and down on her knees, dropping biscuit crumbs all down the front of her dress. Her mother pulled her red curly hair back into a ponytail, or it would be bouncing right along with her.

I laugh and reply, "Well, I saw Him, but He was more of an essence." I look around at the nature around us with a new respect.

The little girl laughs and takes another bite of her

biscuit. Thankfully, we have Apuri with us. I still do not know how he does it, but he is able to create meals that are not only edible but actually delicious with next to nothing when it comes to ingredients. Nothing brightens your mood quite like having good food to eat.

I finish eating and quickly drink a cup of water gathered from the stream. Again, I think back to my dream and seeing all of creation in the beginning. It may not have been the dream I was trying to see, but it was a blessing. I know I need to practice more like Lady Nell said, with fun and feeling the energy, learning to use it. But for now, I focus on our tasks at hand. At this moment, that task is to help Aspen heal Tsar.

Aspen and I sit on either side of Tsar, who is able to remain sitting for this morning's healing. With an audience – everyone else decided to stick around and witness the miracle of healing first hand – it takes me a little longer to clear my mind. Once I am focused, though, everything goes along smoother than I could have ever imagined.

Aspen and I were able to place one of our hands in front of Tsar's chest and the other behind him, focused on his wound. We each find that golden healing light and let it grow. When we release it into Tsar, it joins together and spreads around his torso in a web. I focus my intent to heal into the web knowing Aspen is doing the same. I picture Tsar completely healed, able to walk, and back to his normal self. An image of black fills my mind. Neoinas. I feel the web is weakening. I take a breath and release it slowly, refocusing my thoughts. Yes. Something needs to be done about that, too.

With the healing web back in full motion, I choose to take it further. I let Aspen keep control over Tsar's physical injury, while I move up to take care of what is really bothering him. I cannot take away his memories of Neoinas. If I could, I would have done that for myself already. I think perhaps I can help heal the pain he feels from being there. I remember when I was transferred to the Domain. The overwhelming feeling of happiness and joy to be alive. I remember the beautiful colors within the Domain. I focus on that and allow the web of healing energy to grow and wrap around Tsar's mind.

I am not sure how long we sat like that, focusing healing energy on Tsar, but when I finally stop and relax, I find both of my feet have gone numb. I awkwardly fumble to my knees and hobble over to sit beside Apuri. He rubs my feet to restore circulation, and I cringe at the feeling of pins and needles.

I become aware of voices and look to see Tsar and Lady Nell. They are both standing! He wraps his arms around her and embraces her with a kiss. Tears flow down both of their faces.

"I missed you so much!" Tsar says shakily.

"I missed you too. I thought... I thought...," Before Nell can finish, Tsar kisses her again.

Noni makes a "Yuck!" sound and sticks out her tongue while twisting her face. Idona, sitting beside her, laughs uncontrollably. That musical giggle takes me back to my first day in Reverie. Tilda let me stay at her home, and the first night Idona was quite entertaining at the supper table. She put on a wonderful show of bubbles and flowers followed by a room full of laughter. Hearing that laughter in her faerie giggles now, I cannot help but to laugh as well.

Lady Nell and Tsar, aware of their audience, step apart slightly, embarrassed. "Thank you!" They speak together to both Aspen and me.

I smile, nod, and reply, "Of course! You are welcome. Now that we are all better, what do you say about a little field trip?"

Everyone jumps into motion, gathering their packs, extinguishing fires, grabbing a last bite to eat as they walk. My feet now have circulation, so I get up and head over to Clementine and Tilda.

"The Marketplace Tree would not happen to be in between here and the pixies, would it? I think Pilate could help us out." I say as I walk up to them.

They have still been talking secretly, and I cannot bring

myself to call them out on it. Maybe after we have walked a bit. For now, I would like to know if it is possible to stop by and see Pilate on our way.

Tilda replies, "The Deep Dark Forest lies to the North of our location, and the Marketplace is South of us. I am sorry, Althea. Perhaps we could get a message to him and have him meet us?"

"Okay, yeah. I will do that." It is hard to keep the disappointment out of my voice.

Clementine pats my arm, "It is okay, sweetie. I am sure he can fly up to meet us in no time, and we will still be able to meet with the pixies before it is too late."

Tilda gives her a look and she clams up again.

Clementine's words echo in my head as she and Tilda walk away, still whispering in secret. "...before it is too late."

Things must be worse than I thought, and they obviously know more than they are letting on. I wish they would just talk to me. Still, I know we need to talk to the pixies. What did Clementine say, "...he can fly up to meet us"? Of course!

"Nedra!" I shout through our private link. "Can you speak to Nook from here?"

"There is no need to shout, Althea. Yes, there is no distance limitation to the link, even between dragons. What is it you would like me to tell him?"

"Sorry, I just got an idea from Clementine. If you can contact Nook to get Pilate and bring him to meet us with the pixies it will save a lot of time."

"Okay, that sounds like a good plan. Anything else I should pass along?"

"Yeah, tell them to bring along everything they can find on wild magic."

With Nedra passing along that message, I head back to meet up with Tilda and Clementine so we can head out together. On my way, I pass Noni and Idona chasing after a whirl of bubbles, created by Idona I am guessing. She has grown since I last saw her. I did not realize it earlier. Tilda did say faeries grow at a different rate than humans. She is almost as big as Noni now. Seeing the two of them run around without a care in the world, having fun, makes my heart ache. I do not remember the last time I had fun like that.

I have had moments of fun: when I had tea on the dandelions with Clementine, when Tilda and I had our picnic outside of Inon, when I practiced my magic with Queen Melanomie, Not, and Apuri, and again on the road with Apuri, Not, and Tsar. Flying high with Nedra, allowing myself to forget the world for a brief moment. I have had fun.

It is hard to remember the things that go right when everything seems to go wrong. But, to focus on the positive is the only way to keep a light in the dark. I make it to my site where Apuri, Not, and Nedra are ready and waiting to go. I hug each of them and thank them for being with me. They all give me strange looks, questioning my sanity, but I ignore them and get ready to march out.

Nell and Tilda yell for Noni and Idona. I look up to see both girls running excitedly toward the gathering group.

And just like that, we are all ready. It only takes about fifteen minutes for us to make it to the Gateway Tree's edge. I hold my breath as I step through the thick jelly-like entrance of the tree.

The Painted Forest is just as I remembered it! Beautiful is an understatement. Again, my dream comes to mind. The grass on the ground is so vibrant it takes my breath away. Little flowers can still be seen frolicking to and fro if your eyes are quick enough to catch them. I laugh as I see Indri and Lady Nell grab hold of Idona and Noni just before they run after the little dancing red roses and blue hyacinths. Each tree is unique like the hidden world beneath its bark. Maybe one day I will be able to explore each and every Gateway Tree within the Painted Forest.

The wind blows causing music to play through the leaves of the trees. I glance up at that canopy and catch the violet sky peeking through green leaves just as vibrant as the grass below.

I wonder if the Painted Forest changes with the seasons. Or maybe, since it is Reverie, it is on a different timeline. When I first came through the Glamour, it looked like early summer inside the Painted Forest. It has been at least a couple of months since then and nothing has changed.

We all walk in an unorganized group, admiring the magic around us. Tilda and Clementine are at the front since they are the only ones, aside from Nedra, who really know the way.

I take a minute to talk to Nedra via our private link. He is flying over the canopy in the clouds. I decided to walk with the group and catch up with everyone a little more. It would be rude to go off on my own with Nedra now and leave them behind. Besides, Nedra said he would enjoy getting a proper meal on his own. I would rather not see that sight just yet.

"Nedra, did you get through to Nook?"

"Yes, Althea, he and Pilate will meet us. They are leaving as we speak. Now, it is lunchtime!" I hear the excitement in his voice and let him do his thing. "Have fun!"

I am thankful he does not have to use his glamour now. Our walk from the hegira farm to the Painted Forest was rough on everyone, but Nedra most of all. Being in the human realm, he was not able to fly around free as a dragon. He had to take on his glamour of a dragonfly. After being trapped by the sodocs inside the Pyramid in glamour for weeks, Nedra is not too fond of his dragonfly disguise anymore. I do not blame him.

I catch Apuri watching me as we walk. I guess I have not really given him much attention since I have been back. I have not thought about how he has been affected by everything happening. I smile at him and reach out to hold his hand. It feels nice to walk hand in hand, slightly swinging our arms with every step.

My heart lightens with each swing until I feel as giddy as a child. For a moment, I enjoy walking with my friends without thinking about where we are going or why we are headed there.

We have only been walking a couple hours, but it is time for a break. Most of us, myself namely, still are not up to our normal one hundred percent. I begin to sweat profusely and become short of breath. Apuri, concerned, immediately makes me sit right where I am and alerts the group that it is time to take a break. I am not exaggerating when I say everyone is relieved.

I lean back on a fallen tree. I guess it is not a portal since it has fallen.

"Are all of the trees in the Painted Forest Gateway Trees?" I muse aloud, not really sure if I will get an answer.

"Not all of them are Gateway Trees," Clementine answers. I should have known she would be the one to know the answer. Though I do not doubt that it is common knowledge among all the faeries.

"Some," Clementine continues, "were transformed from the native trees in this forest when the Glamour was created. Others were grown, created for the pure intent of being a Gateway. You can usually tell the difference by size. The native trees are smaller on the inside, accommodated only by the growth of the physical tree. Though they are still a different world on the inside, they have limits. The Marketplace is a native tree. You are able to see and walk through one barrier side and out the other in no time. Inon, on the other hand, was created, grown with intent. The grown Gateway Trees are just as natural as the native ones, mind you; their growing was simply manipulated and accelerated by the magic of earth faeries. There is a map back in Inon, in the Advisor Tree, that marks each of the Gateway Trees, both natural and created inside of the Painted Forest. The deeper you go into the Painted Forest, the stronger and older the magic. Most of us do not go that far anymore since the war with the sodocs. Also,

Reverie does not exist in the same way the human realm does. You could be standing at the edge of the glamour and think you are walking deeper into the forest only to find you have unknowingly circumvented your intended path and come out the other side in only a few paces. To answer your question, though, I am not sure how many of the trees are not Gateways."

"Wow. I would love to see that map sometime!"

Clementine laughs, "Now you sound like Pilate." I laugh too. I can definitely hear Pilate saying something similar.

"Were you able to contact him?" Tilda asks curtly.

"Yes, Nedra was able to reach Nook. They have already left and will meet us there."

"Excellent. I am sorry we were unable to see him at Find It." Though her tone is still serious, I can see by her expression that she means it.

I smile, "It is okay. But I am feeling better, and I know we do not have any time to waste. Shall we continue?" I look not only at Tilda, but the rest of the group as I ask. Everyone agrees with mumbled words or nods of the head. Most do so reluctantly. I am tempted to give them a little more time, but it is true we do not have any time to waste.

Nedra informs me that he has finished lunching his fill successfully. I show him our location through our link, and he tells me we are a little past halfway there. I pass this on to the group for inspiration to keep going. It works!

With a new, if slightly tired, pep in our step, we march on again.

As we walk through The Painted Forest, I pay attention to each of the trees we pass. I personally try to identify normal trees from Gateway Trees and natural Gateways from created. As I begin laughing at Nedra's description of trolls living within a rather gnarled one, I have caught everyone's attention. I tell them of my little game, and everyone decides to join in. I thought the faeries would have a leg up being familiar with which are Gateway trees and not, but the map Clementine told us about must not be available to everyone.

In fact, Clementine seems to be the only one sure of her guesses. She eventually becomes the judge of the game, letting everyone else guess while she announces whether we are on the money or not.

At one point, Apuri and Not actually begin to argue with Clementine about a particularly animated looking tree being a Gateway – created they say. She insists it is not a Gateway and that if they do not believe her, they are welcome to attempt entry.

The two of them attempt to prove their point by precariously pushing against the bark of what looks like the backside of a naked woman. If blushing were possible for either of them, I am sure they would both be glowing like beacons.

As the rest of us laugh, amused by their persistence, they finally admit defeat to a rather smug Clementine.

"I guess I cannot blame you for thinking she was created by us; she is rather beautiful. Though, we all learned from the master, the Creator." Her bright green eyes are full of admiration.

I remember the first time I saw the orange flecks in her eyes light up with her use of magic. It was the first time I had seen a faerie do magic. Heck, it was the first time I had seen a faerie! I smile at the memory and at how far my path has led me. I never would have thought on that day that I would be able to perform magical feats like that and more.

I look down at the mark on my wrist with colors swirling in a clouded rainbow. I focus on myself for a moment. I can feel the magic there, waiting.

I smile to myself as we continue our walk and choose not to play this round of Gateway Tree guessing. Instead I walk in silence listening and observing not only the beauty of the Painted Forest, but also the harmony of my friends as well. I am grateful to hear their laughter as it mimics the cry of birds in the distance.

As we walk, I think of my dream with the street sign.

Wild magic took over, leaving no trace of human existence. Talk about irony. It seems in the world today, humanity has taken over, leaving no trace of nature. It is almost tempting to let it go for a bit.

No! What am I thinking? Even selfish people do not deserve to die. Let's be honest, I was one of those selfish humans not long ago.

So, how do we not only save humanity, but teach them to change their ways without allowing them to know about Reverie and the world of faeries?

I sigh in frustration. Apuri, mistaking it for a sigh of exhaustion, wraps an arm around my shoulders and assures me, "It is not much longer."

A sound from above signifies his truth. We all stop and look up to see Nedra and Nook – with Pilate on his back – fly above the canopy just over us. They drift in a circle as they descend to land.

"Nice to see you made it here safe, Nedra." I greet my dragon through our link while I run to greet Pilate in person.

"Pilate! How are you?" I embrace my furry little friend in a tight hug. "It has been so long. I was not sure if I would ever see you again."

"I missed you too, Althea!"

That is all he says before his emotions get the better of him and he chokes on his words. I wonder at that moment if anyone took the time to tell him that I nearly died inside the Pyramid and now lived again with more magic than before, or if, like my existence, everyone in Reverie just knew.

"Yeah, we are here alright," I hear Lady Nell from behind. "I do not think I will ever forget this place."

Without waiting further, we all walk into the Deep Dark Forest. As soon as I step into the darkness, I am seized by panic. The darkness closes in around me like in Neoinas.

"Nedra!" I gasp both through our link and aloud.

"I am here!" Nedra replies. I hear voices, my friends, but I cannot understand them.

"Light, Althea! Use your magic!" Nedra says urgently through our link.

Light? Magic? Yes, that is right! I focus all of my energy on creating light and lift my hands up letting the magic flow from them.

In seconds, the sky is illuminated by a bright star-like light. My breathing calms and I am able to see and hear my friends again. I realize Apuri is holding my hand, and Not is close to Nedra. I look around to see if everyone else is okay. When my eyes land on Tsar's, my throat closes and I try hard to swallow. It happened to him too.

Aspen, following my gaze, immediately goes to Tsar and sends him a flow of warm energy to lift his spirits. I feel my own mood lifting and wonder if I am near enough to receive the same energy. Apuri gives my hand a reassuring squeeze. Then it hits me, this is his gift. Apuri, like most hegira, possesses powers to manipulate behavior and moods. Apuri is able to temporarily lift anyone's mood. I was wary of Apuri using his gift on me before, but now I am thankful for it.

We all continue through the illuminated darkness toward the cave, walking a little closer now. I keep looking hard in the distance, watching for Mitzi, or a different pixie perhaps, to greet us. They probably expect we will know our way this time. Or maybe they do not even know we are coming.

The longer we walk, the less sure I feel we are supposed to be here. I feel deep down in my gut that something dreadful is coming.

"Should we not be at the cave already?" Tsar asks, not trying to hide his annoyance one bit.

I push the light further ahead of us and urge it to grow brighter. Unfortunately, it does not get any brighter, but I am able to move it higher and forward to illuminate a little more of our path ahead.

"There," I sigh, pointing at the soft gray wall barely touched by the edge of the light.

With relief we all walk a little faster toward the cave.

Disappointment, however, is like a slap in the face as we walk into an empty black cave.

The pixies are gone!

Louveri is gone!

Tilda had assumed they were still here – we all did – because no one had been told otherwise. Where could they have gone?

I fall upon the cave floor in defeat. Why can one of my plans not work smoothly and obstacle free from the start?

Chapter Five ~ The Search

Nook and Nedra stay outside while the rest of us look for clues within the cave. We have built a fire for light so I can save my energy. Using magic in any way is a pull on your personal energy, but something as big as the light I created takes its toll quickly.

Using individual torches, Tsar and Apuri circle the cave looking for any symbols left behind by the pixies or Louveri. This is a specialty of theirs. The hegira, living in hiding, were nomadic, moving through Nashees – abandoned, run-down buildings – for survival. They would carve symbols into door frames and floors as a coded message to future tenants.

Nedra and Nook are still unable to reach the pixies through their telepathic link. Tilda and Clementine look more worried now, and I do not blame them. Pixies are one of the oldest magical creatures in the world, and for them to disappear without a trace at the moment we need them the most is not a good sign.

I feel desperation setting in. We need answers!

I turn to the best source for answers, "Pilate, did you happen to see Feather or Louveri before you came up?"

He drops his head; the light at the end of his antenna dims. "I am sorry, Althea. I have been in my shop compiling all the information you gave me plus what we found earlier into one Dreamer manuscript. I was so absorbed in the project I almost did not hear Nook calling."

He fiddles with a small egg-shaped charm with a book etched into its surface hanging around his neck. I never noticed it before. It blends in well with his soft brown fur. It must be his dragon amulet.

I glance toward the cave entrance to see if I can spot Nook's matching crest. I did not notice one on him before either. Unfortunately, the darkness prevents me from seeing anything except Nedra and Nook's dark shapes pacing back and forth. I guess I could just ask Nedra about it, but I know he is still trying to get through to the pixies.

"It is okay, Pilate." I address the rest of the group, "Does anyone else have any ideas? Where might the pixies be? Or what else can we do about the wild magic? I fear every minute we waste here wild magic is gaining that much more of an advantage."

I turn to Tilda and Clementine. "Should we call an advisor meeting? Maybe someone will know something that will help. Maybe Feather will be there and can tell us about Louveri."

They share that secretive look they have had since I shared my dream about the advisors. I can see them closing up like a clam protecting its pearl. We do not have time for this.

"Stop it!" I shout at them as I feel the control slipping. "We are in a crisis here, and this is not the time for secrets! I know something is going on. Ever since I told you about that dream you have been whispering and hiding something. I am asking you now, as your friend *and* as the Dreamer, tell me what is going on."

You could hear a pin drop. Even Nook and Nedra have stopped pacing outside. Everyone is staring at me open-mouthed. I can hear my blood rushing and my heart pounding in my head. I force myself to breathe, to calm down.

Clementine speaks first. Her voice almost cracks with emotion, "I am sorry, Althea. In your dream you spoke of a new truth advisor. Choosing a new advisor is something that must never be rushed. It is also something we have never known the results of ahead of time. We fear that knowing from your dream who the next truth advisor is may, in fact, alter our path."

"Oh!" I am shocked. I did not expect that answer. Honestly, I am not sure what I did expect. "So, are you saying you know which faerie I saw just from the description?"

"We do," Tilda answers. "And though she is a strong and powerful faerie, she is not in the top candidates to become an advisor. We fear what may happen to those who are before her, for the position to become hers."

"Oh," I say again, understanding their worry now. "So, you are saying we definitely should not call a meeting. What if we speak to the other advisors individually? Someone has to know something."

Clementine sighs, "That would be possible; though it may be a wild goose chase."

"And therefore, a complete waste of time." Tilda rings in with her ever-serious tone.

I sigh and drop my head in my hands.

"I could still check my records, back at the shop that is, for anything pertaining to wild magic." Pilate pipes in optimistically.

I lift my head. "Pilate, that is the best idea I have heard today! Honestly, I do not know why I did not ask you that in the first place."

"It is quite alright, Althea. The pixies were the obvious first choice. I am not sure I will find anything as to their whereabouts," he adds with disappointment, "but perhaps something will pop up while we search for wild magic."

"We?" I ask with a smile creeping in. The last time I was able to do some research with Pilate, we were searching for any records left behind by previous Dreamers. Though tiresome, it was exhilarating. Learning, quenching that inner thirst for knowledge, is something hard to say no to. "I am in!"

"Nook will need help as well. The answer may very well lie within his personal collection. And," he pauses for a minute and looks at our present advisors, "I believe Clementine and Tilda will be able to access the advisors' personal library within the Advisor Tree along with the other advisors, of course?"

He asks the last as a question out of mere formality. He knows there may be answers there, and they are the only ones to search it, along with the other advisors and myself. They both nod their heads silently.

"Okay, so we have a plan B, thanks to Pilate," I smile in his direction. "We need to split into groups. Nook, Nedra, do you think you would each be able to carry four riders?" I ask aloud.

"Yes," they both answer where everyone can hear.

Everyone looks around. We obviously have more than eight in our group.

"I am sorry," I address the other faeries in our group, "We will get you out of here and back into the Painted Forest. After that, you will have to find your own ways home. You should all be well enough. We will leave you provisions and directions. The rest of us will split into three groups. Nell, Tsar, Aspen, and Noni will go with Nook to Dragon Cave. If you find any answers within his books, Nook will be able to contact us through Pilate or Nedra. Nedra will take Pilate, Not, Apuri, and myself back to Find It. We will likewise share any information we find. That leaves Clementine and Tilda. You can start looking through the library in the Advisor Tree."

"Yes," Clementine pipes in, gaining confidence. "We will head to the Advisor Tree, and if we find any answers, Ophidius will be able to communicate with the dragons."

"Tilda?" I have to ask, "I do not mean to pry, but is everything okay in Inon? It is just, with Indri and Idona here," I gesture at Indri and their sleeping child at the back of the cave.

"Oh, it is nothing. Since... well, with what happened to

Verity," she swallows hard. Verity's death is not something any of us are ready to talk about. "We decided it best if the advisors were not left alone. Those of us with families were told to keep them close, and those without, pick a buddy."

That makes sense. And that could mean... A chord of hope strikes in my heart. "Has anyone talked to Feather? Maybe she already met up with Louveri!"

"Honestly, Althea, we have not had any communication with anyone outside of this cave since we met up with you. I am sure that is where she is, but we will not have any certain way of knowing until we get back to Inon."

My heart sinks, but I try not to let it show.

"Hey, sweetie," Clementine reaches her long dark hand out to hold mine. "We will let you know as soon as we see Feather. I am sure she is okay."

"I know," I breathe and sit up straight. "Thank you." I rub my hands on my pants and stand up impatiently. The weight of Louveri's unknown fate sitting in the back of my mind brings back unwelcome memories. The first time I lost her it broke me. I honestly do not know what I will do if it happens again.

"Right, well," I say, gathering my belongings from the cave floor, "we really do not have time to waste. How about we get going?"

Everyone looks tired, beyond tired, worn out. I hate to be the one to push them, but it needs to be done. They each drag themselves up, and we extinguish the fire. I head outside and use my magic to create the light again.

I glance back to see that everyone makes it out of the cave. I see Tsar carrying Noni asleep in his arms. I try to watch him closely to see if he needs more healing, but I am too distracted to tell. Indri steps out just behind him, carrying Idona. Seeing the two of them like that makes me wonder where Apuri and I might end up.

As if sensing my thoughts, Apuri reaches out and holds my hand as we walk back through the Deep Dark Forest.

The walk back to the Painted Forest is a quiet one,

everyone is in his or her own thoughts. I hate that this is happening again. We just battled the sodocs with everything we have. We should all be home celebrating with loved ones, not worrying if we will ever see them again.

Apuri squeezes my hand, and I look up just in time to see the edge of the Gateway Tree before stepping through.

Stepping into the dappled light inside the Painted Forest after walking through the Deep Dark Forest is like coming up for air after deep diving in the dark depths of the ocean. Almost as one, we breathe in the life of fresh air.

After a moment, those of us leaving to research, gather any remaining provisions and pass them off to the faeries traveling on their own.

Trevin, the young lad whose hands Aspen and I healed, has taken it upon himself to lead them. He takes the provisions as well as directions back to Inon.

"I am sorry," I tell him, "If we had the time I would make sure we all traveled by light and returned you home."

He holds his hands up for me to see, "You have done more than enough, Dreamer. The least I could do is help my friends travel within the Painted Forest to our home." He smiles and wraps his warm hands around mine in gratitude.

Knowing the group of faeries is in good hands, the rest of us prepare to leave. Clementine, Tilda, and Indri – still carrying a now awake Idona – wave as they fly up to the canopy.

I watch them from Nedra's back until they disappear into a bright beam of light.

"Just remember," I say loud enough for everyone to hear, "relax and breathe when traveling through light."

Everyone nods, and we lift off. We wave our last goodbyes to the faeries on the ground. There is a gleam in Trevin's eye, a sense of purpose. I am happy to have at least restored that for him.

Back inside Find It, we are busy at work. Not took a quick soak in Pilate's tub to rehydrate and ensure he could stay awake. Meanwhile Pilate put on a kettle of vanilla spiced tea; he ensured us it was the best for energy. With our task at hand, we need as much of that as we can get.

We have each chosen a wall of books to sort through. Anything containing information about wild magic or pixies will be placed in Pilate's private quarters for further examination. Nedra is going to read with me through our link. His ability to read fast and memorize what he reads is much better than my own. I will, with Nedra reading and retaining each book, be able to make it through the books at twice my normal speed.

Many times, as we pace the small shop retrieving new books, Apuri and I bump into each other or graze arms. Every time this happens, I cannot help but think back to the last time we were in this quaint shop searching books for any information on previous Dreamers.

We had just met Apuri and were, in hindsight, unfairly skeptical of his company. We wrongly judged Apuri for being a hegira, connecting his race with that of the sodocs. Now, I could not imagine a day without him by our sides.

I look up from my current book to admire my little band of heroes. With everything that has happened over the past few months, I have not taken much time to look at what I have gained.

Especially in times of trouble, we should stop and recognize those things for which we are grateful. Gratefulness is contagious and should be spread, not only from one person to another, but in our own lives from one moment to the next.

I am proud of how far I have come, how far *we have* come! Now, for us to find another miracle like last time. Speaking of last time, I guess I should do as I did then and get back with you after we have made some progress.

Happy reading!

We still have not found much. There are a total of eight books on Pilate's personal desk containing information about either wild magic, pixies, or both. Nedra and I were finishing up with our second shelf of books when Nook contacted him and Pilate. They made it back to Dragon Cave and have started searching through his books.

Before he joined them in the search through his books, Nook decided to ask some of the other dragons if they might know any information about what is going on. Have they heard from the pixies? Could they pass on any information they might have heard about wild magic?

Unfortunately, their answers only brought up more questions. The pixies were not the only ones who vanished. The Chobudda are unreachable as well. In fact, as soon as the sodocs were defeated, the Chobudda flew off. They left without saying anything. Everyone assumed this was simply part of their demeanor. It was not until they tried to contact Chaz to get information about us that they realized something was wrong. For some reason, Nedra was unavailable, so they thought they could reach us through Chaz.

He, too, was unreachable. They feared the worst, that none of us made it. They tried to contact the pixies to find out what was happening. That was when they realized something was wrong. The pixies were never unreachable. Maybe sometimes individually, but not all of them at once. Not like this.

Nook did not know about it sooner because he was helping to return those who fought in the battle back to their homes. That is what he was doing when we contacted him to get Pilate and meet us in the Deep Dark Forest.

He says all of the dragons have been notified by now, and nobody has been able to get through to either the pixies or Chobudda since right after the fall of the sodocs.

With that new information we are adding the Chobudda to our search.

"Grab that short leather one, Althea, with the rusted brass corners. I remember the Chobudda being mentioned in it." Nedra instructs through our link once Nook cuts contact.

I grab the book and tell Not and Apuri of our update as I carry it to Pilate's personal desk.

"Just great!" Apuri shouts, slamming a book down on the small table in front of him. We all turn to look at him, shocked. He rubs his hands on his head and breathes hard, puffing his cheeks.

"Sorry," he says, embarrassed. "I am sorry. I feel like every time we turn around it is something else. And what are we accomplishing here? We should be out there! Searching!"

I have never seen this side of him. I decide immediately I do not like it.

"We are searching!" I say sternly, trying to maintain my own temper. "I understand if this," I gesture around at the piles of books, "is not your thing. But we are doing what we can, all we know. What do you suggest we do, Apuri?"

He breathes and rubs his head again. "I am not sure." He begins to pace between stacks of books. "I am not sure," he says again, "but maybe I know someone who does."

I look at him, confused.

"The hegira - the rest of us - Tsar's crew, mine, and any others we can find. Some of our elders, like Tsar's mother, were around when the Dreamers first approached Zixus. Maybe they saw something or overheard a conversation that has the piece we are missing. Look, you can stay here with Pilate and look through these books. I know the answer may be here as well. With Nedra helping, you do not really need my help anyway." He tries to smile, thinking flattery will throw me off.

I do not know what to say, so I stand speechless. After all of this, everything we have been through, he is just going to up and leave? I feel the room crushing in around me. My pulse falters and I have to catch my breath. Apuri looks at Pilate with a desperate expression. I follow his gaze.

"Althea?" Nedra whispers through our link, "I know this is hard, but Apuri has family and friends too. You cannot deny him this chance of reunion, as you would wish he would never do to you. Let him go. You will see him again soon."

I grit my teeth with frustration before releasing a sigh in defeat. "Okay, but where will you go? And how will you get there?"

"My crew stayed and fought with the advisors in Reverie. I will start at Lauk. If they are not there, someone in charge will know where they are."

My cheeks flush with anger and embarrassment. How could I be so selfish? Amidst everything that has happened, I somehow let myself forget about Apuri's family. Still, I hate to see him go. I do not want him to leave me!

The day we met, we were gathered in a field to meet with the advisors after I shared a dream with Louveri about her death, her real death. My family and I were told her death was a suicide, that she hung herself in her dorm room closet, but there were too many things that did not add up. The night before I met Apuri, I found out Louveri was the Dreamer before me. She had discovered, through her informant, Apuri, that Zixus was using the Pyramid to extract magic from the Fae. Before she was able to pass on this information to the advisors, Zixus and his goons attacked her in her dorm room in college and killed her, making it look like a suicide.

Apuri volunteered himself to join Nedra and me on our mission to destroy Zixus and his Pyramid and save the world. I let myself forget that he came to that meeting with a group of hegira. He was able to meet and bond with the hegira from Tsar's crew, but that was not his family. He has not seen, or even heard from his family in months. And he has not complained about it aloud even once.

"Okay," I say to Apuri in a much softer tone. "But how will you get there? And how will you contact us once you do get there and let us know if you learn anything?"

He looks between Pilate, Not, and me, "Well, that part I have not figured out." He shrugs. "Any suggestions?"

"I may have a solution," Pilate says softly, not wanting to intrude. "There will be a price, though."

Apuri pushes his hands into his pockets, and drops his shoulders. "I have nothing to give, but a few leftover biscuits from our breakfast."

"That gives me an idea," Pilate says, tapping his small finger on his chin. "Currency in Reverie is based on an individual, not on any monetary items."

"It is true," I say. "I actually purchased these clothes," I run my fingers across the intricate embroidered design of flowers and knots, "with a wish." I laugh at the memory.

"So," Apuri sounds a little worried, "what would I have to pay? And to whom?" He shoves his hands into his pockets, wrinkling the hem of his plain blue shirt, to hide his anxiety. He is not fooling anyone.

Pilate chuckles, "Well, I think you will not have any problems. Sage is quite the connoisseur of anything that satisfies his sweet tooth. Play your cards right, Apuri, and he may let you use one of his mirrors."

I smile at Pilate's tone. I can hear a story coming. Apuri does not bite, though; so, I ask, "And what, pray tell, does a mirror of Sage's do that Apuri could use?"

Pilate's fur ripples with excitement. He leaves the books he is searching and goes to the chair in which he was sitting when I first met him. He climbs up and looks at each of us before beginning. Finding stories and keeping them safe might be Pilate's job but telling them is definitely his passion. He is in his element.

"Long ago, long before the great war and the segregation of humans and Fae it is said Elves walked the Earth." There is a twinkle in his eye as he smiles and clasps his hands together. His antenna begins to glow.

"The Elves are said to have been the most beautiful creatures alive. Their skin was lightly tinted and smooth, glistening like a pearl. They were so in tune with their inner selves, so magical, that they literally shined. The colors of their eyes would complement that of their skin. Their hair, it is said, was white, and as they grew older, and wiser, it began to change. It became highlighted with the colors of the rainbow. At first, it was as soft and muted as the colors of their skin, but as they grew and learned, the colors grew brighter, more saturated. The elders' silky locks are streaked with the most vibrant colors you'll ever see."

His eyes glaze over with the magic from his tale. I feel myself being pulled by the same magic. I am hanging on his every word, but I cannot help myself from interrupting. "Where are they now? What happened to them?" I am sorry I ask as soon as the sentence falls out of my mouth.

Pilate's magical stupor disappears to be replaced by disappointment, even sadness. "Nobody really knows. Some think they were never really here, just a myth. Others say they were weaker than the rest of the Fae and died out. Hogwash, I say! My own belief is that the Elves not only were, but *are* very real and very much still alive. Reverie is a very large realm, and the Painted Forest is a very deep one with endless Gateway Trees. Something I have discovered, and documented," he adds proudly, "is the deeper you go into the Painted Forest, the bigger and more magical the Gateway Trees become. Though, you must know where you are going or you will end up walking out the other side before even passing through the middle," he says with a wink.

He smiles and ducks his head with the shrug of his shoulders as he says in a quieter tone, "Of course, I have not told anyone else about it yet, but I have been doing my own research to find the Elves."

"Wow, Pilate!" I breathe in amazement. "That is a lot to take in. And you have not told anyone about this?"

"You are the first, my friend."

That sparks a little fire in my heart. It is always nice when someone makes you feel special, and Pilate seems to always know what to say to do just that.

"Well, this is all nice, I guess, but what does it have to do with me finding a way back to Lauk?" Apuri asks. One of his quirks is he likes to get right to the point.

"Ah, yes." Pilate says, getting back on track. "Well, it is said the elves created magic mirrors used to not only let you see, but also transport you to other places. The small ones let you gaze upon any desired place. The big mirrors, however, allow you to step through and be transported anywhere you can imagine. The downside is that it is a one-way trip, unless you have another magic mirror, of course. Sage is the sole owner of any and all magic mirrors known to man and fae. So, Apuri, what you will want to do is to use a small mirror first to gaze upon Lauk. If you see the other hegira there, you then will use a big mirror to step through. If, however, the other hegira are not at Lauk, you will have to continue your search until you find them. Unfortunately, the mirrors only work by place, not person."

"Sounds simple enough." Apuri says optimistically. "What are we waiting for?"

"Ah, well, that would be your payment. As I said, Sage's weakness is his sweet tooth. I am sure as talented as you are in the kitchen, anything you create would be to his liking, but you must make enough of it to suffice your use of both a small and a big mirror."

"That sounds doable." Apuri replies. "Any suggestions on what I should make, and where to get the ingredients? I used the last of what I had to make our breakfast and lunch today."

At the sound of food, my stomach releases a loud grumble. I laugh it off, and the others follow suit. Leave it to my stomach. It can never be quiet.

Pilate calms his giggles and turns back to Apuri. "You are more than welcome to use anything here. If there is something else you need, you may have to check in some of the other shops. I am afraid I cannot help you with payment there."

"Thank you, Pilate. And I will whip something up for us while I am at it." He says with a wink in my direction. I roll my eyes in mock annoyance and poke out my tongue. He laughs as he stands to return his current book to its shelf. He then heads to Pilate's kitchen while the rest of us resume our search through the books.

Nedra gets a message from Ophidius before we are able to fully resume our reading. He says the advisors have all arrived. They have been updated on our current situation and are hard at work looking for answers on their end.

"Althea," Nedra adds, "Louveri is well. Feather left her with Indri and all of the younglings." He chuckles, "I bet they have their hands just as full as the rest of us, if not more so."

I sigh with relief. I can feel the worry leaving my body. Louveri is safe! "Thank you, Nedra. And please tell Ophidius and the others thank you as well. Let them know we will update them once we make it through all of these," I fling my hand toward the shelves on the walls around us.

"He says they will do the same. Shall we continue then?"

"Yes! Let's do this!"

With a new optimism, I go back to the shelf and grab a small dark leather book with beautiful silver filigree lining the spine and cover. The silver shines out almost like a light against the dark black leather. I trace my finger over the intricate twisting lines. They look similar to the ones on my outfit, but something is different. Something magical.

I open the book to reveal the first page and disappointment. I cannot read it. It is in another language.

"I can read it, Althea." Nedra whispers through our link. "And I think you should put it on Pilate's desk. Be sure to put it on top where it does not get covered up."

"Okay," I walk through the door to Pilate's private quarters. I go to lay the book on top of the tallest stack of books we have already found, but I find it difficult. Something in the book is calling to me. Unfortunately, we have many more to search, and time is dwindling. I force the book down and turn quickly back to the other room.

Just as Nedra and I finish up with our wall of books, the most delicious smells waft in from the kitchen. Pilate, Not, and I head into Pilate's private quarters to see what Apuri has made for us to eat. Nedra flies out and gets his own meal.

Apuri cooked us a wondrous meal of rice and vegetables smothered in a creamy, savory gravy. As I am savoring each delicious bite, a wall of exhaustion hits me like a hammer. I stifle a yawn and look around at my friends. They, too, look worn out.

"Maybe," I suggest after another yawn, "we should rest before doing anything else."

They all nod in agreement.

We finish our meal and prepare a place to sleep. Before lying down, I go outside to wait for Nedra. I find a nice soft grassy spot between Pilate's shop and the trees to sit while I wait. The moon is just as glorious as last night by the stream.

It is refreshing to sit upon the earth in the moonlight. I am still tired, but not exhausted anymore. I can feel a connection with the ground beneath me and sky above. I cannot help but think of my dream of the beginning and of the Creator.

"Musing in the moonlight?" Nedra interrupts my thoughts. I look around for him, but all I see is treetops. "I have decided to rest in my cave tonight." He answers my question before I can ask it.

"That is fine. I will see you in the morning, Nedra. Let the others know we are going to get some rest, and they should do the same. Goodnight."

I decide to sit out here for just a little longer before retiring for the night.

Chapter Six ~ Elves and Mirrors

The rising sun shines through Pilate's little window onto my body, filling me with golden warmth. I stretch my arms, back, and legs as I prepare myself for the day ahead. I am a little concerned that I do not remember my dream, if I even had one, but then I remember Nedra was not near. I check our link. He is still in his cave; I can feel him. But maybe his continuous proximity is what has allowed me to remember my dreams lately. Trying to not put too much stock into it, I force myself to get up.

I take advantage of Pilate's bathroom and morning mint. It has been a little while since my mouth has been this fresh. I will have to remember to restock my pack with some mint of my own.

I walk out of the bathroom to be greeted by the comforting smell of cinnamon toast. Apuri's cooking. I smile and drift toward the smell. Everyone is already seated around Pilate's reading nook preparing to eat breakfast. A large platter of cinnamon toast surrounded by small wooden cups and a pitcher of juice sits on the floor in the middle of everyone.

I tie my hair back in a ponytail, thankful my trusty hairband has survived this long, and sit down between Pilate and Not, across from Apuri. I glance at his bag, packed and ready to go, lying on the floor beside him as I grab a piece of toast. He is ready to leave.

My heart sinks. I knew he was leaving, but I thought I would have more time. I avoid Apuri's gaze by shoving the toast in my mouth and pouring myself some juice. We all eat in awkward silence until Not takes it upon himself to lighten the mood.

"Althea, have you heard from Nedra yet this morning?"

"Mm..." I pause to chew and swallow my food. "No, I figured I would let him get as much rest as possible. It has been a while since he has been able to sleep in his own bed. He will come back to help us read as soon as he has had breakfast." I see the curiosity in his eyes. "You know, Not, I am sure Nedra would love to let you see his cave; if you would like to, that is."

"Oh, would I! I mean, yes, I would love to!"

I chuckle and say, "I will be sure to put in a good word." I wink and laugh. My eyes meet Apuri's and the laughter dies. I swallow.

Looking for a chance to escape the awkwardness, Pilate and Not decide to clean up. I grab the last piece of toast from the tray before Not takes it along with my empty cup. Being an octopus fae, he is able to carry everything except Pilate's cup back to the kitchen with ease.

Alone in the room and time dwindling, Apuri and I are forced to get over ourselves and talk to each other. I hold on to my last strain of stubbornness, as we both stand. I let him talk first.

"Look, Althea," he says, pacing the floor with a huff. He is never able to be still when he is emotional. Another quirk I have grown attached to. "I do not want to leave you, but if I do not do this, who knows what will happen! You said it yourself, we do not have much time. People could be dying right now, as we are sitting here in the safety of Pilate's home, arguing."

I drop my head, "But what if something happens to you, and I am not there? Or what if something happens to me, and you are not here?" He walks over to me and places his hand under my chin forcing me to look at him.

"We are both strong. We will be okay. And besides, Nedra can just do that mind trick and let us talk to each other, or at least pass messages, right?"

I laugh thinking of our unconventional dragon three-way-calling.

"Besides," Apuri continues, moving his hands to my shoulders, "you are needed here. With Nedra helping you, you can read my share of books and then some. And I am the only one who can do this. Besides, I have been dying to tell my dad about you." He smiles, and it takes me a moment to catch on to what he says.

"Your dad?"

He laughs jokingly, "What? You thought I just sprung up from the ground one day? No, Althea. I have family and friends with whom I grew up. And I would very much like for you to meet them all. So, let me do this. I will get some answers and be back before you know it. Or, if you finish up here first, you can come to me and meet everyone before we have to go save the world again."

I lean my forehead against his chest, and he wraps his arms around me and kisses the top of my head.

I laugh, "So, what are we? I mean *this* between us. How are you going to introduce me to your family and friends?"

He steps back. "Um, I... We... What do you want us to be?"

"That is not what I asked," I say as I playfully hit him in the shoulder. "Actually," I laugh again, "I guess that is what I am asking you."

"Hm." He holds his chin in thought, "Well, I care about you. And I think you care about me?" He raises an eyebrow.

"Yes, I do."

"But we have not really had much time to get to know one another. So, I will introduce you as my friend."

"Friend?"

"Well, we are not *partners* yet. So, yes, friends." He smiles.

"Yet?" I ask curiously. He only smiles in return.

Changing the subject, he grabs his pack and starts walking toward the kitchen. "I do have a favor to ask of you."

"Oh, and what favor would that be, *Friend*?" I put extra emphasis on the friend part, but all he does is smile again.

"I would like it if you came with me to Sage's magic mirror shop. You can help me carry his treats, meet him, and see where I go. Then, you can come back here and read your little heart out."

Now I smile. "Okay, friend. I will do as you wish, but only under one condition."

"And what is that?"

"I get to try some of these sweets!" I grin as we walk into the empty kitchen.

I guess Not and Pilate already went back into the front of Pilate's shop to start searching through books. In our heated discussion, I did not see them go by. I would not doubt if Not used his camouflage to sneak by. The thought makes me laugh.

Apuri looks at me questioningly. I wave it off.

"I am going to miss that, you know." He says as he goes to the little counter and sink in Pilate's kitchen.

"What is that?"

"Your amusing inner dialogue."

I blush in embarrassment then poke out my tongue. We both laugh as he pulls two enchanting silver leaf platters from the back of the counter. One is stacked with a pyramid of brownie squares, and the other is piled high with the same donut bites he made here at the beginning of our first mission.

I grab one and pop it into my mouth. My eyes close in bliss as the deliciousness melts in my mouth. "Mmmm."

"If Sage does not like these," I say as I grab one of the brownie bites, "I am bringing them back with me!"

"Ha, ha!" Apuri replies sarcastically, but a shadow of concern crosses his face and rests within the crease in his brow.

"Hey, it was just a joke. He is going to love them!" He smiles, but the crease remains.

Not sure what else to say, I grab a tray and lead the way to the front of Pilate's shop. Just as I had suspected, Not and Pilate have already begun working again.

"Hey guys," I say as we enter the room, "I am going to help Apuri carry these down to Sage's shop, and then I will be back to help. It will not be long."

"No worries, Althea. We will be here when you return. Apuri," Pilate turns toward the door, holding his place in the book he's currently reading, "do be careful. And do not hesitate to call if you need help. You are always welcome to return here anytime, even if Althea is not here," he finishes with a wink.

I laugh. Not, absorbed in his current book, raises an arm to wave goodbye. Apuri returns the wave, though I am unsure if Not saw it. With nothing else to do, I open the front door to Pilate's shop, and we step out into the Marketplace.

It is not as busy in the Marketplace as it was on my first day here. The only signs of life are a few shop owners bustling about before opening time. A man who looks much like a walking stick strides in front of us carrying an armful of green leaves piled up to his face. He nearly collides with a more human looking fae walking the opposite direction reading a list. I watch with a silent cringe as I wait for the two to crash into one another. At the last second, they each turn a hair's breadth away. Surprisingly, they pass by each other unscathed.

"I could use some agility like that," I whisper to Apuri as we turn left and head down the almost empty path. Apuri laughs in agreement.

We follow Pilate's directions to Sage's magic mirror shop, ignoring the staring eyes of the shop owners we pass. The different shops are each beautiful and magnificent, truly a part of Reverie. Passing them now makes me wish I had the chance to spend the whole day shopping. We pass a sign with markings similar to those Zixus used on The Pyramid and the same ones engraved on the skin of the pixies.

The pixies. I wonder if one of Sage's mirrors would be able to find the pixies. But I do not have anything for payment. Maybe I could make something with my paintbrush, but I left it back in Pilate's shop. Okay, so maybe that is not a possibility at this moment, but I can ask while I am here to know if it is worth coming back.

Maybe I will be able to check out that shop before leaving. It may be of some help.

I see our destination, a cluster of fluorescent blue woodland mushrooms. I do not remember this shop on my first walk through the Marketplace, though my mind was distracted at the time.

Shifting my platter of sweets to my left forearm, I knock on the door - a full body length mirror placed smoothly on the stalk of the largest fungi. There is no answer so I knock again. On my third knock my hand passes clear through the door, almost like going through a Gateway Tree.

Apuri places a hand on my shoulder to steady me; then, we both step through cautiously.

The walls in the round room are covered from floor to ceiling in elegantly framed mirrors. Upon closer examination of the frames, I am shocked to find the pixie symbols again. The language of magic. That is what Nedra called them. Curious.

"Hello? Mr. Sage?" I call out as I look around the shop.

I hear muffled sounds from the narrow hallway at the back of the room. This time Apuri calls out, a bit louder. "Hello? We are here for Sage. We have brought payment." He swirls his tray of sweets around as if luring a fish with a worm. I laugh silently and elbow him in the side. He bends at the waist, recovering from the blow while managing to save his platter of brownies. If he had been holding the donut bites, he might not have been as lucky.

As if following the scent of the sugary baked goods, a fae as blue as his shop emerges from the depths off the hall.

"Mm, smells delicious," he says in a sing-song voice. "What- I mean, to whom do I owe the honor?"

Standing in the full light of his bioluminescent shop walls and mirrors, I am able to see more than just his beautiful blue color. He is about average height, no taller than Apuri, but something about him makes him seem taller. He practically radiates magic; I can literally feel the energy buzzing off of him. He has no hair, and he wears layers of long robes. The bottom layers match the blue like everything else around him, but the top open robe is a silky, knitted white one, draped carefully from his shoulders to his ankles. His eyes match this top robe, white and elegant.

"Hello," I say, extending my hand, "I am Althea, the Dreamer, and this is Apuri, my... friend." I finish awkwardly. Why did I not just say this is Apuri?

He does not seem to mind the awkward introduction. He stretches his blue hand forward to shake my hand.

"Oh, such a pleasure! And such delicacies,"

"Althea," Nedra calls in through our private link. "Sorry I am late, but I am on my way to Find It now. If you would like, I am sure I can read while flying.

"No problem," I reply through our link, "and no need right now, Nedra. I am with Apuri at Sage's shop. Go ahead to Pilate's; I will be there in a bit."

I realize I am still holding Sage's hand and the platter of donut bites which he seems eager to have, stretching his free hand out to grab them.

"Oh, I am so sorry." I release his hand and pass over his payment. "Dragon link." I laugh and point to my head. Sage smiles awkwardly, and Apuri rolls his eyes in exasperation. He is probably wishing I did not help him now.

"Not to worry, Dreamer." He says my title like he knows me. I try to ignore the strange feeling that washes over me.

"Um, Apuri is here because he requires your services, your mirrors. He has baked these as payment. I gesture toward the platters of sweets.

"Mm, excellent!" Sage smiles as he pops one of the donut bites into his mouth and closes his eyes, savoring the deliciousness. "Please, come this way." He turns and walks back down the hall. We follow him as he turns to enter the first room on the right.

"First," Sage sings as he walks around to the other side of a small table in the center of the room – the only thing in the room – "we take care of business. Paperwork, that is." He smiles and beckons us closer as he snaps his fingers and a scroll appears within his hand. He unrolls it on the top of the table. Its white marbled surface feels out of place in the organic room. Still, it is beautiful.

We walk forward until we are in front of the table. Sage pushes his platter of donut bites into the air beside him where it floats effortlessly. He then takes Apuri's platter and does the same to it. Apuri, startled by the sudden movement of the brownies in his hand, holds tight before realizing what is going on. He releases the platter and watches it float over to rest in the air beside the other one.

"Payment is already documented here," he points to a line showing: *Payment – 2*. "Tell me your request here, then you sign here." He points to the corresponding lines. I glance at the top of the paper to see both our names (as well as my title) printed elegantly on the first line.

"Um, just Apuri will be using the mirrors." I say pointing at my name on the paper.

"Oh, not to worry." He smiles as his sing-song voice lingers. I look at Apuri; something does not feel right about this. Apuri, not seeing my look, gets straight to business.

"I need to find my crew with the use of a small mirror and go to them through a large mirror."

Sage simply smiles and nods. The expression on his face makes me wonder if he has been ingesting parts of his shop for extracurricular activities. I find the thought amusing and hold on to it to dispel my unease. "Just sign here, and then we will go back and let you pick your mirrors."

"Do you need to write down his request?" I cannot help but sound a bit irritated. Apuri gives me a look then glances down at the paper, suggesting I do the same. I roll my eyes and follow his gaze. The request is there on the first line. It reads: *1 view; 1 travel.*

"Oh." I mumble, defeated.

Apuri signs his name with the offered pen, and then the scroll vanishes. Sage walks around the table, past us, and back out of the room. We follow after him again. I glance behind to check on the floating desserts to find they, too, have vanished.

"These," Sage waves to the wall on the left of the shop entrance, "are the viewing mirrors. The wall holds more than fifty small mirrors. Each is the size of a classic hand mirror, but the shapes and colors vary widely.

"And these," he shows the long mirrors on the other side of the room, "are for traveling. There are significantly fewer travel mirrors. Only about a dozen, each stretching from floor to ceiling, line the wall from the front door to the hallway. "Take your time and let me know when you are ready."

He stands still in the middle of the illuminated room as Apuri and I walk around looking at each mirror. Seeing my reflection stare back at me from the entire wall only increases my uneasy feeling.

"Are you sure about this?" I quietly ask Apuri, hoping Sage does not have super hearing.

"You know I am," he replies, not as quietly as I would like. He stops in front of a golden bronze frame in the shape of a fish. "This one." He says aloud for Sage to hear.

"Excellent! Wonderful taste, Apuri." He is behind us so quickly, I am not sure he walked. "Ah, yes. He has a match, a mate. She lies just across there." He points straight across the room. We walk over to find a larger version of the fish framed mirror.

"These lovely ladies," Sage informs us in his sing-song voice, "stay on the wall. But I assure you they still work perfectly. All you have to do to use her mate is gaze into his face and focus your thoughts on that which you wish to see. When you are ready, you may hang him on her hook here and step through." He points to a well camouflaged hook within the frame of the larger mirror.

"Nedra, are you still there?" Feeling uneasy about being left alone with Sage after Apuri leaves, but not wanting to leave him in the same situation, I call upon my own security.

"Yes, Althea. Is something wrong?" Nedra replies, concerned – and rightly so – through our link.

"I am not sure. I hope not; I have a feeling." I smile at Sage hoping he does not see through me, knowing I am talking about him within my mind.

Apuri gives me a hug. I hold him, trying to tell him to stay, but his mind is made up. The deal is already done. He gives me a smile of confidence and holds up the smaller mirror. At first, he looks concerned; he does not see them. Then, the features of his face relax and he smiles. There is hope in his eyes. He found them. I smile despite my feelings. He hangs the mirror on the hidden hook and with one last goodbye smile, almost trance-like, he steps into the big mirror.

A tear rolls down my cheek, wiping the smile from my face. I mutter thanks to Sage and quickly leave the shop without another word or thought as to whether I am being rude or not. Without looking at the other shops or faeries, I run back to Pilate's shop and slam the door behind me. I do not stop to chat but instead keep running until I exit the back door to meet Nedra under the trees.

Before I reach him, my knees give out and I crumble into a heaping, sobbing mess onto the grass.

"Althea, what is wrong? Are you hurt?" Pilate and Not's voices call out behind me. I can hear them approaching. Nedra nuzzles my hair.

"Althea, we are here. Let us help you. I know it is hard." I see an image of myself being pulled from the rubble of the Pyramid. I feel the heartache within Nedra and see it upon Apuri and Not's faces. They thought I was gone for good.

"You know he is alive. You know he is well." I hear Nedra's voice, but it takes a moment before the words sink in.

I feel Not and Pilate come up on either side of me. "I have shared what happened with them," Nedra says. I am thankful I do not have to relive all of that.

"I am sorry, dear," Pilate's small voice says in my ear. "I did not think to warn you of Sage's... Well of Sage. He can be very off-putting. Unfortunately, dear, most faeries are similar. Those of us you have met are familiar with humans, or simply have better manners. I am afraid the longer you stay in Reverie, the more you will see the shadows within. Not necessarily bad, mind you, just different," he finishes as I sit silently with my face down. A few silent minutes go by as I stop crying.

Once I am visibly calmer, Not asks, "Did you get to see the location of the hegira? Where did Apuri go?"

I smack my hand against my forehead. Stupid! I was so caught up in my own emotions I did not even look at the location in the large mirror when Apuri stepped through. How could I be so stupid? He could have just walked to his doom, and I let him!

"It is okay, Althea." Nedra growls, upset at my self-insults. "We can simply replay your memory and pay attention this time. And then," he says in a calmer voice, "we can all finish these books."

I sit up and wipe my face. "You are right. The sooner we get finished here, the sooner we can join Apuri."

We head back inside, leaving Nedra in the cover of trees so he is not bothered by outsiders, and begin sketching the scene from the mirror so we can finish reading. If wild magic, disappearing pixies, and mysterious elves were not enough motivation, getting back to Apuri is the kick to speed things up.

Chapter Seven ~ Zoar

We have finished sorting through all of Pilate's books. I am sad to say it took us all day. We only just finished and the sun has already been down for a couple of hours. We only took small breaks to eat – the food was prepared and left by Apuri. If Nedra was not here, I am not sure we would have made it.

He and I finished our wall and Apuri's while Not and Pilate completed their own. We ended up finding a total of sixty-four books that may or may not help us. We have decided to rest for the night and continue with those tomorrow.

* * * * * * * * * *

I am scared!

I look around. I am in a jungle. "Wild magic," my intuition says.

Something is wrong. Something is watching me.

I think wild magic has released more than just fast-growing plants. An image of a shark flashes like lightning.

"Land Shark!" a whispered shout rings through the air.

My heart races. My breathing quickens.

Okay, it is okay. I am okay. This is a dream. I cannot be hurt.

I need to breathe and focus.

Land shark the voice said. I focus my gaze trying to pierce the darkness. I can see shapes of the forest, but I do not see the land shark. I close my eyes. It is here. I can still feel it watching me.

I hear it come out of the shadows. I stand still. I am dreaming, so it cannot hurt me. The hairs on the back of my neck stand on end. I can hear it breathing. I squeeze my eyes tight as it gets closer.

I open my eyes just in time to see its large shark teeth open right in front of my face. I scream and fall back, barely avoiding its lethal bite.

Unfortunately, I did not escape its four-inch claws. It caught my right forearm.

I cry out in pain and shock.

Wake up! Wake up! Wake up!

"Althea!" I hear Nedra's voice.

* * * * * * * * * *

"Althea! Wake up!" It is not only Nedra I hear, but Not and Pilate as well.

I wake in a panic, unable to breathe or speak.

"Nedra!" I shout through our link and aloud. "Nedra what is happening?"

I open my eyes to see Pilate and Not hovering over me.

"She is sweating, she has a fever." I can hear the worry in Not's voice.

Pilate places something cool on my arm. "Here, Not. Let's fix her arm first; that will fix everything else." I glance down to see not only my arm, but the floor and my abdomen where my arm was resting, covered in blood.

"Althea, you need to stay calm. You were hurt... in a dream. I do not know how or why, but the effects reached into reality." Nedra is doing his best to explain what is going on, but I am not following. "Althea, you are bleeding. You are hurt badly."

"Nedra. Nedra, my dream! There was something in my

dream. A monster. No, an animal. There was a voice; it called it... shark? Land shark! Nedra, tell Pilate it was a land shark!"

"Land shark?" I hear Pilate say confused.

I grit my teeth against the pain and try to control my breathing. "Aah!" I cry out through my clenched teeth as Pilate places another cold compress on my arm.

"Althea," Not leans close to my face. "Do you think you can heal yourself? Like you have been doing with Aspen?"

I puff my cheeks and release my breath slowly, trying to focus. I nod. Heal myself. Yes. It takes me a few minutes to block out the pain so I can focus on healing. It is much easier to heal others than to heal myself. I focus on my breathing and find the golden light within my core. I fan it with my breath, urging it to grow and spread. I slowly let the thought of my arm join with that of healing. I push that light there, to my arm. The subtle warmth of the healing energy spreads and wraps itself around my pain, snuffing it like the flame of a candle.

With the pain gone, I allow myself to relax and breathe.

"You did well, Althea. Your arm seems to be healing." Nedra sounds less worried, proud even. "Shall I inform Apuri of what has happened?"

"No, Nedra. Let him be. He has other problems."

"Very well."

"Nedra?"

"Yes, Althea?"

"Could you check to see that he is okay? Without talking to him, that is?"

He hums in response.

"Pilate?" Pilate comes to my side immediately. "Do you remember that tea that helped me dream?" He nods. "Is there a tea to stop them?"

"Althea?"

"If this is what is going to happen when I dream, I do not want it." Pilate's face falls. "I will check, dear." He rises and walks toward the kitchen.

"Althea," Nedra speaks through our link after Pilate

leaves. Not is keeping a watchful eye over me from his bed in the corner. "Althea," Nedra says again. "You must not let fear take over. You are strong. You are a warrior. Remember your magic when you dream."

I roll over without saying anything. Deep down I know he is right, but I do not have the strength to fight right now. Facing the wall, feigning sleep, I remove my amulet, block Nedra from my mind, and allow myself to cry silently in my dark corner of Pilate's home.

I wake with a start as the sun shines through the window. I have been fighting sleep all night. I look around the room to see both Not and Pilate fast asleep. I am not sure if Pilate ever found a dreamless tea. I check the small stove, but there is no kettle on it.

I see movement just outside the window, near the back door to the shop. I rise slowly and tiptoe quietly to the back door. I slowly peek around the edge of the small window set in the door.

"Wha-!" I shout and fall back as I see a large black eye staring from the other side of the window. "Nedra!" I shout aloud waking Not and Pilate. I realize I am still blocking Nedra from my thoughts. I replace my amulet to release the block and allow our private link to flow once more.

"Althea! Serves you right!" I can hear his snort and chortle through the door.

"Shut up!" I shout as I kick the door while lying on my back. Not and Pilate rush in to check that I am okay. I assure them I am as I roll over and push myself up. I walk back to the door and open it to an uncomfortably cramped dragon on the doorstep. The sight sends a shock of laughter through me. Before I know it, I am thrown into a fit of giggles.

"Amused, are you?" Nedra says as he steps back and opens his wings to shake them out. He stretches his front feet forward, wiggling his claws, arching his back, and stretching his tail skyward, much like a cat. The giggles continue.

"I believe, Althea, you are delirious from lack of sleep." He stands up and looks down at me. "It does not suit you." His scales flex showing a glimpse of the deep red core beneath.

"Perhaps," I reply, still using our private link. "I will head back inside and have some breakfast with the others. Maybe that will sober me up enough for our task today." I turn and walk back inside past Not and Pilate to the bathroom.

Breakfast did some good for me. I no longer suffer from hysteria, though the night catches up with me from time to time. I am thankful to have Nedra reading through my eyes. If it were up to me, I would not be able to remember much.

Tired or not, the small book with silver filigree keeps catching my attention. We are going through the books that lay upon the desk, top to bottom. The small decorated book lies eighth from the top. I had planned to keep it at the top of its pile, but with Apuri gone, I lost focus. We simply began stacking books wherever they fell.

We are doing much the same thing we did when we were here at Pilate's all those months ago searching for books, information, on past Dreamers: We are finding every bit of useful information and compiling it into its own manuscript.

Pilate is busily sorting the written manuscripts into some organized method he knows. I am transcribing what Nedra and I have read as he reads it back to me from memory.

I write until my hand cramps and I have to take a break. I grab a cup of tea, letting the warmth seep through my hand relieving its tension. I sip the vanilla spiced tea slowly letting it flow down my throat into my stomach. The warmth spreads through me giving me another kick of energy.

I look over at Not as I set my tea, now half empty, back down and pick up my pen again. He is able to partition his thoughts, writing four separate manuscripts at once. Each of his four arms work independently of the others. He is able, at this rate, to write faster than Pilate and myself combined. That does not stop us from trying to keep up.

I finally make it down to the small book, but when I do, Nedra tells me to set it aside. He says that it is important and must be read last as it will have many answers. I look at the language of magic written on the cover before I set it down.

"Why not go ahead and read it now for the answers we need?"

"Because, Althea, if you find the answers you want in this book, you will no longer pay attention to others you need from the rest of the books."

"Okay, oh wise one!" I mock sarcastically through our link. He only laughs in reply, that deep chortle I find so much comfort in.

We continue through the remaining pile until nightfall. We have been so focused on our writing we have forgotten to eat. My stomach lets out a bear-worthy growl. I look at the desk afraid of how many books will be left. I almost cry when I see an empty desk. The floor around me is piled with parchment upon parchment. The only book remaining is the small one decorated with silver filigree, the book written in the language of magic.

I reach for it, but Nedra stops me, "Not yet, Althea. Help gather the parchments for Pilate. This one we will read tonight."

"But it is night." I argue.

"Wait until you go to bed. I will show you why, I promise." I stubbornly give in and help Pilate retrieve all of the papers. I lay the book beside my bedroll so I do not forget about it.

We organize the transcripts into four groups, one for each of our main topics: wild magic, pixies, and elves, and one for when two or even all three of them cross paths.

I wish Apuri was here with us. But, I cannot focus anymore on my own personal problems or wishes. I need to focus on what is in front of me in these books. There is something deeper at play than merely the release of wild magic.

With all of the papers gathered neatly for Pilate to sew together for his new manuscript, we have decided to retire for the night. Nedra told me to wait for Not and Pilate to fall asleep before he will show me why he wanted me to wait to read the book written in the language of magic.

That is what I am doing now, lying, waiting. I can feel the book, hard beneath my arm, keeping me awake until the time is right. Pilate decided to return to his own room and bed. I do not blame him. Now, I am simply waiting on Not to fall asleep.

I lie still trying to silent my own breathing to listen for Not's. He does not snore like Apuri, more of a heavy breathing.

"Nedra," I whisper through our link, "Do you think you could slip into Not's mind and see if he is asleep? Also," I remember, "you have not told me about Apuri yet either."

"Notyal is asleep, Althea. I am sorry. I, like yourself, have been distracted by the day. Apuri is within the Painted Forest. He has found his hegira crew and they are searching for more. I believe they have made camp for the night. Would you like me to tell him anything for you?"

I contemplate having him send a message to Apuri, but in the end I decide against it.

"Let him rest, Nedra. Thank you. I will be out in a minute."

Careful not to wake Notyal, I slip quietly outside to meet Nedra.

"You brought the book?" Nedra greets me at the tree line as usual.

I hold the book up as I high step over some fallen branches, though I am not sure if he can see it in the dark. The moon is no longer full and at maximum luminance.

"Good. Bring it here and we will discover its mysteries."

"Okay," I reply, thankful I do not have to say the words

aloud and waste breath. "What is the title of this little book anyway?"

He chuckles, "The book is called, *Zoar.*"

I make it to Nedra and hold the book out to him. "Okay," I say aloud, "show me some magic." I smile as I wait for him to show me.

"Step over here, where the moonlight shines through the trees, and hold the book for the silver to catch it."

I do as he says, walking to stand under a ray of moonlight shining through the trees. I hold the book up to let the light hit it. The light touches the corner filigree and within seconds it spreads through every inch of silver until the book seems to be the source of light. I can feel the magic vibrating off the book. It gets hotter with the vibrations, and I am unable to hold it any longer.

I pull my hands back to keep them from being burned. I expect the illuminated book to drop to the ground. Instead, it is still in the air where I held it, floating. It opens on its own and the light changes from white to green to purple to yellow. It flashes over and over from one color to the next, showing every wedge of the color wheel and all the hues in between. It speeds up until it becomes a projection of images and words in the magic language.

My jaw drops in awe. "What does it say, Nedra?"

He chortles, "Let it finish. Then, I will show you in your dreams. For in your dreams, Dreamer, you have no barriers. I believe tonight will be one of enlightenment. Would you stay and watch it with me?"

"I will." I climb up onto his back and lean forward on his neck to watch the show. Before long, I feel the weight of sleep pulling at my eyes.

* * * * * * * * *

I am not sure where I am, but it is beautiful!

It is even more beautiful than the Painted Forest, and that is saying something.

It is an island surrounded by the clearest of teal and aqua colored waters. Corals of vibrant purples and pinks carpet the ocean's floor visible even from the beach. Fish of every color of the rainbow swim to and fro beneath the waters.

The beach between the golden grass and the waters is as pink as an Easter egg. In fact, the entire island seems to be in eternal spring. The sky is a clear blue painted with crisp, white, fluffy clouds. The trees scattered on the island are flowered in patterns of pink and white blossoms.

The island radiates with pure magic, like a song in the air. It makes my hair stand on end, but in a good way. Like static electricity from a balloon.

I leave the beach to explore the land above, careful not to step on any of the immaculate shells scattered along the pink sands.

The ground beneath the golden grass is firm but not hard. The fuzzy tops of the grass tickle my fingertips as I stride through them. I close my eyes, enjoying the smell carried on the breeze from the blossoming fruit trees ahead.

I wish I was more familiar with my trees now. Oh well, I do not need a degree in dendrology to appreciate the beauty that the Creator has made. I smile and continue my walk, almost forgetting this is a dream.

Just as I remember the fact, I hear Nedra whisper, "Use your magic, Althea. While you are dreaming, this is the place."

"Nedra? Are you seeing this? Where am I?"

"Yes, Althea. This is what I wanted to show you. This is what I read in Zoar. Use your magic. Try something, anything."

"Okay,"

I stop under the trees and raise my hand. I feel the breeze blow through my fingers. I close them quickly and flick my wrist. I see the colors on my wrist swirl with white and blue. I look up to one of the flowers and guide my wind around it. It spins, gently at first, then faster until the blossom breaks free of its branch and drifts carefully down to me.

I hold it in the palm of my hand and wrap it in a bubble of

water. It does slow flips as it floats to the center of the bubble. As it rights itself again, I freeze the bubble, turning it into a clear crystal ball of ice. I warm my hand with magic, melting the ball once more into a liquid bubble.

I continue the flow of heat until the water is turned to steam, and the blossom is once again dry.

I take a moment to breathe. That was not so hard. Wind, water, ice, fire...how about we try some earth?

I wonder....

I focus my thoughts on what I want. I picture it in my mind. I see the small white flower change, and I will it to be so. I watch with bated breath as the flower fades from white to gray and changes from light as a feather to heavy as a stone within my hand. When I am finished, I release my breath and look to see a small stone flower resting in my palm.

I did it! I actually did it! I laugh aloud with joy. I toss it up in the air and catch it again.

"Nedra! Nedra, did you see that?" I say the words aloud and through our link. He chuckles that breathy laugh I love so much. "I did! Wonderfully done, Dreamer! Can you do more? I love a good show." He laughs again.

I laugh too and then try some more. I turn the stone flower to sand, I then heat the sand and turn it to glass. I create a chain, attach it to the bauble, and hang it from the tree.

I breathe again and focus my thoughts. I touch the chain where it meets the tree and release my magic into it. It melts into the wood until they are no longer distinguishable. The chain has become a sprig and the bauble has returned to its natural form, a blossom on a tree.

The image brings me joy; my heart swells.

This has been fun, but I need to test myself. I am not sure how much longer I will be able to sleep. How about we start where we left off? I crouch low to the ground, gather some dirt into a pile with my hands. I take a moment to make up my mind on what I want.

I know!

I close my eyes, placing both hands upon the loose soil. I focus my thoughts and let the magic flow into the ground. I feel the roots take place. I urge them to spread and grow. I feel the ground break beneath my hands. I give one big push of magic, move my hands to rest on my knees, and open my eyes. I watch a tree grow within seconds to full maturity and sprout several dark green, drop shaped fruit. Avocados!

I stand and pluck one of the appetizing green fruits. I slice it with my knife and take a piece to eat. It is perfect!

Before I can enjoy it any further, I feel myself waking.

* * * * * * * * * *

I wake with a start and fall hard on the ground. I forgot I had fallen asleep on Nedra's back. I yell when I hit the ground causing Nedra to wake in the same state. He rises up and unfolds his wings only to hit the trees above and behind him, sending him back down to the ground beside me.

We both laugh as I apologize through our link. Once we have recovered, I go and fetch the small book from the ground where it must have fallen after the light show last night. I return to Nedra's side and sit on the ground beside him to flip through the book.

The pages are thick and porous. I trace my finger over the surface of one and feel the faint tingle of magic. Curious, I look at the colors on my arm. They are still a swirling rainbow mix, no one element or power over another.

"I would like to go back there," I say aloud, not sure if I am talking to Nedra, the book, or myself.

"Perhaps tonight when you sleep," Nedra says. "For now, we have a task to finish. Go inside. Notyal and Pilate are waking. I will tell the three of you about this book once you are all fed."

"Okay. We will eat quickly." I laugh and head back inside.

Thankfully, my friends are just as eager to hear what Nedra has to say as I am, though I am sure Pilate already knows. We eat quickly as planned and I pass him the book.

"Ah, this is one of the lovelier books amongst my collection. Sadly, I only know a few words in the language of magic."

"Did the pixies never teach you?" I ask curiously.

Pilate laughs a small laugh in reply. "No, dear. Many things the pixies keep to themselves, their marks included."

"Oh. Well, Nedra, what do you say we hear it then?"

"Very well, grab some parchment to write on."

We do as he says as well as collecting all of the information we documented yesterday. Pilate also grabs his tools for binding. He plans to start the binding as soon as we are able to add the newest pages to what we already have.

Once we are settled, Nedra begins. "The book is called *Zoar*. That may be helpful to your translations and future learning, Pilate. I, too, will teach both you and Nook when this mission is over. It is said – and you have learned some of this from your earlier findings – that elves were a great magical force. As direct descendants of the Creator, they were leaders and lords of all magic, superior to all fae and mankind. Legend says when the Earth was new, wild magic covered its surface; few places were safe for habitation. The elves joined together all of their knowledge and power to find a way to control wild magic and stop it from taking over the world."

"Great! Does it happen to say how they did this?" I ask eagerly.

"Oh!" Not jumps into the conversation excitedly, "I read, and wrote down, that wild magic was weaker in extreme temperatures. Did they burn it or freeze it out?"

"Hmm." Nedra hums. I can hear his irritation at being interrupted. "No, the book does not say how they accomplished this task. It does, however, say that once it was controlled, or rather maintained, the elves left. They disappeared without a trace. There was rumor of a secret island, their refuge and new home. This is the island Zoar, the one you saw in your dream, Althea."

I sit up straighter. I do not remember seeing any elves in

my dream.

"The book speaks of the island in great detail and the magic used to create it. It does not, however, give directions or any description of its location, save that it is an island. There are chapters dedicated to life on the island, one for animals, one for fish, and one for plants. There is reference to more stories in the language of magic. Though I am not sure where to find those. The end, the last page of the book has one single word: Dreamer."

I am speechless, as are my companions. Though it does not last long.

"But...." I take a minute to wrap my mind around this. "The elves were here and disappeared years, centuries, before the Great War. And Dreamers were created by the spirits as a product of that war, to fix what was broken. That is why I had to *destroy* the sodocs!" I cannot keep myself from shouting. This does not make any sense.

Why is it when we go looking for answers, all we end up with is more questions?

Nedra replies to both my spoken and silent questions through our private link. "I am sorry there are no more answers, Althea. But this is still more than we knew."

He is right.

"Okay," I say aloud. "Now what about all the information we recorded yesterday? We are probably not going to have time to read through everything before we have to leave. Really, we should contact the others and meet back with them as soon as possible. Nedra, Pilate, have you heard anything yet?"

"Not yet, Althea, but it is still early."

"No." Pilate says. He retrieves his amulet from within his thick mousy fur. "If you would like, I could contact them."

"Maybe once we finish here. Thank you, Pilate. For now, we have to figure out what we are going to do about this soon-to-be book."

Pilate organizes the newest papers with the others. We all think silently for a moment.

Finally, Notyal is the one to speak up with an idea. "You could...I mean, I have been thinking. Forgive me, Althea. I will be plain. I have been thinking over the past few days of a solution. I may have two."

"Two?!" I reply surprised. "Go on."

"Well, I remembered you talking of the first time you were here searching through Pilate's library, and how you were able to control your dream by drinking a tea so you would not wake and forget it. I am aware that you are stronger, in all aspects, and able to remember your dreams most nights now. But, perhaps you could drink this tea again. Go into a deep sleep so you are not interrupted, and go back to the Pyramid, or its remains. I was thinking you could check on the, er... progress of the wild magic that escaped its walls. Then you would be assured of the urgency of matters."

"That is a great idea, Not!" I grin, but it is gone as soon as I remember the land shark from my dream. I do not voice my concern, though.

"Yes, well," he squirms, "the second one may not be as simple. I am not sure." He pauses to be sure I am listening before continuing. "I have seen you create things a few times now. You are able to create something from nothing using only your magic and imagination with ease, or so it seems." He smiles. "I now have two questions that could be of great use to us all. First, can you change the size and/or shape of an object? And second, would it be easier for you, or faster, to create something already made? Copy it, that is."

I think for a moment. "Copying should not be too hard, as long as I know the elements. I am not sure about resizing. I will give it a shot though."

"Wonderful!" He replies as his face relaxes. "My idea is for you to copy this book," he gestures at the papers, "once Pilate binds them. Then shrink the copy to fit within your pack for travel. You could even make multiple copies for all the libraries and duplicates for our companions."

I grin again, but refrain my urge to wrap him in a hug.

"That is another great idea, Not! Truly wonderful! It sounds, my friends, like we have a plan!"

Chapter Eight ~ More than Land Sharks

I just finished my first successful shrunken copy of Pilate's book!

It fits perfectly inside my pack along with all of my other stuff.

Pilate is contacting Nook, and Nedra is contacting Ophidius and Apuri. Once all parties are informed, we will decide upon a meeting time tomorrow.

Night has fallen, and we are weary from our day. I will make more copies of the book as Not suggested before going to bed.

I am starting on that now while enjoying a cup of sweet rose tea. I hated to break into my own supply, preferring to save it for the road, but Pilate was all out. I could have drunk one of Pilate's other teas, but as exhausted as I am I needed this one.

I was going to only make one for Nook and one for the Advisors, but after further thought, I am making more. I have decided, if I am able, I will make one for each of our companions as Notyal suggested. I will also make one to send to Sengsourya and Ceres. Pilate says he will find messengers to send those for us.

Not is going to inform Queen Melanomie as soon as we find a natural source of water for him to communicate. I have not asked yet how he does that, but I am curious.

To make the books, I am using earth, water, fire, and air to make the paper; earth, fire, and water for the ink; and then earth, water, and air for the cover and binding. It took a few hours of contemplation and careful planning to prepare.

Once I figured out all of the combinations of elements, I decided to approach it like an art faerie. Instead of using a brush or wand, however, I use only my hands and my magic. I sculpt it in midair, drawing with my fingertips and smoothing with my hands.

Shrinking the book was a bit more challenging. It took almost as long for me to shrink it as it did to make it. I decided after the first one I am going to simply create them smaller from the start.

The whole process really is exhilarating!

As I create book after book, Notyal watches me in awe. I even catch Pilate watching, distracted from his conversation.

After my third copy, I decide to mix it up a little bit and challenge myself by creating two books at the same time.

Pilate and Nook have finished talking. Pilate says they have not found anything different than we already have written down. They are all going to rest; Noni is already asleep.

She has been enjoying all of the dragons almost as much as they have been enjoying her. Most of the dragons have never seen a human up close. To have a youngling interact with them, in their own home nonetheless, has really caused excitement inside Dragon Cave.

I wish I could have been there to see that. Nedra said she was already asleep when he returned to Dragon Cave the other night. I am sure he would have enjoyed watching his friends and neighbors play with a human child.

He has finished speaking with Ophidius now. He says they have another book written in the language of magic.

They have not told him what is inside, just that they did not consider it until Nedra spoke to them. They want us to come there immediately in the morning and bring our books with us.

They were very impressed when Nedra told them I was making copies with magic. They have requested that I also make a copy of *Zoar* for them to add to their own library.

I might go ahead and do that for Sengsourya and Ceres as well. Though, I am not sure my copies will work in the same magical way as the originals because I am not sure how that happens or what to include magically.

"Maybe when I retire from saving the world I will come back and help you duplicate your entire library, Pilate." I joke. Really, I would like a simple life, living with books. I had thought of being a librarian when I was a young girl. It is funny how we spend so much time making plans that never unfold. I am not making any more plans for my life now until I know we are safe.

The nightmare flashes through my mind. Right now, we are not safe.

I finish making all the copies necessary and Pilate retrieves a bag for us to carry them. I forget how heavy books become once their number increases.

A memory of a friend and myself moving out of an apartment in college floats to the surface of my mind. When the year started I had only a few books, perhaps half a shelf full. But my love of books was an addiction. As the year passed, I bought books for fun, books for learning, and I am not ashamed to say some books I purchased simply to have more books. Like I said, it was an addiction.

Anyway, at the end of the year, when it was time to move out, my collection had more than tripled. I tried putting all of the books into one big box so I would have less boxes to carry. That was a huge mistake! I could not lift it. My friend and I tried to lift it together, but the bottom started to break. We reinforced it with tape on both ends and all of the corners. We carefully laid it on its side and tried to carry it out sideways - one of us at each end. Just as we made it outside the building, the box split and books spilled out everywhere.

I was mortified. I literally cried right then and there on the sidewalk leaving the apartment. Seeing all of my precious books lying, pages ruffled, on the ground broke my heart.

So, we turned the box with the broken side up and set it on the grass beside my pile of treasures. We picked each one up, placing it carefully back into the box, checking for torn pages in the process. Afraid of passersby taking my books for themselves, I stayed with them while my friend went to get more, smaller, boxes and tape.

Once the books had been separated into several smaller boxes they were much easier to carry. They may have taken a little more room and time to carry, but I had all of my books and they were safe.

I shout up to Pilate, "You might bring several small bags." Better to not make that same mistake twice.

Thankfully he heard me and returns with a handful of smaller, meshed, cloth bags with handles. We divide the books up by destination and set the filled bags by the back door. Pilate will go with us to the Advisor Tree tomorrow; so, we have decided to wake up early, have a quick breakfast, and head out as soon as possible.

Now that everything else for the night is finished, Pilate is brewing the kava tea for my dream. He has been stocking up on the herb since our last experiment worked so well. He figured I might need it again. Pilate has already made himself a bed down here for the night. He says he wants to be here as soon as I wake up to know what happened in the dream. Notyal has already crawled into his bed, as have I, and we are chatting before it is time to sleep.

Not is telling us about a tea they drink at summer solstice, made of a blue and purple plant known as zip that sounds much like kava. They drink it on the night of their festivities to receive dreams from the spirits as to how the year ahead will go. He is curious to know what will happen if I drink that tea. Will I be given dreams by the spirits like the rest of them? Or, since that already happens on a daily basis, would it work much like the kava tea, giving me more control over my dream state? Maybe it would have no effect on me at all.

At any rate, I have told him if we are within Ceres on the summer solstice, I will try this zip tea and tell him the results. I asked if I could not simply try the tea any time, but he was adamant it only works on the night of the summer solstice.

Nedra, amused by our conversation, says he would like to try some of this tea himself, even though he is not much of a tea drinker. He has come up with a plan to spike Apuri's cup, or simply not inform him of the tea's special abilities, when the occasion is here.

I share his musings with Not who wholeheartedly agrees. He has already made the plans of where everyone will sit during the celebration, and he has assured me he will inform Queen Melanomie of our scheme so she does not ruin the surprise.

Pilate breaks up our laughter with a nice large cup of steaming warm kava tea. "I figured you could cool it to your preferred temperature with your powers. Best not to waste time. The night has already gotten a head start on us."

"Thank you, Pilate." I take the cup from him and take a sip. Still too hot, the tea has scorched my upper lip and tongue. I breathe in sharply to cool the burn and send some healing energy to the area. Then, using my fingertips I spread a little frost on the outside of the cup, careful not to drop it.

I wait for the tea to stop steaming before I remove the frost and try another drink. It is still hot, but not so much that it causes damage. I drink it slowly and carefully. After half the cup is gone, I feel its effects kicking in. My brain gets foggy, my eyelids become heavier, and I cannot stop yawning as I tell my friends goodnight.

I add a little more frost and quickly finish the last half of the tea. I hand the empty cup back to Pilate, and my head barely makes it to my pillow before I am asleep.

* * * * * * * * * *

It takes me a minute to adjust in the dream. Once I am to myself again, I get to business. I know straight where to go: the beach at South Carolina where Zixus had his lair, the Pyramid, glamoured as a run-down aquarium. E.G.O.E. were the letters on the sign. I will never forget that sign.

I think of that place and allow myself to go there.

I am not really sure what I expected to find here, but where The Pyramid fell, lies a small jungle.

Trees with rich green canopies stand tall. The ones at the center are taller, stronger. Vines have begun to weave a web between them. As I walk through the lush green world around me, it's impossible to see any remains of the civilized world beneath it.

It has begun.

My heart begins to race.

The Pyramid has only been down for a couple of weeks, and a jungle has already encompassed not only the entire perimeter of what used to be Zixus' lair but the surrounding two blocks in each direction.

Well, I think we can definitely say my dreams are premonitions.

"Nedra, are you seeing this?"

"I am, Althea. You are right. We will inform everyone at the meeting in the morning. Perhaps the Advisors can send a few scouts out to keep a watch on it. If we learn its rate of growth, we will be more prepared to stop it."

It has not reached the pier or the beach yet. Not can inform Queen Melanomie to send some of her scouts as well.

Oh! Petricha can instruct the guards of Sengsourya to keep watch on it from above.

I feel the hairs on the back of my neck stand on end.

"Nedra, something is watching me. What if it is the land shark again?"

"Do you feel prepared to handle it with your magic?"
"No. I do not even know where to start!"
Then you must wake up, Althea. Wake up now!"

* * * * * * * * * *

My body jerks upright as I wake with a gasp. I startle Not and Pilate awake as well.

"Calm down, Althea. You are safe." Nedra whispers through our link.

I look around the room. Pilate and Notyal are sitting up now as well.

"Did you make it? What did you see?" Not asks as excitedly as one can in a sleep drunken stupor.

"What? Oh, uh yeah. It is there; it has already started."

I spend the next few minutes describing what I have seen in my dream to Pilate and Not. They agree to having scouts watch the area and report back any changes. At the mention of the possible land shark again, Pilate gets up and goes into the shop. Curious, Not and I follow after him. He switches on some lamps and goes behind the desk. He opens the bottom left drawer, takes out a small, dusty black book. He blows the dust off and wipes it with his paw before opening it to retrieve a small key from within the back cover.

He sets the book on top of the desk and uses the key to open the narrow top middle drawer. I watch closely, curious as to what Pilate has hidden so well within his desk. He pulls the drawer open, and all that is inside is a stack of papers. Papers with watercolor pictures painted upon each one.

Pilate sorts through the stack of paintings slowly until he comes to a gray and blue one toward the bottom. He moves it to the top of the stack and straightens the papers by tapping the bottoms on the desk a few times. The sound echoes in the quiet, dark shop. Chills shoot up my spine, and my arms shiver with goosebumps.

He turns them around to show us the picture as he asks,

"Althea, I know you said you did not get a good look, but is this possibly what you saw in your dream? Is this the land shark?"

"I am not sure." I take the papers from Pilate to examine the picture closer. The paper is thick and feels handmade. The painted creature is outlined in rich black ink and colored in various shades of gray and blue. Its rows of large, sharp pointed teeth stand out the most, but the eyes give me the creeps. They are beady and black, emotionless. The skin looks smooth with gills right behind the head, just like that of a shark.

Unlike a shark, it has four legs with large webbed feet and even larger claws. I glance down at my forearm. There are no visible signs of the gash caused by those large, fierce claws, but I will never forget that feeling. I thought in that moment when the land shark was attacking me that I was going to die.

It looks like a wolf that was born in an apocalyptic world. A wolf and a shark morphed together; this truly is a creature of nightmares.

At the bottom corner of the paper, it is signed, "Land shark, Pilate."

"Pilate, you drew this?"

"Is that what you saw?" His persistence is starting to worry me.

"I am not a hundred percent sure, but the teeth and the claws do look like it. Why? What is wrong, Pilate?"

I hand the papers back to him. He looks at it like it is a snake about to strike. Still he takes them. He does not return them to the drawer. Instead, he walks back through the door to his living room.

Not and I share a glance of confusion and then, once again, follow after him.

"Pilate, what is going on?" I ask. "How did you draw that painting of the land shark?"

His haunted face looks at me with worry as he says, "I saw it in a dream." He sits in his chair and begins to weep as the papers fall to the floor scattering in every direction. "I saw them all in dreams."

Not and I hurry to pick up the papers for him. I have never seen Pilate like this. We gather the papers, and I ask Not to put on some vanilla spice tea for Pilate. He hurries to the task. I kneel down in front of Pilate with the papers still in my hand.

He looks at me again with haunted eyes. "When you first mentioned the name, I thought perhaps your hysteria made you misname the creature. I am sorry for that. I should have shown you this as soon as you mentioned the land shark. Is this how you felt, Althea, when you first followed me here? If it is, I deeply apologize for the shock I caused you. I assure you, if I could, I would go back and redo everything."

"What? Pilate, no. I mean, yes, I was shocked, but... Pilate, look at me. You are okay. We are going to figure this out together."

Not returns with a steaming cup of vanilla spiced tea. I take the cup from him and cool it before passing it to Pilate. I wrap both of his paws around the cup to ensure he will not drop it. He closes his eyes as he takes a slow, long drink. I am relieved to see the Pilate I know when he opens them again.

"Feeling better?" I ask soothingly.

"Yes, thank you. Thank you both!" He smiles.

I hate to do it, but we need answers. I hold the papers up with an arched eyebrow. Pilate smiles weakly and takes his painted pictures from me. There are at least a dozen, probably two. I should have counted them while picking them up.

As if reading my mind, Pilate stares at his work and says aloud, "There are twenty-four. They started after you came into Reverie." He looks me straight in the eye. "I thought they were interesting. Some I thought were my own ideas until they would show up again in later dreams. If I had known, Althea..."

His voice chokes, and he takes another drink of tea. Once he has calmed down again he continues. "If I had known they were more, I would have told you immediately. I am sorry." He begins to cry silently.

I quickly take his now empty tea cup, and give him a hug.

"Hey," I whisper as I hold him, "this is not your fault. Know that. This is not your fault. We will figure this out just like everything else - together." Not takes the empty cup back to the kitchen.

"I enjoyed painting them," Pilate says as he looks through the pictures. "I had actually been contemplating writing my own book about them."

"And you still can! Why not? Because they may be real? Do it, Pilate! Write your book. I am expecting it now!" I fake a stern, serious look, but break into a smile shortly after. Pilate smiles. That makes me feel better.

"What would it be about?" I ask as I take the pictures he passes to me. Not has returned and is sitting beside me in front of Pilate. I pass the pictures to him once I have looked at them.

"Well, I have not thought out too many details yet. All I know for sure is it would be around these creatures. They are all strong and powerful. Of that I am sure."

"Pilate," I am curious to know, "have you ever dreamt of an island full of flowered trees, surrounded by pink beaches and crystal-clear water?"

"You are talking about the island from your dream? The one from the book *Zoar*?" I nod during his silence. He continues, "I do not remember for sure, I am sorry. I will be sure to let you know if I do."

"Thank you." I look at Not and back to Pilate. "Would you like to try to get some more sleep before our meeting? The sun will be up in only a few hours."

"Yes, I think we should at least try," Pilate answers with a smile.

"I will second that," Not agrees with a stifled yawn.

We all go back to our beds to catch a few hours of sleep before the meeting in Inon.

"Nedra, I think I would like to go back to Zoar this time. Please help keep me on track, okay?"

"I will, Althea. Rest well."

* * * * * * * * *

We did it! I am back on Zoar.

"Would you like to practice using your magic again?" Nedra asks.

"Not tonight, Nedra. Tonight, I am just going to rest."

I walk down to the beach. I do use my magic to create myself a soft grass bed. I lie down and watch the waves in the ocean for a few minutes before closing my eyes.

Even though it is still light out, the sounds of the ocean and the wind in the trees lull me to sleep within seconds.

Chapter Nine ~ A Plan

We are on our way to Inon now. We will travel by light, flying on Nedra's back. After a quick breakfast, Pilate and I agreed I should make copies of his paintings as well. I made one copy to bring to the meeting and one for myself.

Pilate and Not are riding quietly behind me. As we climb higher into the sky, I start a private conversation with Nedra, something I have been wondering about for a couple of nights.

"Nedra, how do you know the language of magic? You can read it easily, but even Pilate barely knows the language. And you said yourself Nook does not know any more than Pilate. So, it cannot be a dragon thing."

He chortles, and his red embers glow bright beneath his bone ivory scales. "No, Althea, it is not 'a dragon thing.' I was taught by the dragon who lived in my cave before me."

"Oh? And how did he learn?"

"I believe he learned from a pixie, but now that I think of it, I am not sure he ever told me."

"How long did it take you to learn?"

"A few years," he answers.

Before I can ask any more questions, we are at the ray of light. I calm my mind and focus on my breathing as we are transported to Inon.

I open my eyes to see the great fountain in the center of the city with its rainbow paths spiraling out in different directions. My heart swells at the sight. I am not sure why, but I expected it to have changed in some way. It has not.

I am the one that has changed.

Nedra lands in the same spot he did the first time we came here together, the end of the path that goes by Tilda's house. I point it out to Not as we walk past it on our way to the Advisor Tree. Pilate, of course, already knows where each of the advisors live. Not falls in love with the liquid spiral staircase at first sight.

"When I return home," he says as we continue our walk, "I may have to have a tree like this made in Ceres for me. To be placed within Mel's castle, of course."

"I am making a note of it now," I say to him with a wink.

As we walk past the fountain – the beautiful structure built to ensure the faeries always remember the war when they learned to work together – I glance at the symbols, the glyphs upon it. This fountain was built by the first group of advisors as a sign of their mutual cooperation and the changes that were to come. How sad that it took war, an attack by the sodocs, and the taking of lives, to open their eyes to equality.

As we approach the Advisor Tree, I instruct Not and Pilate to take my hands to go through, but give strict orders to not let go until we are on the other side.

I will never forget my first time inside the Advisor Tree. I walked through with Tilda. She instructed me to hold her hand. As soon as we stepped through the gateway, we were surrounded by the deepest of waters. I thought I was going to die. Tilda explained, once we were on the other side, that it was a test. Only the strongest faeries can be advisors.

And then when I had to walk through, only a few months later, alone, the Advisor Tree's test for me was Neoinas. Only, I had forgotten it was a test. I thought I died, thought my friends had died. I shudder at that memory. Still,

I remember Tilda's words that she could not tell me about the test before entering or I would not be allowed passage. I do the same now for Not and Pilate.

They both do as I say and take my hands with no questions. I am not sure what we will see once we step through, but whatever it is, I know I am strong enough to make it. I have already faced my biggest fears in real life; I do not need a tree to do that for me.

To my surprise, we go straight into the large round room inside. There is no test. I turn around and stare at the entrance in shock.

"Althea!" Clementine shouts excitedly. I turn around and give her a warm hug. She steps back and looks at the tree's entrance. "We are having guests today, so no tests."

That makes sense. I look around the room. Things look a bit different than the last time I was here. There is a round table growing out of the floor in the center of the room. Chairs surround the table, but nobody is using them. I see Aspen, Tsar, and Lady Nell, but I do not see Noni. I look around again thinking I may have missed her because she is so small.

Someone touches my arm. "Nook took her up to your sister's house," Lady Nell says. I smile and give her a hug.

"Nell! How are you? How is Tsar?"

"We are good. He is good." She glances over at Tsar who is now talking to Notyal. He does look better, healthy. The sight of him makes me miss Apuri. Nell notices and gives me another hug.

"Attention!" Ophidius hisses the command for the meeting to start. We all walk around the table finding available chairs. Not, Pilate, and I place our bags upon the table. It causes our side to look cluttered. I am tempted to move them to the floor, but they are important. We will be passing them out shortly so things will balance out.

Once we are all seated, Ophidius waits for the room to fall silent. I realize as we are all sitting here, that I have not yet thought of Verity.

When I was in college, I went on an art trip to New York City, New York. We went to several museums over the course of a week. That was one of my favorite memories before my life went downhill. That was all before Reverie. One night, we had free time to go exploring. One of my best friends, Elizabeth, and I went to Times Square. We had humongous meat-filled sandwiches at Carnegie Deli, and then we traveled around using the subway, which I was fairly sure we could have died or gotten lost on.

At one point on our fun, free-night we ended up across the way from where the Twin Towers stood. It was late, the sky was dark. We could barely see the tiny silhouette of the Statue of Liberty between the black shimmering water and the black sky. Across the water, though, was a hole in the cityscape. All of those wondrous lights from across the water were beautiful, no doubt. But that hole is all I saw. My heart aches anytime I think about it.

Now, as I look around inside the Advisor Tree, my heartstrings are being pulled again. There is no actual hole in the cityscape, no empty chair, or even a place set for where she would be. Still, I see that hole; I feel that vacancy.

Ophidius clears his throat and looks around the table. He can feel that hole, too. I can tell by the way he is avoiding eye contact. "Let's begin," he says in a commanding tone.

He looks at me. "Dreamer, have you brought the copies?" He looks at the bags on the table.

"Uh, yeah. I mean, yes. These," I hand him a copy of both *Zoar* and the book we have compiled, "are for your library here for the advisors. These," Not and Pilate help me pass out the individual copies to everyone else, "are for each of you to have just in case we get separated on this journey. We all know it can happen." I attempt a laugh at my own joke, but we all know how true it is. Clementine and Nell smile for support.

Notyal has the books for Ceres in a bag and I have the books for Sengsourya in another. I pass this bag to Petricha now. Tilda offers to take the bag for Ceres from Not. He hands it over with a smile. He has been staring at her the whole time we have been sitting at the table and probably for a while before that, too. I know he is homesick. The sight of Tilda must remind him of Ceres. He has not been back home since he joined us to find Nedra. I have dearly appreciated his company and his help, though.

"Do you have the other book written in the language of magic?" I ask Ophidius.

"We do, but I do not think it will be much help in this matter."

I nod. Nobody else says anything, so I start the conversation by asking, "Have any of you heard of an island called Zoar?" I look around the table; everyone, except the advisors, shakes their head no. The advisors look to Ophidius; he has taken the role of their leader.

"It is a myth." Ophidius replies coolly.

I huff, "But what if it is not? What if it is real?" I catch Feather watching me closely. She has not said anything to me yet.

"What if it is, Dreamer?" Ophidius replies in a challenging tone. "How do you suggest we find out? How do you suppose we get there?"

I sit back and purse my lips. "I do not know."

"What do we know?" Aspen asks point blank, tired of waiting for answers.

"Wild magic is loose, and spreading fast," Not volunteers.

Everyone looks at us. I sit up straight and tell them of my dream last night as well as the night with the land shark. At mention of the attack doing real physical damage, Feather looks concerned. I notice but do not say anything.

Pilate tells them of his paintings, the creatures he has dreamt of. We pass the copies around the table.

"This is what attacked you?" Clementine asks when the painting of the land shark falls into her hands.

I nod. Aspen looks over to see what remains of the

wound on my arm after seeing the picture. "Impressive," she mutters to herself.

To stay on track I say, "We also know the pixies have gone, and we do not know where or why."

Tilda's head drops. Mitzi was not only her house cleaning pixie, she was one of her closest friends. As were all the pixies and their faeries I am sure.

I turn to the advisors. "What can you tell me about the pixies? How long have they been here? How long have they been going extinct?"

"They have been here as long as I can remember," Eart says. "I know that is not as long as everyone else, but as far as I can tell, their numbers have been dwindling since before I came here."

"The pixies were a set number," Arsona adds. "They did not procreate. I have never seen one die, but I have been told they simply vanish. They do not age. The only way for one to die is to be killed."

"No," Tilda whispers. Feather rubs her hands together, worried.

"Hey," I say to them in a calm voice, "nobody knows what happened to them. Let's not jump to conclusions. I promise you all I will find out what is going on. But I need to know where to start. Right now, everything we have found points to the elves and Zoar. So, that is the path we are going to follow."

"Where are you going first?" Ophidius asks. I can hear the doubt in his voice.

"First," I say with extra confidence not caring if my irritation shows, "we need to send as many scouts as possible to watch the wild magic in the human realm and search to see if there are any more signs of it. Then, we are going to meet up with Apuri and the rest of the hegira. We need every piece of the puzzle we can find. He has gone to see what he can find from the hegira. Nedra has been keeping in touch with him. As soon as we are finished here, we will join him. We will use these books," I place my hands upon the books in front of me, "as we go and frequently report back any updates we can."

Still, Ophidius is unconvinced. His reptilian eyes blink. I feel his irritation, it is obvious to everyone in the room. There is more to it, though. This is not about pixies, elves, or even the *mythical* island, Zoar.

"We will do the same, Althea," Tilda says, pushing her chair away from the table to stand.

Finally, Ophidius speaks in a hiss, "So, Dreamer, your *plan* is to march out into darkness blindfolded with both hands behind your back and *hope* that you find your way. Forgive me for saying so, but this is the real world, not one of your dreams. If you fail, we all pay the price. This is a faerie problem, for faeries to fix."

Tilda turns to him, "We have done what we planned. Althea gave us all the information she has. She has the start of a plan – that is more than the rest of us have – and she is willing to carry this plan out at her own risk, again. Or have you forgotten that she, too, lost her life in the battle against the sodocs?"

He jumps to his feet and slams his hand against the table. "Yet, here she stands!" he shouts, throwing his hand in my direction while staring at Tilda.

Instead of arguing with him, Tilda smiles, sweetens her voice, and tells the rest of us, "We will send the scouts tomorrow. This meeting is officially adjourned. Thank you all for your help; you may leave."

Everyone gets up and, with their books, heads for the door. Tilda walks over to me, bringing a book similar to *Zoar*. It is the one they found in the language of magic. I can feel its energy as she gets closer.

"Have time to make one of those magic copies?" She asks with a smile as she hands it to me. I glance at the mark on my wrist. The colors swirl quickly at its touch.

"It does not take too long," I mumble as I look at the book. This one is completely silver and the fancy decorations are brown. I levitate the book using my magic to control the air around it with one hand as I begin making my own copy with the other.

"Ophidius did not think it relevant," Tilda whispers, "but I believe you should have it even if it does not help with this journey."

I make a sound which I hope lets her know I am listening but also keeping my focus on the task at hand.

"I am sorry," she continues in a whisper, "you do not deserve the way he spoke to you, treated you. You are the Dreamer; you deserve nothing but our respect. I will tell you why he is upset to help you understand, but please know that his views are his own and not shared by the rest of the advisors." I nod in response as I stitch the pages of the copied book together. Tilda takes a breath and whispers, "Ophidius blames you for Verity's death and for the release of wild magic. When we first heard that you died, none of us knew what to think. We were relieved at the sodocs and the Pyramid no longer being a threat, but we were also still recovering from the battle ourselves."

I have finished the book now, but I remain silent and let her continue.

She holds the original copy against her chest. "I did not know about Verity until the battle was over, but Ophidius... Althea, he was right there with her. He saw it happen. He said there was no time, nothing he could do to stop it. He is angry with you because it is easier. Althea, he blames himself."

I swallow hard; I cannot stop the tears. She gives me a hug and assures me, "It will all be okay."

"He is right." I say in a choked whisper as the tears fall faster. "I saw it too, in a dream. She looked right at me. She knew I would see. She told me to hurry. If I had been there to help fight, she might still be alive. And I am the reason wild magic is loose. If I had learned about my magic sooner and practiced more, I could have controlled it better, and maybe I would have been able to release the spirits without the wild magic escaping."

"You do not know that!" She says. "I do not believe it for a second. This is Zixus' fault, nobody else's. We believe in you, Althea. You were chosen to be the Dreamer for a reason. The Creator brought you back for a reason. Have faith."

I force myself to calm down and breathe. Thankfully, the room is empty. Tilda returns the book to its shelf and gives me a moment to regain my composure. I meet her by the exit when I am ready.

"Indri said Nedra can read it." She says, nodding at the book still in my hand. It reminds me of the others left on the table. I hurry back to grab them and a bag to place them all in before we walk out.

"Yes, he can," I say just before we come down the steps where the others wait in a group. "Can you?"

"Indri has been teaching me. Nedra is the one who taught him."

We decide it is best to not discuss anything more until we get to Feather and Louveri's house to avoid unknown eavesdroppers. Nedra has already flown to meet Nook in their yard.

As we climb up the hill through the woods, the sight of the cabin warms my heart. Just seeing it gives me comfort. The closer we get, the more that comfort is replaced by questions. I shake my head, *there will be plenty of time for questions. Right now, I am going to see my sister and be thankful she and all my friends are here.* My heart sinks. Not all of my friends. Apuri is not here.

"Would you like me to check with him now, Althea?" Nedra asks through our link. "We should know their destination and they should know we are coming their way soon, anyway."

"Yes, Nedra. Thank you." I reply through the link.

I forgot how steep and tiring this hill was. As we reach the top, I must take a break for breath. Thankfully, I am not the only one. Lady Nell and Tsar also pause to catch their breath.

"Magic does not help when it comes to physical activity,

Dreamer?" Arsona jests with a laugh.

I simply give a breathy laugh and shake my head which causes everyone to laugh.

As we file into the quaint cabin, I wonder if it will hold all of us. I walk toward the living room and do a double take. It has expanded to at least twice its normal size and is now lined with warm, comfy sofas. Frost still lines the walls, but I do not see it anywhere else.

"We redecorated for company," A voice says from behind me.

I turn around to see Louveri. "I am happy you are safe!" she says as she quickly wraps me in a warm hug which I gladly return. It takes everything I have to keep the water works at bay this time. I savor the hug for a few more seconds before we finally separate.

"Looks like we are not the only ones who did a little redecorating," she holds me at arm's length and looks at my eyes. "Sweet!" she whispers, noticing the colors on my arm, too. "It is from the Domain isn't it?"

"Yeah," I reply. "Hey, have you been having some strange dreams?"

"Define strange," she laughs and then guides me into the living room, before answering further, to join everyone else on the warm brown sofa. Feather passes out refreshments before she joins the rest of us.

I sip my strawberry orange mango blended juice and eat a few grapes. The room starts to hum with various conversations from each corner of the sofas while we enjoy our snacks. Feather and Tilda talk about their growing faerie children and their ever-developing talents.

Clementine and Aspen are discussing various teas, comparing their flavors and various healing properties. I cannot hear what Petricha and Arsona are saying; they are not exactly whispering, but their conversation looks private. Pilate and Not are reading through their books.

Lady Nell and Tsar seem to be simply enjoying each

other's company, sitting silently side by side watching everyone else in the room. I hear Eart and Louveri say something about eyes and realize they are talking to me.

"What?" I ask, a bit embarrassed.

"I was just wondering," says Eart, "if your eyes were any indication of your powers? I find it curious that they are multicolored like mine, like most art faeries, and yet they are different. Instead of the pattern of a rainbow, they have more of a nebula resemblance."

"Yes, I was telling him about the Domain." Louveri adds.

"Oh, well, I never thought about the change being particular to my power. But yes, the spirits did say my powers had grown. It is like the colors in the Domain as Louveri said. We have found that in addition to the faerie magic, I also have the ability to heal, like Aspen. I am also practicing using magic within my dreams. It started out for protection, but it is becoming quite fun."

"Protection from what?" Louveri asks.

As I tell her about the land shark and wild magic, I feel the room around us go quiet. When I finish, everyone is watching me. It seems I have brought the room to attention. It looks like everyone is refreshed, and it is time we get back to business.

"I have been having some weird dreams," Louveri says. "One of them has been an island, but I am not sure it is the same one you see. I do not see pink beaches. I am always on top of a stone cliff at the edge of a sea or inside of a cave that feels like it is in the same spot. I have not been able to control the dream, only observe. It is beautiful, but something about it makes me feel a bit suspicious."

"Well, be careful. I do not want land sharks or any other creatures getting you. Do you have healers, like Aspen, in Reverie?"

"There is one," Petricha answers. "She is known as the witch. I am not sure of her real name. She lives alone within her own Gateway Tree. She makes up teas, tinctures, poultices, and even spells to help those who come to her. She only leaves her home if it is a real emergency and the one requiring her services cannot go or send someone to her."

"Oh, yes!" Clementine finishes Petricha's story excitedly, "Everyone says she just walked into Reverie one day, physically, went straight to her Gateway Tree, and made her home there. Not many actually go see her, because, well, she is not a faerie. Most faeries do not like or trust humans. Some, still focusing on our histories together, actually go out of their way to trick humans or even lure them into Reverie and trap them within a dream-like stupor inside random Gateway Trees." Aspen and Lady Nell look a bit queasy at this news. I do not blame them.

Arsona, seeing their fear, works to ensure their views of faeries are not altogether tarnished. "Things have changed over the past couple hundred years, though. Since the faeries have come together and Advisors have been around, there have been less and less cases like this. It does still happen; we cannot keep an eye on every single faerie in the world, especially those who choose to live outside of Reverie. We do try, though."

"I have a question." Tsar speaks up unexpectedly. "It is off topic, but I have been wondering what we are going to do about transportation? I mean, walking is fine except when you are in a hurry and have children with you. Althea has Nedra, but he cannot carry all of us. Do you have someone who makes vehicles of any sort? Or perhaps horses or rideable animals for sale?"

He looks from one faerie to the next waiting for an answer. Indri comes in from the hallway. He was in the back with the children and came out to get a snack when he heard Tsar's question.

After finishing his small piece of bread with honey and butter on it, he answers, "How about we have Nedra and Nook ask the dragons?"

Nell sits up excitedly, "You can do that? *We* could have dragons?"

"Well, it would probably be just one. And you would have

to go through the ceremony like all dragon riders. Althea did it not long ago. It is not too bad, is it Althea?"

"Not at all!" I reply. "It is pretty exciting. But how would they get one for all of them? Or would it just be for one and they would share like Apuri, Not, and I do?"

"Well, that would be entirely between them and the dragon who chooses them."

"Nedra," I ask through our private link, "could you find out if it would be possible to have a dragon ceremony for Lady Nell. Explain to them the situation, perhaps."

"Yes, Althea, I will ask."

I thank Nedra and let the others know he is asking about a ceremony. I can see the excitement on Lady Nell's face. I do hope they are able to get a dragon. There is nothing quite like it.

"Okay, so we will go to Dragon Cave first and then head into the Painted Forest to find and meet Apuri and the other hegira. Tsar, do you think the rest of your crew from the farm would come into Reverie? Your mother may know more than anyone if there are any answers."

"She probably will not be too keen on it, but I will do my best to convince her if I can. How will we contact them?"

"Hmm. Well, if you get a dragon, you could travel by light to the Glamour, but then you still have a long walk. Petricha, is it possible to travel by light to get to Sengsourya? If they were to find the farm from above it would not be too difficult to simply fly down when it is night or when they have cover."

"No, light traveling only works within the Painted Forest and the worlds on the ground within the Gateway Trees. To get to Sengsourya or Ceres one must find their Gateway Tree or go the long way around. For Sengsourya that would be up."

Her haloed moon eyes twinkle as she mentions her home, Sengsourya.

"Sengsourya and Ceres have Gateway Trees? Why could we not have just used those on our journey to defeat the sodocs?" I ask as calmly as possible. Why did they not tell us this before?

"Ceres has a few ways to be reached," says Tilda. "You may find the pool guarded by the Piper, as you did. Or you may enter through the Gateway Tree, guarded by his brother within Reverie. The third way, as Petricha was saying, is the long way around. You must swim to the depths of the ocean and find Ceres there."

"Yes," Notyal adds, "There are two reasons the latter is inadvisable to anyone not familiar with Ceres: one, it is easy to become lost and, two, outsiders are not welcome in Ceres. Even traveling through the Pool Tree is dangerous if uninvited. When you first came to see us, Althea, you needed Mel herself to escort you, to be accepted into her kingdom. Now, we could use the Gateway from within the Painted Forest."

"Okay, so once Lady Nell, Tsar, and Aspen have a dragon, they should go to the Gateway Tree to Sengsourya and from there to see his mom?" I ask.

"That sounds like the most reasonable plan to me," Petricha answers. "You can travel by light to get to the Feather Tree, that is what we call it. Once you enter the Feather Tree from within the Painted Forest you will arrive outside the gates to Sengsourya. And you have already met my best guards, so that will not be a problem. The rest will be up to you to find the hegira, though the faeries will be happy to help."

"Great!" I say excitedly. "And your dragon will be able to communicate with us through Nedra so we will all know where to meet up. Then, we can figure out what to do next." I love it when a plan comes together.

"In the meantime," Tilda says, "we will be searching for more answers here. Anything we find out, we will report to you, Althea. If Ophidius is still uncooperative, Indri can help."

"Great!" I say again. "Hopefully at this rate we will have found our answers and fixed the problems in no time!"

"Althea," Nedra says through our link, "I have an answer. Though there was some debate since Lady Nell, Aspen, and Tsar are not Fae, the dragons have agreed to a ceremony. Keep in mind, not all of them will participate, but there are enough for a ceremony. It must take place today, though."

"Thank you, Nedra," I reply through our link. "Let them know we will be there today."

"Great news, everybody! Nedra says the dragons have agreed to a ceremony, but we have to make it today."

Lady Nell and Tsar sit up excitedly. "We should tell Noni!" Nell says. Tsar agrees and goes to get her.

He returns with Noni in his arms and a gaggle of faerie children around his ankles. The sight is quite amusing. At the look on their parents' faces, the young faeries let go and run, squealing with laughter, back down the hall to their room. We all laugh after them as Tsar sits down and stands Noni in front of him and Nell.

Her excited squeal at hearing the news is so high pitched, I am forced to cover my ears to keep the drums intact. I figured she would want to leave at this very moment, but as children do, she has requested more time to play before leaving. Her request is obliged, and our drinks are refreshed while we enjoy our last moments before beginning this adventure.

Chapter Ten ~ Nanoaj

"Are you ready?" I whisper to Nell with excitement as we stand just outside Dragon Cave. I take a moment to admire the magnificent Gateway Tree- an ancient oak with twisted roots topped by a massive trunk. The huge branches, stretching on the sides and the tops of the tree, spread into webs of twigs and leaves. This tree has to be hundreds of years old.

Nedra has already taken Aspen, Tsar, and Noni inside along with Nook, Pilate, and Not. Nell has invited us all to come in to watch.

She nods and squeezes my hand tightly as we walk inside. It looks the same as it did the last time I was here, except all of the dragons are inside their caves, waiting. Even Nedra is going to join in, not to claim them as riders of course, but to watch the ceremony. He says there is no better view. He invited me to join him, but I figured it best to stand with Aspen. Tsar and Noni are already in the center waiting for the ceremony.

I give Nell one last hug as I stop beside Aspen and let her walk to the center of the cave alone. It feels like a lifetime ago that I was taking those same steps. So much has changed since then. I watch from a distance as Lady Nell meets up with Tsar and Noni. As she picks Noni up and stands holding hands with Tsar, the Dragons begin to fly.

Nedra goes first as the tenant of the highest cave. The other dragons who wish to participate follow suit from the top of the large cave to the bottom; they leap from the mouths of their caves one by one, ending with Nook. They fly in a circle as one and then break off into patterns. Again, I cannot help but think of synchronized swimmers. I whisper the thought to Aspen, who thankfully, finds it equally hilarious. We muffle our laughter to not disturb the ceremony.

Eventually, our excitement begins to fade. I mean, it is still a wonderful experience, but we have been here for almost an hour. The dragons continue their patterned flight without err.

"Is something wrong? How long did your ceremony take?" Aspen whispers. I can hear the worry in her voice. Not and Pilate watch silently.

"I am not really sure how long it was, but I do not think it was this long. Nedra says it is taking longer than mine because of the different situation. Not only are they dealing with more than one rider, but they are not faeries."

"You are not a faerie." Aspen replies matter-of-factly.

I laugh, "True. Sort of. Since I am the Dreamer, I am part of Reverie. Ergo, faerie. So, I guess we just wait." We decide it is best to sit and watch the show.

I am not sure how long it has been now. I do know we have dozed off a few times.

Finally, something is happening; there is movement in the center of the cave. We stand up and watch as Lady Nell and Tsar raise their arms parallel to the floor; their hands are held palms up. I begin to bounce on the balls of my feet, giddy at what comes next. I grab Aspen's upper arm with both hands. This must have been what it was like for Clementine.

The light shines from their hands, brighter and brighter. The dragons' flight is more sporadic now. They are flying faster and lower; there is no longer a recognizable pattern.

I watch as, one by one, the dragons break from the flying thunder and return to their homes. They dwindle like this until at last only one dragon is left. I look back at Nell, Noni, and Tsar. They are holding an egg. It looks like it is made of an ice crystal, glimmering blue.

I look up to see the dragon slowly drift toward the floor. She looks like a beautiful majestic snowflake falling on the first day of winter. I look back down just in time to see the egg change not into one amulet, but three clear, blue, frosted icicles. They each hang upon a shimmering white chain of frost. Tsar helps place Noni's on while Nell holds her.

They look up and gasp at the sight of their new dragon. She is a little bigger than Nedra. She looks to be made entirely of ice. She has a pointed snout similar to Nedra's, but instead of horns, she has a small frill topped with three sharply pointed icicles covered in a thin layer of glittering frost just like the amulets. This is their link. Her wings are large, more than double the span of Nedra's, and they are a single webbed mass made of pure sparkling frost. Her body, legs, and tail are made of the glass-like crystal with a thin layer of frost down her spine to the tip of her pointed tail. I watch as she opens her wings for her new riders and lies upon the cave floor for them to climb on. As she stands again with her new riders, she shines and sparkles, much like when Nedra's embers glow.

Oh! I wonder if they are speaking right now! It is so exciting to watch. She crouches with her wings open and kicks off into the air. She flies up just under the top cave where Nedra lives.

"Nedra," I whisper through our link, "What is her name?"

"Her name is Nanoaj, Althea. I am sure you will have a chance to properly meet her." How beautiful! Her name even sounds magical, Nano-ah, I say it over again in my head and tell Aspen, Not, and Pilate in a quiet whisper.

We head outside to wait for them while they become

acquainted.

None of the faeries came with us to Dragon Cave. This was a task which, though pleasant to watch, really required none other than the chosen riders and dragons. So, we said our goodbyes and flew off.

Pilate and Nook will, of course, leave our merry traveling band here. They will stay within Reverie and continue doing their jobs as we will all do ours. Outside of Dragon Cave, I take out the book Tilda gave me and make another copy to give to Pilate. I tell him I will pass on the translations after Nedra and I have had time to read it. We plan to do that tonight.

Aspen has decided to stay with Not and myself while Tsar, Nell, Noni, and Nanoaj go to retrieve Tsar's crew. We, of course, will ride Nedra to meet up with Apuri and the other hegira he has already gathered together.

Nedra says they are still in the Painted Forest. He will pinpoint their exact location before we leave to see if we may travel there by light. If it is too close to the Glamour there will not be a light link. If there was, our first journey may have ended a lot sooner. Nedra would not have been dragon-napped to the evil lair. But that is in the past. Time to focus on the present.

I have not heard anything from Apuri himself. I really thought he would have sent a message through Nedra by now. Pilate informs me, however, that it has only been a couple of days, and Apuri is probably overwhelmed by both his emotions and his task. I reluctantly agree and decide to change the conversation.

"If they were real, the elves, that is, why do you think they left? I know they were supposedly all-powerful and we were all beneath them, but it still does not make much sense to me. If I were to go into hiding, I am sure it would be because I did something bad."

"You think perhaps they are feeling guilty? Or even banished?" Not asks.

"Curious," Pilate joins in,."Althea, if given the choice,

when your adventures are over where would you wish to live? In the human realm, the place you have always lived and known, or in Reverie the place that you feel right in? The place where magic allows you to be who you truly are. Or perhaps you would rather travel between both worlds without limits?"

"I guess my first choice would be both, but if that is not possible, there is no way I could not be within Reverie after knowing it is here."

He smiles. "Perhaps then, the elves have not fled or hidden or even been banished. Maybe this island, Zoar, is to them what Reverie is to you, to all of us."

"Okay, Pilate, I see your point. But why the big secret? Why not simply tell us they are there? Or better still, why not come out and actually help us save the world since they are so high and mighty?"

Pilate shakes his head, "I am sorry, dear, I do not know the answers. My guesses and speculations are merely that. When I find the proof, my dear, I assure you, you will be the first to know." He smiles and his antenna blinks as he winks at me.

Aspen and I laugh at him. The conversation dies for a moment and Aspen looks at the tree and asks, "How long do you think they will be in there?"

"I am not sure. They may be flying, or simply getting to know one another. You know, this is actually when Nedra and I found out we had met before, in the human realm when I was just a small girl. He was in glamour, of course, but it was still cool."

"With the journey ahead, I am sure they are making haste," Pilate says. "Nanoaj is probably just ensuring all her things are in order here before leaving. The dragons rarely leave their homes for more than a few days of fun exploration. Nedra is actually the first dragon to have a real mission and be gone from this cave for as long as he has in years, even centuries I would say."

"Really?" I turn to look at the cave. "He never told me

that. He did say once that the dragons were old, a part of pure magic, like the pixies. Pure magic. Do you think that is wild magic? Nedra," I say both aloud and through our link, "are there any elder dragons in the cave?"

"I hear what you are thinking, Althea," he replies back to only me through the link, "and I am the eldest dragon remaining in this thunder. There are others in different parts of the world. They may still have some elders in their caves. We can add them to our list of creatures to find." He laughs at his own annoying joke.

I huff and tell the others what he said. His joke is true though. We should add them to our list. If dragons were once a part of wild magic like the pixies and even the Elves, they may have our answers.

"We are coming out," Nedra says. Sure enough, within seconds he is outside with us. Nook follows close behind and heads straight to Pilate. He is still a bit shy, I have noticed. Finally, Nanoaj flies out with her new riders upon her back. They fly straight up into the sky above the canopy of the trees and out of sight. At first, I thought they may have traveled by light, but then I saw the bright blue sparkle from Nanoaj coming back toward us. She lands between Nedra and Nook as gracefully as the snowflake she resembled within the cave.

"Hello, Dreamer," She speaks to me as she bows her head in respect and lies down for her riders to climb off. Her voice is soft and musical, almost enchanting.

I bow in return, "Hello, Nanoaj. It is an honor to meet you. Thank you greatly for helping my friends and me on this journey."

She smiles and nods in return.

Nell comes up to me and we hug tight. "That was amazing!" She says in my ear.

"It was amazing to watch as well! Congratulations!" I whisper back in hers.

She then goes to Aspen with an awkward hug, and after to Pilate and Not. Tsar comes over and gives me a hug. Before he leaves me, I look into his eyes. I can tell he is healing. In fact, he is almost a hundred percent his old self, but there is still a part of Neoinas inside him. I do not have to see it; I can sense it, feel it. I do not understand, he should have been healed; he is holding on to something. I really hope he gets it resolved soon. Hopefully, seeing his crew again will help.

"We will see you again soon," I say before leaving his side and going to Noni, who refused to get down from Nonoaj's back for a hug.

We all say our goodbyes and prepare for our separate journeys. Each of us climbs upon our designated dragon, and with one more wave goodbye, we lift off as one. Nook and Nanoaj fly high to a light beam in the sky to get to their destinations.

Before leaving, Nedra and I surprise Notyal with a private tour of Nedra's home. Instead of flying to our destination, Nedra turns and reenters Dragon Cave, flying straight to the top den. Aspen does not question why we are going here instead of heading to find Apuri and the hegira. I guess she knows that we know what we are doing, and she is along for the ride.

We have barely landed on the ledge of Nedra's den when Notyal, figuring out our surprise as soon as we came into the cave, quickly slides down Nedra's side and runs straight to Nedra's nest. From there, he runs to Nedra's enormous rock collection - it fills all of the shelves on the opposite wall and spills onto the floor due to lack of space.

There are rocks of every shape, size, and color. Some are dull, but others sparkle brightly. Most of the ones on the shelves are about the size of a softball or smaller, while the ones on the floor range from the size of footballs to bigger than basketballs, and a few are even the size of small side table tops used to rest drinks on in family rooms back in the human realm.

Notyal carefully looks at each one, memorizing every detail of his hero's home. I glance up on the shelf at the red-cored white rock, a totem of the first time Nedra and I actually met. I was just a young girl in the human realm, Nedra was exploring in his dragonfly glamour, and we both discovered the rare, beautiful rock which mirrors Nedra's own bone white exterior and ruby red embers underneath. Seeing the rock again warms my heart and makes me smile. I glance over at Nedra, and we share a smile.

Once Not is finished internally drooling like a fanboy, we mount up and fly once more. After leaving Dragon Cave, we fly low within the Painted Forest. Nedra has locked onto Apuri's location and we are headed there now. Unfortunately, they are too close to the Glamour, so we are going to take the long way around. Normally, I would be upset about the time we are wasting, but seeing as we have no other choice, I am going to enjoy some of the beautiful scenery along the way.

Chapter Eleven ~ The Reunion

I gasp as we come up to the hegira camp. This is a part of the Painted Forest that I have not seen yet.

The ground is spotted with a vast variety of enchanting fungi. At the edge of their camp are some Prussian blue mushrooms that look like twisted witch hats. Nedra lands just beside them, and we slide off of his back to walk the rest of the way.

Aspen closely examines each species of mushroom as we walk by. A small grove of oak trees is blanketed in a bed of snowball mushrooms – soft white mushrooms that grow directly on the ground with no stems that look just like small snowballs. At the edge of these are some soft pink fungi resembling a thousand tiny fingers. These stretch out and fade into a web of silver. I cannot tell if this is one large specimen or a cluster like the ones before it.

We continue walking, slowly examining the magic around us. There is a small patch of what looks like tiny dragons or lizards. Upon closer look, I am surprised to see they are mushrooms. These are followed by some foul-smelling ones that each look like a miniature exploded octopus. Not looks a bit uneasy as he passes by them. I do not blame him.

A slender hollow log is covered in an orange fungus that looks like tiny wings attempting to lift it from the earth.

I look around the ground between us and the camp. There must be at least a thousand or more different species in every color, size, and shape imaginable. Before I have time to inspect them further, I spot Apuri headed our way.

He is happy to see us! That makes me feel better. When Nedra notified him that we were coming, his only reply was a simple, "Okay." He has not sent any messages to me. I asked Nedra if Apuri has checked in at all since he left only to be sorely disappointed by the answer.

Nedra has continuously assured me that Apuri has been busy, but it is still a bit depressing to feel like he does not care. What am I saying? I do not know why I care so much; we just had this talk before he left. We are just friends, remember?

But none of that matters now that he is here. As he gets closer I see how busy he has been. He does not just look tired; he is down right exhausted. I am not sure he has slept at all since walking through that mirror. Oh, I hope the mirror does not have anything to do with this. Thinking about Sage again makes the hairs on the back of my neck stand on end.

Apuri quickens his pace as he gets closer; he rushes up and picks me up as we spin together in a tight embrace. He sets me down and steps back to look at my face. Time slows down. I realize Nedra, Not, and Aspen are still here, and my cheeks burn with embarrassment.

"Hi," I say to Apuri to break the awkwardness. "So, um… What is with all the mushrooms?"

"They are great, are they not? They work as a sort of battery, a magic enhancement, if you will."

"Whoa."

"Yeah," He grins. "We needed a safe place to work that was as close to the other realm as possible without actually being in it. We also did not want to risk the Glamour failing at any moment and exposing us. I have sent a few scouts to check on the progress of wild magic." He smiles and nods to answer my question before I ask. "Yeah, Nedra told me about your dream." A tight crease appears between his brows as he frowns and adds, "I am sorry I did not say anything back. I have been pretty busy. Not that that is an excuse."

"Apuri, it is fine. I will admit I have missed you, but I am glad you are safe."

"Apuri," Aspen steps closer, pushing us to step apart more. "Do you think it would be okay if I gathered some of these mushrooms? They could prove beyond valuable in an emergency."

He looks around at all the mushrooms on the ground. "Go for it," he shrugs.

She smiles and pulls a bag and knife from some hidden pocket in her skirts. She wastes no time; without another word she marches off into the thick of the fungi to start her work.

Apuri, remembering his manners, greets Nedra and Not, then welcomes everyone back to the camp. Aspen assures us she will join us shortly, just as soon as she finishes collecting. I am not too sure on how "shortly" that will be.

We follow Apuri into his camp where busy hegira are bustling in every direction. It looks like Apuri is not the only one who has been losing sleep. I feel like I have walked into a zombie camp. There is no energy here. It is a stark contrast to their beautiful surroundings.

Like the Painted Forest itself, the magical energy coming from this place is breathtaking. The surrounding fields of a thousand species of mushrooms only enhance that energy. Apuri was right. Now that I am paying attention, I can feel it. I can almost see it.

I look at the structures, plain but beautiful temporary cottages made from the nature provided within the Painted Forest. The walls are built with mud and sticks and even leaves. They are all covered in vibrant blue, purple, green and white mosses. There are no roofs atop the structures. Hmm, surely it rains within the Painted Forest.

Nedra waits outside while we follow Apuri into the

largest structure. I am not surprised to find a table with chairs around it in the center laden with food. If there is one thing Apuri is passionate about, it is food. What does surprise me is the food that is on the table. All I see are berries and greens gathered from within the Painted Forest, most of which have begun to decay. Now I know how bad it has been. Apuri has not even made time to cook anything.

He sees the realization in my eyes and turns away before I say anything. He walks down the long side of the structure toward the left end away from the opening toward a small group of hegira. Thankfully, with no tops on the structures, it is light enough to see every corner.

Not and I follow after him. I smell the berries and greens on the table that have started to sour and wilt and hold my breath. I wonder when was the last time he ate. When was the last time any of them ate?

As we reach Apuri, I say, "Tsar went to get his family. With any luck they will be here in a couple days."

He rubs his hands together. "Good," he says without enthusiasm. He turns to the hegira who have stopped whatever it was they were doing and now stand staring at us. "Althea, this is my dad, mom, and sister." His introduction takes me by surprise. I stand silent for a moment until his words sink in. I quickly and awkwardly raise my arm to give a wave.

Looking at Apuri's dad is like looking at a future version of Apuri himself. His sand sculpted hair has a slight curl to its shape instead of the straight form of Apuri's. The curls are mirrored in his grandfatherly beard giving him a warm, kind face. His eyes are a soft grayish blue. They hold a glimpse of a full life, full of pain, sadness, and – as he looks at his family – love. I bet he has some stories to tell.

Apuri's mother is quite a bit shorter than him and his dad. Instead of sand, her skin is made of a dark red clay. As soon as I see her, the word *home* comes to mind. She is the true vision of a mother: stern, fierce, compassionate, warm. But her eyes are like Tsar's mom's: dark, black, soulless.

Apuri's sister is tall like him and their father. Her skin is clay like her mother's, but instead of red, it is a dark warm gold. Her long hair falls in dark tight curls down her back. I see sadness in her smile.

They each nod as he says, "Guys, this is Althea, the Dreamer!"

"I saw her that day with the Advisors, Apuri," his sister says. "Though she did look somewhat different then. Anyway, it is nice to meet you, Althea."

His mother places her hands on my shoulders, looks me in the eyes like she is judging me, then steps back, and says, "Nice to meet you, Dreamer."

His dad smiles and wraps me in a hug while mumbling, "How are you, Althea?"

I catch my balance as he lets go and reply, "I am well, thank you, sir."

Apuri, slightly embarrassed by his family, gets right to business. "We think there is a book... Zixus had a private library before the hegira. When it was time to leave, he could not take all his books with him; he had to carefully choose a select few. There was one book in particular he would never let anyone else see or touch. Althea, this could be our answer!"

Apuri's family returns to their work at the table; I step over to see what they are looking at. It is a map. It is a map covered with multiple X's.

"Uh, X marks the spot?" I ask sarcastically.

Apuri, not in the mood for humor today, rolls his eyes in response and points at the map. "This is a map of all the known, or remembered, Nashees the crews here have lived in. It was rumored some hegira spies stole a bunch of Stick's books. We have been searching every known location touched by a hegira looking for that book."

I look at the rough sketch of a map. I do not recognize the area, but then again, I am no cartographer. There are at least a dozen X's, most grouped close together. Is this what they have been doing the whole time? No wonder they all look exhausted. It must take them days to get to each place and back to the Painted Forest.

"Any luck?" I ask Apuri, knowing the answer.

He shakes his head silently. "Momma keeps saying, 'It can't be nowhere.'" He laughs and says, "I am tempted to disagree. I think that is exactly where it is."

"Okay, what has been your plan? How have you been searching? Do you even know the hegira who took the book or if they took that book?"

He rubs his hands on his head and begins to pace. Finally, he shouts, "How! How are we supposed to know any of that?"

"Hey!" I say sternly, "Calm down. That is why we are here, to help! So, who are your elders, the first ones to leave and become hegira?"

Apuri bites his tongue and looks at his parents. His mom looks at his dad. He closes his eyes and breathes slowly for a minute. Then he turns from the map and leans back against the table. "I was sodoc."

"But your eyes..."

"Yes," he stops me, "I am the only grown sodoc turned hegira whose eyes have changed. I suppose that can happen when you have gone through as much as I have. Now, I cannot confirm if this particular book was taken, but there was a siege on Zixus' library. It was just before the Pyramid was finished. We wanted to stop Sticks." He gives a coy smile. I have the feeling that referring to Zixus as Sticks was his idea..

"He had all these books, you see," he continues, "written by your kind, all them girls he kept locked up. He thought he was being clever, but we all knew something was going on. That is why we left. He went crazy, thirsty for more power. He kept saying he was going to make them pay, everyone who did this to us. After that night... the battle..." He rubs his eyes and clears his throat. "We decided to leave. The plan was to steal the books. We had an informant on the inside; she planned everything. We found out from her that Sticks was getting suspicious. His insanity was growing. He killed all of the girls already, needed their blood. After the last one died that night, no more came. He was restless. He decided it was time to leave, to find a new spot, *his spot.*" He stops talking for a minute.

I do not think he has ever told these memories. I hate to bring that struggle up for him now, but we need to know. I wait patiently for him to continue.

"We left without getting the books we needed. A while after we left, after we knew we were safe, we separated. Our informant had a son; she took him and some others who wanted to raise families. The rest of us began working on another plan to stop Sticks. A few of our friends stayed behind to act as spies for us. They told us when Sticks was planning to travel again. We knew he always took the most valuable books with him, so we split into two groups. One would go back to the fortress; the other would infiltrate Stick's new camp. I was part of the former. We retrieved all we could, but the fortress was mostly cleaned out." He swallows.

There is more he is not saying, but I know now is not the time to pry. If it was important, he would tell us.

"As we met up with the other group, Sticks and some of his goons had figured out what was happening. They were hot on our trail. Some of us stayed behind to fight them off, giving the others a chance to escape with our treasures." He adjusts his stance, switching the positions of his feet and propping his arms on the table behind him, then crossing them across his chest. His face grows somber as he continues, "We were not ready for a fight. We had no training. We did not want violence in our lives; that is why we left in the first place. I am the only one of us who stayed behind to make it out. I heard the rest of them die. Thankfully it was a dark night; I did not see much. I was hurt pretty bad myself; they thought I was dead. They went back to their camp. When I knew they were gone, I began crawling back to safety."

We all stand speechless for a minute. I am not sure what

to say. I look at Apuri; he is in just as much shock as I am. This is the first time he has heard this story, too. He stares at his dad with a mixture of surprise and pride.

"So, Althea, the Dreamer, I do know the hegira who took the books. I do not know if the particular book we are looking for was one of them. I could not read, and even if I could, by the time I was healed enough to do anything, the books had been moved and hidden in case Sticks came looking for them."

"Oh," I say. I feel dumb not knowing what else to say. "So, that is why you are searching all the places hegira, I mean you, have been? You think they would be there?"

"They have to be somewhere, and I cannot think of anywhere else. The others who were with me that night are all gone now. It seems, once again, I am the only one of us to walk away from a fight with the sodocs."

Apuri's mom steps in, "Well, I think that is enough for now. Apuri, why don't you and the Dreamer head out to the Glamour. The next batch of scouts should be coming back soon. Perhaps they have what you are looking for. Come on, dear," she says to Apuri's dad, "let's get you some water and perhaps something to eat?" She says the latter with an honest smile, and I see where Apuri gets his love of food.

He nods in agreement and they walk back to the long table and find a seat on the far side to be left alone.

"I am sorry," I apologize to both Apuri and his sister.

"He will be okay," Apuri's sister says. "Mom gets this way anytime Daddy talks about the past."

"You knew this?" Apuri exclaims, surprised.

"Well, not in so much detail, but I have heard pieces. Come on, she is right; the others should be getting back soon. Maybe seeing the Dreamer will lift everyone's spirits."

She leads the way out as Not, Apuri, and I follow quietly after. I sneak a glance at Apuri's parents as we walk by. They bicker over what and how much he should eat. I smile to myself and quickly catch up to the others.

I walk up beside Apuri and grab hold of his hand.

Apuri's sister and Not begin a conversation walking just ahead of us. Aspen is still diligently gathering mushrooms. Nedra is watching her.

When he sees me watching her he tells me through our link, "She is quite amusing when she is caught up in something. Every once in a while, when she sees one she likes more than the others, her hair gets more feathers in it." His breathy dragon laugh lightens my mood after hearing Apuri's dad's story.

I glance at Apuri. He looks even more exhausted than when I arrived only a few moments ago. I gently nudge him in the side with my elbow. "Hey, you okay?" He nods, but I can see the truth. "What is wrong? What has been going on since you left? I thought maybe you would tell us something through Nedra."

He looks up at the tree tops around us. "There is so much I want to tell you, but I am not sure what to say, how to start."

"The beginning is always a good place. What happened after you stepped through the mirror at the creepy shop?"

He glances down at me and laughs, "Got that vibe too, did you? I honestly thought about turning around after we walked in, but then he came out. It seemed too late then. When I stepped through that mirror, a part of me feared I would never see you again..." he trails off in thought. Shaking his private memories from his thoughts, he continues, "But, here you are." He squeezes my hand and smiles. "Nedra said you and I needed to find some time to talk about the past few days. I guess he has been checking in on me?"

Now I laugh, "How else was I supposed to make sure you were okay? He is right, though; we do need to talk. Maybe after we greet your scouts?"

His brow creases with concern, "Althea, what happened? Are you okay?"

I squeeze his hand and nod, "Yeah, let's just do this first okay?"

He nods and we continue walking until we are no longer

in the mushrooms. Apuri's sister and Not are still leading the way. They seem to be getting along quite well.

We make it to the Glamour just in time to see three hegira come through. One of them looks like a dark fox boy. I wonder how old he is but do not voice my question aloud.

The two bigger hegira behind him actually look more human than any hegira I have seen. Their skin is still dark like the rest of the hegira, but instead of the nature-like features of most of the hegira and fae, they have human skin. Their ears are pointed. One of them has medium length, greasy, black hair, and the other has no hair at all. It is easy to tell they are brothers.

Apuri's sister greets the boy while the brothers walk straight to Apuri. It is clear who is in charge here. He releases my hand and steps forward to meet them. He greets each of them with a strong clasp of hands and slight nod.

I never stopped to think of Apuri's influence or status among the hegira or even who he was to them before we met. I never questioned his volunteering for my mission. I was too self-absorbed to worry about anybody else.

Suddenly, Apuri's dad's story comes to mind. He was with Zixus when they first tried to invade Reverie. He was with Tsar's mother when they decided it was time to start their own path. He was not only part of the group that sought to stop Zixus, but he was the only survivor. It is no wonder that he would be deemed their leader after his recovery. He even said he is the only elder still here. Apuri is the son of this hegira crew's leader.

I stand back with Not and watch Apuri and his sister converse with the hegira about their travels. The fox boy hands over some folded papers, but I do not see any books.

Suddenly, three more hegira come through the Glamour. They shake their heads regretfully when they see Apuri. They did not find the book either. Apuri greets them as he did the brothers and sends them all back to the camp.

He walks back to stand by my side again. It seems as if

each minute is chipping away at him a little more, like he is holding on by a thread. I think if I were to poke him, he would crumble into nothing more than a pile of sand.

Seeing him like this breaks my heart. His sister comes over, followed by the fox boy, with the papers in her hand. She hands them to Apuri and takes the boy back to the camp.

"Are we going with them?" I ask Apuri.

"There are two more scouts out there. We will wait for them." He flips the papers open.

I look over his shoulder. It is a list. He goes through the pages and stops when he reaches the last one.

We have sent them with the others. They will keep them safe.

"Who are the others?" I ask.

Apuri shrugs, "I do not know, but I know who might." He refolds the papers and sticks them in the back pocket of his tattered shorts.

Before I have a chance to ask him how long until the others might get back they emerge through the Glamour. They are two small girls about the same size, and probably age, as the fox boy. Instead of fox-like features, however, they remind me of Clementine. They have crape myrtle bark for their skin, only it is dark like it has been burnt. When they stand side by side, they actually look like one tree. I am going to have to ask Apuri why he is sending children out on these missions.

They run up to Apuri and perform a double curtsy, spreading their black petaled flower dresses out around their ankles. He bows in return causing them both to grin from ear to ear. Their grins disappear when he asks if they found anything. He quickly reassures them it is not their fault, and they did a fabulous job trying. Before running off to the camp, they both stare at me until Apuri shoos them off. Whether their stares were of admiration or jealousy, I am not sure. Hopefully the former.

Apuri takes the papers to his father while Not and I go back to the abundance of mushrooms with Nedra and Aspen.

After the hegira discuss the papers, they are supposed

to take a break for the rest of the evening until tomorrow. Apuri assured me we would have time to walk and talk about everything then.

Aspen has now made it all the way up to the camp. She has finished collecting mushrooms and is sitting on the ground beside Nedra sorting through them. She does not notice the suspicious stares from passing hegira. Nedra is watching her closely as she empties a few out of her bag and contemplates which of the many piles around her feet to put them. Not and I walk over and sit down beside them.

"Need any help?" I offer as I sit across from Aspen.

"Um, sure. For now, I am sorting by properties. These," she points to a bunch of long, stringy-looking specimens, "will help with problems inside the body: upset stomach, muscle cramps, headaches, things like that. These," she directs our attention to the pointed blue mushrooms, "and those with similar physical traits, will help with mental disabilities. Sometimes you do not function properly if you cannot clear your mind. That is where these come in handy. Just the smallest drop of tincture made with one of these mushrooms can help clear your mind and refocus your energy for hours, even days. But you must know which one to use. This group," she points to a pile of short, moss-like fungi, "is for topical use only." None of them look like something you would want to ingest, either.

"What about those?" Not asks, staring at a pile not knowing how they are grouped. They are pretty, but abstract..

"These are for more *spiritual* healing. Oftentimes the things that ail us cannot be seen. It is more the energy around us and the various ways you can be affected by its lack of balance."

Not and I both let out an "Oh!" of wonder.

"There are, of course, many other plants with similar properties, but the shelf life of medicine made with mushrooms is much longer. I suspect being in Reverie might even add more quality. Well, now you know how to sort them;

here you go." Aspen passes over an unopened rucksack full of unsorted mushrooms.

Not and I look at the bag then to each other. He holds up all four arms with a smile and says, "Shall we begin?"

I laugh and nod as we shake out a small pile, careful not to damage any of Aspen's harvest, onto the ground between us. I pick up a couple of strange fluorescent green blobs and say, "I will take topical and spiritual; you get internal and mental." Notyal nods in agreement and we begin.

Helping Aspen sort through the mushrooms is actually quite relaxing and fun. I came across one that resembles an exploded octopus. Notyal got a bit squeamish at seeing it; so, I quickly added it to the spiritual healing pile. I would say the exploded octopus is definitely abstract.

We have almost finished with both bags when Apuri comes over and crouches down beside me. "Hey, I am sorry that it took so long. What is going on here?" He looks around at the piles of mushrooms.

"We are helping Aspen sort medicine," I explain as I look at the piles around us. "Has it really been that long?"

Not dumps out one more pile and tosses me the empty bag. "I think it has," he says, surprised himself.

I hand Aspen her bag and turn back to Apuri, "So, what took so long?"

"Momma," he says with a shrug. "She did not want us to bother Daddy, but I had to show him that list. She insisted on seeing it first. Finally, she admitted to not knowing about it and went to fetch him from his nap. He said the only thing he can think of is that the books are with the other original group of hegira – that would be Tsar's crew – and we either have to send someone to them or wait for them to come to us. We have already sent messengers asking for all hegira to meet us here, but I do not know if they will come. You have met Tsar's mom," he says with a quirked eyebrow. Indeed, I have. "After the loss in the battle with the sodocs, she will probably be even more apprehensive to help us again. After that, they argued a little bit about their own opinions on the matter, and I left."

"Wow, okay. Well, Tsar is already on his way to the farm with Lady Nell, Noni, and Nanoaj, their dragon. He will probably find it and bring it back. If it helps, we can contact them and let them know about the list."

"Yeah, that would help." Apuri replies without saying anything about Nanoaj. He still sounds worried.

"So, once we finish sorting these," I hold up a neon pink mushroom that is tipped with tiny white spots, "will we have time for that walk?"

He looks back at the camp then sighs and answers, "I guess."

I contemplate telling him not to worry about it, that we can do it later, but I know we will not have time.

We finish sorting in silence, not the peaceful, relaxing silence we had a few moments ago, but the loud silence that you wish you could shut out. Once we finish, Apuri and I leave the camp on the opposite side of the mushrooms to get some time together. We walk in awkward silence for a while until I finally ask Apuri, "What do you need? What do they need? Rest, obviously, but what else? Food?"

"That would be a start. But I have not had time to do anything, and the second I stop working, my mind gets the better of me." He quickly stops talking and closes his eyes.

Seeing his trouble, I speak up, "Okay, food I can do. But nothing else is going to get better until you tell me what is going on."

"Okay," He says, and we continue walking.

Chapter Twelve ~ Laughing Frogs

Apuri and I have been walking for a while now. The walk was, unfortunately, a quiet one. I was hoping he would talk more while we walked, but he continued to lose himself in his own internal battle.

We left the mushroom protected campsite and found our way to a small pond filled with laughing frogs.

"This place never ceases to amaze me," I say as I watch the giggling frogs hop to and fro.

"What?" he asks. I give him a stern look and point to the laughing frogs. How could anyone not be amused by this?

He follows my finger and smiles a little. "I wonder what is so funny," he remarks.

"How about what is not?" I bark. "You have to let me in. What happened after you walked through that mirror, Apuri?"

We find a solid place to sit and watch the frogs. Instead of pushing again, I decided to wait and enjoy the chorus of laughter. I do wonder what they are laughing at. What if it is us? I watch closely to see if they look directly at us when laughing, but that does not seem to be the case. From what I can tell, laughing seems to simply be an innate part of the creatures.

Finally, Apuri sighs and says, "I am sorry. I was uncomfortable in that shop, too, but I knew this had to be done. When I walked through that mirror, it took every fiber of my being not to turn around, grab your hand, and dash out of that place. I braced myself, thinking stepping through the mirror would be similar to stepping through the Gateway Trees. It is not." He looks me straight in the eye for the first time all day. Seeing the fear behind those eyes makes me want to tell him to stop, but I cannot. I need to hear this just as much as he needs to get it out.

"You know how traveling by light is hot, almost unbearably so? Well, traveling through the mirrors is the opposite. When you first step through, you feel no difference. After your entire body is inside, however, everything goes ice cold. It is like a million needles stabbing every inch of your body. I could not stand to keep my eyes open. It hurt so bad. I thought for sure I walked into some sort of trap set by the crazy blue man. I even tried to call out to Nedra, but nothing happened. I wanted to give up so bad. I tried once; I stopped walking and waited for something to happen, sure I would die. When nothing happened, I knew I had to get to the other side. I am not sure how long I was actually inside that mirror, but when I finally stepped out onto the other side, I made up my mind to never go back through another one. Feeling the fresh air was like being born again, like the first time I used my magic."

"Oh, Apuri! I am so sorry." I reach over and hold his hand hoping to comfort him. He does not respond.

"I stood there breathing," he continues, "feeling my body return to its normal self, when I heard a *crack* in a nearby bush. I jumped behind the closest tree and peered around it cautiously, taking in my surroundings for the first time." He finally squeezes my hand and places his other hand over the top of it before going on. "Do you remember those faeries you helped heal on our way here? Althea, the pain and devastation we saw on the faces of those faeries does not even hold a candle to the destruction and terror at Lauk. I do not know how I thought the air was fresh when I walked through. After seeing the slaughter, all I could smell was burnt bodies. I almost gagged with every breath."

Not sure what else to say to all this, I ask the question on my mind, "So were the hegira there? That is why the mirror took you there, is it not?"

Apuri takes a deep breath and lets it out slowly. He releases my hand and rubs both of his upon his thighs. "Yes," he says, "I was not sure at first, but I kept watching to see who or what made that sound. Finally, Fen – the fox-like boy you met earlier – showed himself. I stepped out from behind my tree and gave the poor boy such a fright he threw a knife and nearly sliced my ear off." I look at his ear and see a line on the top curve. I touch it gently; it looks mostly healed.

Apuri goes on with his story, "Once he realized who I was, he apologized profusely. I assured him no apology was necessary; that I was proud to see he was prepared. I asked him where the others were. He said everyone except him and the twins was in the Painted Forest. The three of them were sent back to search for any survivors. I helped them search. It was impossible to differentiate between Fae and hegira with the state of the bodies. Most of them could not even be called bodies." He drops his head and slumps his shoulders. "There were no survivors. By the time we left Lauk to return to the Painted Forest I felt like one of the dead. Everyone you see here is all that is left. I told my dad what was going on, and he quickly rounded the others up to help. We have all been so focused on trying to find these books as an escape from the horror we cannot forget."

I sit quietly for a moment absorbing Apuri's recent events. I feel foolish for ever getting upset about not hearing from him.

"I am so sorry, Apuri. I was being selfish, and only thinking about my own troubles. I should have been there for you, too."

"Hey," he says as he grabs my hand again, "do not beat yourself up about it. I should have told Nedra, or at least told you when you got here. So, now that we have talked, what do you say we head back with clearer heads and be productive?"

I lean my head on his shoulder and give his arm and hand a squeeze. I want to tell him about my dreams, but I guess that can wait. "That sounds like a plan," I say. "But you know what would make the work more enjoyable?"

"These laughing frogs?" he jokes.

"Well, that might help, too," I laugh, happy to see his sense of humor returning. "But I was actually thinking more along the lines of something to eat. What do you say? I will provide the ingredients, and you whip up something delicious to lift everyone's spirits. Hey! Maybe that is why you are such a great cook! Because you are a lifter."

"You know, I never thought of that before. I guess it makes sense, though it does hurt my pride a little. I thought it was pure talent." We share a good laugh and stand up.

Before heading back, I go over to the pond full of laughing frogs. They are all different colors, shapes, and sizes. There must be a group of every species of frog on the planet here. Reverie has changed them from their safe, camouflaged colors, though. They all resemble poisonous jungle frogs with brilliant colors. I watch them admiringly. Maybe laughing really is simply the way they croak here in Reverie. I crouch down and, feeling a bit silly, ask them if any of them would like to accompany us back to our camp to help make everyone happier. Surprisingly, they not only understand, but they agree. They begin to hop toward us and continue following us back to the camp surrounded by magical mushrooms.

Their laughing really is contagious. By the time Apuri and I make it back to the camp, my cheeks and sides are splitting with pain from laughing so much. I begin to question my decision to invite the frogs with us.

[1]The mood of the camp when we get back is more akin

to that of a cemetery, dreary and somber. I know immediately that I made the right choice. A few curious hegira, as well as Not, Aspen, and Nedra, come out to see what all the noise is. The laughing frogs' bright colors blend in with the mushrooms surrounding the camp. I watch the faces inside the camp; curiosity quickly turns to smiles which grow into giggles. By the time we make it to the center of camp everyone is laughing in chorus with the frogs who are now jumping jovially around the entire camp.

The hegira children chase after them excitedly, but the laughing frogs are much too quick to be captured.

Aspen walks over to me with both her eyes and teeth shining with laughter. "Laughter is the best medicine," she says. "Thank you. We all needed this. How did you find them?"

My cheeks still hurt from smiling and laughing, but I do not complain. I know too well the difference between a good pain and a bad one. This is definitely a good pain, one that I welcome with a smile plastered on my face.

"They were enjoying themselves in a pond not too far away," I answer. "That is where we finally stopped to talk. Before we came back, I asked them if they would join us to cheer up some friends. Here they are." I smile as I sweep my hand in a gesture to encompass the whole camp. "And now, Apuri and I have another surprise to lift everyone's spirits. Have everyone wait out here until we are ready."

She looks confused but agrees. I nod to Apuri and we head into the now empty structure in the center of camp. We quickly clear the long table and begin working hard to make a soul healing meal.

I begin by building a carved out stone oven similar to those seen in authentic pizzerias. This will be crucial to our meal. We will use the hollowed-out mouth for baking and the flat surface like a stovetop. I start the fire with magic, not having time for the old-fashioned way.

My next task is growing ingredients for Apuri. He starts preparing foods as soon as they are available. I tell him to get everything measured and laid out together, and I will help after the growing is finished.

I worried that using my magic so much for growing all the food would drain me and make me tired and useless. The opposite is actually happening. The more I use my magic, the stronger and more energetic I feel.

As soon as I finish growing everything on his list of ingredients, I go to the table to help mix. He tells me what each set of ingredients will become, what kind of dish it needs to be in, and how to mix and cook it.

I step out and ask Aspen to see if she and the hegira will help gather medium sized, strong logs and rocks from within the Forest and bring them back as soon as possible. It will be easier to manipulate these to make dishes than to create everything from magic alone.

I use magic to help mix everything together quickly. Still not trusting myself with the actual cooking of the foods, I leave the mixes on the table for Apuri and move on to the next one. It works efficiently for us as he is able to circle back around after putting out all the ingredients and begin cooking. He leaves all of the berries and vegetables to be eaten raw at the end of the table for me to clean – though, I am not sure that is necessary - cut, and place on the table after all the mixing is finished.

I am able to help with some of the cooking, like the delicious stews. Instead of placing them in the oven or on top of the hot stone, I heat them directly with my magic until they are done.

The side table at which Apuri's family was studying the map when we first arrived became the drink station. We really were not sure how to approach drinks. Making cups for everyone was possible but would have been time consuming. We also were not sure of the exact number needed. Instead we created long deep basins of magically smoothed stone and filled them with magically created water bubbles like the ones Tilda and I had at our picnic in Inon. I make sure to place extra air around the bubbles to keep them from popping when picked up.

Seeing such an elegant meal makes me wish we had more elegant drinks. Apuri suggests my tea, but I am reluctant to give up the last of my personal stash. At some point during the growing of the herbs, Apuri asks why I do not just grow the plants for my teas. I had not thought of that.

I grow a few roses, some mint, and chamomile for just that purpose. In separate bowls I combine the ingredients with water and heat them directly until they boil. I then stop the heat and let them steep for a few minutes while we continue working. We fill three other basins on the drink table with balls of each tea and a small piece of the plant from each in front for labeling.

I tell Nedra through our link that the food is done, and he leaves the camp to go in search of his own meal.

When we finally set the last dish upon the long table, Apuri and I are both beaming with pride.

We check that all the cooking fires are fully extinguished and all messes cleaned up before going to get everyone. As quiet as it is outside, I hope they did not fall asleep while waiting on us to finish. Hopefully the delicious smells wafting out of the structure kept them awake.

I look at everything on the table as we walk the length back to the door. We have made everything fresh, growing fruits and grains, herbs and edible mushrooms, to use as our ingredients. I needed practice using my magic; Apuri needed to relax and cook again; and everyone at the camp needed a good meal. This has been a project to help everyone.

Fresh baked bread rolls brushed with oils and herbs are placed on several trays all across the table. On either side of each bread tray are small bowls filled with more herb-filled oils for dipping. These range from rosemary to garlic to parsley. Beside each bowl of oil are dishes of jams and preserves including grape, blackberry, strawberry, plum, pear, apple, and yimi berry.

Growing each of the fruits was actually kind of fun. At

first, I was not sure the plants I grew were going to produce any fruits, but as I kept pushing my magic into them, they quickly blossomed. The blossoms just as quickly became luscious fruits ready for picking and preparing.

There are several bowls overflowing with steaming vegetables like broccoli and carrots as well as our own version of fried rice. This truly is the greatest buffet of all times.

There are two big wooden pots I created to hold the stew. The savory smells drifting from the blend of carrots, potatoes, onions, garlic, celery, mushrooms, and brown ginger sauce makes my mouth water and my stomach growl with hunger. I know as I pass the large steaming pot that the blend of vegetables and herbs inside that stew is going to be like heaven in my mouth. I close my eyes and imagine dipping a piece of the fresh bread into that stew causing my mouth to salivate even more.

Apuri laughs, seeing my fantasy clear on my face. I laugh, too, and continue following him to the door of the structure. My stomach rumbles again as we pass the middle of the table. Between two trays of bread, the very center of the table is piled high with desserts.

A tiered stand almost three feet tall is the main focal point. It holds a variety of little cakes. Piled around the bottom of the stand are several dozen of Apuri's famous donut holes. On one side of those lies a couple loaves of banana bread; on the other side are some of his scrumptious brownies.

I admit I snuck one of the brownies just as it started to cool after baking. I pressed it down between my fingers into a fudgy brown ball and popped it into my mouth savoring its soul melting goodness.

Between the jams and the edges of the table are several long skinny dishes of cobblers made of blackberry – my personal favorite – apple, pear, and peach. The only thing missing now is some vanilla ice cream.

The rest of the table is filled with fresh fruits and vegetables of every kind. I tried to place them close to foods of complementing colors to make the table setting not only smell and taste wonderful, but to look as glorious as possible too.

As I reach the end of the table and the door, I glance back at our extravagant display and smile. Together, Apuri and I step through the door and motion to Aspen who is already watching the door closely. I imagine she has been sitting here like that the whole time we have been cooking. It is a good thing we used magic to rush everything along. I can only imagine how long everything would have taken without it.

Aspen, Not, and Apuri's father lead the way into the structure, followed by the rest of the hegira. Apuri and I stand at the door and hand each of them one of the smooth, wooden circles we made for plates. Each one takes a plate then turns to the table, shocked by what lies before them. Some smile, some close their eyes and smell the delicious aroma coming from the long table, but a few – Apuri's mother included – look cautiously, even suspiciously, at the food.

Nothing easy nor extravagant has ever come to the hegira, especially while they sat and waited on it. To see something like this created, and in such a short time to boot, was bound to cause suspicion. I notice, not surprisingly, that most of the latter group are the elders, Apuri's dad excluded. I choose to ignore their skepticism and focus on those faces beaming with joy.

Once the last of the hegira in line, the young boy named Fen, gets his plate and begins filling it with food, Apuri and I walk together on either side of the table carefully piling our plates high with a sample of each dish. Knowing we had stew, I intentionally created a bowl-like dip in the center of each plate. They resembled miniature upside-down sombreros before any food was on them.

We let everyone know there is plenty of food to get seconds and desserts. They all fill their plates and head back out to find a place to sit and enjoy the meal. I notice when we finally emerge from the structure with mountains of food upon our plates, that even the skeptics are eating bite after bite without worry or caution. It is not long before Apuri is headed back for seconds.

If there is anything more impressive than Apuri's ability to cook, it is his ability to eat quickly. Notyal is not far behind him. One by one, hegira begin rising with clean plates to return for more food.

As I sit here with my friends, eating savory filling food, watching everyone in the camp eat and grow happier with every bite, my heart fills with joy. This is why I am the Dreamer. I can help. I can do good. I can save people. With that affirmative thought in mind, I finish the food on my plate and lie back on the ground to watch the canopy above me.

Chapter Thirteen ~ The Dreamer

Everyone finished eating and fell asleep, full and happy, right where they were. Once I was sure everyone was finished with the food, I returned to the large structure in the center of the camp, our new feast hall as I like to call it, to see what remained.

There was not a lot compared to what we started with, but there was still plenty for breakfast for everyone. I use all of the stone and all of the wood from the cooking and drink storage – all the drinks are gone – to create a makeshift freezer. Once I have made a pretty good-sized rectangular structure I freeze the whole thing solid. I then magically float all of the remaining food into the freezer and freeze it quickly with magic as well before placing the frozen lid on.

This way, the food will still be edible after thawing it in the morning. Waste not, want not.

I return outside to find Apuri, Not, and Nedra waiting for me on the other side of the mushrooms. I check that everyone else is still asleep. They are.

"I thought you were asleep," I say to Apuri as I walk up to him and grab his hand.

"I was," he says before turning to Nedra. "Then I heard

Nedra land, and I woke up. He was standing out here, so I came to join him while waiting on you. On my way, Notyal woke up and came, too. What were you doing anyway?"

"Putting the food up," I say dismissively with the wave of a hand. "What is it, Nedra?"

"Come with me," he says. I tell the others and they both climb on Nedra's back behind me. We all sit between his silver-maned neck and his large webbed wings. Apuri wraps his arms around my waist. I cover his hands with one of mine and hold on to Nedra's mane with the other.

We lift off the ground and fly through the lush green canopy. As soon as we get up above the trees, Nedra bends to fly back down into the Painted Forest.

"Nedra, what are we doing?" I ask through our link, thankful I do not have to speak with the wind blowing in my face.

"Have you told Apuri about the book?" he asks.

"Not in detail, just that we found it and it has some answers, but more questions."

"Tonight, we will show him. We will also read the second book."

"Oh. But do we have to have moonlight for that? As far as I can tell, it does not get dark inside the Painted Forest."

"It will actually work with any natural light, but moonlight is best so you have the darkness to see the story. For that we are going to travel inside a nearby Gateway Tree. That is why we are flying. It is easier for me to fly up over the canopy than to meander through all the trees."

"Oh, okay. Have you told Apuri any of this?"

"No. It is not as easy for us dragons to talk to those who are not our riders or others with old magic."

"But you have done it before," I protest.

"I know," he cuts me off before I can say more. "I am a strong dragon, but it still wears on me. It uses great energy and focus. That is why I made a detour while I was out hunting."

He shows me an image of his den and the rocks on the

shelves. "I am giving Apuri his own amulet. It will not be the same as yours. Your amulet is part of me, like all amulets given to riders. Since we do not have time to do another ceremony for Apuri, I am going to give him one of my oldest and most precious stones embedded with bits of my magic to create a link. I have one for Notyal as well."

"Oh! They will enjoy that. Thank you, Nedra." I feel his body hum slightly beneath me and see the red embers glow beneath his ivory scales.

When we land back in the Painted Forest, I look around to see the hegira camp, but it is nowhere to be seen. I guess we did not go up and back down like I thought. Of course, Nedra knows what he is talking about.

"In here," Nedra says as he steps into a nearby tree. It is odd watching a dragon step into a Gateway Tree about half his size.

We quickly follow after him into a world of night. It is not black, like the Deep Dark Forest, it is just night. The sky is more of a midnight blue speckled with bright, twinkling stars. It feels soothing to be here.

I tell Apuri and Not what is going on, but leave out the amulet part, simply saying Nedra had a surprise for them before we started. At my request, they both shut their eyes and stand silently. I take each of the amulets from Nedra. He told me for whom each one was, and I place it around the neck of its new owner.

Each of them opens their eyes and looks at the new treasure with wonder, appreciation, and confusion. Confusion, that is, until Nedra speaks to each of them and explains that these will be their amulets linking them to him as I am.

Apuri thanks Nedra with a bow. Notyal looks like he is about to faint. I cannot help but laugh at the sight. Remembering himself, he quickly bows and thanks Nedra repeatedly until Apuri nudges him in the side to make him stop.

"Now," Nedra says to all of us, "You all should get comfortable so we can read and watch the show.

I take out both books and leave the second one beside Nedra while I take the first to the moonlight. The silver filigree catches the light like before, and the book begins to vibrate. I release it and let it do its thing while I go back to sit beside the others.

We fall asleep and Nedra shows us all the island of Zoar. It looks just the same as before, magical as ever. Once Not and Apuri understand what is going on, Nedra wakes us up for the second book.

Apuri walks with me this time to get *Zoar* and take it back to my bag while I take the second book to the moonlight.

This book is black with pearl white filigree in the same pattern as the last book. As I carry it to the moonlight, I cannot stop looking at it. It draws me in like a magnet. I wish I could read it. I gently touch the title written in the language of magic.

"What does it say, Nedra?" I ask through our link without speaking aloud.

"This book," Nedra says to all of us, "is called *Dreamer.*"

We all look up, surprised. "Are you kidding me?" I shout aloud. What about when we were doing all that research looking for any information on Dreamers? Why did the advisors not help us out then and share this information?"

"They all did not want to share it this time either, remember?" Not says. He makes a good point.

Ophidius. He did not want me to have this book, but Tilda allowed me to make a copy and bring it so I would learn whatever I should from inside. Now I know that this book is somehow about me and my predecessors.

I calm myself down so we can hurry and see what this book has to say. I hold it up, like I did the first one, so the filigree can catch the moonlight. The elegant twisted knots along the top of the cover catch a beam of light and begin to sparkle. It spreads quickly to the rest of the lines as the book vibrates and heats faster and faster. Finally, the entire cover is sparkling with moonlight. The book becomes too hot to hold, so I calmly release it. I know that it will float like the book before it.

I quickly walk back to sit with the others.

The book shines and opens like the first one, but instead of flowing through a rainbow of colors, it shines with pearl-white sparkles. It makes me think of pixie dust. I wonder if the pixies had a part in making these books? It would not surprise me. We all nestle in against Nedra, getting comfortable. Our bellies are still full from the meal Apuri and I prepared aiding in bringing sleep our way.

It is not long before I find myself drifting.

* * * * * * * * * *

I am disappointed to see I am not on the island, Zoar. I look around to find out where I am instead.

Everything is dark, but not so dark that I cannot see. I am standing in the middle of what was once a warzone. Now, it is nothing more than a wasteland. Everything looks to have been burnt and destroyed.

"Nedra?" I call for him aloud in my dream.

"I am here, Althea," he answers.

"What is this? Where are we?"

"This is the first location to perish during the Great War between humans and faeries."

"Oh." I think I am going to be sick from the smell of death everywhere. I wonder if this is what Apuri experienced when he first found the hegira.

"Nedra, can Not and Apuri see this as well? I do not see them."

"Yes, they see it just as you do."

I walk around in silence thinking about all those lives lost, all the pain that would follow for hundreds of years. I notice movement in some nearby bushes. I cautiously step closer, remembering the dream with the land shark.

I raise my hands, ready to use whatever magic I need in case of an attack. Before I can move the shrubbery aside, a small, round, dirty face with bright blue eyes speckled with white sparkles peeks through from the other side. Her dirty round face is streaked with the tracks of tears. I stiffen, unsure if she can see me.

She glances from side to side before crawling out on hands and knees. She crawls right past me; I am invisible to her. Her green gown is so tattered and torn, its color is almost unrecognizable. Her once iridescent gossamer wings lie dull and folded on her back. I see as she turns to crawl to the left that one of them is torn in the middle. Blood drips from its frayed end and runs down her back and side.

Crying, she crawls until she reaches a smooth spot upon the earth. She uses her hands to wipe away the ash and char on the ground until clean earth shines through. Once she has cleared a circle about a foot in diameter, she places her right hand over the left and threads her fingers together while keeping them outstretched.

She places them in the fresh dirt and curls her fingers down, folding them deeper into the soil under her palms. Her tears fall down upon the back of her hands and roll off into the soil.

She leans her mouth close to the earth and whispers, "If you still care, please send help."

A bright light shines from under her hand and goes into the earth.

The small faerie girl sits back on her feet, letting her hands fall limp upon her thighs. She does not even worry about dusting the soil off of them.

Still crying quietly, she stares intently at the circle of fresh soil she has just sent her message through. I watch, too. After some time, the dirt begins to move. There is something coming up from within the earth!

The round-faced faerie girl stiffens, waiting for her answer. With an almost audible pop, *a small green sprout appears in the center of the cleared-out circle. The girl does not move.*

I look back to the earth. The plant is growing rapidly. It quickly blooms into a large orange and yellow hibiscus bigger than the girl's face.

Confused, I keep watching, waiting for something else to happen. I look back at the girl.

"Creator," she whispers softly. She is not crying anymore, but her face is still streaked with the dry, dirty, tracks of tears. Her lips tremble as she speaks, "Please, Creator. Help us!"

The flower begins to glow and emits an ethereal sound. The blossom shifts, turns to face up toward the dark, gloomy sky above. The faerie girl and I shift our gaze to follow. I am not sure what we are looking for, but all I see is a gray overcast sky. The wind begins to blow, gentle at first, but it picks up quickly.

My hair is thrown in a frenzy across my face. I glance down to see the faerie girl's hair doing the same. I look over at the flower to find it has gone. In its place stands an orange, glowing pixie!

It has no inscriptions carved into the surface of its skin. The androgynous features make it impossible for me to tell if it is a boy or girl, unlike with Mitzi and Scrit. The eyes are a pale clear blue, almost white. A bob of purple and white streaked hair lies in a frizzled mess upon its head.

"We will help, child, but we require a price."

The small girl is obviously frightened, but nods to the pixie.

The pixie holds out a small orange hand to the child. The faerie child extends her shaking hand to the pixie. The pixie's features remain void of emotion. As the faerie and pixie hands touch, a blast of wind and light explode from the point of contact.

Suddenly, time stands still. The faerie girl's hair remains floating in the air, extended behind her, from the blast. A fat transparent tear sits frozen, balanced upon the edge of the lower lid of her left eye. The pupil in her bright blue eyes is nothing more than a pinpoint against the light from the blast.

I do not even see a pulse in the vein in her neck. I cannot tell if she is breathing.

My own heart races as my breathing becomes heavier. I lift my hand; I am not affected by the blast. I look at the pixie. It moves, releasing the girl's hand as she remains frozen. It floats *right up in front of her and extends both hands into her chest.*

I watch in horror and amazement as the pixie pulls a bright golden light, magic, from within the faerie child's core. I watch as the glow within those bright blue faerie eyes dulls to nothing more than a hollow glassy stare.

The pixie just took her soul.

I cry for the little girl. My chest aches until I cannot breathe.

The pixie holds the faerie's soul in one hand, and with the other, makes the faerie's body disappear with a simple wave. "No!" I shout, but I am not heard.

The pixie gathers some of the soil from within the circle the girl cleared to send her message for help.

With soul in one hand and soil in the other, the pixie floats to a nearby creek. With both hands full, the pixie uses nothing more than thought to control magic pulling water from the creek. Without hesitation, all three ingredients are combined and molded under the magic prayers of the pixie.

Something tells me the pixie is speaking in the language of magic, but being in the dream, I can still understand every word:

"From horror and pain, hope will rise.

This star shines through from the darkest night.

The world filled with hate has one need.

Let love and balance be the seed."

The mold becomes the shape of a person, a girl. She looks just like the faerie girl would if she was a human instead of a fae.

The pixie takes the molded girl to the edge of the creek and leans in close over the water. This time I am unable to hear the words whispered. I am able to see, however, that the water's surface now reflects the faces of what can be nothing other than the elves Pilate told us about.

There are three of them. Each one has sharp elegant cheekbones. Even through the water's image, they radiate pure magic. The one in the middle with pale blue skin and pink eyes strangely reminds me of Mitzi. She seems to be the leader, as the two elves beside her say nothing during the conversation with the Pixie.

They both have blue skin as well, but instead of a soft Easter blue, it is more of a prussian blue. They have no hair, and their eyes are a swirling gold. I think perhaps they are her guards. They stand stoic, watching and listening, nothing more.

"Is it done?" She asks the Pixie.

"It is," the pixie replies with a nod. "All that is required are the finishing touches."

"You are ready," she says in a powerful voice. It is not a question. Still, the Pixie nods. "More of us will follow your lead, Smaul. With the cover of glamour, we will reside, watch, and help when needed. We thank you, and the Father thanks you for this sacrifice."

She then begins to chant in a whisper. It begins the same as the chant the Pixie said while making the mold of the girl,

"From horror and pain, hope will rise.
This star shines through from the darkest night.
The world filled with hate has one need.
Let love and balance be the seed."

A light emits from within the pixie.

The Elf continues,

"A Dreamer is made from sacrifice.
She will take what is wrong and make it right.
If by chance her mission does fail,
Her next in line, this path must sail.
Until the wrong is made right,
All upon the earth shall fight.
When at last peace has come,
All her children will live as one."

With the elf's last words, the pixie's body is transformed into sparkling white pearl dust, pure magic. It floats into the molded girl giving her life.

She gasps with her first breath of life. When she blinks, I see the eyes of the faerie child. She leans over the water where the image of the elves remains.

"Hello?" She says softly to the elves.

"Hello, Dreamer," the Easter blue elf replies. "You know your

mission?"

"To save the world," she says automatically. "To find and spread love. To restore balance to all."

It sounds strange hearing the words spoken by a child.

"We will join you on this mission, Dreamer. We will come to you in the form of pixies as our brother did before us. When the number of years of your life have passed, another will be born with your abilities. With each new cycle, a new Dreamer will be born to help you on this mission. Earth is grand and holds much life. If we increase our allies on this mission, the task at hand will be easier.

"We will bring the remaining dragons with us. They have agreed to join our mission. You must know, if you die before completing your mission, your soul will be trapped, unable to pass into the Domain until another Dreamer succeeds."

"I understand," the child Dreamer says.

"You will be called Una, as you are the first of your kind. Go now, Una. We will be with you soon."

* * * * * * * * * *

We all wake when the dream is over and sit quietly taking in what we just saw.

"So, pixies are elves?" Apuri asks aloud.

"And they are the ones who created Dreamers," Not adds.

"With the sacrifice of one of their own *and* a faerie child turned human!" I add, not wanting her sacrifice to be forgotten. Though I know, already, their stories were forgotten long ago, either intentionally or simply by time passed I am not sure.

"Nedra," I say aloud for everyone to hear, "did you know the dragons came here with the elves?"

"No, Althea. Much like the rest of what happened that day, those details were lost with the years."

I yawn, still tired from the extravagant meal Apuri and I prepared, not to mention the busy day leading up to finding the hegira camp.

"Nedra," I say through our link, too tired to speak aloud through yawns, "do you think we will have time to get some restful sleep when we get back to the camp?"

"Yes, Althea," he replies through our link, "you will have plenty of time to rest. The darkness was not the only reason I chose this place to read the second book. Time is different here. You will see, when we return only minutes will have passed."

Chapter Fourteen ~ To The Feather Tree

It has been two days since we arrived at the hegira camp in the Painted Forest. Nedra just received word that Lady Nell, Noni, Tsar, and Nanoaj are on their way back from the farm. Tsar was not sure exactly which book we were looking for; so, he took all of them. His mother and the rest of the hegira from the farm are headed this way, too. I am not sure how I convinced them to leave the farm, but I am glad they are going to help.

Nedra spoke to Nanoaj this morning. She said they would wait for night in the human realm before flying back to Sengsourya. They plan to return to the Painted Forest through the Feather Tree so they were not spotted by humans. I am still not sure it ever gets dark inside the Painted Forest which makes tracking time a bit difficult.

Nedra and Not have become my clocks. They are used to the strange way time works in magical realms.

Nedra assures me I, too, will learn how to feel the passing of time with my magic. I have my doubts.

We have been cleaning up camp here and planning what

our next move will be. If Tsar has the book, then we will find what answers we need to stop wild magic. If not... Well, that is what we are trying to figure out now.

The hegira have decided to speak to the advisors. They are seeking their place, purpose, and acceptance. They helped the faeries in the battle against the sodocs; maybe the faeries will now help them.

For now, Aspen, Not, Apuri, his family, and I are meeting inside the feast hall. Nedra, keeping his much-too-large body outside, pokes just his horned head in through the door to listen and join the meeting himself. Though the sight nearly sends me into a fit of giggles every time I look at him, I know he often feels left out of our important meetings even with the ability to listen in through our link.

"There is really only one more place to look if Tsar does not have the book," Apuri says.

"The Pyramid," I say it without emotion, but deep inside, every alarm is going off.

That is the last place I want to see. It literally killed me the last time I was there physically, and wild magic almost did the same when I went there in my dreams. But wild magic is getting stronger by the day. We have to stop it.

With a plan in our back pocket, we are ready when Tsar, Lady Nell, Noni, and Nanoaj arrive.

Nedra gave Nanoaj our location, and she found us with ease. Nedra tells us when they are getting close so we can wait for them outside. As soon as they land, Noni jumps off of Nanoaj's back with a squeal of excitement and runs to greet us, red curls bobbing all the way. Nell slides down gracefully with a grin at her daughter. Tsar gathers their bags and brings them after the girls.

I nod a greeting to Nanoaj, which she returns before turning her attention to Nedra. They let us know they are going to fly for a while, but they will be listening when we are ready for them.

Noni, now used to being around faeries and hegira, runs off to play with Fen and the twins.

Inside the feast hall, we tell Tsar and Lady Nell everything we know thus far. Nedra is even able to share glimpses – a sort of synopses of events – of the books with Nanoaj so she can in turn share with her riders.

The other two books give us an idea of what we are looking for.

With every book that is not *the book*, worry sets in. "What if Sticks changed or damaged the cover somehow to keep others from knowing what was inside?" I say, voicing my concerns aloud.

"Do they *have* to have the light show?" Lady Nell asks. "I mean, can't you just read them like a normal book?"

"I am not sure, really. Nedra is the only one I know who can read the language of magic fluently. I will ask him to see."

Nedra answers through our private link, "It would take a long time to translate and read the book the way you are thinking. It is possible though. My fear is, if Zixus has done as you say, we will not have the time required."

"How long are we talking?" I ask, afraid of the answer.

"It took me about a month to translate one full page when I was working with Vidas. I am more efficient at reading the language now than I was then, but it would still take time. That is time we do not have."

I relay the message to everyone else and receive the same disappointment on their faces that I feel in my gut. It seems finding the book damaged would be almost as bad as not finding it at all.

Once we have made it through one full bag of wrong books, we take a break to eat. Lady Nell calls for Noni, and the rest of the hegira to come eat. We have set the table up outside of the structure today so our work will not be disrupted.

It is not an extravagant meal like the other night, but the food is still good and filling. We decided the stew and bread was the most popular part of our meal the other night, and the most filling – it also works well for feeding a crowd – so naturally, it was our choice for everyone today.

For dessert, we have provided jam as well as honey that we gathered ourselves from some very nice and colorful bees to spread on the bread.

It was my first time trying animal faerie powers. It was Nedra's idea, but Apuri and Not quickly encouraged it. I was not too sure about it myself. Animal powers are not something I practiced with Queen Melanomie in Ceres.

I felt so silly trying to call a swarm of bees with my mind. I left the stares of the camp to venture past the mushrooms to a more secluded area. After several failed attempts, I asked Nedra for help. He brought Apuri and Not along.

It turned out Not was actually the fae I needed. He has experience speaking to animals in the sea. He explained it is less about speaking and more about feeling and intent expressed through emotion and magic.

I still used words, because that is how I am used to communicating, but it works out pretty well. Just like the other magic, once I pictured in my mind what I needed or wanted to happen, it got easier.

Not long after I clearly pictured bees with us in my mind, we heard buzzing. It was hard for me not to flinch away when they flew too close. I had to remind myself that they are creatures, too, that I called them here, and we are here for their help. I tapped into my magic, feeling it in my core.

I glanced at my wrist as I bowed to the bees and thanked them for coming. It looked like a hot summer sunset, deep gold and warm. I wonder if it changes according to what animal I am working with. The bees buzzed and danced to show us how happy they were to help the Dreamer any way they could. I expressed my gratitude and told them if they ever need my help, all they have to do is call.

We climbed on Nedra's back and followed the bees to their hive where they instructed us on the proper way to collect the honey. I was having trouble creating the glass jar in my mind with my hands, so I pulled out the paintbrush Eart gave me. That did the trick. I was able to focus the magic exactly as I saw it in my mind and create a glass jar big enough to hold the honey needed for the camp.

After finishing our lunch, we head back inside to work again. Noni and the hegira children begin a game of *around tag* – a basic game of tag, but instead of running willy-nilly, you have to run around in a circle.

With the thought of Zixus altering the cover to make it harder for others to read it, we are paying extra close attention to the content inside the books as well.

Lady Nell holds the book she is searching up in front of her face with the pages hanging open like a calendar and her head turned. Her face pales; she looks like she might be sick. "Sticks was into some really freaky stuff." She turns the book around for us to see.

The double page spread depicts the form of a man's body. The upper page shows the muscular structure, red meat accented with white tendons, and blue veins drawing the eye from one joint to another. I have seen such diagrams in biology books in school. The bottom half of the body is where it gets disturbing. This half shows only the vein work upon the skeletal structure of the man. From head to toe, there are small lines – pinpoints – instructing the reader of every key place on the body to cut for optimal bloodletting.

"Looks like he did his homework to ensure he got every drop," Tsar says, not bothering to hide the disdain in his tone.

Every drop of the blood of my predecessors. The thought makes me pale as my own blood rushes back to my heart with fear.

Nell sets the book down and cautiously picks up another, holding it at arm's length to read the title scrawled upon the spine. "How many languages did Sticks speak?" She scrunches her nose and squints her eyes as she attempts to sound out the foreign word upon the book.

"Not sure, why?" Tsar replies while flipping through his

own book. She holds the book out in front of his face and says, "Because I have no idea what this says."

Curious that it may be the language of magic, I lean over to peer at the cover. There is no filigree. The language looks to be Russian, perhaps. This is not the book we are looking for.

After some time, Noni comes in and lies down between her mother and Tsar for a nap. We continue reading, but in a quieter manner.

* * * * * * * * * *

I toss the last book upon the pile of others with disappointing failure. We have been looking through books for what feels like an eternity. I know it has really only been a few hours; still, I feel time slipping through our fingers.

We all sit back and sigh as one. There is only one thing left for us to do. We have to go back to the Pyramid. The mere thought of it fills me with dread. I sigh again, alone this time.

I sit up with a forced attempt at enthusiasm and say, "Well, let's get to it, I guess."

"We should have a plan," Aspen says. "You did say there were monsters in there. Monsters that can physically hurt you even when you are dreaming. If that is the case, I want to be prepared when we meet them."

"I agree," Lady Nell chimes in. "Also, I think we should go back to Sengsourya to get there. It would be our fastest route, and it was pretty advantageous the last time we had to go to the Pyramid."

Tsar nods his agreement.

I look at Apuri and Notyal, both of whom simply shrug.

"The Feather Tree actually is not too far from here," Tsar says. "It took longer for us to get from the Farm to Sengsourya than it took to get from The Feather Tree to here."

"Okay," I agree, "Sengsourya will be our next stop. Then, we head to the source of this wild magic and hope we can find the book that may or may not be the answer to stopping it. As for a plan once we get to the Pyramid, that is something we will have to work on."

Nedra and Nanoaj have been listening in silently. They grabbed their own meal while they were out. Now, they are flying within the beautiful clouds above the Painted Forest.

Lady Nell and Tsar stiffen a bit; they are listening. After a few minutes, Lady Nell says, "Nanoaj has suggested we ask to use some of the tools within Sengsourya before deciding on a plan for the wild magic. When we stayed there before going to the farm, Petricha showed us around a little bit. I did not think of it at the time, but maybe something there can help us like the tower did last time."

"Okay," I rub my hands together, "sounds like we have a plan, then. Apuri, what about the crew here? I hate just running off and leaving them." Apuri's family left the research a while ago to help tend to their crew.

"I have already talked to my mom about it. She says not to worry; they have always taken care of themselves and will continue to do so now. They are not giving up on helping us, either. They are going to continue their own search to find a solution for wild magic."

"Okay." I look around at my companions. Once again, I feel the dread of going to the Pyramid, but their faces give me some comfort. "I guess there is no reason to procrastinate. If we leave now, we will make it to Sengsourya before nightfall. That will give us time to rest once we get there and work on the rest of this plan with the help of the sky faeries."

Nedra and Nanoaj return with a swift, but graceful, landing in the center of the hegira camp. We all get our things together as quickly as possible and prepare to journey to Sengsourya. Tsar gently picks Noni up and carries her out to Nanoaj. The hegira will remain here and wait for Tsar's crew to come from the farm.

Apuri and I prepared some lasting foods for the hegira to ensure they keep their energy up over the next several days until the rest of the hegira arrive. We leave the books with them as well.

With everything in order, Apuri says his goodbyes, and we take off. Tsar was right; the Feather Tree is not too far from the hegira camp. I was not really sure how I expected the Feather Tree to look, but it is beyond breathtaking.

Its trunk resembles a catalpa tree, but instead of the green, bean-pod fruits, this tree is filled with millions of feathers! There are feathers of every color, shape, and size. Just like everything else within the Painted Forest, they all coexist to blend into the most beautiful composition.

The way the different colors blend together seamlessly reminds me of the rainbow nebula of the Domain and the mark on my wrist. As we circle the tree before going into it, I get a new sense of hope.

I let that hope fill me to the brim as we enter through the rainbow feathers of the Feather Tree.

Chapter Fifteen ~ The Rescue

I forgot how fresh the air in Sengsourya was! It is like breathing for the first time. I take a deliberate, slow, deep breath and enjoy every second of it. It is intoxicating.

It is not just me, either. The elation coming off of everybody reflects that same sense of hope I feel inside. That hope continues to grow as we reach the gates of Sengsourya to find Petricha and her guards, Leslie and Dianna, waiting for us.

Nedra and Nanoaj land gracefully upon the clouds, and we dismount our dragons to greet the faerie trio.

"Hi!" I hug Leslie, Dianna, and Petricha. "How did you know we were coming?" I ask with a smile.

Petricha looks at me. Her haloed moon eyes are filled with a dreadful haunted look. "We did not know." Her nostrils flare slightly as she inhales sharply. "Althea, things have taken a turn for the worst." She leans over the edge of the cloud to gaze down with a spyglass like the one in the tower we used in the battle against the sodocs. She passes the spyglass to me.

I carefully lean over the edge of the cloud and hold the spyglass to my eye. It does not zoom right up to the structures upon the earth but reveals a bird's eye view as if looking at a topographic map.

The wonderful sensation of hope I was feeling only moments earlier stops dead in its tracks; frozen by the horrific sight before me, it is replaced with dread. I stumble back into Apuri's arms and pass him the spyglass before stepping over to Nedra. I rest my arm at the base of Nedra's shoulder for support as each of my friends takes a turn to see what is happening below.

I feel as if the clouds under my feet will slip away at any moment. We have wasted too much time. Wild magic has spread. It now covers the whole town, the entire beach, and it has even crept into the ocean.

Notyal nearly drops the spyglass when he sees the beach and the ocean. "My lady!" he gasps in a horrified whisper. If wild magic has made it into the ocean, Ceres is in just as much danger as the Painted Forest, maybe even more so.

Petricha takes the spyglass back from him and turns us to enter the city gates without another look below. Her guards lead the way to the city center where we stayed before while she walks at the back of our group by my side.

"Something has changed, Dreamer. We have been keeping watch on the wild magic below. It has been spreading at a steady pace, but a slow one. Althea," she lowers her voice. I can hear the frustration in it as she continues. "That beach was not touched by a speck of green last night. This morning that jungle had just started to creep onto the boardwalk. We have been rotating watches every hour. You remember Leslie and Dianna? They just started their shift when they noticed how much it advanced since their shift last night. They fetched me immediately. That is why we were on the ledge when you arrived. I had just seen the view below when we saw you appear in the sky.

"I assumed you knew about whatever event triggered the wild magic to increase its rate of growth and came to tell us about it. By the look on your face when you peered through that spyglass, I am guessing that assumption was completely inaccurate. If you did not come here about wild magic, why did you come? Does it have to do with those books Lady Nell and Tsar were bringing back? Did you find the book you were looking for?"

The truth of what it means to see wild magic spreading sinks in, and I feel like I may drown in fear, in terror. Petricha's questions pour on top of me suppressing all but my last breath. I turn my face down to watch my feet step upon the white and blue-gray clouds. "No," I whisper without meeting her eyes. "Quite the opposite, in fact. We came here looking for your help. I actually was hoping you would be able to help us figure out a plan to get into the middle of that jungle so we can look for the book."

"Oh," she sighs. "Well, of course we will help!" she says with forced enthusiasm. But the creases at the corners of her eyes and between her brow remain. "Would you mind extending your stay until we figure out what happened down there? I would hate for you to go down there and it end up being nothing more than a suicide mission. If, however, we have time to figure out what is happening down there, you may be able to not only get the book but stop the wild magic, too."

"Yeah!" I do not hesitate to answer. "I figure at this point the more answers we can find the better."

She seems relieved as she says, "Good. Have you had any more dreams lately? Anything helpful, perhaps?" She raises a brow in hopeful curiosity.

Again, I avoid her gaze out of embarrassment. "No, actually, I... I have been going to Zoar every night." I rub my arm self-consciously. "Honestly, I have been purposely avoiding the Pyramid in my dreams because of what happened last time. But I have been practicing using magic within my dreams. I am pretty good now."

She laughs and says, "Well, that is good news. Do not worry about the dreams. You do not have to handle all of this all on your own, Althea. That is why we are all here, to work together. Maybe you can even train with me and my guards some time. To perfect not only your sky magic but fine tune your fighting skills as well. We would enjoy that."

I accept her offer, and we stop talking as we walk into the cloud formed building. Nedra and Nanoaj head to the same stead that Nedra went to the last time we were here with Chaz.

I wonder, again, what became of the large majestic Chobudda thunder, and why they abandoned us along with the pixies. Something in my gut tells me that is what really happened. They are not missing or hurt; they are just gone.

Petricha, her guards, and the other sky faeries are most accommodating. They show us to our rooms, the same ones we had on the top floor the last time we were here. They give us some time to freshen up while they prepare lunch on the main floor.

I immediately collapse onto the soft cloud bed. "I wish we could stay here one night without the pressure of eternal doom looming over our heads," I say aloud to Apuri. He falls back upon the bed beside me. "One day we will," he says with a certainty impossible for me to doubt.

"How do you do it?" I ask softly, "How do you stay positive when every time we turn around, the world is crumbling beneath our feet?"

"I do not give myself a choice," he laughs. "When everyone in the world tells you everything is horrible and there is no hope, you have two choices. You can believe them, or you can prove them wrong. I have chosen to do the latter. That is actually how I met your sister, you know?"

"Really? No, I did not know. With saving the world always at the forefront of our agenda, we have never had time to actually talk about just us."

He reaches over and holds my hand. We lie quietly like that for a few minutes before we finally decide it has been long enough for lunch to be done.

For the rest of the day there is a knot in my stomach that will not unwind. We make casual conversation while eating. Our lunch is a truly magical one. The meal is not normal by any means; there is no food cooked and placed upon the table. Instead, we are each given a white porcelain plate and cup decorated with a golden sun or silver moon and lined with a circle of stars. The length of the table is spread with serving dishes of similar décor filled to the brim with different colored cloud tufts.

Each color cloud represents a different food type: red clouds are meat; yellow clouds are dairy products; orange clouds are grains; purple clouds are fruits; green clouds are vegetables; pink clouds are dessert; and blue clouds are beverages. You grab a tuft of cloud and place it onto your plate or inside your cup with a clear thought of what you would like it to be.

Thankfully, Dianna explains how everything works when we all arrive to eat. I make a chicken salad with a tuft of red and a couple tufts of green for the vegetables and even some purple to add some strawberries. For dessert, I grab a couple tufts of pink cloud to make a brownie-bottom cheesecake topped with crumbled blueberry donut cake and some cool whip.

During our magical dinner, we actually find ourselves having fun creating our food. I wish I could say it is so much fun that I am able to forget about the trouble brewing below and the knot in my stomach, but unfortunately that is not the case. I did enjoy the meal and had fun not only creating my own food, but watching my friends create theirs as well. But I know on the ground below us, wild magic is growing stronger by the minute.

We all eat our fill and return to our rooms for a post-meal nap. Once everyone wakes, we will meet again to begin a plan.

* * * * * * * * * *

Everything is foggy and dark. It is not night, though; it is a storm.

I hear screams. So many screams!

I cover my ears with my hands, but it does not help. The screams vibrate to my very core making my teeth rattle.

A small, barefoot child stands in the middle of a neighborhood street crying. A deafening boom thunders, momentarily blocking out the child's shrieking. The crackle of lightning that follows illuminates the scene allowing me to see what is actually happening.

Wild magic. I should have known.

The house that the child is watching crumbles before our eyes as trees, vines, and other greenery shoot up from the ground.

"Mommy!" The child screams even louder and runs toward the house.

Another boom of thunder and crack of lightning bring forth a shower of heavy raindrops. We are soaked within seconds. I run after the child. If he goes into that house, he will die.

I cannot let that happen.

Someone screams from within the house. It is a woman. She is at the front door, but she cannot open it. It is blocked by debris from the side of the house that was destroyed. I use my magic to trap the debris in a bubble of air and lift it out of the way.

Seeing this, the child stops, unsure whether to keep going or not. The woman knocks the door open and runs out with a baby in her arms. Seeing her child so close to the house, she begins waving with her free arm and shouts, "Turn around! Go back!"

The child does not listen, instead, he waits for his mother to reach his side as he asks, "Where is Daddy?"

Without answering her son, the woman grabs his arm with her free hand and drags him along with her, back toward the street. I turn back just in time to see their house completely demolished by the jungle. Now, it is racing our way.

We make it to the street and stop. There are no cars passing by. There are no more houses nearby. If the family had a car, it was destroyed along with the rest of the house.

The small boy asks again, "Where is Daddy?" The woman turns back to where their house stood only moments ago. She swallows hard and says with the most normal voice she can attempt, "Daddy wants us to keep going, sweetie. We have to stay safe."

She turns to look down the street. The east end is already blocked by the oncoming wild magic. She looks again at her house. It looks like a mountain is beginning to erupt from the location. The ground rises quickly, shaking the earth as it grows.

Without another thought, we all make a run for it down the west end of the street. We are not going to make it. We are not fast enough on our feet. I have to save them.

"Stop!" I shout; running is not going to help anything.

It is no use; they cannot hear me. I am dreaming.

I do the first thing I can think of to help. I start a fire behind us to cut off the wild magic. They stop running to see what has happened. This is my only chance. I quickly create a hollowed-out tree trunk and do my best to shape it into a canoe before floating it in the air until it reaches the family where I gently place it on the street. The woman and child look at it in shock, with fear on their faces. I focus all of the rain in the area around the canoe ensuring the inside stays dry.

"Get in!" I shout through the rain. They still cannot hear me.

The woman is about to run again; I can see it on her face. If she does that, none of them will survive. I run my hands through my hair in a frenzy. I look back to the fire. The magical flames are flickering, straining to stay ablaze in their current circumstances. It will not hold long.

I need to tell them to get into the canoe, but they cannot hear me. Maybe they can read a message I write! I rub my hands together. It has to be obvious, something in front of their faces.

I wipe the rain off my face. Maybe I can use the rain. No, it would just blend in too much. It might be too dark to see anything in this storm.

Darkness... That is it! I need light!

I have seen photographs of moving light; complete words and shapes are formed by moving sparklers or flashlights while the person remains a blur from the extended exposure.

If I can pull off something to that effect with magic, I can write a message right here with light. I do not have to worry about them seeing me anyway. If I get it right, I can use magic to speed up the light and make words.

I flex my hands and calm my breathing, ignoring the rain. I extend both arms with open hands and create a fiery spark. My magic allows it to burn without being extinguished by the rain, just like the fire wall I created to keep wild magic back.

As fast as I can, I write "Get in the boat!"

They hesitate, but it works. With the water now almost as high as our knees, it takes the woman a little effort to climb into the rocking canoe after placing her crying children into it.

I use my magic to give her some help with a boost of air. Once they are all in the canoe safely, I increase the water and push them out with magic as fast as I can.

"Nedra!" I shout through our private link. "I need your help! I have to get this family out of here, and I cannot do that if someone wakes me up. Also, I have no idea where I am taking them. Any ideas?"

"I will inform the others you are not to be woken up. As for where to take the family, are you sure this is happening now in the real world?"

"Yes. I am not sure how, but I know it is. Is there any way to find out where we are, so I know where to go?"

"The others are aware of what is happening," Nedra replies. "If you are certain this is happening right now, I have an idea. The sky faeries can use a spyglass to find your location, but they will need a beacon of some sort."

"I made a wall of fire to hold back the wild magic to give us a little time. Do you think someone can spot the smoke?"

"I will let them know and get back to you. For now, just keep doing what you are doing. I am just a whisper away if you need me."

I add water below us to speed up the trip out of here. We are sticking to the streets to avoid obstacles. We turn onto a street heading north and finally see some lights ahead. Maybe someone here can help. I guide the boat toward the light.

Unfortunately, it is just a closed service station. I let the water recede as we float into the parking lot, allowing the canoe to rest on the rough gravel.

"Althea." It is Nedra. "We still cannot find you. The wild magic is growing too fast. You will have to make something stronger for us to see."

"Okay, Nedra." I look around the vacant parking lot. I do not see anything useful here. Even the lights that brought my attention here, now seem dull and hopeless. "I know! I can use magic to create a light and focus the beam upward for a beacon. Look for the beacon Nedra!"

I create the bright beacon quickly and rejoin the family. They are sitting by the door of the service station now. As much as I hate to have spooked them with the fire, the canoe, and the floating words, I would hate even more for them to meet the same fate as the boy's father. I wonder if she has told him yet. They are quiet, probably in shock.

We do not wait long before faeries start showing up. "Nedra, they are here! Tell them to be careful. I will meet them at the gates. I am waking up now."

* * * * * * * * * *

I wake up and immediately go to the door. Apuri follows without any questions. Nedra has already told everyone what was happening. I run downstairs quickly and out the doors toward the gates.

If I can get there as soon as they arrive and explain everything to the human woman, hopefully it will help her understand what is happening.

Petricha meets me on the way. "Althea, we have never had humans in Sengsourya, in Reverie, other than dreams. Most of us have never even been around humans or seen one, let alone interact with them. On the flip side, at least we know they exist. How are they supposed to handle this? Humans do not even believe we are real."

I continue walking with determination. I answer her with the same determination. "I am not sure, but we cannot just sit back and let them die. How many have died already because we have been too busy looking for the answers from the safety of our own magic?"

We arrive at the gates just in time to see the group of faeries from my dream bring in the woman and her two children from my dream.

She looks so frightened and confused I feel bad about bringing her here for a moment. The thought of her missing husband, and the reason he is missing, stop those feelings. I hate that I was not there in time to save him, too. I run up to the humans and do my best to explain what is happening.

"Hi," I say as I reach out to shake her hand. She automatically raises her own hand in a habitual motion but with a face frozen in shock. "I am Althea. I know this is a lot to take in, and we will do our best to help you understand. The most important thing you need to know is that you are safe now." The little boy clings tightly to his mother's leg. She drops her hand to hold him against her while still carrying the baby on her other hip.

We usher them away from the gates and toward the city center.

Thankfully, Apuri is not far behind. He quickly catches up and joins me beside the humans. He is a lifter; his magic ability is making people feel better. I can think of no better situation in which to have that ability. I give him a nod to go ahead and use that gift. In an instant the woman and children stop crying. They are still confused, but maybe their lighter moods will allow them to understand where they are and who we are.

When we reach the building, everyone else is waiting on the main floor. The room now contains a bunch of sofas and small tables. We guide the woman and her children to the largest one in the middle. Aspen quickly starts making some tea for them using the kettle and cups on an octagonal shaped table centered between all of the sofas.

After a few minutes, I notice the family begins to relax a little. The woman starts to warm up to Aspen and Lady Nell, though the two seem to have some problem between them. They have not spoken since I woke up from the Domain. Noni's presence seems to help the young boy. He does not say anything, but he watches her constantly.

It is natural to cling to the familiar, especially when faced with a traumatic event.

The woman's name is Nicole, the baby is Joshua, and the little boy is Tim, after his father.

"Nicole," I say, keeping my voice calm but serious, "can you tell us what happened?"

She nods, "We were home, watching a movie, when the house shook like an earthquake. We do not get earthquakes, though. Timmy woke up scared, I went to check on him while Tim turned on the news and checked out the back door. He yelled back at me that it looked like a storm coming, maybe it was thunder that shook the house. Before he could come back inside, this tree just shoots up out of the ground, fully grown, right where he was standing." She continues to stare at the floor as she whispers, "One second, he was there, the next he was gone.

"I told Timmy to go wait by the door, and I ran to check on Tim." She swallows, and her nostrils flare with emotion. Her lip quivers like she is about to cry, but Apuri's magic and Aspen's tea prevent it. She continues in a lowered voice. "He did not make it. I still have not told Timmy."

She catches her breath and says, "I ran back to get Joshua. The garage and the whole side of the house suddenly fell splintering everywhere. I yelled at Timmy to run. 'Run to the street, and don't stop until you get there!' I told him. After he made it out, more of the house fell in. I got Joshua, but I could not open the door. Something fell in front of it. I kept trying and yelling, and suddenly, it opened. Whatever was in the way moved. I grabbed Timmy in the yard and ran for it. We got to the street, but nobody was around. Our house was the last one on the street; all of the other houses were already gone, swallowed by the trees.

"I had no idea what we were going to do; we began running when, suddenly, a wall of fire appeared between us and the trees. And then out of nowhere this boat shows up and the rain starts to flood the ground, but only around us. I was scared to get in. I did not know where this boat came from. And then, these words appear in midair telling me to get in. I did not have any better ideas or time to argue otherwise, so I got in the boat. We began floating down the street. We made it all the way to the old station when the water went away and the boat landed. I took the boys to sit under the awning covering the door, and then, this bright light appeared, followed by them." She points to the faeries who rescued them.

"Nicole, I am the one who helped you. It is a pretty complicated story, but what you need to know is that we are here to help. These are my friends. The sky faeries who saved you knew where to go because I made the beacon. I have the ability and magic to see things in my dreams. I saw you and helped you get out. I wish I could have made it there sooner; I am sorry. What you saw down there is wild magic. We are trying to find a way to stop it. I know this is a lot to take in at one time. I promise we will do our best to answer any questions you have. We will give you a room, food, and anything else you need."

She nods but does not say anything. She probably thinks this is a dream. Lady Nell and Noni excuse them from the group and show them to their new room. Aspen sends some of the tea with Nicole.

The rest of us have more business to continue discussing.

Chapter Sixteen ~ Plan B

We are postponing our trip to the Pyramid. We are contacting the other advisors about Nicole's family and the danger of wild magic to the other humans. Petricha has her own office of sorts in a loft in her home. She invites us there after Nicole and her children are safe and resting in their room.

Apuri and I join Petricha to contact the other advisors. Lady Nell and Aspen choose to stay behind in case Nicole needs anything. They are the most human and therefore most familiar to Nicole. That is what she needs right now. The thought hits me that I would be trusted as well if not for my transformation after dying, the changing of my eyes and the mark. No human has rainbow swirling eyes and a moving, color changing tattoo. Everyone else decided to rest or tour Sengsourya. We have promised to pass on any information we learn.

We leave the building at the city center and follow Petricha around it and past the dragon's structure. Nedra assures me he will be listening in and provide any help if needed. I thank him and continue following Petricha through Sengsourya. The sun is going down, so the clouds are a warm orange lined with purple. The sky is already darkening making it difficult to see exactly where we are going.

We pass a lot of interesting buildings on our walk through Sengsourya. This is no time for a tour, though. Instead, I quietly admire the city in the sky until we have made it to what feels like the farthest edge of Sengsourya itself. Petricha's house is more like a watchtower sitting higher than all the other buildings, except for the city center, to keep them safe.

We walk into her home, a plain, undecorated space with white walls and minimum furniture. There is no kitchen; though with the ability to make any food you wish out of clouds, I doubt kitchens exist anywhere up here.

Petricha wipes her rainy locks out of her face and heads straight to the back of the house where a ladder stands alone on the wall. She does not seem to have any emotional attachments to the home.

We follow her up the ladder to her office loft. I am surprised to see a beautiful silver crescent moon mirror decorating the wall behind a desk with a full moon lamp on it. A couple small sofas line the walls, and two comfy chairs sit in front of the desk while one plain chair sits behind it.

Instead of sitting behind the desk, like I thought she would, Petricha goes to the silver moon on the wall. She removes it from the wall and turns around, taking it back to the desk. She beckons for us to come over. We sit in the two chairs right in front of the desk as she holds the moon upright just above the desk. She holds it at the top with her index finger and thumb and sits in the plain chair behind her.

Still holding the silver moon, she leans in close and blows on it like you would blow a candle out on a birthday cake. As she releases her breath, her eyes light up with magic. The full moon pupil brightens a deep orange like a magical harvest supermoon; the halo lining the iris glows a faint blue, perfectly complementing its moon. Between the two, in the dark abyss resembling the night sky, several small stars begin to shine and twinkle.

Petricha removes her hand from the silver moon as it ripples and shifts into a smooth, liquid mirror. The silver frame now pulsates in a glowing blue light similar to the ring in her eyes.

Petricha sits back and says, "It will not be long. We just wait for them to answer the call."

"So, it is like a magic mirror phone?" I ask, amused.

Petricha smiles but does not have time to answer before the first Advisor picks up our call. The mirror's surface ripples with vibrations. Petricha reaches out and touches it with her finger. The mirror's surface splashes into a billion tiny droplets that soar through the air to cover every corner of the office. It is as if the mirror became a massive sprinkler.

As fast as the mirror splashed apart, the mist droplets changed even faster to show us in the company of Clementine. She is sitting in the room with us on one of the small sofas, but it is just an illusion.

She looks at us and says, "Petricha, Althea, what is it? What is wrong?"

Petricha smiles and answers before I have a chance to say anything, "We will explain once the others have answered, but it seems we have run into more trouble. A danger we overlooked, or frankly did not even concern ourselves with, about wild magic."

Clementine looks worried but waits patiently for the others to answer. We do not have to wait long before Eart and Feather answer at the same time. They, too, appear to be in the room with us, sitting on the sofas. Before long, all of the advisors are in the room with us, except Ophidius.

Arsona was in the middle of a drawing. She appeared still holding her flame-tipped pen in her hand. I guess the others put down whatever they were doing before answering the call.

Each advisor has an office space exclusively for advisor work in their home. In each office is a message mirror for the advisors to easily communicate. Petricha and Clementine told us they are usually used to calling a meeting at the Advisor Tree in Inon. Not many emergencies have happened that require an emergency call.

Clementine later admits, however, that she and Tilda use theirs to plan personal dates sometimes as it is the easiest way to communicate since Clementine does not live in Inon.

We wait a little longer for Ophidius, but when it is clear he is not answering the call, we have no choice but to continue without him.

"Have you found the last book?" Feather asks when the meeting officially starts.

"No," I answer, "we arrived in Sengsourya this morning to find wild magic had grown significantly overnight. We intended to construct a plan to go into the heart of it, to the Pyramid, in search of the book. But I had a dream that changed our plans. Really, I feel horrible for not realizing it earlier, but humans are in terrible danger with wild magic consuming their realm.

"In my dream, a house was being destroyed by wild magic. I was barely able to save a woman and her children. Unfortunately, I showed up too late to save her husband. We have them here with us now, but there is a reason I had that dream. How many other humans have already died? Wild magic has grown into the sea now and twice as far on the land side. When the sodocs had the Pyramid there, people were walking the streets and visiting the beaches. I can only pray that they were all smart enough to get out of dodge when the Pyramid was destroyed, but that is not likely.

"Our goal is not to save only faeries. We are supposed to save *the world,* all of it! That being said, I have a plan. It is a plan I am not sure you will like."

"Maybe it is a good thing Ophidius is absent," Eart says to Clementine in a whisper that is loud enough to be heard by everyone. Arsona smirks, but Tilda cuts off her laughter with that mother look she bears so well.

Business first as always, Tilda asks, "What is your plan

Althea?"

"We need to create a sanctuary in Reverie for humans."

Everyone sits speechless for several minutes. Finally, Eart is the one to speak up. "All humans?" he asks.

"Yes." I answer. "Well, all of the humans we can convince to come with us. I have not thought out the details of how we will do that, but I do have some ideas of what to do once they are in Reverie. Eart, I will need all the art faeries who will help. Clementine, the same with nature faeries. We can create temporary shelters for them in the Painted Forest while we get rid of the wild magic outside the glamour. We will also have to create some sort of blockade around each Gateway Tree to keep them from going in."

Again, the room is filled with silence. I had not shared my ideas with anyone prior to the meeting, not even Nedra or Apuri. Now, I wish I had.

Clementine leans forward with her elbows on her knees. Her bright green eyes look concerned. "Althea, are you sure you have thought this through, Sweetie? I mean, bringing humans into Reverie really goes against the whole reason it exists in the first place. I know you are worried, but maybe there is another solution, another way, a better way to go about this."

I look at each of them. Their expressions are all the same. None of them accept my idea. Even Apuri doubts my plan.

I do not understand. I thought they would want to help me. I can feel my anger growing. I cannot just sit by and let this go. I shout, "So, you are just going to sit behind your protection of magic and watch as the human race dwindles on the other side? Even you, Feather? What do you think my sister would say? We still have family in the human realm! If we just let them die because of our own selfishness, we are no better than the sodocs. In fact, we are worse!"

When nobody replies I jump up and shout, "Really?" The room remains silent. My hands begin to shake with anger and I leave the loft and Petricha's house as fast as I can. I need to go somewhere I can think straight.

I am so angry, I begin to cry. I fiercely wipe the tears from my cheeks, but that just makes more follow faster. "Nedra!" I cry out both through our link and aloud.

"I am on my way, Althea," he replies. Within seconds, he is flying over me. He dives down to the edge of the clouds past Petricha's house and hovers to let me drop onto his back.

As soon as I am seated, he takes off flying straight up into the night sky. It is a new moon tonight leaving the sky dark to show off the twinkling stars. I bury my face into Nedra's mane and allow myself to cry until the anger passes. After I stop crying, Nedra continues to fly around. He knows I am not ready to go back yet. I do not know if the other advisors are still there or if the call has ended. Right now, I do not care.

"What are we going to do, Nedra?" I ask through our link, thankful I do not have to speak aloud after crying. "We have to help them somehow. It is our job. It is *my* job!"

"Yes, it is. I will help you think of another way to save the humans, Althea. But if no other way shows itself, we will carry out your plan. Even if we have to stand against all the faeries in Reverie, it will be done."

I lie down on his silky mane and wrap my arms around his smooth scaly neck. "Thank you, Nedra. Thank you for trusting me."

He hums in reply and his embers glow a deep, bright red in the night sky. Nedra flies through the calm night until I fall asleep on his back. He lands back in the dragons' shelter without waking me, and we sleep there through the night in silence.

With Nedra's support, the morning finds me in a confident mood. We have to stop wild magic while at the same time saving all those who live upon the Earth, including humans. While I slept last night, I did not dream. Instead my brain was working constantly to find a solution. When the first rays of light shone through the window and woke me, I immediately headed to Petricha's house to inform her of the one I developed. Nedra flies me over to save time.

I dismount Nedra and march right up to Petricha's door intending to break it down if she does not answer. I raise my fist to knock and almost fall inside as the door swings open before I make contact with it. Apuri catches me with a flinch. He thought I was striking at him.

My first reaction is anger and jealousy, "What are you still doing here?"

He holds my hands and talks calmly, "After you stormed out last night, we waited for you to come back for a while. When it became apparent you were not coming back, we ended the meeting with the other advisors, and I went back to our room hoping to find you there. I waited and waited, but you still did not come back. I figured, perhaps, you would come back here to finish the meeting. Since I was not getting any sleep anyway, I came back to wait for you. And I was right. Although I did not think it would take you this long to show up. And next time, you could at least have Nedra tell me what you are doing and not keep me blocked from the link."

I can tell from his expression that he really was worried. I choose to respect that by not replying with any of the smart remarks flying through my mind. Instead, I push past him and head straight to the loft.

"Althea," Apuri calls from behind me. "Althea, hold on." He quickens his step to catch up with me, but I am already up the ladder by the time he catches up. I step into an empty loft. It looks exactly as it did before we started the magic meeting last night. The chairs are moved back, aligned perfectly in front of the desk. The silver moon hangs once more as nothing but a decoration on the wall. Petricha is not here.

I turn around and look back down in her house to see if I can find her. Apuri's head emerges from the ladder hole. "She is not in here. She is out there." He points toward the back of the house.

"Well, get her." I say as I turn again and walk past the desk to get the silver moon off the wall. "Tell her I am calling the advisors again, and if she wants to hear what I am doing, she better hurry."

He looks at me in disbelief. "Althea, come on…"

"Get her, or don't. I am doing this," I say, and without another word I stand the moon upon the desk and sit down in the plain chair. Focusing on sky magic, I lean forward and blow on the moon like Petricha did the night before. I think of calling the other advisors. I am not sure if intent matters with this magic or if the mirror simply responds to magic by default, but I figured better to go ahead and think about it just in case.

The moon spins and changes into the liquid mirror like it did last night. Now, just to wait. I sit back in the chair and go over my plan again with Nedra to make sure I have it all worked out when the call is answered.

It is not long before Apuri returns to the loft with Petricha following close behind. As soon as they arrive, the call is answered. Eart is the first to show up this time, followed by Arsona. The others answer one by one until everyone that was here last night once again sits in the room. Again, we wait for Ophidius. Again, he does not show.

I know he is not exactly my biggest fan, but as an advisor, I thought these calls would be something he would have to answer. When it is obvious he is not going to show, I get on with the meeting.

"I have called you all to tell you I have another idea. Mind you, if this does not work, I fully intend to carry out my first plan with or without your help. It is my job as *the Dreamer* to save the world. I will do that any way I can. Now, the solution is to stop wild magic. We have no idea where to start, right? Well, instead of us marching up and risking our lives to see what will or will not work, resulting in needless deaths, I suggest we use what is at our disposal. Before we fought the sodocs inside the Pyramid, we used a weather tower here in Sengsourya. I think we may be able to use that tower again. If we aim it at the center of the wild magic, we may be able to kill it off for good."

Everyone stares, speechless. Finally, Tilda stands up and says, "Well, it sounds like a plan to me. Keep us updated and let us know if there is anything else we can do. And Althea, we are sorry about last night. We should have listened to you. When you are expected to always have the answers for so long, it is hard to keep an open mind to new ideas. Of course, we do not want our history with humans to repeat itself, but you were sent here to save us all. We know that, and we will trust you. Now, Idona will be awake soon, and without Mitzi, simple tasks take more time to accomplish. A youngling even more so." She smiles, says goodbye, and disappears.

The other advisors also offer their apologies and support before leaving the call.

Once they are all gone, Apuri, Petricha, and I leave the loft. "Let me grab something, and then we can tell Leslie and Dianna your plan." She goes through the back door and leaves it ajar for Apuri and me to follow. Walking out to her backyard from within the plain house is like walking into Reverie from the human realm!

Instead of just clouds, her backyard is filled with a beautiful crystal garden! The path from the door to the far end of her yard is made of solid hematite lined with breathtaking shards of purple, sparkling amethyst protruding from the clouds below. Scattered throughout the yard are clusters of diamonds, clear quartz, rose quartz, pearls, opals, sapphires, turquoise, and blue topaz. And those are just the ones I can see and identify from the doorway. Some of them are as small as lichen while others tower over us like trees and every size in between.

At the end of the hematite path sits an elegantly small white table surrounded by three matching chairs.

I gasp at the sight before me. All of the magic in this garden makes up for the lack of decoration inside. "Wow!" I say as I look from one precious stone to the next.

Petricha smiles and says, "Wonderful isn't it? To be honest, though, I am surprised this is the first crystal garden you have seen. There are several in Reverie. Come on, I have something for you." She waves for us to follow her down the path.

Apuri and I walk down the path in circles admiring every inch of the garden we can. I get so caught up in looking at all of the crystals that I bump into one of the chairs and almost fall over into the amethyst shards lining the path. Apuri quickly grabs my arm and pulls me back upright.

I thank him, and we both go to the table and stand across from Petricha to see why she wanted us to follow her. She picks something up from the table and holds it in her hand. She grins excitedly, "I wanted to give this to you as a thank you gift after you defeated the sodocs. Unfortunately, things have not gone too smoothly and this is the first chance I have had."

She holds her hands out to display a clear quartz crystal about the length and thickness of my little finger.

I take the crystal and hold it up in the light to admire it. "It is beautiful! Thank you, Petricha!"

She smiles proudly, "Now, shall we?" She turns and leads the way back down the hematite path. We go back to get Leslie and Dianna, and see who else will come with us to the Guard's Tower.

We find Aspen, Tsar, and Not lounging on soft fluffy cloud sofas on the main floor. I ask if they want to help us fight some wild magic. They eagerly agree. Lady Nell and Noni decide to stay with Nicole and her children. The rest of us head outside to find Leslie and Dianna guarding the gates.

Petricha walks up to them alone. I am not sure what she tells them, but they immediately close and lock the gates and follow her. We all head back in the direction toward the Guard's Tower. Petricha leads the way across the path of flat-top clouds.

The rest of us follow with more energy than we had the last time we jumped across these clouds.

Nedra decided to stay back with Nanoaj to inform us if anything happens at the city center.

As we walk into the upside-down watchtower, I run my hand across the cold brick walls along the spiral staircase. The round room at the bottom looks the same as it did the last time we were here.

We each return to the window we controlled before.

Not grabs the condensation orb for rain; Apuri picks up the palette. Aspen holds the tuft of cloud, squishing it gently between her fingers. Petricha takes over the stardust in place of Lady Nell. Tsar picks up the little bellows and looks at it admiringly, like seeing an old friend. I resist the urge to laugh at his intimacy with the object. Dianna gets the sun, and Leslie holds the web of lightning. I, once again, take the role as leader using the spyglass to watch and control the storm as a whole.

I plan to focus every ounce of my magic into this storm and destroy wild magic once and for all.

Standing here, I look around the room and remember standing here before the fight inside the Pyramid. I was not sure then if this plan was going to work, and I am not sure it will work now either. All I know is hope got me through the last time. I am going to hang onto that hope once more.

I look around the room again and realize I have no idea what has happened to Serena, the hacket – a woman with the ability to see through others' eyes and the curse of having polymorphic faces. She was here with us in the tower before we flew down to fight the sodocs.

She watched through the eyes of the people on the street to let us know when it was clear to attack.

"Hey Aspen, what happened to Serena? Did she…?"

Aspen drops her head and says, "She did not make it through the battle with the sodocs. I am sorry; I thought we told you."

"No," I reply, swallowing my guilt at having not realized it sooner. "I understand it has been pretty chaotic since then. Who knows, you may have told me, and I just forgot. Still, I am sorry to hear it. She helped us a lot."

"She did. She managed to take down four sodocs single-handedly before she fell. One of them snuck up behind her and stabbed her through the back of her shoulder. She reached around, pulled the knife out, and stabbed the sodoc through the throat with it. Another one ran up and hit her in the head. She fell to the ground, but never got up. I think it killed her instantly."

Everyone else in the room is silent as Aspen finishes telling me of the fate of Serena. Without saying anything else, I turn to the window and look through the spyglass. It is hard to see anything through the jungle of wild magic. The location of the Pyramid is easily found by locating the tallest, thickest, and most vibrant trees. What would naturally take hundreds, even thousands, of years for these trees to grow took mere weeks.

"Okay," I say aloud for the others to hear me clearly, "let's do this!"

Starting with Aspen and moving in a circle, everyone uses the tool at his or her window. We quickly create a chaotic storm using everything we have. I focus all of my power on controlling the storm and guiding it to the heart of the wild magic.

I see the trees bend and twist in the storm. Shadows move beneath those trees. I think of the land sharks, and my heart skips a beat with fear. I clench my teeth and focus harder on my magic.

"Not this time!" I whisper to myself. I will not freeze with fear or be attacked and vulnerable like that again. "This time, you freeze!"

I close my eyes, no longer needing to see the storm below. I can feel it. I let the feeling of the storm and my magic's connection to it flow through me like a battery on charge. Once it is strong enough, I release every force of my magic through the storm at the target. This is not just any storm; it is an epic winter storm. I feel the ice spread upon the flora below. The bite of the icy wind on my skin and the sharp cut of it in my lungs urges me to keep going.

I send it into the dirt, attacking the roots, the life source of wild magic. I feel leaves and branches freeze and break from the sudden weight of the ice. I keep pushing, but that tree in the middle seems to have its own warmth. It is fighting back.

We keep this up for nearly an hour. I can feel the energy in the room draining. I use the spyglass to look at the wild magic below. As soon as we stop the storm to take a break, it begins to flourish again.

I sigh with frustration. It seems all that did was give everything below a nap. One from which it awoke even more refreshed and invigorated. Even more wild!

I step away from the window and say, "Okay, let's try a different approach. Petricha, Leslie, Dianna, and Tsar, just us this time. Let's light it up." This time we are going to burn it down. Fire worked to keep it at bay temporarily when I was saving Nicole; maybe that is what we need now.

We let loose with every fire power tool we have. I guide it all to the center of wild magic. Falling stars and lightning hit the target, igniting and splintering one of the trees with a bone rattling quake and our desired spark.

Remembering my training with Queen Melanomie, I latch on to that fire, that spark. I connect with it and urge it to grow. Something is wrong. I feel another energy, but not that of the fire. It is strong. Familiar. It is pushing against the fire, trying to extinguish it. I push back even harder. I release all of my fear, anger, and grief from the past few months and allow those emotions to fuel my fire. I keep pushing back, but as I feel myself grow weaker, the wild magic below only grows stronger.

"Althea!" Someone yells my name, but it sounds a million miles away. Still I push harder. This has to work!

"Althea!" It is Apuri. He grabs my shoulder and shakes me until my eyes open. I feel the link weakening. He turns me around to face him and says, "They are coming straight for us. You have to stop; it is not working!" I look out the window to where he is pointing, but I do not see anything. I pick up the spyglass and look through it.

There are large, dark creatures flying out of the wild magic straight for us. I reach out with my magic still connected to the storm and aim at the flying creatures. I hit one, knocking it out of the sky. It becomes a falling ball of fire. I recognize it from one of Pilate's paintings, but cannot recall the name. More of its kind begin to fly in after it. There are dozens of them. We aim and hit them all, burning them out of the sky.

Finally, they stop coming. I look through the spyglass again to see several creatures and shadows moving around within the wild jungle below. It does not look like anything else is coming after us.

I take a break and sit down on the floor. My face feels wet. I wipe the sweat off my top lip only to discover it is not sweat. It is blood. I pushed myself too far.

"Althea, are you okay?"

Aspen kneels down in front of me. She holds my wrist between her thumb and fingers feeling for my pulse. She uses her other hand to pull a cloth out of her pocket and hands it to me to wipe my nose. I hold it against my nose and pinch to stop the bleeding. I sit quietly on the floor with my hands in my lap while Aspen checks me over to make sure everything else is okay. A million thoughts race through my mind, but one is prevalent among the others: It did not work.

"It didn't work," I whisper in hopes that if I speak the thought aloud it will leave my mind. It does not.

I look up at Petricha and say, "I am sorry. I really wanted it to work."

I do not wait for a response. Once Aspen clears me to leave, I walk back up the steps in silence, not worrying if everyone follows after me or not. Instead of jumping across the flat-top clouds, I simply create more in between them to build a full bridge. I walk back to the building at the city center without saying a word.

"I am sorry the plan did not work, Althea." Nedra whispers through our link.

"Thank you, Nedra."

When I get inside the building, I collapse upon one of the sofas on the main floor.

I lay my head back, close my eyes, and try not to cry. Something presses against my hip as I lean back against the couch. I reach in my pocket. It is the crystal Petricha gave me. I hold it tight in my hand and close my eyes again as the door opens and the others file in and join me on the sofas. Apuri sits down and places my feet on his lap. Leslie and Dianna sit on the sofa beside my head. Their armor catches some light and reflects it around the room as they walk by. I can see the brightness through my closed lids.

They sit down, and Dianna leans over to say, "This is not your fault, Althea. It was a great idea!"

"Yeah," agrees Leslie, "at least nobody went in there like the first plan looking for that book."

I do not respond. I honestly do not know what to say. Apuri pats my leg and says, "It will be okay. We will figure it out; we always do."

I open my eyes and look around at my friends. I push myself up into a sitting position but leave my feet on Apuri's lap. I say, "I know, and I thank you all for sticking with me." My stomach rumbles loudly interrupting my words." Does anyone know what time it is? I am starving!" Apuri laughs and pats my foot as he stands up.

"Petricha, how do we get this place to change into that wondrous dining table again?" Apuri asks.

She laughs and asks the rest of us to move out of the way. Once we have all stepped out of the way, she waves her hand, and the sofas disappear. With her hand still in the air, she snaps her fingers, and just as quickly as the sofas disappear, the food-cloud laden table appears with chairs all around it.

As we all begin to pull out our chairs, Aspen heads for the stairs. "I am going to let Nell and Nicole know the food is ready," she says. She returns shortly with the two women and their children who look more eager than me to eat.

We all make our plates and savor every bite of the foods of our choice. Timmy watches Noni and quickly follows suit creating a plate full of donuts and chocolate cake. Nicole gives him a stern look but does not say anything.

Taking a page out of Timmy's book, I create a blueberry cake donut topped with strawberries and whipped cream to place on top of my French toast. I think if I stay in Sengsourya too long, I may have to triple my exercising.

Timmy sees my plate and grins. I return the grin with a wink.

Inside I still feel the bitter sting of failure, but I am not going to share that stress with children. I think about telling Petricha that we need to go ahead and call another meeting after we eat, but another idea hits me instead.

"Nicole," I say after swallowing a bite. "I have something to ask you. You know firsthand what is happening down there. Unfortunately, that is not changing anytime soon. Until we can figure out a solution that works, we have to do something to keep everyone safe. We just tried to destroy wild magic at its core with a magical storm. We tried freezing it and burning it, neither of which had a positive effect.

"The way I see it, we only have two options: The first is we evacuate everyone to the most remote areas and do all we can to keep the wild magic at bay, kind of like I did with the fire in the street. Or the second is we can build a sanctuary within Reverie, where wild magic is not attacking yet. With everyone safe, maybe we can focus more on the proper solution to getting rid of wild magic. My question for you is, which option would you personally choose?"

Nicole takes a moment to think about it. Before she has time to answer, Timmy says, "Can we stay here until the bad stuff is gone? I like it here!" Everyone laughs, but Timmy is serious.

Nicole says, "I think Timmy is right. You said you already tried to destroy it, and that did not work. If you go with the first choice and this wild magic changes and speeds up, then what? Best case scenario, you find out in one of your dreams and create beacons for everyone to be picked up and brought here before it is too late. If you will be bringing us here anyway, why not do that from the start?"

"Thank you. I agree with you. I just wanted to hear your opinion. Now we just have to figure out how we will execute this plan. I do not think everyone is going to go easily with strange faeries into a land they did not know existed." I get another piece of French toast on my fork and say, "But for now, let's finish enjoying this meal."

I finish my last bite and grab some more clouds to make some apple slices and grapes.

Chapter Seventeen ~ A Glimmer of Hope

We decided to bring Petricha's mirror into the lounge on the main floor at the city center. All of the children have been put to bed and the rest of us are waiting for the other Advisors to answer the call to officially start the meeting.

Petricha sent a message earlier to let them know we would be calling tonight, so it did not take them long to answer the call.

We introduce Nicole and the advisors and then quickly sum up the events of the day. When they hear that we lost against wild magic, the disappointment is clearly written on their faces. Arsona smirks when we get to the part of burning the flying creatures. She is proud of her element.

"Well," says Tilda, making sure we stay on track. "It sounds like your plan is our only choice. We will all help in any way we can. How do you want to start?"

"First, we have to find the perfect place, or places, to build the human sanctuaries within the Painted Forest. I also had another idea. We can use glamour magic to make it look like normal human buildings. This will help keep them more comfortable, but it can also work to our advantage. We can hide the Gateway Trees, or at least place something around them where humans do not accidentally travel in and out of them."

"That sounds like a solid enough plan," Feather says. "But, how do you plan on getting the humans to come here in the first place?"

I smile and wave my hand to Apuri. "Leave that to the hegira!" he says with a sly grin. "As you know, our abilities are more of the social type and affect humans easily. It is part of the reason we choose to live in Nashees and have remained nomadic."

Arsona sits up straight and says, "Wait, you are going to use your magic to influence them to come here? I know their lives are at stake, but that still does not sound like the best idea."

Tsar laughs and replies, "No, we are going to plant some ideas; that is all. We are going to spread the news that there are some safehouses with locations, to escape the wild magic. We may come up with another word for wild magic, as well. Once it is shown on all news stations and spread by the public, we will not have to do the convincing. Then, we will just have to ensure everything is ready at the locations."

Nicole raises her hand to speak; I nod for her to go on. "Is it possible to make these sanctuaries hotels? There would be less panic and more privacy for everyone if they think they are going to stay at hotels for free. Also, does the glamour work on the inside of the building as well as the outside? Who will act as staff? It might get weird fast if strange looking faeries start showing up. No offense."

"I think that is a great idea!" says Lady Nell. "What about you, Nicole? Would you want to be in charge of one of the hotels? We can still have faeries helping behind the scenes, but you will be the familiar face they see. Aspen and I can do the same. Maybe some of the faeries who look more human can help as well."

"Perhaps," adds Aspen, "as humans move in, we can offer them jobs, as well. That way the faeries will be able to step back and not have to be seen by the time the hotels are filled."

My stomach begins to knot. "I do not know, guys," I say, "if we constantly try to hide the faeries, what happens when they are spotted by accident? We do not want to frighten anyone; I get that. But I think it is best to be honest about what is happening up front. I know it will be a lot to take in, but that does not make it impossible. I mean, look at us."

I wave my hand to Nicole, Lady Nell, and myself. I intentionally leave Aspen out as I am not sure if she is not really from Reverie to begin with. "We all were introduced to the world of Reverie in not so subtle ways, and we have survived and adjusted well. I understand that not everyone is open minded, and when we add more numbers into the mix, things are going to get chaotic. But lying about it will not help anything."

"What if they start to blame us for what is happening?" Eart asks quietly. He looks worried, afraid.

"Hopefully we will have time to prepare ourselves for that, but for now I do not have an answer." I say to him gently. "We can start looking for the perfect sanctuary location first thing tomorrow. While we work on the sanctuaries, I am going to check in with Pilate to see if he has come across any more clues to help us with wild magic, the Pixies, or the Chobudda. Also, I am going to need some practice with glamour magic before we start building the structures."

"It is actually not unlike using art magic," says Eart. "You picture what you want everyone else to see, but instead of actually creating something new, you are using your vision to paint over, or cover, something existing. We can practice when you get here. I am sure you will master it in no time."

I smile and thank him for his confidence in me. With nothing else to discuss, we adjourn the meeting and head to bed.

Apuri falls asleep almost instantly; I hear his snores

gently grow louder with each breath. I toss and turn on my own side of the bed a few times, not from discomfort but restlessness, before settling in for the night.

As I lie here trying to numb my mind and ready it for sleep, I cannot shake this feeling that I am missing something. There is a familiarity, a connection, that is hiding just outside my grasp.

The more I try to search for the answer in my mind, the more I feel myself spiral into a void of confusion.

I decide to go ahead and go to sleep for the night. Before I even drift off to my dreams, I know I am going to the island, Zoar. My plan is to go ahead and start practicing with glamour magic. I feel more confident practicing magic on the island.

* * * * * * * * * *

Eart was right; Glamour magic is a lot like art magic.

I spent a little bit of time practicing with art magic before attempting my first Glamour.

Since hotels are what we are going to be creating, I decided that was what I should work on tonight.

Easing myself into the process, I decide to start by creating a dollhouse sized version of a hotel. Creating the outside was easy; making it an actual hotel with rooms on the inside, was harder. Once I created it and split it open, I was a bit disappointed in myself.

Instead of recessed blocks for rooms, all I created was two dimensional representations of rooms. I continue practicing on the pink beach, working my way up to creating an actual glamour.

Since a Glamour is created to hide or disguise something, I decide to move up to the orchard to practice. I smile when I see my avocado tree thriving among the island's deciduous residents.

It saddens me a bit, but I have decided to use the avocado tree as my subject. First, I simply copy one of the other trees in the orchard to make my tree blend in. After several tries, I finally made the avocado tree's trunk resemble its neighbors.

Knowing the importance of mastering this magic, I keep at it. After I successfully copy one of the trees beside my avocado tree, I work on using glamour magic to make it completely invisible to anyone looking at it from any direction.

I am not sure how long I have been working, or sleeping for that matter, but I finally made my tree completely invisible. It reminds me of Lara and the other Clariits using their invisibility during the battle against the sodocs.

Hmm, I wonder if the Clariits' magic is simply glamour magic?

As I step back to admire my work, I hear something.

Someone else is on the island.

My guard is up. The glamour on my avocado tree falls away, and I stealthily walk amongst the trees to see who else is here.

I have to stop repeatedly and listen for the sound again to pinpoint the direction from which it is coming.

I reach the other side of the orchard, where I discover the seaside cliffs that Louveri talked about in her dream. Maybe Louveri is here!

I wonder for a moment why I have not taken the time to explore more of the island until now.

I stiffen and quiet my breathing as much as possible to listen again.

Nothing.

Maybe she already woke up. I leave the cover of the orchard and walk out onto the grass covered cliffs. I can smell the ocean as the breeze blows over the cliffs and lifts my hair from my face and neck.

This side of the island feels like a different world. I know it is the same island because I just walked out of the orchard, but if I were to see an image of the pink beach next to these cliffs, I would never assume they were on the same island.

I look out to sea searching for any other islands, something to give me a hint to Zoar's location. There is nothing. It is like the ocean itself simply fades out of existence.

I close my eyes and listen to the waves crash against the

rocks at the base of the cliff below. I let that soothing sound wash through me.

At first, I think I may have imagined it, but after hearing the distant sound again, I know someone else is on the island with me. The wind carries their voice away. I open my eyes and, without thinking, run after the sound.

My mind races as fast as my feet. There is a reason someone else is here. I have stopped believing in coincidences. If anything wanted to hurt me here, it would have done so when I first arrived.

I yell, "Hello!"

I am hoping the wind will carry my voice to whomever else is here.

I stumble and fall as the cliffside turns into a steep hill. I quickly pull my hands together on my chest so I do not break my wrist rolling down the hill.

Thinking quickly, I reach out with my magic and grab all of the air around me, pulling it in a protective sphere. It worked. The force brings me to a sudden stop.

I slowly stand and turn to look back up the hill. I have rolled almost to the bottom, at least three quarters of the way down the hill. I place my hand on my chest, urging my racing heart to calm itself.

I turn back to the bottom of the hill to listen for the voice again. All I can hear is my breathing and my pulse drumming inside my head. I cross my wrists in front of my chest and close my mouth and eyes.

Breathing through my nose and feeling the rise and fall of my chest allows me to control my breathing.

Once I catch my breath and feel back to myself again, I carefully run the rest of the way down the hill and find myself in front of another beach. This one is made of glistening black sand. I can feel the heat radiating off of it from at least four feet away. I am careful not to step on it.

The bottom of the hill flattens into a forest of glorious mushrooms. It very much resembles the one at the hegira camp inside the Painted Forest, but these mushrooms have had extra magic exposure or extra time to grow. The smallest is a cluster of thin-stemmed, cream-colored fungi standing as tall as my shoulders.

What a sight, and just when I thought I could not be surprised by magic anymore.

"Hello?" I yell once more, this time into the mushroom forest.

There is an answer! I cannot make out the voice or the words, but whoever is here, definitely went into this forest.

I climb up onto the cream-colored mushrooms and use them to reach an even taller specimen growing nearby. I am hoping with a bird's-eye-view I will be able to spot the other end of the mushroom forest and finally locate the stranger.

Unfortunately, that is not the case. The only thing I can see from the top of the mushrooms is more mushrooms. Some of them stand several feet above my head, almost as tall as trees.

It looks like there is only one way I am getting through this forest. I slide down the curved mushroom tops and drop to my feet with an audible, "Oof."

"Hello!" I shout again, "Can you hear me? I am over here!"

I continue shouting frequently as I walk deeper and deeper into the darkness of the mushroom forest. The beautiful curved tops are only separated in random spots here and there making the way dark with dappled light at unexpected moments. The further I walk, the more difficult it is to see. The dappled lighting gets less frequent until finally, there is no light at all.

I stumble blindly with my hands outstretched feeling the trunks around me to find my way. Focused on walking, I have stopped calling aloud.

I wipe my sweating forehead in the dark with the back of my hand. I start to walk again and hear a sound to my left. I turn, and in the distance, I see a small bright light. It is a brilliant sign of hope!

I begin to run toward it as best I can in the dark mushroom forest. It gets closer and closer until BAM!

I have run smack dab into someone and knocked us both

down.

Rubbing my elbows and my bottom, I sit up and apologize.

"Althea?" the voice inquires with a quiver.

"Pilate? Pilate, is that you?" I crawl forward and feel for him. His light went out when I ran into him causing us to be completely submerged in darkness.

"Yes, it is me," he says, as his light comes back on.

Sure enough, below the glow of his antenna his mouse-like face shines with a smile. Overwhelmed with excitement, I hug him close.

"It is so good to see you!" I say. "But how are you here? What is going on?"

"I... I don't know," he says." I went to sleep, and here I was. At first, I thought it was just a normal dream, but then something felt off. This place has a familiarity to it. It was the same feeling I got when I dreamt of those creatures. Once I put two and two together, I figured this must be the island, Zoar. The description you gave of the pink beach was quite different, though, so I was not sure. I have been running around calling for you in hopes I was not here alone. Althea, I am so happy you are here!"

"Me too," I say. I grab his hands and help him stand. "Come on, let's find our way out of here."

"Why not use your magic?" he asks.

"I was so caught up in finding out who I was hearing, I did not even think of that." I extend my hands out in front of me, and with the flick of my wrists, create a floating orb of light, a tiny star, to light our way. I close my eyes for a moment and let myself connect with the ground below me.

"Come on," I say, "the beach is this way."

We follow the light out of the forest of mushrooms and into a real forest with giant, towering trees. Another new sight for me on the island.

As we walk, I tell Pilate about Nicole, our failed attack on wild magic, and our plan to save the humans. He tells me the flying creatures we fought back are called worcs. They are certainly one of the creatures he has painted from his dreams.

The other side of this forest ends in another hill. This hill is not smooth and grassy like the one on the other side of the island. This is a mountain.

We climb the rocky terrain in silence to save our breath and energy. We stop at a beautiful clear stream to get a drink before continuing. When we finally make it to the top of the mountain, I am relieved to see the orchard.

"This is such a strange island," I say aloud. "Why would it have so many different areas together like this?"

We stop when we arrive at my avocado tree.

"I assume it is because the elves created it this way," Pilate replies at last with a smile.

I laugh at his attempt at sarcasm and say, "Touché. But why would they create it this way?"

"I am not sure. What have you learned about it since coming here?"

"Not a lot really. I have mostly been using the island to practice my own magic within dreams. I made this tree." I point to the avocado in front of us.

"Very nice." He smiles proudly as if the creation was his own. I smile, too.

"I do know," I say, "the magic here is like nothing back in Reverie. It is strong, raw magic. The elves must have really been special."

"They really were," Pilate says with a dreamy smile.

* * * * * * * * * *

Chapter Eighteen ~ The Search for the Perfect Location

It takes me a minute to realize what happened. I woke up! I did not get to tell Pilate goodbye, and we did not figure out why he was there!

I grunt in frustration and slam my fists down on the bed beside me. The clouds absorb my hit with no effect. My grunt, however, wakes Apuri with a start.

Thinking something is wrong, he quickly sits up and pulls his knife from beneath his pillow ready to attack.

I cannot help but laugh. I know it is not a laughing matter, him being prepared for danger and ready to protect me, but seeing him jump with his knife that fast just because I was so upset that I made a sound, sends me into a fit of giggles.

Once he realizes there is no danger, he sheaths his knife and rubs his face to fully wake up. "What are you doing?" he asks with a still sleep-filled, scratchy voice.

"I was dreaming," I say calmly, "with Pilate. Then suddenly, I woke up. Apuri, he was on the island with me. We did not get to figure out why, though."

"Weird," is all he says. He stretches and turns to get out

of bed. I look out of our window to see the sun is already up. That is probably what woke me. I scrunch my nose and poke out my tongue at the sun for waking me too early.

Apuri laughs. I sit up and follow him out of the bed. We get ready for our day ahead and leave our private room in Sengsourya's city center.

"Nedra, do you have any ideas on the dream and why Pilate was there?" I ask through our link.

He yawns through the link and answers, "Not yet. Give me some time to think about it."

I tell Apuri Nedra's answer as we meet Petricha, Leslie, and Dianna at the table on the main floor. Nobody else is here yet.

The sky faeries look as if they have been waiting on us to arrive.

"Morning." I say with a not-so-cheery voice as we approach the table and pull out some chairs. I quickly begin grabbing at the colorful clouds to make some breakfast. My sleep was cut short; I will make sure I eat before my meal is, too.

"Dreamer," they all say as one and nod in greeting.

"Early risers?" I ask with a smile.

Leslie and Dianna laugh. Petricha smiles and answers, "We have been waiting on you, Dreamer. The three of us would like to accompany you on your mission to help the humans, if that is okay with you."

"Oh," I say. I was not expecting that. The advisors have never asked my permission for anything before. Maybe I made an impression on Petricha yesterday morning. I figured Leslie and Dianna always had to stay here to protect Sengsourya.

"We have other guards who will watch over Sengsourya in our absence," Leslie answers my unspoken question. Petricha says nothing.

"Okay, then, sure. The more the merrier," I say with a smile as I finish constructing my breakfast. I glance at Apuri who shrugs in response.

The others string in to join us at the table. First, Notyal shows up, followed shortly by Aspen. Lady Nell, Noni, and Tsar sleepily stride in a few minutes later. Finally, Nicole and her children are the last to the table.

Other than morning greetings, we eat our breakfast in silence. We all know there is a lot of work in store ahead. Now is the time to savor the peace of the moment.

After eating, Petricha turns the table into a collection of sofas and tables. We all sit on the comfy cloud sofas to discuss the game plan for the day.

Once we are all situated, I go ahead and update them on what I learned last night. "I saw Pilate on Zoar in my dream last night, but I was not able to ask him if he has found anything new about the Pixies, Chobudda, or the Elves."

"How and why was Pilate on the island?" asks Not.

I shrug and reply, "I heard him while I was practicing glamour magic, which I think I have almost got the hang of. After I found Pilate, we were able to walk and discover the entire island. It is even bigger than I ever could have imagined. In addition to the pink beach, grassy pasture, and the orchard we already knew about, I discovered the island has rocky cliffs which is where I am assuming the cave Louveri saw is located. The cliffs connect to a steep grassy hill which leads to a black sandy beach. A forest of the most gigantuous mushrooms ever butts up against the grassy hill and black beach. That is where I found Pilate. On the other side of that is a forest with trees even bigger than the mushrooms. Through that forest is a steep, rocky mountain side which leads back to the orchard."

"Wow!" says Lady Nell.

"It sounds like maybe Pilate should have come to the island and shown you around sooner," Aspen says with a laugh.

"Maybe that is it, Aspen. Pilate was my guide in the beginning, the one who showed me the way into Reverie. Maybe he was just there last night to be my guide again. I am not sure how long it would have taken me to get all the way around the island if I had not heard him there."

Aspen makes a surprised face then smiles proudly and says to Lady Nell, "Maybe you have started rubbing off on me."

Lady Nell shakes her head and mutters a sarcastic, "Sure."

"So," I get the conversation back to the business at hand, "I figure we can go back to the Painted Forest and fly just above the canopy to easily see the biggest clearings. If we stay just inside the glamour border we should be able to keep the locations easy to access from the human realm. Once we find our spots, Eart and Clementine will send faeries to help us build our *hotels.* We will drop a marker to let everyone know the spots we choose. I think I have something in mind for that. As soon as we finish with the hotels, the hegira will make sure the news spreads like wildfire throughout the human realm. After that, we just have to ensure we are ready for them."

Tsar asks, "Since Reverie flows throughout the world in its own way, how will we know where all of the locations are?"

"I am not really sure," I say.

"Oh!" Petricha says, excited to add something to our plan. "The dragons can help us there. Arsona is actually quite the cartographer. The dragons can all fly over once we give word that we have found the right locations. The dragons can then relay those visions to her to compile into a map. Her maps are really quite extraordinary!"

"That's brilliant!" I say. "I think I actually have one of her maps. Pilate gave it to me before I left to find the Pyramid. It shows the owner any location they wish to find within Reverie. That was our intended tool to get to the Adler brothers and the mer pool. Unfortunately, things went a little sideways, and we were not able to use it much. Also, Nedra knows the Painted Forest pretty well. I trust him to get us safely to our designated locations there."

"Well," Petricha says, "I guess that is all, then. Shall we?"

"Actually," Apuri interrupts before she can stand, "I was going to ask if there was any way we could pack some cloud food for the ride?"

Petricha laughs and looks around. Everyone is in agreement with Apuri. "I will do you one better," says Petricha. "Follow me. We will go straight to the fields and harvest our own. The sky faeries here will need what is already available. We can leave straight from the fields and travel by light to the Feather Tree."

Excited about our little detour, we all get up and grab our things. Nedra and Nanoaj meet us outside the doors.

"You might want to fly," Petricha informs us. "The fields are a good way past the first tower, the one you are familiar with."

Apuri, Not, Aspen, and I climb up onto Nedra's back. Tsar, Nell, Noni, Timmy, and Nicole – still holding Joshua – climb onto Nanoaj's back. Leslie and Dianna unfold their long sleek starlit wings and take off toward the field. Petricha simply lifts herself into the air and follows after them. The dragons push off the clouds at the same time and follow after the sky faeries without wasting any time.

Petricha was right; we fly well past the first tower – we actually lose sight of it – before we see the fields lining the horizon. I am glad we flew, not just to save time, but also because the view as we begin descent toward the field is breathtaking.

A massive quartz, as big as Nedra, stands in the four corners of each field. There are at least two dozen fields. A rainbow blankets each field from edge to edge, connected at the corners by the tips of the quartz crystals. The fields here aren't very different from the ones I grew up around back home, other than the fact they are made of clouds, that is.

Instead of each field being one crop, or color in this instance, each plowed cloud row in the field mirrors the color above it in the rainbow. Each field starts with a red row on the left and works through the whole rainbow ending with purple. Each field is a different size from the one next to it.

The field we land by is about four hundred yards wide

by eight hundred yards long. There is a path at the head of the field and between each row allowing us to walk where needed without damaging the fluffy produce. We each gather as much as we want of each food type and place it in our personal packs.

"We usually harvest on rainy days," Petricha says. The moisture allows more weight to go into each cloud produced. That will allow them to double in size once we take them back to the dryers, yielding twice the produce. Once the field is fully harvested, the rainbows will be released from the quartz. That is why you're able to see rainbows from the ground after it rains."

"That is amazing!" I say. "Though, I will be honest; I will not be able to look at a rainbow without getting hungry ever again."

We all enjoy a laugh and go back to the dragons waiting at the edge of the field.

I hear Lady Nell calling back to Nicole, "Nicole, remember what we told you about traveling by light? Make sure Timmy is ready." Noni reaches back and holds Timmy's hand tightly. I smile at the sight then give Nedra the go-ahead.

We all fly off toward the nearest light beam, our route back through the Feather Tree and into the Painted Forest. One by one we go through to the other side. In the Painted Forest, we land between the Feather Tree and a tall, smooth, white sycamore.

"Nell, you fly North with Leslie, Dianna, and Petricha. We will fly South and pick up Pilate and Nook on the way."

"What about your idea for marking the spots?" Lady Nell asks.

"Oh yeah! Petricha, I assume you can make small stars, or orbs of light?" She nods that she can. "When you find a suitable location, drop a couple orbs. Just make sure they will shine bright for a while. Once we're finished, Nedra and Nanoaj can contact the other dragons. Then they can fly over and give Arsona the locations to map out."

"Sounds like a good idea to me," Petricha says. "What do

you say we all meet back in Inon when this is finished? I would like to see the other advisors in person at the Advisor Tree."

"Okay. We will see you there."

With that, we take off in our separate directions.

We do not see any viable hotel spots before we get to the Marketplace Tree. We go inside and head straight to Pilate's and let him know what is happening. Eager to help and have more time to talk about last night, he quickly closes his shop and calls Nook to meet us in the Painted Forest.

I ride with Pilate on Nook so we have time to talk. This will also give Nedra a break from carrying everyone. I have wondered to myself why Aspen does not simply morph into her beautiful painted hawk form to fly around on her own.

"I thought she told you," Nedra answers my thoughts through our link.

"Told me what, Nedra?" I ask silently.

"Althea, Aspen was hurt pretty badly during the battle at the Pyramid. She tried to fly into the Pyramid in her animal form to help Not, Tsar, and you. We are not sure of the details, but she came out with both wings broken and bloody. She was barely able to turn back into her human form before the Pyramid began to crumble. Once we all made it back to that camp where you woke up, she immediately went down to the stream alone and stayed there for a while. When she finally came back, she acted as if nothing had happened and immediately began to heal others. You were her first patient, followed by Tsar. She healed others as well, but she never gave up on the two of you. She still has not spoken of her injuries, but I am afraid that whatever happened to her wings inside the Pyramid could have been permanent damage."

My heart breaks at the news. How could I not have noticed? Does Lady Nell know? I wish she would have talked to me about this. I will have to address this later with Aspen herself. Right now, I need to take advantage of my time with Pilate while simultaneously looking for sanctuaries for the humans.

"Pilate," I lean forward to talk where he can hear me while we fly, "have you been able to find any more information on why the Pixies and Chobudda disappeared or where they may be?" I want to ask him about the elves, about the island, and why he was in my dreams last night, but I figure it is better to keep it simple and cover one question at a time.

"I have been looking nonstop," he says, "but I am afraid I am no closer to any answers than the day you left my shop."

"That is okay. What about the elv- Oh my gosh! I have it! Pilate, I have a brilliant idea!"

"That is wonderful! How would you like to tell everyone about it down there?" he points to an expansive clearing below.

"Oh, that looks nice, and it is not far from the Glamour border at all. Great watching, Pilate!"

We all land in the clearing and have a look around.

"I think we could fit at least two, possibly three, hotels here. Unless we find bigger areas, this may be our sanctuary headquarters." I head to the middle of the clearing and create a handful of small stars to place upon the soft, thick grass. I place the stars and walk back to my friends.

"Now, what is the big idea?" Pilate asks excitedly.

"Oh! Yes, well it just hit me all of a sudden. We have been looking for the pixies and Chobudda, not only to find answers about wild magic, but also because they have all simply disappeared. Well, I was thinking about the elves and that made me think of the mirrors." Apuri makes a face to show he's not sure about where this conversation is going. "I know, Apuri, but hear me out. You were able to successfully find the hegira you were looking for. Why can we not do the same thing to find the pixies and Chobudda?"

"Okay, you have a point," Apuri answers. "But who goes through the mirror? I am not ready to do that again, and I do not want you to either." His tone of voice tells me not to argue.

"We will figure it out," I say. "For now, we should focus on the task at hand. We can share the idea with everyone else back in Inon. Maybe someone else will have some good ideas to help, too."

We all mount back up on the dragons and continue our search for sanctuaries. We eat our lunch of cloud food on the go to save time in our current task. Pilate has a blast with the cloud food. He creates a sweet grained cone with orange clouds and uses a couple paws full of purple clouds to fill it with a variety of berries, including the tiny blue strawberry shaped yimi berries I have come to love.

I cannot help but laugh at his excitement. I tell him, "When this is all over, Pilate, you will have to close your shop for a little while."

"Why is that?" He asks, perplexed at the idea.

"Because, my friend, you are going on a vacation!"

We laugh together as we continue flying over the canopy of the Painted Forest.

Part II

Chapter Nineteen ~ Sanctuaries

We meet back at Inon with eight successful sanctuaries, including the potential headquarter location, on the south end of the Painted Forest. Nanoaj is already resting in the clearing outside the city where Nedra and I landed on my first trip here.

She informs Nedra that they have been back for a while. The others are already waiting for us at the Advisor Tree. We thank her and head straight there to see how many sanctuaries they found and tell them of our newest idea.

When we get to the Advisor Tree, I cautiously step through first. Just as I expected, the tests are down again today due to a high number of guests. It is strange how a tree knows who is coming or not.

We step into the room, ready to share our news, when all of a sudden, my heart skips a beat. I grab my chest; it feels like someone just knocked the wind out of me. My mind is foggy. I find it hard to focus on anything. My ears are ringing. I close my eyes to try to regain focus.

Then, just as suddenly, my ears stop ringing. One single thought pops into my mind and will not go away until I speak it aloud. "I wish we had all of the advisors, and they would tell us what is going on."

Apuri guides me to a chair and eases me into it. Everyone else gathers around to see if I am okay.

I say it again, and this time I can feel the magic in the wish. "I wish we had all of the advisors, and they would tell us what is going on."

I look around the room, scared. I do not know what is happening. All of the faces staring back at me reflect my own confusion.

I rub my forehead to clear the residual fog. When I lower my hand, Tilda gasps and whispers, "The clothing peddler!"

"The what?" Apuri asks. "What is wrong with her? What happened?"

"When Althea first came here," Tilda explains, "she paid for her clothes with a wish. Normally, a wish given is stronger than if you were to use it yourself. Since Althea is the Dreamer, there must have been even more power, and it looks like attachment as well, with the wish she gave. From the sounds of it, the peddler she gave the wish to has wished for us to fill our vacant advisor seat and update everyone on what is happening." Her brow creases as she heaves a sigh and says, "To be fair, it is something we should have done already."

The wish has finally drifted to the back of my mind allowing me to stop repeating it aloud. I drink some tea offered by Clementine. It is sweet rose tea. I grasp the smooth wooden cup with both hands and sip it slowly, letting the energy flow through me as my strength renews.

When I paid for my clothes that day using a wish, I doubted it was real, let alone something that would work. Now, I know not to pay with my wishes anymore.

"So, what do we do about it?" I ask after I hand Clementine the now empty cup and thank her for the much-needed pick-me-up.

"The only thing we can do is grant the wish," Feather says with a concerned look on her face.

"Then, let's do it," says Apuri. "What are we waiting for?"

The advisors look at each other. I look around and realize

Ophidius is not in the room. Missing the calls is one thing, but not showing up for a physical meeting at the Advisor Tree is serious.

"Ophidius is missing," Tilda says, answering my questioning gaze. "Nobody has seen or heard from him in a couple of days. We have to have all advisors present to induct a new advisor. We have questioned some of the faeries closest to him. Apparently, after your story about the land shark, Althea, he decided to investigate the creatures within wild magic himself. We have sent a few scouts to search for him, but with strict orders to preserve their own lives and return to us with any information. We are still waiting for them to return."

"We may have to induct not only one but two new Advisors," says Eart bluntly.

Everyone is silent for a moment before Petricha cheerily says, "We found several nice spots to build the sanctuaries!" I cannot help but laugh at her childlike enthusiasm with the change of subject.

"Great!" I say, almost guilty at continuing her conversation just to avoid talking about Ophidius. "We found about eight. The one closest to us could be the headquarters; it is big enough to hold at least three full sized hotels. How many did you find?"

"Twelve," says Aspen. I realize after Aspen's answer that Ophidius is not the only one absent. Lady Nell, Nicole, and the children are not here. That makes sense. The children stayed with Indri and Louveri before; I bet that is where they are now, too. Lady Nell must have stayed for Nicole.

"Do you think it will be enough?" Not asks, bringing my attention back to the conversation.

"I honestly do not know," I say. "We have to try something, though. Eart, I wondered if we could use glamour magic to not only make the sanctuaries look like human hotels, but also increase the size inside? If so, we would be able to save many more humans."

Eart makes a contemplative face and replies, "I do not

see why not. It is similar to the way a dragon's glamour and even the Gateway Trees work. If we can fit entire worlds within the boundaries of what looks like a normal tree trunk, we should be able to increase the room size inside of these hotels. How will we make them permanent enough to last until we figure out something for wild magic, though? Art magic fades over time."

I smile and answer, "That is where the nature faeries come in. Once the art faeries have constructed the basic design, the nature faeries can come along and add the required materials, stone, wood, or whatever else we may need, to make them last. After that, all we have to do is add the glamour."

Petricha pipes up again, "We can use clouds to help with the basic construction, if needed."

Feather adds, "And the rest of us can help with the glamour magic to allow the others more time to work on the structures."

I smile and say, "That is wonderful; we are going to need all the help we can get. If there is nothing else on this matter," I look around the room to ensure that there's not, then continue, "I may have a partial solution, or at least a start, to finding answers on what to do about wild magic. Apuri was able to find the hegira by using a pair of mirrors made by the elves. We may be able to do the same thing to find the pixies and chobudda. The only downside, other than the creepy vibes, is there will be a price to pay, maybe even two prices if the pixies and Chobudda are not together."

Everyone mumbles to one another about the idea until Tilda says loud enough for everyone to hear, "It is the best idea I have heard so far. What is the price, and who is traveling?"

"I have not figured that out, yet," I admit reluctantly.

I really hate having half-made plans. Maybe one of these days I will come up with one grand plan to fix everything without any questions.

"None of the advisors can do it," says Arsona, somewhat disappointed. I guess she was looking forward to the adventure. "We all have to be present to induct a new advisor, or two, as soon as the scouts return. If not, the Dreamer's wish is only going to get stronger as time goes by."

"Any volunteers?" Tilda asks. She has stepped into the role of the lead Advisor pretty well. She is always ready to get straight to business, but she is also patient and fair. The room is silent for a moment until someone steps into the middle of the room.

It is Leslie. "We will go," she says as Dianna steps up beside her. "You are all needed here, and if anything goes wrong, we know how to protect ourselves well."

Petricha looks both proud and sad at the same time. She does not say anything to her guards. She simply nods to give them her approval, even though they did not ask for it.

"How will we know what you find and if you are okay?" asks Clementine.

"Nedra," I ask through our link, "can you link up with Apuri and Not so they can hear my thoughts?"

"We can all hear you now, Althea," Nedra replies.

"What if we give them your amulets?" I ask Apuri and Not through the link. I do not have to expand on the question; they know where I am going with this.

"Yes, of course," they answer immediately.

"I have a solution for that problem!" I say aloud to everyone in the room. Apuri and Not remove their amulets and pass them to me. I extend them one at a time to the sky faerie guards.

"As long as you are wearing these, you will be connected to Nedra and me. Nedra will be able to see and hear everything that happens. He can open the link between us at any time so I can see as well."

They each accept the offered amulet graciously and handle it like the most valuable treasure they have ever touched.

"You can leave when this meeting is adjourned," Tilda tells them. They nod their agreement but say nothing. "Does anyone else have any more business to discuss while we are here?"

Aspen steps forward quietly, "I would like to make a request of the Dreamer."

Everyone looks at me. Not sure what else to do, I say, "Okay, what is it?"

"I would like to travel to see the witch. I can find her Gateway Tree on my own with directions. I know what you are doing here is extremely important, and I understand if you would rather I stay to help."

"Of course!" I say without hesitation. This is the first time she has let any sign of her injury be known, and she still has not said anything about it even now. I know that is her reason for wanting to go, though. "Do you have any way of staying in touch with us though? If anything serious happens, I would like to have you near."

She wrings her hands and says, "I am not sure. You do not have any more of those amulets lying around, do you?" She smiles.

"I do not," I say, "but I know someone who does." I return the smile with a raised eyebrow, hoping she will put two and two together.

I have noticed a distance between Aspen and Lady Nell ever since I woke up in that camp after the battle at the Pyramid. I know now that Aspen was in the Pyramid right before it fell. I would bet my magic that she blames herself for what happened to Tsar just as much as I do. Because of that, she has distanced herself from her best friend, Lady Nell. I am hoping that this will give her reason to trust her friend and open up a little more to begin the healing process for herself and their relationship.

She casts her eyes down in embarrassment. "Thank you, Dreamer. I will ask her before leaving."

After that, nobody else says anything. After several awkward minutes of silence Tilda announces that the meeting is adjourned.

Leslie and Dianna prepare to go to the Marketplace to ask for a price.

Aspen thanks me for granting her request and heads to talk to Lady Nell before heading out to find the witch.

The rest of us prepare ourselves for hotel building.

We go back to Louveri and Feather's house to wait for the dragons to finish sending Arsona the final locations, so she can compose a map for all of us to use.

Louveri made buttered squash bites for the kids to eat while we were at the meeting. As soon as we walk through the door, images of my childhood flash through my mind of Louveri and I running after each other down the hall or watching the newest released cartoon snuggled together on the couch sharing one blanket. I close my eyes to savor the memories and the smell. The smell of home.

Louveri comes to the door to greet everyone. She wraps me in a warm bear hug. I wish I could bottle her hugs and carry them with me everywhere. One of her hugs can melt away all my worries in an instant.

Still holding me tight she whispers in my ear, "You did good, kid."

"Ha!" I laugh sarcastically, "If you count getting myself killed and releasing a tyrant form of magic upon the world good, then sure."

She steps back and holds me at arm's length. "Do not do that!" She says sternly. "Do not discredit all the good you did, all of your success, just because the universe throws you a curveball."

I try to shrug her off and go into the other room with everyone else, but she does not let me. "Hey," she says sternly. "Remember, everything happens for a reason. Have you thought about that?"

"What do you mean?" I ask, curious.

"Come on, Althea." She taps a finger on my head and says, "You are one of the smartest people I know."

When I do not say anything in return, she simply smiles

and releases my arm. "You will get it, Sis," she says as she hooks her arm through mine and leads me into the other room. "For now, let's enjoy the company."

We march into the room arm in arm with smiles on our faces. Despite the travesty in the world outside, I am happy. I have my sister on my arm and a room full of friends. We have a plan, and we are working together. I am choosing to focus on the little things, my blessings.

The squash Louveri laid out on a platter is devoured in no time. When the platter is empty, we decide to fill it with a few portions of cloud food from our bags. Arsona pulls out some of her special paper to make the map. She keeps it on a side table so she is able to add in each location as the dragons send it to her. Instead of a pen or even a brush to draw with, she uses her finger, tracing it along the paper to create the thin burning lines.

We decided to start at the headquarter's location together so we all know what to do. After we complete the first sanctuaries together, we will split up and tackle the rest individually to make the most of our time.

Once we finish discussing business, Arsona says she has half the map completed. While she waits for the remaining locations from the dragons, we lighten the mood with casual talk and snacks.

Louveri and I share a few stories from our childhood about playing in mud holes and exploring through the woods with long sticks in hand as we pretended to be Amazonian warriors.

When Arsona announces the completion of the map, I take it and create normal copies of it for everyone in the room. We would be here all night if Arsona had to make all of the copies herself. And I have no clue how long it would take me to learn the craft of pyro-cartography.

We hurry out to start on the first structures immediately.

On our way, I ask Nedra if he will check in on Leslie and

Dianna to see if they have struck a deal with Sage yet and what the price is.

"It seems he wants some of their armor," Nedra replies. "But he will not accept theirs; he wants them to make him his own. That is the only payment he will accept."

"Great!" I reply in a huff through our link. "That does not sound like something quickly done."

"I do not think it is. You can ask Petricha to be sure, but it sounds like Leslie and Dianna must return to Sengsourya regardless of the time it takes."

I catch up to Petricha as quickly as I can and whisper what I have learned. The expression on her face tells me I am not going to like the answer.

"That armor is forged from the stars themselves, Althea. It is no easy task, and it is definitely not something done quickly. My guards are wearing armor passed down from their predecessors. I am afraid Leslie and Dianna's mission just got extended whether we like it or not."

I nod in reply. There is nothing else to say. It is not like we can argue. That part of the mission will have to be left up to the guards of Sengsourya. Now, we have our own mission to execute.

Eight art faeries and eight nature faeries meet us at the first location for the sanctuaries. Eart and Clementine make quick introductions and explain what we're going to do. I burn lines on the ground to frame each hotel and create a small-scale model for everyone to use as a guide.

The Art Faeries – Libby, Dawn, Chelle, Bee, Jay, Papaya, Dustyn, and Hollye – really are talented artists. Eart, Dustyn, and Hollye simply use their hands, measuring and pinching the air. Once they have a desired length, they snap their fingers with a flick of their wrists and push their palms out into the air sending creations forward building the frames. As soon as they finish with the first building, they move on to the next one.

Jay, Papaya, and Bee come behind the first group of artists to use clay and build walls from the ground up. They are able to use their magic to spread the clay up the hotel's bones. They use their magic, waving their hands in the air to spread the clay in smooth strokes back and forth like spreading icing over a cake. When they finish, they lower their hands and gently exhale. As the air passes between their lips, the clay begins to dry. When they finish, they move on to the second building, picking up behind the first group to cover the bones. I walk up to the clay and gently stroke it. It's dry. Solid.

Libby, Dawn, and Chelle use paintbrushes as their tool of choice, painting strokes directly in the air like Eart did at the meetings. Their work is mesmerizing, soothing to watch. I find myself falling under a trance with each stroke. In a matter of minutes, the four-story building in front of me looks exactly like my miniature hotel.

I cannot help but grin with pride not only for myself, but for the faeries' work in front of me. They have beautifully executed the perfect hotel, something that would take humans several months minimum, within a matter of minutes. But there is still work to be done. The art faeries continue their work until the base of all three structures in this location are complete.

Clementine steps forward with her Nature Faeries; they are ready to work. The Nature Faeries work differently than the Art Faeries. Instead of breaking off into groups, all of them approach the first building at once. One faerie stands at each corner, one at each wall, and Clementine flies up to the peak of the roof. Simultaneously, they touch the building with one hand. All of their eyes light up with magic. They reach down toward the Earth below them with the other hand, fingers outstretched, and begin to move it in a circular motion.

If they were building the hotels from scratch it would take them more time than it did the art faeries to put it all together. This way, all they have to do is take the materials already in place and use their magic to make them permanent.

Clementine told me earlier that nature faeries are able to change the material of any object to something from the earth.

She thought my example of turning a person to wood or stone was extremely crude but agreed that was the basic idea. Since the creations of the art faeries are actually the materials they will be using, it makes their job easier. All they have to do is transfer their nature magic into the materials to replace the art magic.

The entire building begins to sparkle and glow a faint green where each faerie's hand touches it. They continue swirling their hands toward their power source. The magic grows; it spreads until each pool of green magic meets up with the next and the whole building is aglow.

I stand about eight feet from the hotel, and the magic radiating off of it is electric. I can feel it surge through my entire body from the hairs on my head to the tips of my toes.

When the nature faeries finish, I walk forward and cautiously open the door to the first human sanctuary hotel. It works. I walk inside and see that, just like on the outside, the inside matches my model inch for inch. I cannot believe it.

I walk in circles trying to take everything in: the large, open lobby, complete with a lounge and diner big enough for all; the elegant wooden staircases leading to the upper floors; and each room's oval-shaped oak doors, their frames painted with the best colors of spring and numbered with intricate vine-like digits.

Even though the structure is based on human hotels, there is no denying the whimsy and magic inside this hotel. I personally do not know how anyone could be unhappy in a place like this.

I step outside the door to a crowd of waiting faces. They are wondering if it is good enough.

I nod with a face-splitting grin and say, "It is wonderful!"

Everyone cheers. We do not bask in the celebration, however, because there is more to be done. The next two hotels are completed just as the first one. Again, the faeries all make quick work with their magic. I check each one after it is finished and emerge with the same pleasing results.

After the headquarters were finished, we split up to save our time. Eart and Clementine assure us that their faeries are already waiting at the locations with beacons as per their earlier instructions.

The rest of us simply decide which direction we want to go and start breaking off at locations along the way until they are all set with at least four of each faerie.

Nedra flies Not, Apuri, and me to the last location in the south side of the glamour beside a nature faerie named Buckeye and the art faerie named Libby.

When we arrive, we discover only one art faerie and two nature faeries waiting for us. Since it does not look like anyone is going to show up, I volunteer to fill the third art faerie spot and the fourth nature faerie spot.

Libby has a very enthusiastic personality and is more than happy to teach me how to use my art magic to create the frame of the building as she executes it. I will also be doing the last step, painting the final details with the magic paintbrush Eart gave me before I left to fight the sodocs, but I am always eager to learn more about my magic. If Libby is willing to teach me, I am not going to pass that up.

She has such a passion as an artist. The way she plans the frame tells me she is smart, and the way she quickly executes the structure without pause shows her confidence. "It is not unlike painting with the brush," she says. "You still picture what you want to create, only you have to be more precise because it is all created in one shot. You do not go back and add details with a brush. That is why I plan everything in detail before I even start. Once you have the image complete in your mind, you pinch, like this, to mark the starting point. You are defining your canvas here. Now, when you pull away from that point, that is when your visualization comes to life. It does not matter how far you really pull. Your intent is what matters, like with all magic."

She pulls her arm through the air making the beams appear with perfect precision. As she continues creating the frame, she continues teaching as well. "There is no way my arms could really make the beams as long as they need to be. It is physically impossible. With magic, however, I can figure that length in beforehand and that is what comes out. That also means there is no room for error. Distractions could destroy your entire creation causing you to erase it completely and start over. That wastes precious time, especially with a project as important as the one we are doing now. By the way, I am honored to be a part of this. Thank you."

She steps back from her finished product and gives me a hug. I return the hug and tell her, "You are welcome, and thank you for helping. I honestly was not sure what the faeries would think about us bringing humans into Reverie, but we cannot sit by and do nothing."

"That is true," she says and the conversation ends there.

The next art faerie steps up to add the clay. "Oh! watch this," Libby says. "Clay is always one of those mediums that look easy peasy when you watch someone else do it, but it really makes you get to know yourself when you attempt it."

I smile at her artistic passion, especially when it is not even her work. Standing here, watching the second art faerie smooth the clay walls up over the bones of the hotel, I feel like I have known Libby all my life. She has a comforting familiarity about her.

Once the clay walls are dry, it is my time to step forward. With my paintbrush in hand, I raise my brush, relax my elbow, and feel the magic bubbling just beneath the surface. Taking inspiration from Libby, I picture what I want to paint before allowing it to flow from the brush. Once I am certain on the details, I allow the magic to start. With each stroke, I am pulled further and further into my own mind, my own world. I release my worries and stresses of the outside world. Nothing remains but my brush and me. We dance around and around until, what feels like too soon, I am finished.

I step back and realize I am grinning from ear to ear like a fool. Libby comes up to give me another hug and says, "That was wonderful, beautiful, magical artistry! Very well done!" I smile and thank her for her compliment.

My job is not finished yet, though. I step up to the front of the hotel. Since we only have four nature faeries instead of eight, we each take a wall. The magic will work the same way it did at the headquarters; it will just take a little more time to finish.

Using nature magic is less entrancing and more meditative for me. Instead of a flow, a dance, with magic, there is a stillness, a calm. The magic emits a different vibration of energy, one that feels like it is breathing all on its own. I know from feeling the source that it is the Creator lending trickles of energy to each of us. We are not doing this alone.

Chapter Twenty ~ The Advisor Test

As we sit inside the Advisor Tree waiting on Tilda to return from her meeting with the scouts, I cannot seem to keep myself from yawning. I have already hit a record of thirty yawns in half as many minutes.

We worked on the hotels all night, and just as we were getting ready to retire for the night, Tilda got news that the scouts sent to look for Ophidius had returned with news. She immediately called a meeting and said she would meet us here.

Just as I catch myself dozing off again, someone enters the tree. I look up to see Tilda stop just inside the door, keeping her distance. She does not look like herself. Her eyes hold a look of hopelessness, something I have never seen from her. Instead of her usual flowing skin, the water is still, motionless. Nobody speaks. We are all thinking the same question, and she knows what it is.

She swallows and opens her mouth to speak, but nothing comes out. She shuts it, clears her throat and tries again. "Ophidius is dead." It comes out as barely barely more than a whisper, but it feels like it was shouted and continues to echo around the room.

A million thoughts flood through my mind, but I am

unable to speak any of them.

Everyone is quiet. Eart casts his eyes to the ground. I know he is thinking of his earlier comment about inducting two new advisors. It looks like he was right.

Finally, Clementine breaks the silence. "What do we do now?"

"We have to start an induction as soon as possible," Tilda says without emotion. "That is why I have called you all here. We should have all of the advisor positions filled before the humans are invited in. Everyone inside the realms of Reverie needs to be prepared for this."

Feather stands up and walks over to stand by Tilda. She turns to look at the rest of us and holds Tilda's hand. "Let's begin. We do not know how long this will take, and we do not have any time to waste." She holds up her free hand to cover her mouth as a yawn creeps in. "We can sleep when it is over," she says when she lowers her hand.

The other advisors follow Feather and stand side by side around the tree facing the center of the room. They stand evenly spaced apart and reach their arms to clasp hands closing the circle, except for two vacant spots on each side of the entrance. The walls behind them shift. There are no more shelves. The surface looks smooth, but behind each faerie the wall is a different color to represent each type of magic. They each look up to the ceiling.

Together they say, "Through unity we are free."

The walls behind them begin to glow. The entrance and the two vacancies keep their natural wood appearance.

My whole body begins to tingle, like a sudden chill that blows in when the door is opened on a cold day. This is strong magic!

My curiosity peaks, knocking my exhaustion down for the time being. Tilda told me after my first trip through the Advisor Tree that the entrance into the tree is a test to ensure only the strongest faeries become advisors. The details of that process were never mentioned. I wonder how the other faeries even know that an induction has started.

The time for questions has passed, though. The induction has begun, and nobody knows how long it will last. Those of us in the center of the room watch with bated breath as the advisors continue to chant, "Through unity we are free."

The magic grows stronger.

Nedra whispers to me through our link. "What you are feeling, Althea, that is an energy wave sent throughout Reverie. Only faeries with the strongest magic can feel it. They all know when it happens to come here if they want to take the test. The first faerie of the power, or powers, needed to pass through the entrance successfully becomes the new advisor. This induction will, of course, see two new advisors so it could be awhile before it is over. Nanoaj has already informed the others of what is happening."

"Thank you, Nedra," I reply through our link.

It is not long before the entrance shifts to allow our first new advisor through. I am shocked, but pleased to see Indri walk in. Without saying anything he walks to Tilda's free side and takes her other hand. He, too, looks up to the tree and begins to chant. The wall behind him instantly lights up like the others.

I wonder if he already knew what to do because Tilda is his partner, or if it is common knowledge for all faeries.

I find I have actually dozed off when both Apuri and Not begin nudging me awake just before the next advisor walks in. I am not sure how long I was out, but I am thankful for the sleep I got.

The entrance shifts just as it did with Indri. This time I see the truth faerie from my dream. Her long night black hair rests at her lower back just like in my dream. As she walks over to take her place in the circle, I look at Clementine and Tilda. Looks like my telling them ahead of time did not interfere with this faerie becoming the new truth advisor.

As Indri and the new truth advisor take hands, closing

the circle, the magic shifts. It is still radiating strongly, but instead of the cold chill, it feels warm, much like when I feel my own magic or that of the plants or animals. This is not a call, it is simply a presence.

Together, they all chant one last time, "Through unity we are free." Then, they unclasp hands and lower their gazes. The induction is over.

Tilda walks to the center of the room with Indri and the truth faerie.

"Dreamer, I would like to introduce you to Sue, the new truth advisor. And you already know Indri." I can tell she tries to sound unbiased, but her pride for her partner is obvious.

I glance over to see his own pride shines just as brightly. Both of his sharp K9 teeth gleam from his gray lion-like face.

I give a slight bow in recognition and greeting to Sue. She returns the gesture then asks, "I am afraid, Dreamer, we have no time for friendly conversation. What is our first line of business?"

I am thrown off by her bluntness. "Um... We..."

Tilda steps up and answers Sue for me, "We have just finished the human sanctuaries in the Painted Forest."

She does not look surprised. "I expect the next step will be to bring the humans in." It is not a question. She knows. Of course, she knows; she is the truth faerie advisor. "And what of the wild magic?"

"We are still working on that," I say. She nods. She stands still for a moment, looking at me. Her eyes are white, ethereal, like Verity's, but there is a difference. Her eyes do not chill me to my core.

"May I?" she asks, still looking at me. She is asking permission to see into my mind, read my thoughts. Verity never asked permission. Sue is different. I nod.

I can feel her presence in my mind. There is a shift in energy. I know right now I could stop her from going any further. I could close my mind tighter than the most secure safe in the world. I do not. She needs to know everything, and this is the quickest way to update her.

I can feel when she leaves. It is like a breath of fresh air.

"It seems you are on the right track," Sue says after seeing everything. I will take that as a compliment. Suddenly, my yawns are back. I apologize, but Sue says there is no need.

Tilda gathers everyone around and says, "Our work for now is finished. Let's get some rest, regroup, and meet back here tomorrow morning."

We all congratulate Indri and Sue on their new positions and head to find comfy beds.

* * * * * * * * * *

I am back at the Pyramid, or what is left of it. The heart of wild magic.

Remembering my last time here, I quickly check my magic. I want to be ready in case anything decides to attack again.

I walk around the dark overgrown jungle for a while with no incident. I have a strange feeling in the pit of my stomach. I am not sure what it means.

I work on clearing my mind as I continue walking. I am not sure which direction I am headed, but I do not focus on that. I just walk.

As my arm brushes against leaves from trees and bushes, I feel the tingle of their magic. I am reminded of my first time in Inon, when I felt that tingle from the touch of a fern. I did not know at that time what it was.

Now, I know what I am feeling is magic, energy. Energy is in everything. It connects everything and everyone.

This magic is different from that of the fern in Inon, though. This is wild magic, raw and pure. It feels powerful and dangerous. It is.

As I continue walking, I smell something different in the air. I close my eyes and breathe in deeply. It is the ocean. I must be walking in the part of wild magic that covered the beach.

I reach out with my magic, feeling around me for any of the creatures from Pilate's paintings. I do not sense anything else, but the magic of the creatures is the same as the jungle, so it may just blend in.

I am careful not to let my guard down.

Still, I must be here for a reason. I find a place to sit down and close my eyes. Using only my magic, I reach out. I am not really sure what I am searching for, but I have been practicing on Zoar with my magic.

Maybe this is the reason.

I feel the danger, the power, of the wild magic. I fight the urge to throw up my guard. Still cautious, I push on.

There is something new. I still feel the danger, but it is more like a mask or a cover. Underneath the threatening veil, is pain, fear, and despair.

Immediately, the wild magic reacts. It knows I am here. I can feel the creatures coming for me.

I quickly leave, waking myself up.

* * * * * * * * *

I wake up after a good sixteen hours of sleep feeling like a brand-new person. It is amazing what some good sleep will do for you.

It takes me a few minutes to realize where I am. When I see the small turtle pond by the door I remember Apuri and I stayed with Louveri and Feather. Not returned with Nedra to his cave, and Nicole and her boys, Lady Nell, Tsar, and Noni bunked with Tilda, Indri, and Idona.

I look beside me to see an empty bed. Apuri must already be up.

"Althea, are you okay?" Nedra asks through our link.

I remember the dream. That must be what he is asking about. "Yeah, Nedra. I am fine. I need to go tell the others what happened though."

I head to the living room, but nobody is around. The house is quiet.

"Nedra, where is Apuri?" I ask through our link.

I hear him hum through the link before replying, "They are all at the fountain. Would you like me to talk to Apuri or link him in?"

"No, I will just go down to them."

"Not and I will join you shortly."

I quickly make myself presentable and leave the cozy cottage. Before I make it to the bottom of the hill, I hear laughter and voices. I pass the Advisor Tree and head straight for the fountain.

I am greeted by Lullabay, Dante, Idona, Timmy, and Noni in the middle of a game of tag. Idona circles around my legs with a high-pitched giggle and creates a poof of flower petals to distract Noni for a quick getaway. Noni twirls in the petals with a beaming smile then picks up the chase again back toward the fountain.

I follow after them at a leisurely pace.

Apuri walks up and greets me with a good morning hug. When it becomes awkward, I pull away before anyone else notices. I look around him to see everyone else sitting and standing around the fountain chatting away like the world outside is not in danger.

"What is going on?" I ask Apuri as we turn and walk together the rest of the way to the fountain.

"We knew you needed your rest. When you did not respond the first time I tried to wake you up, I thought it best if we just let you sleep until you woke on your own. Louveri, Feather, and I had just finished breakfast when Tsar showed up. He said the kids wanted to play outside for a bit and wondered if Lullabay and Dante wanted to join them. Louveri and Feather agreed it sounded like a good idea. I figured I would tag along and chat with Tsar a bit. We have actually been waiting for you to show up. Come on."

Everyone extends morning greetings even though it is not morning anymore. I thank them and quickly move the conversation forward. Small talk makes me awkward. I have enough awkward moments on my own; I do not need to make any more for the rest of the group. I need to find out why they have been waiting on me, so I can tell them my dream.

"Thank you all for letting me sleep. My body is most appreciative. I did not realize I needed to sleep that much. Apuri says you have been waiting on me though. What is going on?"

As I'm talking, I glance up behind Tilda. I realize something is different about the fountain.

The conversation disappears in my mind as I step closer to it. Tilda moves out of the way without me asking, and I walk right up to the edge of the fountain. It looks the same as it always has, but there is something different.

"Althea, are you okay?" Clementine places her hand on my shoulder.

"Huh?" I turn to look at her. When it is clear nobody else sees or senses anything different about the fountain I decide not to say anything. I reply, "Yes, sorry. I do not know what came over me. Maybe I had too much sleep." I finish with a laugh to put her at ease.

"What was it you were saying?" I ask Tilda.

"Pilate says he sent Tsar's message to the hegira camp this morning. Althea, it is already working. The news is buzzing through the human realm like fire. We expect the humans will start showing up within a day or two. Are you ready for this?"

Wow! I did not expect it to work that fast. I suppose, though, that the people closest to the wild magic are already experiencing its dangers, like Nicole. They would be grateful for refuge.

"I guess I am." I say with emphasized spunk. "Let's go run some hotels, friends!"

Before I have a chance to call on him, Nedra flies overhead and lands with Not in the clearing past Tilda and Arsona's homes. Not long after, we see Nanoaj fly in from the same direction.

"Are you going to tell them about your dream?" Nedra asks through our link. I reply, "I will bring it up later. We have to make sure we are fully prepared to welcome the humans right now."

Unlike most of our ventures, the faerie children do not have to sit this one out. Everybody comes along to the sanctuaries. Lullabay and Dante look like they are on their way to an amusement park, grins stretching from ear to ear.

We arrive at the sanctuary headquarters in quick time and with no problems. I say that is a good start.

After the induction last night, we had each advisor spread word of the sanctuaries, wild magic, and everything that was happening in as few words as possible, leaving out any information about the island.

We made it clear that the humans were coming to the sanctuaries for survival. Both humans and faeries would be protected by the Dreamer and her friends personally. We asked for any willing faeries who wished to volunteer their time to help with the sanctuaries to contact the advisors or simply show up to the locations in a couple mornings.

As I said before, we did not expect the hegira's plan to work as quickly as it did.

Honestly, I am not sure how many faeries will be on board with this plan. Considering their history, I cannot blame them for not wanting the humans in Reverie. With this worry on my mind, I am excited to find a handful of faeries outside each of the structures at the headquarter's location.

Among them is the peddler to whom I gave the wish when I first came to Reverie. I cannot help but give her a stern glare when our eyes meet.

The wish is no longer echoing in my mind. It stopped instantly when we inducted the new advisors and shared the news of our current events. Still, it played over and over in my head long enough that I do not think I will ever forget her words.

Having someone uninvited in your head like that leaves a mark. It is something I will strive to prevent in the future.

Seeing my glare, she quickly loses the smile and casts her eyes down at her feet. I walk into the first building with a quick greeting to all the faeries except her. I know I am being petty, but she needs to understand what she did was cruel and worth way more than a few pairs of clothes.

I will pull her aside and have a real conversation when the time presents itself, but for now, I must rally what troops we have and start this business.

Chapter Twenty-One ~ Running Out of Time

We were able to set up a proper welcome station at each sanctuary and even slept in one of the hotels ourselves the first morning before the humans started arriving.

We placed a sign in front of each *hotel* describing Reverie Inn's whimsical features and even added bits about faeries and enchanted trees.

The guests simply read it and smile or scoff like it is another sideshow attraction gimmick. The first faeries they see actually appear more human, so the humans think they are simply costumes and makeup along with special effects.

I wanted to say something, to tell them the truth, but Lady Nell said, "This is actually a blessing. As long as none of us tell them the faeries are not real, and the idea of costumes and such is entirely their own we cannot be held accountable or accused of lying when they discover the truth. And with any luck," she added, "we will solve the problem of wild magic and have them out before any of them do discover the truth."

I decided to go along with it for the time being, but it still leaves a sour feeling in the pit of my stomach. The fountain in Inon flashes through my mind. The feeling it gave was different than this, but still uncomfortable. We have been so busy with the *hotels,* I never had time to tell anyone about the fountain or my dream.

Right now, I am helping pass out keys to arriving guests. We actually made all of the locks and keys identical to save time. They are more for room identification for each guest than anything. Nicole brought up the possibility of theft, but the faeries assured us that would not happen here.

I was unsure what the humans would think of my eyes and the mark, but most of them think they are special effects, contacts, and makeup. I am okay with that. Still, their stares make me uncomfortable sometimes. I realize, ironically, that I was here not very long ago staring at Reverie's residents just like the humans are staring at me now. I feel a pang of guilt at the memory.

I glance over to see my friends chatting with more incoming humans about our unique hotels. "I could not find anything on the internet," I hear an older couple say to Clementine. She simply smiles and hands them their keys. The man glances up and down her body. "It is like they just popped up overnight. Must have been planning these costumes for a few decades, though. Too much work if you ask me."

The couple take their keys and follow the crowd out of the lobby and toward the rooms.

I head back to the staff room behind the front counter to get more keys. While I am gathering a few from some hooks on the wall, Notyal comes in from the back entrance in a state of frenzy. He is practically tripping over his tentacles. He rushes over to me saying, "Althea! Althea! I have news from My Lady!" He grabs my hand and pulls me toward the back entrance causing me to drop the keys I had gathered to the floor in a scramble. "We have to hurry; Queen Melanomie has news."

I do not have time to get a word in before we make it out the door. Not continues to pull me past the corner of the building and heads toward the line of trees. I pull my hand away and stop walking.

"Not, what is going on? We cannot just run out like this."

Not's mouth opens then closes. He looks like he is ready to run in the direction he was taking me, but he wants me to come along. He knows he has to explain what is happening. Wringing his tentacles, he speaks as fast as he can, trying not to leave out anything important.

"I was walking around the sanctuaries in camouflage to make sure the humans did not go where they should not be. A few of the faeries have been doing the same."

He points to the trees we were headed to. "When I got close to those trees, I heard someone talking. I thought it might be someone who had wandered too far, so I went to check it out. I heard the water before I heard the talking again. When I got closer, I realized it was Queen Melanomie. She was calling for us! I rushed to the water to speak to her. She said she did not have time to say everything twice, and not that she did not trust me to deliver the message properly, but she had to say it to you directly. Now, please let's go!"

"Okay, let's go." Without any further delay, we run as fast as we can to the source of Mel's call.

I hear the babbling brook before I see it. We come to a stop just by the water's edge. I look around and listen for Mel's voice but hear nothing. Not clears his throat and points down into the water. I look down to see an image of Queen Melanomie floating in the water in front of me.

It looks just like when the elves spoke to the young faerie during the war.

"Mel, what is going on?" I ask.

"Althea! It is good to see you. I know you have been looking for anything that will help you find a way to get rid of wild magic. We have been keeping an eye on the shore where it started as well as scouting for more breakouts. It is spreading faster, Althea. I do not know if you have checked in on it recently, but South Carolina's entire shoreline is overgrown. At this rate, the whole East Coast will be gone in a couple weeks, tops."

I let out an exasperated sigh. If it has spread that much on the beaches, I can only imagine how far it has gone on land.

"That is not why I reached out, though," Mel continues. "We were not sure what to expect once it came into the ocean. I honestly thought the water might make it grow faster, make it more dangerous. That is why we were surprised when a few of my scouts swam to inspect it closer. Althea, when wild magic hit the water, it stopped."

"Wait," I reply, confused, "what do you mean it stopped?"

"Just that. Instead of continuing to grow into the ocean and take over here, too, it stopped. Once it made it past the shallow waters, it did not grow anymore. We have been keeping an eye on it to be sure. But Althea, it has not grown into deep water at all. I am not sure why or how, exactly, but I think the ocean may be key to stopping wild magic. I know you are busy up there, but I think you need to check it out personally. It might help you figure out the answer

"Yeah, okay. Let me tell the others and make sure Nicole and the advisors have everything handled here. Then, we will be right on our way to you."

Mel replies, "I will send some of my scouts to meet you when you get here."

Her face disappears from the water, and its surface returns to its normal bubbling self, flowing over the rocky terrain below.

I look at Not and say, "Are you ready to go home?"

He answers with a smile.

Together, we head back to the staff room to tell the others. We have to be careful not to let the humans hear anything. We have to keep up our guise of a whimsical hotel resort.

Back in the staff room, I pick up the keys I dropped on the floor.

"I will take these out so nothing looks suspicious and

come back with Apuri and the others. We can get some of the other faeries to greet guests and pass out keys while we meet with the advisors."

Not waits in the staff room while I go get the others. It takes me a moment to spot Apuri and the others amongst all the people wandering around the hotel. You would think they would stick out like a sore thumb, but they actually blend in quite well. Clementine is the first one to catch my eye.

Smiling at guests as I pass, I make my way over to her. I wait to get her attention until she finishes talking to a woman with a young girl.

"Clementine," I say with a smile, "I need you in the staff room as soon as you are able."

A worried look flashes across her bark textured face. I smile again and she quickly resumes her cheery expression. Without saying anything else to the humans around her, she walks, still smiling, toward the staff room.

"I will meet you there after I get the others," I whisper to her before breaking off on my own,

I head to get Apuri and the advisors inside this building so we can all meet together. We have to tell everyone in the other *hotels* as well, but for now I take what I can get.

I return to the full staff room several minutes later. I was able to find more faeries walking around helping with odd jobs to replace the greeters I removed from the lobby. I gave them the keys I had and told them they were doing a great job.

Inside the room, everyone looks a bit anxious. I was not able to tell anybody any details before sending them in here.

I make the speech as short as possible. "Thank you all for coming in. Not and I just received a message from Queen Melanomie from Ceres. They may have found a way to stop wild magic, but we have to go there to see for ourselves. I hate to just up and leave the hotels, especially in the early stages, but I do not think we have a choice. Wild magic is spreading even faster now; I am not sure how much time we have left. If we are going to do anything to stop it, now is our chance. I need to know who is going with me. We will leave immediately to go to the other hotels and tell them the same. We hope to be on our way to Ceres before nightfall."

The sky faeries were actually able to create a sky glamour to make everything seem as normal as possible for the humans. It would get a bit suspicious if they began to notice it never got dark here.

Apuri, Not, and I leave the hotel using the staff room back door. Nell, Tsar, Noni, and the dragons will meet up with us on the way.

The advisors, of course, stay behind to run things in the Painted Forest. I expected as much, but they needed to be present to hear the news as well. They return to the lobby to carry out the necessary jobs while we head to the next building to pass on the message.

Again, it feels like time is slipping through my fingers. It is already dark and we are just now making our way to the Pool Tree to Ceres. Notyal and I are lighting the way for easier travel. Nedra is flying above the canopy to meet us at the tree.

I am surprised to see patches of glowing flora along the way. The first plant we see resembles a purple iris, but it is much larger. The petals glow a deep rich purple, while the stems balance perfectly between blue and gray.

We also see a spiraling patch of small white illuminated mushrooms and, my favorite, a tree with small teardrop shaped flowers that glow in a rainbow of colors. Even though we are still not there and we are rushing to reach the tree as fast as possible, I cannot help feeling a sense of relief that this might be it.

If we find the answers we are looking for in Ceres, we could wrap this up and be on our way to returning the world to normal, or even something better.

I hear the sound of bubbling water, like from a fountain.

"We are close," says Not. "This way." He makes an abrupt turn to the left. As the rest of us stop to figure out what is going on, we are suddenly knocked off our feet as something slams into us from behind.

My light goes out as I fall to the ground in a tangle with my companions. "What is going on?" I say as I fumble to create the light again. I see Not's bioluminescent glow headed toward us. He must have realized we were no longer behind him and came back to investigate.

I manage to shut out the voices around me and reignite a ball of light for us to see by. I pull my legs out from under Lady Nell's torso and manage to roll over into a sitting position. I ready my magic for whatever it was that attacked us.

As I raise my hands in a defensive position, I am shocked at what I see in front of me. Not just one, but two familiar faces stare back at me with wide eyes, Sil and Tag.

The Syx twins, along with Nedra, were rescued from the Pyramid by Tsar's hegira crew before we fought the battle with the sodocs. They are the fastest creatures I have ever met. They must have been running at full speed to have created such a calamity.

I realize I have not seen the twins, let alone any of the other band of misfits we trained for the battle against the sodocs, since I left Lauk headed for the Pyramid. A flash of guilt surges through me. I should have been more concerned. I should have asked about them sooner, especially after hearing Trevin's story of the battle.

I will have to worry about that later. Right now, something is wrong. "Sil, Tag, what is going on? Are you okay?"

They take a moment to catch their breath then answer in their usual manner of finishing each other's sentences.

"We are okay," says Sil, "we just- "

"-ran a long way without stopping," finishes Tag.

It turns out the twins have been living with the hegira at the farm since the end of the battle. When Tsar and Lady Nell went there to ask the hegira for help, the twins naturally volunteered. They knew they would not be able to help in influencing the humans with magic in the way the hegira planned, but they were determined to be useful. Surviving the battle gave them a new sense of purpose, and living with the hegira gave them a place to call home.

Considering their unique skills of speed and telepathic communication, the Syx twins became the designated messengers for the hegira as they carried out the plan of persuasion.

That is why they are here now. They are delivering a message from the hegira that we are out of time. Wild magic is spreading too fast. The hegira are falling back. The farm is being evacuated to the Painted Forest as we speak. All other hegira have been instructed to do the same.

We can only hope they were able to spread the word about our hotels as much as possible.

"They said the glamour must be completely closed off and reinforced," Sil finished.

I sit in silence for a minute, mulling all this over. Everyone else has dusted off and stands waiting on my answer. Apuri gives me a hand and pulls me to my feet. Not is understandably impatient to get to Queen Melanomie, but I cannot just leave everyone in a panic.

Still, we are so close to Ceres' Gateway Tree. I grit my teeth and breathe through my nose as I try to debate this out in my mind. If we go ahead through the Pool Tree to Ceres, we can stop wild magic for good and save everyone. But that could mean more lives lost up here. If we stay, we can help get everyone over into Reverie and aid in closing off and strengthening the Glamour to prepare for the coming of wild magic.

I look at Notyal, "I am sorry, Not. We have to help them. We do not know how long we will have to be in Ceres. By the time we get back, everything up here could already be gone. I understand if you would like to go ahead without us."

I have to give him the option of returning to Ceres without us. He is here voluntarily and I will not make anyone stay against their will. That being said, I do hope he decides to stay with us. I have grown quite fond of Not, and I would hate to lose another companion.

I understand Aspen's reasons for going out on her own to the witch, but we still feel her absence every minute.

I wait with bated breath for Not's answer. He spends a few minutes looking in the direction of the Pool Tree.

"I will stay with you, Althea. I do wish to see My Lady again, but you need me here. With my help, perhaps we can work faster and be on our way to Ceres sooner."

Anything I think to say does not feel like enough, so I just smile.

Without wasting any more time, we head back to the hotels to get the advisors.

Chapter Twenty-Two ~ Velmae

We immediately returned to the hotel to tell the advisors Sil and Tag's news. They decided to return to Inon with us to officially discuss matters.

We left the hotel greeting and running to a couple of faeries per building while the rest of the faeries headed to the glamour border to speed things up there.

As soon as we entered the Advisor Tree, Sue was adamant that the glamour must be sealed immediately. I have been arguing that they need more time to get people inside.

"There are not only humans out there, but faeries and other creatures, too! You cannot just leave them out there like this, trapped."

"We have to think about the lives we are responsible for inside Reverie," Sue responds coolly. "The faeries and creatures out there are there by choice. Your hotel plan has worked; the humans have almost filled them already. They will be able to repopulate once their side is safe to live again."

Sue raises her hand and arches an eyebrow to stop my response. Instead she allows each of the other advisors to voice their opinion. They are to vote "Now" if they agree with Sue or "Wait" if they agree with me. They go clockwise around the room, allowing each advisor to cast his or her vote. Only the advisors are allowed to vote.

Arsona votes "Now;" Feather votes "Wait;" Eart votes "Now;" Petricha votes "Now;" Clementine hesitates before voting "Wait;" Indri and Tilda look at each other for a long, tense minute before they both vote "Now."

Hearing that last "Now" is like a blow to the chest. I force myself to remain composed. I am the Dreamer. I have to be responsible and do my duty to save everyone, even if that means saving only the ones I know will have a chance. As I bite my tongue and clench my fists to keep from crying, I sense something in front of me. Someone. I look around, but nobody else has entered the room. I look back at the advisors.

"The decision is made," Sue says with an air of finality.

Hearing those words brings it all back. This is it. This is the dream I had after I woke up from Neoinas. I reach out, knowing my dream self is there, already turned back to the conversation, about to wake up.

Lady Nell stands up quickly. She does not look happy either.

"We should tell them the news as soon as possible," I say aloud at the same time she does.

Everyone looks at me like I have finally gone crazy. Maybe I have. Or maybe they just now see what I have been feeling since this whole journey started.

"This was my dream," I whisper, not caring if any of them really hear me or not. "Oh, dear spirits, they were trying to tell me what to do. I should have tried harder. We should have done this sooner, moved faster. Everyone could have already been saved."

Warm tears begin to fall down my cheeks. I turn and run out of the Advisor Tree with a million thoughts flooding my head. If only I could have figured out the time travel in my dream. I should have tried harder. Why did I slink away and hide on that stupid island? I should have been searching, fighting for an answer. And now I have failed.

Sure, Sue is right that those here can be saved. But that is maybe a couple thousand humans at the most. What about everyone else out there? We are slamming the door in their face, denying them sanctuary, denying them their lives.

Why did I not just go to Ceres? We could have been there already. We might have even had the answer by now. They would have made the same decision without me.

I know they are doing what they think is best, and they have loved ones to think about. But I have to do what I know is right, too.

I head to the clearing to get on Nedra's back and set this right.

Apuri shouts from behind me, "Althea, stop! What are you doing?" I turn to see everyone has followed after me.

We are almost to Arsona's house. Nedra is not much further.

"I have to do what I can!" I shout back for all of them to hear. "It is my responsibility to save them!"

Apuri, now standing right in front of me, reaches out and grabs my hand. "Well, you do not have to do it alone," he says.

"We are coming, too," says Tsar, carrying Noni. Lady Nell is not far behind.

"As I said before," Not says through gasping breaths – running on land really is not his thing – "I will stay with you."

I look past my companions at the advisors. Clementine smiles and says, "Go ahead, save the world! We have this. Besides, we are all more experienced at glamour magic than you." A tear falls from the corner of her bright green and orange speckled eye. "You would just slow us down," she says with a laugh as she runs forward and gives me a hug. I embrace her and feel her loving energy spill out around me.

Feather and Louveri come to me next. Louveri wraps me in a hug that threatens to bring up old memories. "Remember, you are stronger than you know. You can do this." I hate that I always end up leaving her. Every time it reminds me of the worst moment in my life. I will never forget the last time I told her goodbye in our old lives, when she never returned. I still feel like every time I tell her goodbye that it may again be our last. I am not sure I could handle that again.

Finally, Tilda and Indri come forward. She is crying. It is strange to see tears fall on a liquid face. "Althea, I am so sorry. We had to. Idona…"

I wrap my arms around her and whisper, "It is okay; I understand." I tell them all goodbye and turn and start back on the path toward Nedra.

With a quick glance back to the advisors and Louveri, I turn back to my companions and say, "Let's do this!"

When we reach our dragons, Apuri asks, "So, what is the plan?"

I speak loud enough for everyone to hear, "First, we are going to go pick up a friend. Then, we are going to get a little wet."

Notyal smiles. He is ready to be home. I smile back. I am ready for answers.

"Alright, Nedra, take us to the witch," I command silently through our link

Nedra and Nanoaj push off the ground simultaneously, throwing bits of dirt and grass into the air from the force. "Everyone, think of the witch!" I shout as we lift into the air.

We fly straight up to the light. I hold my breath as we enter the warmth. I am not sure what is waiting for us on the other side, but the light changes while we are still in it. It cools down and becomes more refreshing.

When we come out on the other side, the sky is dark and cloudy. It is night here. The dragons find a clear place to land, and we start our search for Aspen and the witch.

My ears are instantly filled with nature's song of chirping crickets and croaking bullfrogs. There are trees all around but few enough that the stars in the sky are still clearly visible. It is warm, but not uncomfortably so. A soft breeze tickles my neck as we continue our search for Aspen.

"Perhaps we should call for them?" Lady Nell suggests. "It may save us some time."

"Sure," I agree. "Go ahead."

"Aspen!" Nell calls with a loud clear voice. There is no answer so she calls again.

This time there is a response, but it is not Aspen.

"Who is there?" the new voice calls back. The tone in the new woman's voice says she is not used to having visitors, and she will not put up with any shenanigans. "Show yourself now, or I'll release the hounds! Then, I'll brain you myself!"

"Hello," I call out to the voice as we head in her direction. "My name is Althea. These are my friends. We have come for our friend who left to seek guidance on her own."

"Dreamer? Is that you?" the stranger calls back but now in a tone of delighted surprise. "Come, come, I'll make us all some tea!"

In a split second, the darkness changes. About three yards ahead of us is now the glow of a warm light, a lantern to be exact. We follow the light to what can only be described as a witch's cottage.

The lantern hung to light our way looks like something from the eighteen hundreds. It casts its warm glow upon the most curious door I have ever seen. It looks like a great dragon. Nedra becomes an instant fan of the witch.

On the ground, next to each side of the door, sits a fierce white pit bull. These must be the hounds the witch spoke of. They look like they could easily take down any unwelcome trespassers. Careful not to be their next victims, we walk cautiously to the witch's cottage.

It is not much bigger than a typical garden shed, but it is tower shaped with eight equal sized walls. The roof itself mimics the iconic witch's pointed hat. Each wall, except the one with the door, has a different shaped window in a different spot. To the left of the door is a star-shaped window located about half a foot from the base of the wall. On the wall to the right of the door, the window is about normal height on the wall, but the shape is a squiggly blob, like a bubble coming off of its wand. The more I look at the shack, the more I fall in love with its whimsy.

We all stop awkwardly at the door unsure to knock or simply wait. The witch knows we are coming, but it would still be rude to just walk into her house. I decide to knock on a smooth spot of the door near the lantern.

"Come in!" the witch calls.

I grab the small besom-shaped door handle and give it a push. The door creaks slowly open.

The inside of the witch's cottage is warm and inviting. I do a double take as we step inside the door. There is no way she has this much room in such a tiny building. There is only one room, but it holds everything in such a way it must have been built from the inside out.

Each of the eight walls seems to serve a different purpose. The wall directly opposite the door is made of stone and has a deep recess housing a fire and a hanging iron cauldron bigger around than a car tire. The smells drifting from that cauldron are heavenly. My mouth begins to salivate, and my stomach releases a loud roar announcing its approval of the food cooking across the shack. I am thankful nobody says anything, and the witch does not seem to notice.

Instead, she directs us to a table in front of the smooth tiled wall beside the one with the cauldron in it. It looks entirely too small for our party of six. As we get closer, however, I see there are actually eight chairs placed evenly around the smooth wooden table.

This witch is not what I expected. Honestly, I am not really sure what I expected, perhaps something straight out of Hollywood or Halloween stories. The woman in front of me is pretty average. She is not old, but she is not young; she is not tall, but she is not short; her skin is not pale, but it is not dark; her hair is not brunette, but it is not blonde; her eyes are not blue, but they are not gray. Everything about her seems to be *in-between.*

The wall behind the table is a hand-crafted mosaic depicting a great tree with full branches reaching tall and wide across the top half of the wall. Symmetrical roots twist across the bottom half of the wall. I wonder at first if it is a gateway tree, but as I look at it, I get the feeling it represents something more. In the center of the tree is a window in the shape of a spiral.

I am learning perhaps things may not be what they seem here.

"Um... We have come for our friend, Aspen," Nell says to the witch as she turns to the next wall containing a set of shelves full of jars from floor to ceiling. In the left corner of the third shelf down is a window in the shape of a crescent moon.

The witch smiles. "Yes, dear. She will be down shortly; she's just finishing up a session. I'll take care of y'all while you wait, though; don't you worry."

She grabs a few jars from different shelves then bustles over to the wall on the other side of the cauldron. This wall is also shelved from floor to ceiling, but instead of jars, it is filled with a variety of dishes – bowls, plates, cups, and utensils, all made from wood, stone, and even clay. The back of the utensil shelf, in the middle of the wall, has a long horizontal besom shaped window carved into it.

She holds the jars between her left arm and her body as she uses her right hand to pull a hidden sliding slab of wood from the left side of the cauldron wall. She places the jars upon this makeshift counter and retrieves eight cups from the top shelf in front of her. She places these cups beside the jars on the slab and proceeds to add a small sprinkle of the herbs from the jars into the cups.

I glance around, looking for a kettle or some other source of water. I find it hidden in a carved-out niche on the inside of the fireplace. There is also a cauldron shaped window almost as big as the real thing at the very bottom of the back wall. Interesting.

While the witch continues to prepare our tea, I continue to explore her cottage with my eyes.

The wall on the other side of the dishes features a bay window with a seat smothered in pillows. The small walls on either side of the seat are filled with numerous well-used candles in every color. The white candles are the biggest followed by the black ones. There are more of these candles than the colored ones. These two colors are obviously used more than the rest. The rest of the colors are of equal size and number. There are also some smaller shelves in between the candles holding smoking bundles of different herbs. Through the window, I am barely able to make out some sort of body of water in the distance.

The next wall is the one behind the dragon door. This wall is shelved like the others from floor to ceiling. These shelves are packed tight with books of all sizes. I'm sure Pilate would approve of her collection. At the bottom of the shelf is the star-shaped window.

The wall on the other side of the door has a ladder that looks to be built into the wall, maybe even grown from the wall itself like some of the faerie houses. Behind the ladder is the bubble shaped window. The ladder leads up to a loft that wraps around the whole shack, save for the wall with the door and half the wall with the ladder.

I guess that is where Aspen is, in the loft. The witch said she will be down when she finishes her session. I wonder what that means.

Our host returns with a tray of full cups and steaming bowls before I have time to ponder anymore.

We all accept our bowls and cups graciously as she places them in front of us on the table. I glance around as each of us receives our meal. It looks like we have different teas. The bowls, however, seem to be filled with the same thing, chili. It smells delicious!

As the witch begins placing wooden spoons by each of our bowls, I get an idea. What if there is something in the tea?

"Nedra," I whisper through our private link, "how much do you know about this witch? Are you certain she is a friend?"

"I am not. Has she given you reason to think otherwise?" He replies.

"No, but..."

"I understand, Althea. You should be able to use your magic to get your answers. Earth faeries are able to detect if there is poison in food or drinks, even after it has been brewed or cooked."

"Okay," I reply, trying not to look suspicious, "how do I do that?"

"I believe you just look for anything poisonous using your magic. Only you will be able to see it, and I am not really sure what you will see."

Here goes nothing. I wave my hand under the table where it will not be seen. Carefully, I examine each cup and each bowl for anything out of the ordinary. I make it all the way around the table without seeing anything.

I whisper the results back to Nedra. "I guess that means it is safe. Thank you Nedra."

I look up to see our host watching me curiously. Does she know what I was doing? Will she be offended? What if she knows magic that would counteract my magic to detect anything?

I realize everybody is looking at me. I smile and say, "Thank you so much, w- um…. I am sorry. I guess we never got your name."

"Oh, look at me; where are my manners? I'm Velmae," she does something between a head nod, a bow, and a curtsy.

The clumsy greeting echoes her whimsical home and sets me at ease. With the energy in this house, I do not think anyone bad can live here.

I smile and nod before saying, "It is very nice to meet you, Velmae. Thank you for your hospitality. I do not mean to be rude, but we are in a bit of a hurry and do wish to see Aspen as soon as possible."

"Ach," Velmae scoffs with the wave of a hand. "We already knew you would be coming. Saw it a few days ago. Aspen is finishing her last session, now. We expected you would show up a little later, though. I apologize for the wait. Please eat, drink, relax for a moment." She holds her hand up to stop me from saying anything and arches an eyebrow with a knowing look as she says, "You never know how many *moments* you have left, dear. Always best to take them one at a time and savor the life out of them when you can. You don't want to look back on your life and see one big rushed blur. Life is all about balance, dear. Now, eat up, and don't forget to drink. The tea will help."

I take her advice and pick up my wooden spoon and take a bite of the chili. I close my eyes as I savor every detailed flavor rolling over my tongue. There is a bit of spice and a touch of sweet bundled in a blanket of savory. Every breath through my nose brings a new scent, a new flavor. By the sounds around the table, I guess that everyone else has followed suit, and they are enjoying the chili just as much as I am.

"Velmae, this is delicious!" I say enthusiastically. She just smiles. I take a drink of my tea. It is not one I have had before. I swish it gently over my tongue, trying to figure out what it is. As I swallow, I try to hold on to the scent, but it is no use. I have no idea what this tea is made of.

Velmae, still watching me with a curious smile, says, "It's dandelion. Does wonders, really, like a detox." She looks deliberately at Tsar but says nothing.

She looks at Noni. I follow her gaze. Her red ringlets frame the cup as she takes a big drink of her tea. I take another bite of my chili and another while we watch Noni. She places the cup back on the table and smacks her lips. A purple tinted liquid dribbles down her chin. "Mmmm. My dandelions taste like strawberries!" She says with a grin.

"Ah," says Velmae to Noni, "That's because it is strawberries. And blueberries, and blackberries. It will help keep you strong so you can help your mother and her friends.

Do you like it?" She asks with a childlike gleam in her eye. Noni nods her head enthusiastically. "Good. And how about your chili, dear?"

Velmae knows Noni has not taken a bite of her chili yet. In fact, Lady Nell has had some trouble getting her daughter to eat anything since we have run out of the cloud food from Sengsourya. Just as Lady Nell lets out a stressed sigh, expecting another *you have to eat* argument, Noni picks up her spoon and takes a bite of the chili.

"Mmmm!" She closes her eyes and grins from ear to ear as she chews her food. I laugh thinking that must be what I looked like when I took my first bite. Soon, she eats bite after bite, barely leaving herself time to breathe in between. Lady Nell's jaw drops as she watches her daughter scarf down the food like it was candy.

She turns to Velmae and mouths, "Thank you!" Velmae closes her eyes in a compassionate nod of understanding. Lady Nell takes another bite of her own chili before saying aloud to Velmae, "I may have to get your recipe before we leave." She casts a sideways glance at her daughter to show the real reason she asks for the recipe.

"Ach!" Velmae scoffs, "It's really just a little of this and a pinch of that. Easy to whip up with whatever you've got laying around. The trick is when you stir it. You don't just put ingredients into your food when you cook, dears. Your intentions go in as well, whether you're aware or not. Same with your tea, though the ingredients will matter a bit more there."

Before anyone has time to say anything else, we hear a crash from the loft above us. Everyone gets in a defensive position and gazes upward. Everyone, except Velmae that is. She simply stands with her hands folded, gazing up to the loft with a proud smile. After another crash, a screech, and some fumbling, she places a hand on the table and says, "I'll be right back, dears. Aspen has finished with her session and will be on her way down. She already knows you're here."

She walks back over to the herb wall and grabs an almost empty jar before walking over to the wall of dishes. She begins preparing a meal for Aspen as she did for us.

"I want to see Aspen!" Noni says with a chili stained grin.

"I know, Sweetie," says Lady Nell, "wait- "

There is a sudden flapping sound, and a dark blur of colors falls from the loft. The beautiful rainbow feathered hawk flies around the tiny room a couple of times before landing in the middle of the room. Right before our eyes, the bird transforms into Aspen. She opens her arms with a face-splitting grin and says, "And I cannot wait to see my Noni bug!"

Noni jumps from her chair and runs to Aspen. They squeeze each other in the tightest of hugs until Noni finally says with a gasp, "Aunt Aspen, I can't breathe!" Aspen sets the child back on the floor and takes her hand. Together they walk to the table and take a seat.

Velmae brings Aspen's food and tea to the table as well as some for herself.

"Mmmm, thanks V. It smells amazing!" Aspen says enthusiastically as she picks up her spoon. Before taking a bite, however, she uses her other hand to pick up her tea and takes a big drink, swallowing half the cup at once. She sets it down and proceeds to eat.

"As it should," Velmae says. "We should all be thanking you, though. Couldn't have made it without your help."

We all look between Aspen and Velmae trying to guess what she means. Velmae drinks half of her tea like Aspen did. When she sets the cup down she gestures toward Aspen with her spoon and says, "Aspen gathered all of the ingredients and seasonings for tonight's supper."

She smiles but says nothing else about it. Aspen continues her meal in silence.

I hate to be rude, but I think of the outside world. Time is slipping away and we are still here eating. I know Velmae said to enjoy these moments, but I just feel selfish sitting here with my friends and good food, while the outside world is withering away. I fidget in my seat thinking about the best way to rush things along.

I notice Velmae and Aspen share a look as they watch me. Aspen raises an eyebrow, and Velmae smiles and nods.

Aspen sets her spoon in her half-empty bowl and folds her hands on the table in front of her. She is sitting across the table in front of me; she squares her shoulders, and says, "Althea, stop worrying!" She uses the same tone of voice as when she heals someone who will not be still or listen to what she says.

My jaw drops. Everyone else stops eating and looks at Aspen. She keeps her eyes on me and says, "Sometimes you have to get out of your own head in order to see what is best for you." She casts a sideways glance at Velmae. I inhale, ready to argue my point, to explain why we have to hurry.

Aspen takes a breath and says, "I know what is going on; you do not have to explain. Nanoaj has been sending me updates, and…" she looks at Velmae. "V already saw it a couple weeks ago, when I first arrived."

I am taken aback, "Aspen, you have only been gone for a couple of days, not weeks."

I look at Velmae. She smiles and asks, "D does time always work the same in gateway trees as it does in the outside world?"

I smile, feeling foolish. Of course not! That is one of the wonders of the gateway trees. They each contain their own worlds, working separate from everything around them.

"So, how different is the time here?" I ask.

"Well," says Aspen, "from my own figuring using my time here compared to Nanoaj's messages this is how I have broken it down: one week here is about one hour in the outside world. I was shocked to find out you guys had just retired the night I left when I checked in after being here for a week. So, using that guide, the time roughly translates to one full day here is about nine minutes in the outside world. When we leave, time will barely have passed out there."

I try to wrap my mind around that. "Oh," I say, "so that means..."

Velmae interrupts, "That means enjoy your meal and some company with friends before rushing into the unknown, dear."

I smile and pick up my spoon. I wonder, as I eat, how long Velmae has been here, and how old that makes her. She does not look a day over forty, but I know that is not the case.

After we finish our chili and tea, Velmae carries the dishes outside to wash in a nearby stream. She refuses any help, insisting we use this time to catch up and relax before we have to leave. She opens a cabinet under the bay window seat and takes out several pillows and blankets "to sit on" she instructs, pointing at the floor in the center of the room.

We all move to the floor, sitting on the pillows and blankets provided by our hostess.

"Have you found what you were looking for, what you needed?" Lady Nell asks Aspen. I know she is not talking about just her wings.

Aspen smiles, "I have. And I am sorry." She holds up her hand to stop Nell, "Not for before, but for distancing myself after, for shutting you out. That was not fair to any of us."

I look at Tsar while Nell and Aspen continue their conversation. I realize he has not said anything since we came into Velmae's home. He sits with his back to the bay window and his empty cup of tea still in his hand. I wonder why he did not give it to Velmae. He is lost in his own thoughts. He still has not made peace with his time in Neoinas; honestly, I guess I have not either. I have been keeping myself busy with tasks like the sanctuaries and wild magic partly to keep those thoughts at bay.

Maybe that is something Tsar and I both can ask Velmae about. I look up at the seat behind Tsar. There is a lot of energy, a lot of magic in this place, but that spot is the strongest.

Tsar looks up at me. When our eyes meet, I am thrown back to Neoinas in a flash of light followed by darkness. My first instinct is to panic. My pulse races; my breathing gets heavier.

Suddenly I hear Aspen's words, but in Velmae's voice, "You have to get out of your own head in order to see what is best for you."

But what does that mean? I close my eyes and instantly see the bay window covered in its purple seat and rainbowed pillows. The walls are lined with candles and smoking herbs. This time all of the candles are burning. I follow them up and then back down to the seat in the window. I cannot see anyone or the rest of the room. I am scared to open my eyes and see that dark void again. But Velmae's words must mean something.

I open my eyes to the darkness, but this time I am not alone. Tsar is here too! He is sitting just as he was on the floor, but his eyes are shut tight.

"Tsar?" I am not sure he can hear me. I call him again, "Tsar?" He brings his hands up to the sides of his head. He thinks it is part of Neoinas, part of the insanity. I am not sure if it will work, but I reach my hand out to touch his arm. "Tsar, I am here, too. You are okay."

He slowly lowers his hands and opens his eyes. "Althea? How?"

I shrug my shoulders and say, "I am not sure, but I will take this over the alternative; how about you?"

He nods. I look around the black void, unable to see anything other than Tsar and myself. "Why do you think she brought us back here?" I ask aloud.

Tsar shrugs and replies sarcastically, "Crude sense of humor? Maybe she really is a wicked witch, but she tortures her guests according to their biggest personal fears instead of things in the stories. I think I would rather be eaten."

I laugh. The thought of someone trying to eat Tsar brings the image of a dog chewing on a stick followed by a person chewing on a stick.

"Find that funny, do you?" He tries to sound upset, but I

can hear the smile in his voice.

I force myself to stop laughing and say, "I think you may be onto something."

"Still hungry, Dreamer?" he asks with a huff.

I laugh, "No, not that. The part about our personal fears, but I do not think she is doing this to torture us. I think she is trying to help us the same way she helped Aspen." He sits up straighter and listens; I have his attention.

"Tsar, do you know the reason Aspen came here, the reason she has been distant since the battle at the Pyramid?"

"Nell said she was hurt but never went into any more detail than that," he replies.

"That is part of it," I respond. "When we were inside the Pyramid with Zixus, Aspen came back for us, to help. Tsar, we both saw you die. I did not know she was in there, but I also blamed myself for your death. I should have destroyed Zixus sooner. Aspen felt the same way. She thought she could get you out safely, and I thought I could save us all. Instead, we were all hurt when the Pyramid came crashing down. Because she blamed herself for what happened to you, she distanced herself from her closest friend. She came here to heal her wings, but also to heal her heart. I think that is why we are here now, to do the same."

He sits quietly for a moment then says, "Okay, that makes sense, but how exactly are we supposed to do that?"

"Talk about it?" I suggest with a shrug.

He lets out a big sigh then asks, "Has that helped you any? You told everyone about your time here already."

"No," I answer honestly. "But I also do not think that is why I am here."

"What do you mean?" he asks, curious. When I hesitate, he says, "Okay, I will go first; then, you go." I nod my head in agreement.

He begins, "My biggest fear growing up, especially after I came into my *power*, was that I would turn out just like him. I did everything I could to make sure that did not happen.

When I walked into that place to confront him, to kill him, I thought I could erase him. I thought it would help. When I was fighting him, though, I liked it too much. I could feel the power building, growing within me. I was bloodthirsty. I wanted to tear him to shreds with my bare hands. Althea, I liked the way that felt. I almost did it; I could have killed him in a split second with nothing but a touch, and he knew it. He encouraged it even. That is what stopped me. I saw the same bloodlust burning in my veins reflected in those dark soulless eyes. That is why I stopped. I decided I would just keep him distracted until you could do your thing. And then he hit me. Everything went black. Then, all I saw was my life flashing on a reel, showing me everything I had never accomplished in my life because I was letting my fear control me. That is, until you woke me up."

He rubs his hands together nervously then rubs the back of his neck and says, "I have not told anyone else that, not even Nell. So, what about you?"

I let out a big sigh. "I am not even sure where to start. I was terrified in Neoinas. But once I woke up and learned about wild magic, that was not my biggest fear anymore. Yes, I am still terrified of letting everyone down and risking the lives of my friends. But now... I thought by destroying the Pyramid, I would save the world, and we could all have our happy ending. That is not what happened, though. Instead, I released something just as bad, if not worse, than Zixus and the sodocs. Wild magic is not worried about hiding in the shadows or executing a plan. It answers to no one. Its power increases by the second, and nothing can stop it. I have tried fire, ice... But the part that scares me the most is not even my dreams are safe from it. Sure, I am learning to use my magic inside my dreams. And I am grateful to the elves for creating that island for me, well for all of the Dreamers, but what if I fail again? Or even worse, what if I succeed again and something else bad happens? Louveri was supposed to be the Dreamer, not me. I keep thinking, if she had friends like I have, she would not have died, and she could have saved everything and defeated Zixus before the Pyramid was that powerful. I know the elves created Dreamers to save the world, but what if I am broken?"

As soon as I stop talking, the darkness vanishes. Velmae's cottage is once again wrapped around us like a sheltering hug. Tsar and I look at each other and then at the others. They all stare at us. Lady Nell, Aspen, and Not are crying. Noni has fallen asleep. Apuri sits silently, but I can see on his face that they heard everything we said. He reaches out and grabs my hand. Nell does the same to Tsar. Aspen reaches both hands out, one to me and the other to Nell. Not does the same to Tsar and Apuri.

We all sit like this, silent, hands linked as one, for what feels like an eternity. I can feel the energy flow through us, from one hand to the next, in a clockwise motion. Nobody says anything, but I feel better. I feel like a door has opened and let in fresh air. I am not worried anymore. I know I am going to do my best, and I am not doing any of this alone. If I do fail, others will keep trying. We will not go down without a fight.

Chapter Twenty-Three ~ Ceres

I am not sure how long we sat on the floor hand in hand until Velmae came back, but it felt like an eternity. It was refreshing and energizing in the same way the Domain was. It was pure.

Velmae returned to her house not with the bowls and cups she left with, but with a big dish of blackberry cobbler. The smell of it was enough to wake Noni. She was the first to get a piece of "berry cake."

Velmae never said anything about the time she was gone, but I have a feeling she not only knew what happened inside her tiny cottage, she conducted it.

While sitting at the table eating our cobbler and drinking juice, I ask Velmae, "What is your story?"

She shrugs and says in a matter-of-fact tone, "I never fit in anywhere. Growing up, I was always a loner. I realized from an early age that I had gifts, gifts that not everyone else had. I would spend as much time as possible in nature fine tuning those gifts. The Creator would speak to me, guide me. In the human realm, though, things were hard. I always lived in between two worlds. When I was younger, I could balance those worlds with finesse, but things changed when I grew up.

That is what happens when you are not allowed to be who you are meant to. To truly honor the life you are given, you have to find the balance and strive to not only live that balance every day, but to serve it."

She refills all of our cups and continues her story, "I saw Reverie in my dreams. First it was the Painted Forest. Then, I found this place. It called to me. I knew it was real. So, I dedicated every minute of my life to finding it. I knew this would be a safe place. When I found a crossing through the glamour border, I left everything behind, except the clothes off my back, and came straight here. I am sure those who knew me say I ran away, or worse. But I see it not as running away but as coming home."

She explained that her gateway tree contained several thousand acres of land made of every terrain around the world and the flora and fauna that goes along with it. She is still learning her craft and will continue to do so until the day she dies. She does her duty by offering healing to any good soul who comes her way. She has learned over the years that that does not always involve tinctures, poultices, and teas.

She does not advertise. If someone truly needs her help and is worthy, they will find her, or she will find them.

"Now, before you go," she says as she goes to the ladder and climbs to her loft, "I have one last thing to give you." We all look at Aspen, but she is as clueless as the rest of us.

We hear Velmae rustling around in the loft upstairs. We finish our juice and cobbler and wait for her to come back down.

She returns a few minutes later with her arms full. She places carefully wrapped packages in front of each of us and keeps two, one in each hand. "These are for the dragons when you go back out."

I smile. Nedra will love getting a gift, and I am sure Nanoaj will, too.

"Well, go on," she says, "open them."

Noni tears into hers first. It is a tiny besom that fits

perfectly in her little hand. "Your own personal besom to sweep away your worries whenever needed," Velmae says with a wink. Noni hugs it to her chest with a smile.

Nell opens hers to find a small heart shaped pink rock. "It is rose quartz," says Velmae. "To remind you that you are always loved and to keep those in your heart close to you."

Tsar gets a small black stone. He holds it up to examine it. Velmae tells him, "Black tourmaline. It helps banish negative energies from you by absorbing them into itself and neutralizing them."

Aspen opens her package and smiles before the wrapping even falls all the way off. It is a pocket-sized book. "Thank you, V," she says with a smile. It is a magic book of herbal properties. Even though it is no bigger than Aspen's hand, she will be able to use it to identify any plant she comes across and learn all of its properties, good and bad. Velmae gives her a hug and says, "You're welcome. Now, you will never forget me or what you learned here."

Notyal has already opened his package and is holding a black and gold conch shell with a cork in the opening. He uses the suctions on one of his arms to pull the cork out, and the shell immediately fills with water. "It is enchanted," Velmae says. "I received that from a friend when I first came here and still did my own travels of adventure. You will be able to appreciate it more than I ever could." I wonder privately if he could also use it to communicate with Queen Melanomie.

Apuri opens his gift and holds it up for me to see. It is a small string of wooden colored beads. Like a rainbow, it starts with red at the bottom and ends with purple on top. "Uh, thanks," he says, unsure about the gift but still showing his gratitude not wanting to be rude. Velmae laughs, "You may not need it now, but there will come a time soon. It will teach you, guide you, to unlock and balance your energies. When the time comes, find a quiet place to meditate with the beads." He holds them in his hand and puts them in his pocket.

That leaves me. I unwrap my present with care. I have

never been one to just rip into the wrapping. This gift is wrapped in prussian blue flower petals, so I really want to take care. After I remove all the petals, I am left holding a metal sculpted flower. I turn it over after feeling the smooth back to reveal a mirror. I do not sense any magic of its own, but it definitely has a lot of energy attached to it. I look at Velmae and tell her, "Thank you, it is beautiful!" She places her hand over mine and says, "This is one of my most precious treasures. I don't even remember when or where I got it; I've had it for so long. Let it remind you that you can do whatever task you come up against."

I swallow the lump that forms in my throat and give her a silent hug for fear that emotion will take over if I speak. She hugs me back, and in that hug, I can feel her energy, her power. It is like hugging my grandmother when I was a small girl.

With no further business, we each say our goodbyes to the witch, Velmae. She passes on the gifts for the dragons and tells us to send them her well wishes.

Once we are past the reach of her lantern's light, Not and I relight our path back to the dragons. I am not sure how long we stayed inside the whimsical witch's cottage, but it is still night here. That should mean we have not been out of the Painted Forest for more than a handful of minutes at most.

You would think after all that, we would be tired, worn out, and drained dry of energy. But actually the exact opposite is true. We all feel more energized, optimistic, and prepared for whatever may lay ahead.

We give the dragons their gifts with the well wishes from Velmae. Nanoaj immediately tears hers open with a claw and gulps it down with a hum of approval. Nedra smells his first, smiles with a gleam in his eye, then carefully opens it with one claw. I do not see anything special about it; it is just a dried piece of meat. He gently bites it with his large mouth and uses a claw to tear some off before gulping it down.

He holds the piece on his claw out to me and asks through our link, "Althea will you hold onto this for me. I do not want to use it all at once. I may need the rest later."

"Sure," I reply. "What is it?"

"Ah, it is a boshckey, one of the rarest, tastiest, and most magical creatures in Reverie. It is a delicacy for us dragons. When eaten, its magic enhances our own, making us stronger and more powerful. With this in our bellies, we will be stronger and faster than ever." He laughs his dragon chortle as he looks at Nanoaj licking her chops like a dog who has just finished eating a steak. "I figured I would save some of mine in case circumstances in our future call for it."

"Sounds like a smart plan to me!" I place the meat in my pack and climb onto his back.

Once we are all mounted and ready for take-off, Noni shouts, "Next stop, mermaids!" The excitement in her voice makes the rest of us laugh as we lift into the air.

We arrive at the gateway tree to Ceres in no time at all. Nedra was right that the boshckey would enable them to fly faster.

This tree is one of the most beautiful trees I have seen in the Painted Forest. And that is saying something because there is an abundance of beautiful trees here.

I see immediately why they call it the Pool Tree. The tree itself is a large straight oak with full branches. The trunk and roots do not go straight down into the ground though. Instead, they curve and warp out into a large circular base with an eight-foot diameter creating a natural pool at the base of the tree. I have seen small pools like this before, but they have never been more than a foot at most in diameter. This is extraordinary! I am happy to see Reverie still surprises me with its enchantment.

I walk forward to look into the surface of the pool. I expected to see a dark tree-textured bottom in the pool, but the water shines from the surface all the way to the bottom. In fact, the more I look, the more I think there is not a bottom at all.

Not steps up beside me and gently grabs the top of my arm to pull me back. "It is best not to get too close until you are ready," he says.

"Oh, sorry," I reply.

"It is the fastest way to Ceres," Not continues, ignoring my apology, "but there is still plenty of time to drown if you are not prepared.

I think back to when Apuri and I traveled to Ceres with Queen Melanomie. I wonder if this pool will change once we go under the water, too, or if its waters are enchanted to allow us to breathe. Perhaps not, since Notyal just mentioned drowning.

I just remembered the piper's brother is supposed to be guarding this entrance to Ceres. I look around, but do not see him anywhere.

"What are you looking for?" Apuri asks, confused.

"The piper's brother," I answer. "The Adler brothers guard the entrances to Ceres, one on each side of the glamour border, remember? I expected to see him here."

Everyone else, except Not, begins to search for the missing Adler brother, but there is no sign of him.

"You won't find him out here," says Not.

"What do you mean?" asks Tsar.

"The Adler brothers do guard the pools, but only the piper guards from the land. His brother guards this pool from the inside. Not many know their story. The Adler brothers were, like most humans, ignorant to our world right under their noses. The one we call the piper, would play his enchanting songs by the ocean regularly. Before Melanomie became queen, she could be found traveling the waters at her whim. On one of her travels, she heard the piper's music and could not help but be drawn in by him."

Not takes a seat by the pool to finish his story. Looks like we are not going anywhere until he is finished. We get out the waterproof wrappings Pilate added in our packs and pass them for everyone to seal their belongings.

Notyal continues his story while we prepare for the trip. "One late afternoon, the piper's brother was on a small boat in the ocean. A terrible storm blew in, and he didn't stand a chance. Melanomie, recognizing the man as one of the Adler brothers, tried to save him. She was unsuccessful. She carried his body back to the beach. The piper was on the beach looking for his brother and saw Melanomie carry his body out of the water. Desperate to save his brother, he cried out to the Creator, offering himself in his brother's place. The Creator, seeing the deep love he had for his brother, made a deal. Both brothers would live in exchange for their service to protect the balance of both worlds. The piper would protect the entrance in the human realm, but his brother's body was badly damaged. In the healing process, the ocean somehow became fused with his very essence. He became a mer and would, from that day on, guard the other pool from within the water."

"Wow!" I say, enchanted by the story. "I take it Mel and the piper have a relationship. I mean, when we entered his pool, there was definitely some chemistry."

"Yes," Not answers with a smile. "My Lady is loyal to no other to this day. She visits him as much as possible, which I am sad to say is less and less since she became queen. I really do not even know if many in Ceres know their story." He stands and says no more about his Queen's story. Instead he asks, "Now, is everyone ready?"

I look around at everyone and tell him, "It looks like it, but what are we going to do about breathing? We cannot risk any of us drowning."

"Ah, leave that to me!" He excitedly takes a jar out of his pack and proceeds to smear a clear slime from inside the jar all over his body.

"Eeeww!" squeals Noni, and I have to agree.

Not laughs and holds the jar out to me saying, "It is to help you breathe underwater. Smear it all over, and it allows you to breathe until we reach the waters in Ceres.

"Not," I say curiously, "can't you already breathe

underwater?"

He giggles and replies, "Indeed, Dreamer, I can. But I have always wondered what it felt like to rub this stuff on oneself. Also, I figured you could use a visual example on how best to apply it."

We all laugh and reluctantly rub the slime on our own bodies as quickly as possible. Nedra and Nanoaj have to enter the pool in glamour form because they are too big to fit in their dragon forms. We wait until they have reluctantly shifted to apply the slime to them. Notyal assures them the slime will continue to work even after they shift back into their dragon forms underwater.

Nanoaj is a beautiful light blue dragonfly with frost tipped silver wings. Nedra does not say anything, but I can tell he is ready to get out of his glamour as quickly as possible. I understand. He was forced to remain in his glamour form for far too long under the capture of the sodocs.

Once we are all slimed up, Notyal steps up onto the root edge of the pool, looks at me, and says, "We should meet the Adler brother not long after we enter. The slime will allow you to talk underwater as well. He will take us straight to Ceres." He slides into the pool and disappears into the shimmering water.

Without waiting any longer, Apuri is the first one to jump into the pool. I am not convinced he really had to add the slime either. Maybe he did it like Not, as an example for the rest of us and an experiment for himself.

I watch as he jumps off the edge of the rounded root and into the middle of the pool sinking to its depths. The smile on his face reminds me of our time in Ceres. I often forget that water is a part of who he is as well. Even though his powers are different, he is very much like a water faerie himself.

I go in after Apuri. Standing on the tree's root, I am not really sure how to go about this. I try to step off, but my stomach tightens. I cannot do it. I clench my teeth, squeeze my hands into fists, and close my eyes tight as I plunge into the center of the pool after Apuri. I hold my breath by instinct. The water rushes around me in a whirl of bubbles. I remind myself to breathe.

Nedra says he and Nanoaj will enter the pool last to make sure everyone else enters without any problems.

I am surprised to see the water does not change like in the other pool. I guess since we are already in Reverie there is no glamour in the pool. The sparkles are still here. They go down as far as the eye can see.

I look up to see Not and Apuri talking to a mer. He looks like the mer-people from our fairy tales, with a human upper body and a fish tail instead of legs. I can tell, even from this distance, that he is the piper's brother.

I swim over to meet him. He smiles and welcomes me with a bow. He has a scabbard with an elegant pirate sword hanging around his waist. "It is an honor to meet you, Dreamer. Once everyone is here, we will go straight to Ceres. The Queen is waiting for you."

One by one, my companions enter the pool until, finally, the dragons enter. They are so small, they do not make a splash upon entry. Once they are well in the depths of the waters, though, they both shift back into their natural forms.

With the Adler brother in the lead, we swim further away from the small pool and closer to Ceres.

It is a strange thing to see dragons swim underwater. They are not as graceful as they are in the air. They move their legs and wings to propel themselves forward. The leg movements are what make them uncoordinated.

"Could you just use your wings like when you fly?" I ask Nedra through our link.

"I will try that, Althea. Thank you," Nedra replies with a tense voice. I can hear the struggle in his voice.

He passes the information on to Nanoaj, and after putting enough distance between them and the rest of us, they flap their wings. At first, it is a struggle for them to find balance, but once they have the hang of it, they are swimming like pros.

With one push they are propelled forward so far, they pass us all completely, leaving us in a trail of bubbles. That gives me an idea.

"I wonder," I say slowly, not wanting to offend the Adler brother, "if it would be okay for us to ride the dragons into Ceres? They could get us there a lot faster than we can on our own."

"You have a point, Dreamer. Queen Mel said you were full of ideas," he says with a smile. "Go ahead, get on your dragons. I will be right with you." He swims down away from us, places his thumb and index finger in his mouth and whistles a short tune. It reminds me of his brother.

I wonder if this Adler is musically talented as well. By that whistle, I am inclined to say he is.

Not sure what he is doing, we go to our dragons. We wait for him, though, instead of swimming ahead.

We do not have to wait long. In a matter of seconds, the whistling tune is echoing back at us from the dark depths. In a rush of bubbles, a creature as big as Nedra and Nanoaj, maybe even slightly bigger, swims out of the depths of the ocean.

It looks like a giant brown and white patterned seahorse but with extra fins and a longer tail. It closely resembles a large piece of seaweed. It swims straight to our guide and nuzzles under his arm. The Adler brother laughs and announces, "This is Inugo. He is my closest friend. If you will ride dragons into Ceres, Dreamer, I will join you." He grins and quickly swims a loop-the-loop, stopping just behind Inugo's head. Using one hand, he grabs onto one of the dragon's leafy fins on his spine and makes a clicking noise with his tongue.

"Let's go!" I say aloud to Nedra and Nanoaj.

We all take off in a flurry of bubbles.

It is a strange feeling to fly underwater with the bubbles in your face yet still have the ability to breathe.

It does not take long to reach Ceres. Not was right; this is the fastest way here. Our dark shimmering waters transform in an instant from a void of ocean to the underwater city made of a giant sandcastle.

We stay on our dragons as they walk out of the water and up to the castle doors. I turn to see if our guide is going to join us, curious at how that would work with his tail, but he's already turning around.

"Best of luck, Dreamer!" he shouts back and waves with his free hand as he rides Inugo back to the pool he guards.

We all wave back and shout our thanks. Once on the beach in front of the castle doors, we dismount our dragons and walk up the steps. Before we have a chance to knock, the large castle doors swing open in front of us.

A pair of Queen Melanomie's turtle guards stand at these doors and the next ones. The set of dark pearl double doors leading to the throne room are also already open. We enter the room to see Mel waiting for us on her white throne.

Her multi toned green seaweed hair is tied back under an elegant pearl crown. She wears a matching shimmery pearl dress with only one sleeve attached to a sheer drapery that melts into a thousand folds upon the floor by her feet.

She may look more like the queen of the seas, but in her smile, I see she is still the Mel we met at the piper's pool.

She jumps up from her throne and runs over to greet us. She wraps Not in a tight hug, and says, "Oh, how I have missed you, my friend!"

She then greets Apuri and me with a hug and says, "Thanks for coming".

While everyone else is making introductions, I notice Not looking around the room. I walk over to him and ask if he is okay.

"Yes. It's just... I've been away for so long. I thought when I came back, everything would be the same as it was before, but..." Before he has time to finish his sentence, Mel comes back and loops her arm in one of his. I know what he was going to say. It is not the room or the castle that has changed; it is him.

Smiling with her friend on her arm, Queen Melanomie

leads us out of the throne room.

Not may feel different being back in the castle, but by the look on his face, nothing has changed about his love for his queen. He does not miss a step as they walk arm in arm down the hall together.

I smile for him. I know what it feels like to be reunited with a friend. It is one of the best feelings in the world.

They lead us to the meeting room we were in last time where I identified the location of the Pyramid from one of Mel's scouts. The giant bubble is already floating above the table. There are no scouts here this time, just us.

Mel goes to her seat and picks up a pearl. She turns it between her thumb and forefinger as she looks at me and says, "The scouts brought me this and returned to their search not long before you entered the Pool Tree."

She gently tosses it into the bubble where it ripples and changes into a projection. We see the image of a jungle appear in the bubble. I feel the tingle and know immediately where this is. It is the source of wild magic, the location where the Pyramid fell.

It is completely unrecognizable. The beach is no longer visible at all; neither is the town.

Mel watches my reaction as she holds her hand up to the bubble and slides it down. We watch as the view drops into the ocean, beneath its surface. The tangle of vines and wild growth continues into the water. The scene moves out, the scout recording this was swimming back, deeper into the ocean.

I keep watching. I begin to notice as the water gets deeper, the growth gets thinner. When the scout reaches the point of drop-off or as we would say, "over my head," there is barely any wild magic growing at all. It continues like this until it just stops altogether.

"That's strange," I say aloud.

"Is it doing this in all water?" Apuri asks.

"No," Mel replies, "only in this ocean."

"Wait," I say, worried, "you mean it already reached the other oceans?"

Mel looks upset as she says, "I am sorry, Althea. I thought you knew. Wild magic has spread across your land from one ocean to the next and is covering the connected lands as we speak. The Atlantic is the only ocean it has stopped in. It is spreading into the others just as fast as it is on land."

I grab hold of the back of the chair in front of me to stay on my feet. I did not know it was this bad! The advisors made the right decision to close and reinforce the glamour. I honestly doubt there are many survivors out there at this point, if any.

I feel like I am going to be sick. How many bodies are buried in that wasteland of a jungle because of me? Thousands? No, millions! I feel the lump forming in my throat. My emotions are taking over. I squeeze my eyes shut and feel the surge of energy building. I cannot control it. Anger and despair burn through my core like a wildfire and even the tears leaking from my shut eyes burn my face. Just when I feel I am about to literally combust, it stops.

Everything goes black.

I find myself groggily waking in Apuri's arms. I struggle to stand and look at my friends. "I am sorry," I choke out, trying to keep it together, "I… I need to lie down."

My head begins to spin, and if not for Apuri by my side, I would have fallen to the floor.

Nedra is waiting in the hall for us. Apuri helps me onto his back, then climbs on behind me.

Mel sounds worried as she tells Apuri, "Your room is the same as before. I will show the others to their own."

My body feels alien, like it is not my own. I see a flash of color as my head drops onto Nedra's silky soft mane - the mark. It is active, but I am not sure what magic I am using.

Blood pounds in my head like an ominous drum.

I keep seeing bodies, both human and fae, flash in visions through my mind. It is not my imagination. It is a dream. I am dreaming while awake. I struggle to catch my breath. I feel their pain. Apuri places a hand on my back. More dreams flash through my mind. I feel wild magic, too. It is everywhere, and it is stronger than ever. I squeeze my eyes shut again in an attempt to remove the images, but it does not work.

I am not ready. What am I going to do?

I barely remember Apuri carrying me into our room before I lose touch with my other senses.

* * * * * * * * * *

A bright light causes me to open my eyes. I smell the ocean before I hear its gentle waves crashing on the sand not more than ten feet from me.

I sit up to see I am on the island, Zoar.

I can breathe here; I do not feel the weight of all those lives lost to wild magic. I still feel the loss, and I grieve for them, but I no longer feel their pain as if it is my own. I do not feel like I have to fight. As I sit on the pink beach enjoying my moment of peace, I hear a noise behind me.

I turn to see what the noise is, thinking maybe Pilate has joined me on the island again. I fall over in shock when I see an elf standing in the tall grass between the beach and the orchard.

This is a tall pale green-skinned elf with rainbow streaked hair. She has soft, kind eyes full of great power. Beside her stands a Chobudda, the biggest I have ever seen. His scales are the same pale green as the elf's skin, and his feathers match her rainbow streaked hair.

I recover myself and stand up. Slowly, I walk forward to meet the elf and Chobudda.

There is a gentle breeze blowing the tall grass, the Chobudda's feathers, and our hair. I stop at the edge of the tall grass. It tickles my fingers as they rest gently on my thighs. I ignore it.

I am not sure what to say. Should I say hello? Maybe I am supposed to bow? I have so many questions, I do not know where to start. I open my mouth, and the first thing that comes out is, "I thought you were all gone!"

Great! Way to go, Althea!

You have just met the most powerful creature on the planet and you start the conversation with I thought you were all gone!

The elf smiles and says, "My brothers and sisters are already gone. As are Daurey's," she inclines her head gracefully toward the Chobudda. In fact, seeing as we are here," she raises her hands to show she is talking about Zoar, "we are already gone, as well."

"Uhm…. Okay. What exactly does that mean?"

"Dreamer," the elf says, "in my time, your kind has just been created. This island," she gestures around, "does not exist yet. It remains nothing more than an idea suggested by one of my own. Something happened to you, in your timeline. Your magic is so strong it is making waves back to my time. Dreamers' magic is something given by us elves and enhanced with that of the faeries and humans to create a new species. That is how I am here, using the same dream magic that runs through your veins. I was sent to investigate and help if possible."

"Oh," I say, trying to wrap my mind around all of this. "But, if Zoar has not been created yet, how do you know the elves and chobudda are all gone by the fact that we are here?"

"The elf who presented the idea of this island to us told us that it would be the answer for future generations if wild magic got out of control and threatened the lives of the innocent."

I huff and mutter, "Too late for that," under my breath.

The elf continues as if she does not hear me, "He told us this would have to be a last resort plan as it would require a great sacrifice from all elves and our beasts. That sacrifice would be our magic, therefore our very lives. The details have not been explained yet, but that is the plan. Seeing it here in your dream tells me that plan will be carried out. Now, child, what is it I can do to help you? What caused your magic to spiral and ripple through time?"

I force myself to speak as slowly and calmly as possible. Starting at the beginning of my journey in Reverie, I tell the elf all that has happened. She listens patiently and does not speak until I *am completely finished.*

"I see," she says after I tell her about my breakdown in Queen Melanomie's castle. "I am sorry that we left your kind so unprepared to carry this burden. I assure you it was not our intention. It is hard sometimes, when things come so easy to you, to relate to others and see things from their perspective. We should have realized you would need more guidance and training. I am afraid there is nothing we can do to change your past or my future now. To do so may alter the course entirely and cause more harm than good. You may not even exist in my future if the things I learned here are shared with the others."

"Great!" I huff. I can never catch a break! Why can't things be easy just once?

"But perhaps," the elf continues, raising her hand to catch my attention, "there is still time to change your future. I will tell you two things and two things only. The first is about this place. The elf who created it did not intend it to be for the Dreamers. It is to be a sanctuary for wild magic, a safe place for it to remain in the world without harming others. The second is about wild magic and you, though this advice applies to all. You will find your peace when you learn balance. You yourself are the product of a balance of two worlds. Your magic is no different. Yes, you must allow your emotions to fuel your magic. That is what makes it real, after all. But do not let them consume you. Emotional reactions are much like fire, it is fast and dangerous, and once the damage is done you cannot undo it. All you can do is wait for the rain and new growth."

I ponder the elf's words. I still have a million questions, but I cannot bring myself to ask even one of them. By the time I feel like I know what I want to say, I can feel myself waking up.

"No! Not yet!" I shout up at myself. But it is too late. I look back down to see my visitors have vanished. I am standing alone in the grass beside the beach on Zoar. With a heavy sigh, I allow myself to wake up and return to Ceres.

* * * * * * * * * *

Chapter Twenty-Four ~ Treasure and Trouble

I do not wake up with a gasp or a jolt this time. I wake up calmly, as if it is the easiest thing I have ever done. My eyes open with no forced effort, and I sit up in bed.

The room is dark. I feel the space in bed beside me, but it is empty. Feeling refreshed and energized, I get out of bed and leave the room to find Apuri.

"Nedra," I call out through our private link. "Where is everyone?"

"Althea!" He calls back filled with excitement and relief. "You are up? Are you okay? We are in Queen Melanomie's throne room. Would you like us to come to you?"

"No," I reply with a laugh, "I am fine. I am coming to you."

It does not take me long to follow the hall back out to the front of the castle where the throne room is located. I find it strange to see the doors are slightly ajar, and the turtle guards are not here.

I push one of the doors open more and enter into the pearl throne room. Everyone is seated around a large white pearl table that matches Mel's throne. I have never seen it here before. I wonder where it came from.

At the sound of my footsteps, they all turn and look at me like I have risen from the dead.

"Nedra," I say cautiously through our link as I look at him, "why is everyone looking at me like that?"

"I thought it best not to tell them you were coming, to let you surprise them yourself," he replies with a laugh at his own attempt at being sly.

"Okay," I say back through our link as Apuri slides his chair back on the pearl floor and takes off running toward me. "But why are they all being so dramatic about it?"

"You don't know?" he asks, this time in a serious tone. "Althea, you have been in a magic coma for nearly two weeks."

"Two weeks!" I shout aloud. Apuri stops in his tracks. Everyone from the table watches me closely. Aspen leaves the table and walks my way in no hurry.

"Althea," Apuri says as he continues walking toward me, now at a normal, deliberate pace, "are you okay? You should not be up like this. Let Aspen take a look at you."

"Apuri, I am fine. I just woke up and I need to tell you about my dream..." He stops me from talking, wraps his arm around me, and takes me toward the table. Aspen meets us halfway and walks on my other side until I am seated in one of the pearl chairs around the table.

I look over at Nedra and say aloud, "You couldn't have just told them I was awake?"

Everyone looks at him with accusing glares. His head droops and he casts his eyes to the floor in shame.

"Really, though," I say to everyone in the room, "I am fine. I know I freaked out earlier, but I promise it will not happen again. I went to Zoar again, in my dream..."

Nobody is listening to me. They all watch Aspen as she uses her magic to check me over. She started at the top of my head and is now in front of my face. I raise my hands to stop her, and I notice my mark. It has changed again. This time, the pale white markings of the symbol have turned black.

The elf's words about magic being like fire echo in my head. It looks like I am the one that got burned. I gently rub my fingers over the mark. Nothing feels different. I decide to go ahead and let Aspen finish her checkup. Maybe more happened that I do not know about.

Apuri takes hold of my hand, his eyes on the mark, and whispers, "I thought I lost you."

"Lost me?" I reply, confused. "What are you talking about?"

"Althea," says Queen Melanomie, "what do you remember?"

I think back to the meeting room and the beach covered in wild greenery creeping into the ocean. For just a second, I think it is beautiful until I remember what it really is and the terrible thing it has done. I feel my face pale as I look back at Mel and whisper, "You told me how fast wild magic is spreading." I swallow the lump in my throat and breathe deeply through my nose to keep my composure. Slowly, I continue, "It was too much. All I could think about was all those that died because I failed. I blacked out, and Apuri and Nedra carried me to our room."

Everyone shares a worried look, like there is a secret I do not know, and they are wondering if they should tell me. They are worried I might freak out again.

"Just tell me what it is!" I shout, causing them all to jump a little in their seats. "The sooner we get this over with, the sooner I can tell you about my dream!"

"Well..." starts Apuri. But he cannot find the words to continue. As I look at him, I see there is something different, something has changed inside him, but I cannot tell what that is.

"It was a little more than that," Tsar says. He has changed as well, but for the better. I no longer see the haunted look in his eyes. He seems more sure of himself.

"What do you mean?" I ask, still confused.

Nedra lets out a dull rumbled growl from his throat as he slams one of his front clawed feet on the table.

"Let me handle this," he says for everyone in the room to hear him. Then, to just me through our private link he says in a much calmer tone, "Althea, I am going to show you what happened. Do you remember when we first met and shared our memories of finding the stone from your world? It will be much like that. Are you ready?"

"Yes," I answer, though part of me is still unsure.

I am standing in the hall outside of the room Mel took us to. I look through the door to see my friends. Standing right beside the table is Queen Melanomie, Apuri, and me! That is right, I am looking through Nedra's memories.

Okay, Mel just showed us the beach. Next, she is going to tell us about the oceans and how wild magic has spread across our continent without mercy. I watch myself in the memory, expecting to see my panic attack and removal from the room.

Here it goes, my breathing just increased. I turn and place my hands on the back of a chair for support. I am about to black out. I watch the other me and see the magic of the mark is activated. I see it swirl from the hall. Something is wrong; I can feel it in the energy. Suddenly there is a silent but deafening boom accompanied by a bright light.

I recognize that magic. It is mine. It is the same magic that was released when I was standing in the center of the Pyramid. I released everything that was inside of me. The last time I did that, I died. It is a miracle I did not die this time.

Queen Melanomie quickly throws the drapes from her gown around herself for protection. It works. The magic simply bounces off of her like hitting a mirror. Everyone except Apuri falls back into the hall before it reaches them.

I watch in horror as the chair I grab melts beneath my fingers. Apuri is not protected. The magic not only hits him, it goes right through him. I watch as it knocks the wind from him. He takes only a moment, however, before recovering himself in time to catch me before I fall to the floor myself.

Together we stand before I fall into him again.

I can see the pain in his eyes as he carries me – nearly unconscious – from the room.

Suddenly, I am back in the throne room with my companions. They all watch me silently, waiting for me to speak. I open my mouth, but I am not sure what to say. I see now why they had such a hard time explaining it to me. I cannot even explain it to myself.

"I tried to heal you immediately," Aspen says from beside me. "But your magic was too strong. You would not let me in. I came back every day to try again. Each day you were calmer than the last. Finally, I was able to do enough to stop the destruction you were doing to yourself. After that, you just had to heal on your own until you woke up."

"What do you mean? What destruction?" I ask, still trying to understand what happened.

"Do you remember the magic you used inside the Pyramid?" Aspen asks. "It freed everything that was trapped there, yes, but it was a destructive magic." She unconsciously flexes her shoulder blades. I realized at that moment that I was the reason Aspen's wings were injured when she was inside the Pyramid. I gasp in shock and horror.

"Oh, Aspen," I whisper as tears well in my eyes, "I had no idea! I am so sorry!"

She smiles with sincerity and assures me there is no reason to apologize. "It was my own fault for flying too close," she says with a shrug. "Anyway," she continues, "what you did here was the same thing only..." she hesitates as she looks at my mark. "Only this time, you were targeting yourself. The magic that hit the room was simply overflow. You took the brunt of it. It really is a miracle you are sitting here in front of us."

"Althea," says Apuri, still holding my hand, "we thought you were going to die. You were unresponsive. Even Nedra could not get through to you."

I am not sure what to say. I look at everyone around the table. "I am sorry," I say as tears fall down my face. As I wipe them away, I realize I interrupted a meeting. I breathe and regain control of myself before asking, "What is happening? What have I missed?"

Mel smiles, happy to get back to business. I think of Tilda. I wonder how well the two know each other. "Well, Dreamer," she uses my official title to indicate business is back in order, "more scouts have returned, but I am afraid it will still be a few more days before the viewing room will be completely renovated. In the meantime, we were discussing our other options of dealing with wild magic. Just this morning Nedra received word from the sky faeries. They have finished making the armor for the one with the mirrors and are on their way there now."

"No," I say in a hurry, pushing my questions about the viewing room to the back of my mind, "Nedra, we need to stop them. There is no need for them to do that anymore. I know what happened to the pixies. They are not going to find them in a mirror. Quickly, catch them before they go back into Sage's shop. I really have a bad feeling about him."

"I will tell them." He replies curtly through our link.

"Okay," I say, "what else has happened?"

Mel sits back in her chair with a smile and says, "Perhaps this is the time for you to tell us."

"That's right," says Tsar, "you were saying something about your dream when you came in. What did you find out?"

I am relieved to finally tell everyone what I learned from the elf in my dream. "Well, as I said earlier, I went back to *Zoar*. Only this time I was not alone. Standing in the grass by the pink beach was an elf and a Chobudda! She said she came to me because I used magic that was so strong it rippled back through time. So far back that the island had not even been created yet. It was only a theory, a mere suggestion, being presented to a group of which this elf was a member."

Everyone's jaws drop. Satisfied with the reactions, I continue, "It turns out the island is in fact not at all created for Dreamers, though I have appreciated its use. The island was created as a last resort emergency protocol to save the world in case wild magic ever got out of control. Do you get it?" I laugh as I say the words, "The island has been our answer all along!"

I feel on the verge of hysteria as I finally deliver the punchline to be followed by no reaction, not even the drop of a jaw. I guess my delivery was off.

Lady Nell finally speaks up, "Did this elf and chobudda happen to tell you what to do with that information? How are we supposed to get wild magic to it when it is killing everyone who comes near it, even you?"

"No," I say honestly, "they were gone, or I was awake, well, both actually, before I could ask. They did say, though, that for the island to be possible, it would take the sacrifice of all of the remaining elves-turned-pixies and chobudda. When they sensed wild magic was loose on the world, they knew they had to work quickly to create the island. That is why they all disappeared without a trace, without a word."

"Okay, so that's two questions answered," says Mel in her business tone of voice. "If we don't have the answer for how, I guess it's time to move forward and contact the faeries in the Painted Forest."

She places both hands upon the smooth table top and closes her flat silver eyes. Water begins to flow from the tips of her fingers. Each vein continues on its own separate path until they all pool together in the center of the table. The table begins to vibrate. It makes a strange sound.

I realize as I listen harder, that the sound coming from the table is an echo of our conversation. Everything that we said here is being put into the pool of water.

Notyal, happy to be back at his Lady's side, promptly presents a sleek glass bottle. When the vibrations stop, she lifts her hands bringing the water back to her. She takes the bottle from Not and clasps it tight between both hands. The water goes straight into the bottle without spilling even a drop. When it is full, Notyal corks it and takes it from the queen's webbed hands.

I watch as he carries it out of the room as quickly as possible.

"He will send it directly to Tilda," says Mel. "She will be able to play back our entire conversation for the rest of the advisors to hear and send back a reply. We have a magical current that flows straight to the water advisor's house. There is no need to send it to the others as they will not be able to use it without a water faerie. I will also add a message for them to seal off all water entrances into Reverie to prevent wild magic from entering that way. At the rate it is growing, we need to be diligent in our security. This private current, coming straight from Ceres, has waters from all oceans in it. That means whatever is in the Atlantic waters will also be here and in that current, so it will be safe. Unfortunately, it is too small of a current for anyone, save perhaps a shrimp, to travel." She taps her chin in thought and mumbles, "Perhaps I will recruit some shrimp to be scouts."

I start to laugh, but realize she is not joking. I quickly bite the inside of my cheek to stop from laughing. I glance over to Apuri to see if he saw. My urge to laugh subsides immediately. Something is different about him. His eyes. I cannot quite figure it out, but now I know the cause. Me. Or at least my magic.

I give his hand a squeeze which he returns without any emotion. He is distancing himself from me, already. This is exactly what Aspen did. It is not just the pain, it is my magic. It is like a poison. I drop his hand for fear of hurting him more.

Aspen is the only one who notices. She looks at me with a sincerity that tells me she knows what is going on. I shake my head with a quiet subtlety to tell her not now. Nobody else has noticed that I can tell, and I would like to leave it that way. She nods once and refocuses on Queen Melanomie.

"Nell," I change the focus of my thoughts before

everyone else catches on, "where is Noni?"

"Oh, she is with some of the other children in the castle. Mel has a giant conch shell building on the beach that is made just for children. There is a small pool to play and relax in and plenty of perfectly moist sand for building sand sculptures. The children build whatever they like, and when they are finished, the sculptures are magically relocated all over the beach for everyone to enjoy. Noni has been there nonstop when she is not eating or sleeping."

I smile. I am happy she is able to retain her innocence in all of this madness.

"It sounds like a place I might have to visit before we leave." I say. Everyone laughs. Everyone except Apuri, he just smiles.

Mel stands and says, "I will assemble some of my best scouts so we can start doing more research on the Atlantic waters and Zoar. We can meet back here before retiring for the night, maybe after we have all eaten." She waits for everyone else to leave and calls for me to stay back.

I walk over to her after telling Apuri to go ahead and get some rest. He does not argue. I watch as he slowly exits the throne room with a squint at the brighter light from the hall. I find myself cringing in empathy.

I whisper to Nedra through our private link, "Nedra, stay with him. Alert me immediately if he gets worse."

"You can count on me, Althea. Would you like Aspen to keep watch as well?"

"I will get her if needed. Thank you, Nedra."

Mel places a webbed hand on my arm. I turn to look at her. "Keep a close eye on him," she says with sincere concern in her voice. I feel the pit in my stomach grow deeper and the knot in my throat tighter. She sees it, too. Unable to speak, I nod in response. I breathe through my nose and force myself to swallow the ever-tightening knot without crying. I look at her for any sign that she, too, was affected by my explosion of magic.

As far as I can tell, she looks as healthy as when we arrived. I guess she successfully shielded herself against any harm from my magic. I wish Apuri could have done the same.

"How are *you* feeling?" Mel asks. Her silver fish-like eyes glisten as she watches me.

I open my mouth to reply but realize I do not know the answer to that question. I do not feel any pain, physically, but emotionally and mentally I do not feel stable. I shrug my shoulders silently.

"Do you feel up to helping me?"

Finding my voice, I reply, "Yeah, I think that would help honestly."

"Wonderful!" she says with a cheery smile. "I have a theory I want to test." She winks and guides me out of the throne room.

She loops her arm through mine, and we walk like this down a hall I have never traveled. The walls are still made of packed sand, but the floor in this hall is a mural made of sea glass. It starts as simple swirling water waves made of blue, green, and white on a sandy brown background.

"Beautiful, aren't they?" Mel says admiring the art as we walk slowly down the hall. "You would never guess by seeing this hall that these were not one of nature's creations."

"What do you mean?" I ask, curious to know what she is talking about.

"Sea glass," she says as she gestures to the floor with her free hand. "The ocean may have tumbled it enough to smooth the surface and make it appear natural, but it is man-made glass. Broken bottles and such from the human realm find their way into the seas. Over time, this is what happens to them. Notyal and I used to scavenge for them. That was a lifetime ago, before I became queen. If my father knew about it, he would not have been happy. He always said our job was to protect the waters, not the humans. That was God's job." She rolls her eyes at her father's quote.

"I, on the other hand," continues Mel, "feel it is our duty

as living sentient beings on this earth to help any and all that we can. I keep the glass as a reminder that anything can be transformed, and there is beauty in even the harmful and unwanted."

The floor mural shows a few fish between the waves guiding us down the hall. The fish get bigger as we walk further down the hall until we walk on dolphins, sharks, and finally, a whale. We are nearing the end of the hall now. After we step past the whale's head, the mural spreads up onto the wall as well. The hall is now decorated with mer creatures from ceiling to floor. Some are the iconic half-fish half-human creatures we are familiar with. Others are more like Mel and Not, with a prominent sea creature form.

"This mural was not made until after I was crowned Queen. It was a gift from Notyal. He secretly instructed all scouts to gather sea glass every time they were out. I had to travel to a distant sea for my first birthday on the throne. I was upset because I usually spent that day with..." She stops herself from finishing the sentence. "When I returned home, Notyal rushed me straight here to see the mural."

We reach a door at the end of the hall. On the left side of the door, the mural depicts a man, the piper. The framing on the opposite side of the door shows Queen Melanomie. They both face inward toward the seashell lined door frame and each other.

"It is beautiful!" I say. It really is. The color palette was limited to white, blue, green, brown, and a few red and purple sea glass pebbles. The artistry in this mural, though, makes you think they were not limited at all, but instead chose this particular palette intentionally.

"This was my room for the majority of my life," Mel says, breaking me from the trance of the mural's beauty. She opens the door and steps inside. "When I became Queen, I had to move into the royal chambers as did all of my predecessors before me. I still come here, though, when I want to be alone and remember."

The walls inside the room are not decorated with sea glass murals. They are packed sand as in the rest of the castle, but they are decorated here and there with shells or drawings and the occasional scribbles. It is weird to think of Queen Mel as a teenage girl, but that is exactly what this room shows.

Mel walks straight to the other side of the room to a large treasure chest. It looks like it was plundered right off of a real pirate's ship. Something tells me that is exactly where it came from.

She kneels down in front of the chest and unclasps the lock. She opens the chest with a mighty push to reveal her treasures inside. I want to see what is inside, but I feel intrusive. I stand awkwardly by her large clam shell bed while she rummages through the chest.

"Got it!" She says excitedly. "Althea, come here."

I am surprised to see the chest is not filled with jewels and gold. Instead, there are papers, books, and an array of knick-knacks. She pulls out a small wooden box from the very bottom of her treasures.

Before she has time to open the box or hand it to me, an alarm goes off. It is a shrill cry, like that of a banshee. Clasping her box tight, Mel takes off in a sprint down the muraled hall. I quickly shut her door, cover my ears, and do my best to catch up with her. That is much easier said than done as she knows these halls like the back of her hand.

She turns a corner some distance ahead of me. I push harder to catch up, but I am too late. I turn the corner after her to find the hall splits into three different directions. I look down each hall, but Mel is nowhere in sight. Moving as quickly as possible, I decide to stay straight and run as fast as I can. The alarm is still screaming in my brain.

"Althea!" Nedra's voice drowns the alarm in my head and causes me to stop short. I trip over my feet and barely catch myself before slamming face first into the sandy floor.

"Nedra, what is it?"

"It is Apuri. Bring Aspen quick!"

I feel the blood drain from my face. Apuri! I run again, this time with every ounce of energy in my body.

When I reach the end of the hall, I turn without thinking. After another turn, I realize I have no idea where I am. I am hopelessly lost. Tears fall down my face as, once again, I feel time slipping through my fingers.

"Nedra, I do not know which way to go."

"Clear your mind, Althea. Follow our link. Remember, we can find each other from opposite ends of the earth with our link."

"Unless it is blocked by sodocs inside a magical pyramid constructed with wild magic," I answer sarcastically. Nedra simply huffs.

"Nedra," I change the conversation to a more serious one, "do you know what is happening? Why are alarms sounding?"

"Give me a moment. I will see what I can find out. You follow the link, get Aspen from her room – I believe it is four doors down from ours – then, get here as quickly as possible. He does not look well at all. "

I stop running to close my eyes and focus on my link with Nedra. I feel a pull at my back. I turn around. The pull is now in front of me. I follow it, running as fast as I can while still focusing on the link. At the first intersection of halls, the link pulls to my left. I turn left and feel it in front of me once again.

I go on like this, following the pull of my link with Nedra, for what feels like an eternity with the banshee cry blaring around me and Nedra's words blaring inside my head.

"He does not look well at all."

I feel like a hamster running loops in tunnels. Just when I think I will never reach them, I find myself in the hall with our rooms. I quickly count doors and run to the one I hope is Aspen's.

"Nedra, I am almost there." Without stopping to knock, I open the door and rush in to find two beds on the left side of the room. Tsar sits holding Noni on one, while Lady Nell lies on the floor at the foot of the other with Aspen leaning over her. Her hands are hovering over Nell's body.

"Aspen," I call. She holds up one of her hands telling me to wait. I feel the link just down the hall. Apuri is waiting.

"Aspen!" I shout. Again, she holds up her hand. Tsar looks at me. I see dread in his eyes. I wish I could stay and ask what happened. I wish I could help take care of Lady Nell.

I can't.

Without another word, I turn back into the hall and run four doors down to the link, to Nedra, to Apuri.

"Turns out that was Nell's room," I say to Nedra. "But Aspen was there. She cannot come." I answer before he has time to ask where she is. "Something happened to Nell, too. I will have to try this without her."

It is hard to get to the bed with Nedra cramped into the small room. I wonder how he got in here anyway.

My heart stops when I see Apuri still and pale on the bed.

"Nedra, is he?"

"He is still alive," Nedra answers. "I believe he just passed out from the pain. He has only been like this for a few minutes."

"What pain?" I ask. I hate not knowing what was going on with him. The lingering guilt of knowing my magic is what caused his pain makes me sick.

"In his head," says Nedra. "He had the blankets pulled up over it when he first laid down. When those alarms went off, I thought he was going to die. His hands were pressed on either side of his head like he was trying to keep it from splitting open from the inside. He kept screaming in pain. He began to cry. I am sorry, Althea, I did not know how to help him. I felt foolish just standing here, but I dared not leave him alone. Finally, he just stopped. I do not think the pain stopped, though. I think he just passed out."

I walk over to examine Apuri closer. I gently sit on the edge of the bed beside him.

I rest my hand on his chest. He is breathing! It is shallow, but he is breathing.

I lean close to his ear and whisper, "Apuri, it is me, Althea. I do not know if you can hear me. Apuri, I am so sorry. I promise, I will fix this." I kiss his forehead and whisper, "I love you."

I stand up beside the bed and turn toward him. Using my magic, I feel with my hands inches above his body for any ailments. With one hand above his head and the other over his chest I take a breath and open myself up ready to let my energy flow. As soon as I open the flow I feel his pain. It feels like someone stuck a fork into the energy source of a power station. My hands are searing with pain. I clench my teeth in an attempt to push through the pain and heal him.

I feel the golden healing energy building inside me. I just hope I can hold on long enough to help Apuri. It spreads from my core to my arms and then my hands. It is not powerful enough. The energy is zapped as soon as it leaves my hands. Whatever is inside Apuri is absorbing my energy and using it as fuel to make itself stronger. Apuri groans.

I quickly cut off the energy flow. I fall back on the floor and begin to weep. Not only did I cause this pain, but I cannot even heal him.

Suddenly, the alarms stop. I do not know whether to be relieved or not. The silence that fills the air feels suffocating.

"Nedra, did you ever find out what triggered the alarms?"

"The glamour in Sengsourya is failing. Petricha and all of the guards are evacuating as quickly as possible. Any time the glamour fails, an alarm sounds to alert all faeries so they can seek safety and reinforce the glamour. Once Sengsourya is evacuated, a glamour will be placed around the feather tree to seal it off for protection."

I wipe my tears away and stand up. "I need to talk to Mel. Nedra, will you keep watch over him? Let me know as soon as he wakes."

He nods with an ember glowing rumble.

I thank him and squeeze by to find Mel.

I push open one of the massive throne room doors to find Mel sitting on her throne in front of a crowd of mer.

At first, I was not sure where I would find her, but I took a moment to think like a queen might. If the queen was needed by her people, she would have to be accessible to them. The throne room would be the best place for that to happen.

I slip quietly into the room and wait at the back while Queen Melanomie handles business. I am not sure how long she has been speaking, but it sounds like she is about to wrap things up.

"The Atlantic and Ceres are safe, but you will no longer be able to travel. We will have to move all creatures here and to the Atlantic. Keep close watch to prevent chaos. Go! Save as much life as you can."

The turtle guards open the doors, and the mer flood out of the room in a frenzy. I wait until only the queen and I remain in the room before I approach her throne.

"Althea!" She rises to greet me. "I apologize for earlier. When duty calls." She claps her hands together and raises them in a motion to show it is out of her control.

"I understand," I say with a laugh. "I had to go check on Apuri. Nedra explained what was happening. Has everyone made it out of Sengsourya safely?"

"Not yet, but they should be out soon. It is terrible, being forced from your home in order to survive. We are doing the very same to all the living in the seas as we speak. It is now up to us to ensure as many creatures as possible survive. I fear to know how many have already been lost. But enough of that for now. How is Apuri?"

I resist the urge to cry as I shrug and shake my head. "Nedra," I instruct him through our link, "try to contact Aspen again. Maybe she is finished with Lady Nell and can help Apuri now."

"I will, Althea," he replies.

Mel, seeing my distress, walks toward me and says, "Come, we have business of our own to finish." She once again loops her arm through mine and leads me to her treasure.

This time the little box is sitting in a secret hole inside her throne. She leaves me at the bottom of the throne steps while she fetches it. She quickly steps down to bring me the box, holding it up between both palms. I take it from her open hands. It is a plain little box no bigger than the palm of my hand. I undo the small clasp and lift the lid to see a shimmering pastel green scale. It fills the box from edge to edge. It is the shape of a shell with a tuft of rainbow feathers at the top.

I take it out of the box gently and examine it.

"Is this what I think it is?" I ask in a whisper.

Mel's silver eyes are inches from my own and the scale. "I have never been sure. I have heard stories but never seen one myself. I was hoping you could confirm it."

"It is much larger than any I have seen. And to have these many colors...he must have been one of the elders. It almost looks like... Where did you find it?"

"I do not remember the exact place, but many years ago when I was just a wee guppy swimming the seas, I ventured far from home. I was gone, alone and afraid, for many days. I thought I was going to die without ever seeing my father again. I told myself to just keep swimming. Finally, the waters changed. Everything seemed brighter, happier. I cautiously swam to the surface. The sun was so bright I had to quickly go back under. Before I did, though, I swear I saw something flying away from me. When I went back to see again, I found this floating on top of the water. Somehow, I found my way home within a few hours. I was back at Ceres before nightfall. It is something I still question the reality of today. If not for that scale, I would not trust my own memories."

"Well, as far as I can tell, you saw a chobudda flying over the ocean." As soon as I say it, it makes me think. "Why would a chobudda be flying over the middle of the ocean away from any land?"

"I have always wondered the same thing," Mel says. "That was until you told us about your dream with the origin story of the island, Zoar. There is not an island in all the oceans we do not know about, even ones hidden by glamour, unless said island was only created say, a couple of weeks ago. My theory is this, what if on that day I was lost at sea, there was a chobudda, and possibly even an elf with it, scouting for the location of the future island?"

I stand silent for a moment processing her theory in my mind. I am not sure why they would wait so long to scout for the island. And if that is what happened, how do we find that location now? Mel said she did not know the place. We cannot just allow ourselves to drift aimlessly at sea until we float upon the location by chance. By chance...

"Mel, you said you were just a small child when this happened?" She nods. "And how old are you now? What I'm thinking," I rush to explain when she looks taken aback, "is that maybe you getting lost was not an accident. I have truly believed all my life that everything happens for a reason. Sometimes it is as simple as cause and effect, but sometimes there is a deeper influence, maybe even from God Himself. Call it fate, destiny, or what have you."

"Okay, I understand what you are saying, but what does my age have to do with it?" She does not sound offended, even though she still has not answered my question. Instead, she sounds curious.

"Well, I am not sure. I mean, I am thinking if you were old enough, you could have been alive when the sodocs first released wild magic from its original sources. If that is the case, that could have been why the chobudda was out scouting for the island. The time had come to put their plan, or at least the foundation for it, into action."

While still withholding her age, she replies, "Well, I cannot argue with that one. I may not have proof that you are right, but I definitely do not have proof you are wrong. So, how do you suppose we find this mystery location?"

I laugh and say, "That, I am still not sure of."

"Do you think any of your friends might be able to help?"

"First, I need to check on Lady Nell and then Apuri again." .

Mel smiles and says, "I will meet up with you later."

Without another word, I hand the box with the scale inside back to Queen Melanomie and head out of the throne room.

"Nedra," I say through our private link as I run toward the hall with our rooms, "I am coming back to check on Nell. How is Apuri?"

"Still resting," he hums. It sounds like Nedra was resting as well. I leave them both to it while I head into the room four doors down from my own.

This time I knock and wait for an answer before opening the door.

"Come in!" Aspen's voice echoes from the other side of the door. I push it open to find Lady Nell, tended by Aspen, lying in her bed.

I look around the room but nobody else is here. "Where are Tsar and Noni?" I ask as I approach the bed.

Nell pushes herself up into a sitting position. "They went to play on the beach. Tsar said Noni did not need to be cooped up too long. I think he needed the air more than Noni, honestly."

I laugh with them. "How are you?" I ask Nell as I sit at the foot of the bed.

"Better." She says with an attempted smile. "Somewhat," she adds after Aspen scoffs while pressing a damp cloth to Nell's head.

"She had a vision," Aspen says in a serious tone. "First one since the fall of the Pyramid. It took its toll. I am afraid we will not be able to join everyone tonight."

"We won't either. Apuri is still not well, and I cannot leave without him. I will speak to Melanomie. I wanted to check on you first."

"Thank you," says Lady Nell.

I stand and walk to the door. Aspen follows me into the hall. "I am sorry about earlier," she says in a quiet voice. "I did not mean to ignore you about Apuri. She just collapsed and I had to take care of her. How is he?"

"I am not sure. Nedra said his head was hurting something terrible. The alarms made the pain so bad he finally passed out from too much. Honestly, I am worried. I do not know what to do about it though. I tried to heal him and it was like a thousand volts of energy grabbed hold of me and would not let go." I begin to cry. "Aspen, that is what he feels inside his head, and it is all my fault."

"Hey, don't say that. You must not blame yourself for this. It will be okay; he will get better."

I wipe my face and say, "Nedra said he was still resting. I guess I will return to Queen Melanomie for now and inform her our mission tonight will have to wait. Before I go, what was Nell's vision?"

She frowns and drops her head. "I don't know. She said it was only a fragment and it did not make sense. She hopes she will have another one to understand. As soon as she does, I will let you know."

"Thank you," I say sincerely.

Aspen heads back inside Lady Nell's room, and I turn back the way I came. I hope Mel is still in her throne room. I really do not want to get lost in these halls again.

The throne room is empty. Instead of searching through the maze of halls, I ask Nedra if he can relay the message through to Mel or Not. He agrees and I return to my room to check on Apuri and get some rest.

At first, I worried about even lying in the bed beside Apuri for fear of hurting him further. Nedra assures me that it is only my magic that has any ill effects on Apuri, and he will alert me at the first sign of change, better or worse.

I thank him and allow myself to slowly drift off to sleep.

Chapter Twenty-Five ~ A Bird's-Eye View

I am on Zoar. I look around for any elves or chobudda, but it seems I am alone. I walk the island slowly and intentionally.

I want to soak in every detail of this place and never forget it.

I am not sure if I will still be able to return here after wild magic takes up residence, however that is going to happen.

I suddenly get an idea!

Maybe I can use my magic to lift myself up high above the island. With a bird's-eye-view I may be able to see further out to the sea. If I can see far enough to spot any other islands or some sort of landmark, we would know where to go!

I walk to where the orchard meets the mountain top, the highest point on the island.

Once there, I use my magic to gather all of the air around me in a large bubble. Slowly, and with careful focus, I begin to lift myself off the ground.

I make it no more than a foot into the air when my throat tightens, my stomach and hands clenched tight, and I fall straight *back to the ground, hard.*

I land on my backside and scrape my elbows on the mountain's rocky surface.

Fighting the urge to cry, I roll over onto my knees and push myself back up.

I dust off, take a few deep breaths, and give it another go.

This time I fall before my toes even leave the dirt!

Frustrated, I sit down on the ground. I think back to the day in the woods with the hegira when I first tried this trick on some food out of my pack.

I have to focus better! I rub my hands on my thighs and stand up again.

Okay, focus. I want to be up there. I look up to the clear blue sky above me.

Maybe that is it. I need to literally focus on where I want to go.

I give it a third try, but this time, I keep my gaze skyward. I only look down when I am certain the ground is far below me.

Slowly, I let my head fall back into its normal position. Careful to keep my focus and breathing steady, I chance a glance below.

I clench my teeth and breathe fast through my nostrils as I look back at the sky for a moment.

I lifted myself up so high that the trees below me are nothing more than soft green dots.

Once I have control of myself again, I return my gaze to the island below. This time I look at the whole island.

My breath is taken away by the sight below me. The island is perfectly and completely circled by a bright rainbow-colored reef able to be seen clearly through the water. Not only that, but the island itself is actually in the shape of an equilateral triangle.

What I see below me is an exact replica of the mark on my arm!

It is hard to believe. If I was not seeing it right now with my own two eyes, I probably would not believe it.

I wish I had thought of this sooner!

Though, to be honest, I still am not sure what to do with this information. It is beautiful and curious, and I am sure it means something, even if that something is what we have already discovered about Zoar.

But as of this moment, I still do not have any answers.

I squint as I look out as far as possible over the ocean. Nothing.

I turn myself in the air and look again. Again, nothing.

I feel myself waking up and lose my focus.

My heart races as I begin to plunge through the air back toward the island.

* * * * * * * * * *

As quick as it happened, it ends. I jolt upright in bed and place my hand over my racing heart. I am still alive. I glance around the room to see what caused me to wake up, but I see nothing different than when we went to sleep.

I look at Apuri; he is still sleeping heavily. I use my link and feel for Nedra. He, too, is still asleep. I get myself a drink of cold water out of our bedside spicket then return to bed.

I lie down, cover up, and close my eyes. I am not sure what woke me from the dream, but hope this time my sleep is more restful.

Chapter Twenty-Six ~ Gratitude in Chaos

has been two days since the alarms of Sengsourya have sounded. We are eating breakfast together, all of us.

Apuri and Nell both seem to be better. Apuri has not said anything about his headaches, and I do not know how to approach the subject with him. I can feel the distance growing between us. It makes me sick to my stomach.

Queen Melanomie and I told everyone else about the chobudda scale and our theory of its connection to Zoar yesterday morning. Not knowing what to do with that information, we decided to put it back in its box until we could figure something out.

The rest of the day drug on. Lady Nell still did not feel well and was resting except for meal times. She still has not recalled her vision either. She and Aspen apologized and explained, "Unfortunately, these things cannot be forced or rushed."

I told them I understood. We will just have to wait. Aspen and Nanoaj watched over and tended to her until this morning when she assured us she "felt more herself."

Apuri had another headache as soon as he woke up yesterday. He was not out of bed for more than ten minutes when he ran to the bathroom to throw up. He went back to bed without breakfast and slept most of the day under Nedra's watch. Notyal also frequently popped in to check on him when he was not needed by Queen Melanomie.

I spent the day walking the beaches alone with my thoughts. I do not think I was as productive as I should have been. To be honest, I spent more time looking at the mark, feeling guilty about it, and wishing I was back on Zoar.

Notyal has put himself in charge of caring for Nedra and Nanoaj. When they were playing the roles of caretakers inside the rooms, he would bring them food and ensure they were getting enough rest.

This morning he has taken them out to stretch their wings and mingle with some of the sea dragons. He said Inugo has been asking if they would have time to get away. He never saw dragons of land and sky before we came through the gateway tree. He is eager to learn as much about them as possible before we have to leave again.

I could tell it was hard for both of them to leave their wards this morning, but "one must take care of him or herself before being able to fully care for another." That was Not's argument to get them out of the castle this morning. He gave me an accusing glare as he said it. I know he was talking about me, too. I simply ignored him and urged Nedra to go so he would leave me alone.

Now, the rest of us are sitting at a table together eating our breakfast as we mull over our own thoughts in silence.

I want to ask Apuri about his headaches, but I know he does not want to talk about it. Honestly, I am not sure I really do either, but the guilt is gnawing at me from the inside. I glance across the table at Lady Nell. I can tell she, too, is dealing with her own guilt at her inability to recall her vision.

Noni and Tsar look to be half asleep still. They spent

most of the day playing at the beach. I am not sure when they returned to their room, but from the looks of it, I would say it was later than it should have been.

Aspen is watching Nell close like she expects her to fall to the floor again at any moment.

Just after Apuri finishes his second plate and returns with a third, I decide to break the somber silence.

"I went to Zoar in my dreams again."

"Was one of them there again?" asks Apuri in a serious tone. I know he means the elves.

"I looked for them when I first got there; but no, I was alone. I had a thought, an idea. If I could lift myself up somehow to fly over the island and get an aerial view, I may be able to see further out to sea and get some sort of clue to its location."

He nods as he chews on a piece of shrimp, "Sounds like a good idea. I take it by the look on your face it did not work." I shake my head to confirm his guess.

"So, are you going to do anything today?" The question comes out in a harsh accusatory tone. I am not sure if it was intentional or merely a side effect of the damage I caused.

It takes me a moment to refocus my thoughts before replying, "I did not see anything that gave me clues to the location, but I did discover that the island itself is shaped like my mark. There is a rainbow ring around the island which is a triangle. It is impossible to notice from the ground. To answer your other question, Mel and I will be in her chambers. We are going to talk with the advisors to check in about Sengsourya, the hotels, and the glamour. We are also going to see if we can ask some of the Sky faeries to help out in the search for Zoar."

"Sounds like a busy day; mind if I join you?" he asks in a milder tone than his previous question.

"I don't mind at all! You may all join if you like. You may think of something to say that we don't. The more the merrier."

"I think I will take Noni out for the day if you do not

mind," says Nell. "I feel the need for a little bonding." She looks at her daughter who has now fallen asleep on the bench between her and Tsar. "Though, we may return to the room for a morning nap first."

"That is fine. Have fun! We wil update you with any information tonight at supper."

"I, too, will pass," says Aspen. "I need some personal quiet time for meditating."

"We will see you all tonight, then," I say with a smile.

We finish our breakfast and get started on our day. Nell, Tsar – carrying Noni, and Aspen head back toward the hall with our rooms while Mel, Not, Apuri, and I make our way toward Mel's chambers.

As we walk the sandy halls toward her private chambers, I cannot help but remember our time here when I learned to use magic. I smile at the memory. I was so nervous, afraid, and excited all at once. I am surprised I did not explode from all the emotions. The image of the melted chair and Apuri from my emotional magic combustion comes to mind. Poor choice of words, perhaps.

I think back to that little flame dancing in my hand. My magic seemed so fragile then, so innocent. The Spirits did say my magic has grown. We reach Mel's chambers and follow her to a four-foot wide by two-foot tall well. She tells us to sit on the floor around the well. I sit upon the floor, cross my legs, and lean over to look into the well. It does not look like anything special.

"What now?" Asks Apuri.

"Now," says Mel, pulling a small plain shell from a bag at her side, "we make a call to Tilda."

She says, "Tilda, Mel's calling for the advisors," into the concave side of the shell, then *plinks* it into the water with a swift toss. We all watch as it sinks deeper and deeper below the surface of the water into the depths of the well until it disappears completely.

We wait quietly for a few minutes until I begin to think

nothing is going to happen. Suddenly, the surface of the water begins to ripple. Mel touches it with the tips of both her index fingers and pulls her hands up creating an arch with her fingers meeting at the top.

An arch-shaped non reflective mirror-like surface appears above the rippling water. It reminds me of the moon in Petricha's loft.

"Hello?" Mel says to the non reflective mirror. When there is no answer, she touches it. It begins to ripple before splashing apart into a convulsion of water. When it finally settles down, it takes on a new form.

Now, the surface of the well's water holds the shape of tiny advisors.

"Mel! Althea!" says Tilda, "How are you? Is everything okay?"

Mel responds, "Yes, well, as okay as it can be considering what is going on out there."

"How is everyone there?" I ask.

Sue answers, "Sengsourya has been successfully evacuated and the Feather Tree has been sealed off until wild magic is fixed. The sanctuaries are still running smoothly, but I am not sure how long the humans will keep telling themselves we are not real. It may go poorly when that thought process stops. You really do not have much time. Have you found the location of Zoar yet?"

"No, that is actually why we are calling. We have learned more about Zoar, but in order to find it, I believe we will need the help of some sky faeries. If we are looking from both above and below we have a better chance of finding Zoar faster."

"Very well," she replies, "Petricha, take whomever you choose and leave for Ceres at the end of this call. Is there anything else we can do to aid you, Dreamer?"

"I am not really sure, but I do want to inform you of the dream I had last night."

I explain my dream on Zoar to them as I did to my friends this morning, careful to not forget any details.

"Interesting," says Eart, "Dreamer, I will do more research into the symbol to see if that helps unearth any answers."

"Thank you, Eart."

Apuri impatiently asks, "And what about the hegira? Have they all made it back safe inside the glamour?"

"They have," Sue answers. "You may speak to them later. They are scattered throughout the Painted Forest. Inform us which of the hegira you wish to speak with, and we will let them know."

"No, that is okay," replies Apuri in a somber voice, "I just wanted to make sure they were safe."

Feather speaks next, "Lou says she is unable to visit the island. She has been there a few times without control, but something has happened. She said she felt something, like energy blasting across the world. It rippled for some time. Since then, she has not dreamt of the island anymore. We heard your conversation, the one Queen Melanomie sent to Tilda. Lou wants to make sure you are okay. She thinks your... episode is what she felt."

My chest swells with worry, love, and appreciation. "Tell her thank you for checking on me, but I am okay now." I feel guilty for the words as soon as I see Apuri.

"Althea," Clementine says, "how long do you think it will take?" She pauses before going on. I can hear the sadness in her voice as she says, "The earth is not well, Sweetie, and it is getting worse by the day. These beautiful weeds are killing our precious garden. She needs your help."

"I know," I say sincerely, "just keep hope; we will find it!"

Sue takes over the conversation again in her authoritative tone, "If that is all, Dreamer, we have order to keep here. The sky faeries will be on their way to you as soon as they are assembled."

Queen Melanomie replies, matching her tone, "We will have our guard meet them, and we will not waste any time once they are here. Send any updates, and we will do the same."

We say our goodbyes to the advisors and head back to meet the others just in time to grab a hot meal and share our news.

Noni is excited about seeing the sky faeries again.

We still do not have a fully hashed out plan, but everyone agrees to stay with us and help find Zoar. We wrap up our meal with a lighter topic of sand sculptures as Noni describes, with a bit of toddler excitement and charades, all of her favorites from the day.

She also told us about when she saw the thunder of sea dragons swimming around with Nedra and Nanoaj. She stood on the bench and jumped, twisting in midair before Tsar caught her, to show us how they dance when they swim.

Once Noni's stories are finished and our bellies are full, we exchange "Goodnights" and head back to our rooms to retire for the night.

I wish Nedra a goodnight through our private link as we walk down the hall. He sleepily replies, and I end our conversation there. He and Nanoaj are spending the night with the sea dragons.

After I make it back to my room, I decide to soak in the tub for a short while before going to bed.

A beautiful pink conch shell rests on the edge of the tub by my head. I hold it to my ear and listen to the sounds of the ocean while my body slowly relaxes in the warm, fragrant water.

I'm staying with Apuri tonight since Nedra's not here. He is already asleep. He does not seem to be in any pain at the moment. I am thankful for that. As I feel myself drift off to sleep, I wonder how we will accomplish our goals.

My thoughts are interrupted when Apuri rolls over and lays his arm around my waist. I lay my hand on top of his and allow myself to relax. Even though he is not well right now, I am thankful he is here with me.

My last thought before falling asleep is, *At least for now, everyone is safe inside Reverie. Tomorrow, we will find Zoar.*

Chapter Twenty-Seven ~ Majesty

Some time through the night Apuri's head started hurting again, and I was not able to sleep well anymore. I wandered the halls in an attempt to calm myself. I walked around without any real direction or purpose, but I was not surprised when I found myself in the mosaic sea glass hall leading to Mel's childhood room.

I walk slowly down the hall, carefully examining each colorful pebble and the picture it makes. Mel's words about the glass starting as man made trash and turning into something this beautiful by nature ring in my mind. I let the thought soothe me as I continue walking down the hall.

I stop in front of the door with the pictures of Mel and the Piper. As torn up as I am about what happened to Apuri because of me, I am thankful he is able to be here with me. I cannot imagine how Mel must feel.

I cannot help but think about the conversation Apuri and I had at Pilate's before he left to go through the mirror in Sage's shop. I cannot let things stay this way. I need to tell Apuri how I feel.

As I make my mind up to do just that and turn to walk back down the hall, Mel's door opens and I jump in surprise. I expected Mel to be sleeping in the royal chambers. I catch my breath as I turn back to the door to greet her.

"Althea, are you okay?" Mel's face is full of concern as she looks me up and down.

"I do not know," I answer honestly. She puts her arms out and pulls me into a hug. Her cool skin reminds me of Tilda. She opens the door the rest of the way and invites me in. We sit side by side on the edge of the clam shell bed.

"I am sorry if I woke you," I say. "I could not sleep so I decided to take a walk."

She waves her hand at me in dismissal as she says, "Nonsense, I have been up for a few hours myself. I was trying to figure out our plan before the sky faeries arrive in the morning."

I look around the room as if looking for a clue to help us in this situation. My eyes land on the little box holding the chobudda scale. It sits on top of the pirate treasure chest that it originally came out of. Mel follows my gaze and goes to get the scale and bring it back.

She opens the box and hands me the scale. "I have been looking at this thing for hours hoping an idea would come to me. Maybe you will have better luck."

I carefully take the scale in my hand. I can feel the slight pulse of magic in it. "Strange," I mutter under my breath as I examine it closer. Mel gives me a questioning look.

I do my best to explain my thoughts, "This scale is no longer attached to the chobudda. It has not been for a long time, and its host is in fact actually gone. But I can still feel a slight pulse of magic in it. It is similar to wild magic, but not exactly the same. I wonder, though, why it still has magic in it."

"Maybe," Mel replies, "you can feel it because your magic is linked. I am not sure why the magic is still present in the shed scale. You said the chobudda was gone, but that is not entirely true. The body may be gone, but the magic still exists in Zoar. Their spirits are still alive through their power on the island."

"Hmm, that makes sense I guess." I give her the scale back. She returns it to the box and carries the box over to the treasure chest. I look at the chest and wonder what its story might be. How many times was it plundered and passed from one chaotic vessel to another?

"Want to see something cool?" Mel interrupts my thoughts.

The question throws me off, and I'm not really sure how to answer. "Um, yeah. Sure." She skips over to me with a new gleam in her eye. I have not seen her this excited since she taught me to use magic! She offers her arm with a wink and I see I have no choice but to take it.

As soon as our elbows link, she skips toward the door dragging me along.

"Mel, where are we going?" I ask as soon as we near the end of the sea glass hall. I do not wish to dampen her spirits, but I really dislike not knowing what is going on.

She looks at me with her big silver eyes full of excitement and whispers, "I saw you musing over my chest, and I figured I would give you something better to fill your thoughts." She leans in closer and whispers, even quieter, "We are going to see a pirate ship!"

I let out a gasp unable to contain my own excitement now. "What? Really? Where? Whose was it?" I am unable to stop the flow of questions running through my mind from spilling out of my mouth. Mel just giggles and places a finger over her mouth to shush me. It is still early hours and nobody else is out and about yet. I press my lips shut and begin skipping along with Mel to the castle exit.

Before we leave the castle doors, Mel goes over to a dark cranny hidden behind the entrance. She soon returns with the same water breathable slime that Notyal gave us before we entered the Pool Tree to Ceres. "Put this on first," she says, handing me a small jar. I apply the slime as quickly as possible and we proceed out of the castle.

As soon as we are well out of the castle, Mel releases

my arm and takes off running toward the dark abyss of water surrounding the castle's underwater island. I follow after her as fast as I can, but I still find myself falling a great distance behind.

I watch in awe as Mel leaps and dives into the wall of water. I clumsily follow after, splashing my way into the liquid wall. "This way!" She waves eagerly as she turns to the left and swims with determination. I push myself forward with my hands and kick my legs at a steady pace. I know I will not catch up with Mel, she is a mer. Instead I focus on pacing myself. When I feel my energy fading, I know I have to find another way to get to my destination. I close my eyes and focus on the water around me. I feel it. I let it become a part of me. I know if I look at my arm right now, the mark would be surrounded by aquatic blues and greens.

Instead of using my own physical energy to swim through the water, I use the water to push myself forward much like when I lifted myself above Zoar with air. Tiny water bubbles cascade down my face and arms. I feel the same rush that I did when I rode the vine from Clementine's tree to the Painted Forest on my first day in Reverie.

I come up beside Mel and see my excitement mirrored on her face. "How far?" I shout. She smiles and shouts back, "Not long!" She points ahead and I see a pile of grayish rubble and unrecognizable shapes on the sea bed. As we swim closer, I come to a stop. I knew from watching movies that pirate ships were big, but seeing this in person is not something I was prepared for.

Even in its waterlogged and ruined state, the vessel in front of me is still one of the most magnificent things I have ever seen. Cruise ships of today's time may be huge, but they lack a certain quality of the heart. This ship was handcrafted; it is art!

"She's a beauty isn't she?" Mel says as I slowly swim up to the craft. All I can do is nod in response. What should be the top half of the ship is mostly gone, decaying or ruined in the wreckage. The bottom is covered with various amounts of sea life from barnacles to coral.

As I swim around the sunken pirate ship I find myself dreaming aloud, "I wonder what it was like to actually travel in one."

"I've often wondered the same myself," Mel chimes in as she swims up beside me.

Suddenly, Mel and I look at each other with the same fire in our eyes. "Are you thinking what I am thinking?" We say it simultaneously and begin to laugh.

"Seriously though," I continue, "do you think it is possible?"

"With your magic and mine combined, I don't see why not!"

"Should we tell the others? Maybe we should surprise them! Where should we do it? Here or at your castle?"

Mel thinks for a moment before replying. "I think we should take it back and let the others help. They would appreciate getting to tell us their input, and they may suggest something neither of us would ever think of. Besides, they will all be waking soon if they are not already, and they may begin to worry about us."

She is right. I forgot we left without telling anybody. "Alright then. How do we move it?"

She looks at me with a smirk and replies, "How about using that water trick you used to get yourself here? Shouldn't be too different. I will help, and we can take our first test drive."

I laugh at her suggestion. Still, it is our best bet. Using our water magic combined we manage to get the ship back in a sailing position. We both swim aboard, turn the magnificent water vessel around, and head back to Mel's castle.

We decide to park the ship on the back side of the castle where it will not be so easily seen or disturbed while we go in and join the others for breakfast.

We are pleasantly surprised to see everyone is up and eating when we approach the table.

"Where have you two been all morning?" Not asks with the most serious facial expression I have ever seen on him.

Mel and I look at each other with excitement and giggles. "You will find out soon enough," I say, not wanting to give anything away just yet. Apuri arches and eyebrow in question as I take my seat across the table from him. I am glad to see he is feeling better. I smile and shake my head in response. He will find out soon enough with everyone else.

Mel and I rush through our breakfast as quickly and quietly as possible. It is hard to make conversation when the only thing on your mind is the epic pirate ship sitting in the backyard. At the same time, we drop our utensils on the table with a clank and stand from the table.

"Let's go!" Mel says to everyone with more authority than the situation calls for. I laugh. She looks at me and eases up some. "Eh, sorry. What I mean to say is, if you are ready, let's go."

Our friends look at each other then slowly start to rise from the table and join us. I laugh again. They all look as if they may be sheep going to slaughter. "Relax!" I say with a laugh. "I promise it is nothing bad."

We lead them through the halls and toward the back of the castle to a small and very seldom-used back door. Mel and I used the door to come into the castle earlier. I go ahead and mentally call Nedra to meet us outside and to bring Nanoaj.

Mel pauses before opening the door and looks at me with a grin that reflects my own excitement. She turns to our friends and announces, "Althea and I have been thinking a lot about our upcoming mission, and after putting our heads together, we believe we have found one of the major puzzle pieces. After today we will have transportation for everyone when we go search for Zoar. Are you ready to see what is on the other side of the door?"

Noni eagerly nods her head with a grin. Apuri rolls his eyes impatiently. The others simply nod their heads or mutter agreement that they do indeed wish to see what we are going on about.

Without further ado, we open the door to our treasure.

"We are aware it needs some work," I inform them. "We already have that figured out, but we wanted each of you to have a chance to share your own input."

Noni twists her face and pokes out her tongue at the sight of the wrecked ship. I laugh and assure her we will use our magic to fix it right up. She reexamines the remains and nods, but I can tell she is not convinced.

Lady Nell, Tsar, and Aspen look interested in the new project. Perhaps they are glad to have a distraction from current events, as am I. Notyal actually does not seem all that surprised. I guess being Mel's closest friend he would have already seen sunken pirate ships firsthand.

I look at Apuri and my heart leaps in my chest. I have not seen him smile like that since we saw his family. He walks up to the ship and gently strokes the corroding boards. A little decaying wood would not phase a hegira; they have lived in houses with worse conditions. The memory of my first visit to a Nashees with Apuri and our surprise of meeting Tsar surfaces in my mind. That feels like a lifetime ago. I guess in a way it was.

I focus back on the now and realize everyone is walking around the ship to examine it closer. I decide to join them. I meet up with Mel and ask, "Think we should give them a little example of what we are thinking?" She rubs her hands together with excitement and grins before answering, "Definitely!"

Together we walk to the bow of the ship and each place a hand upon the remains. "I will take the water out," Mel says, "you rebuild the wood. Just focus on the hull for now, and, Althea, think of a strong, buoyant, wood."

"Okay, let's do this!" I focus on the wood under my hand and see the colors on my wrist change to greens and browns as I think of different trees. I do my best to recall any information I can remember about wood or boats from my lifetime. Only one comes to mind. Gopher wood. I laugh at myself as I wonder for the first time on this crazy journey if God has a hand in all this. And if so, what would He think about our own Noah's Ark rendition.

That is a thought I will have to come back to later. For now, I have a ship to restore! I feel the warm tingle of energy flow through my hand into the ship's wooden planks. They begin to change right before our eyes. What started as gray, washed out, rotten wood is becoming an almost golden hue of rich wooden planks. It takes a while to replace the whole ship hull just because of the size of it.

We finish and step back away from the ship to admire our work. Everyone else comes over to join us.

"Impressive," Apuri says, rubbing his hand along the new shipboards.

"Now is where you all come in," Mel says as she begins making steps from the sand that lead up to the top of the ship. "We will all be living on this ship together for a few days until we find Zoar. I invite each of you to walk around the ship, carefully, and think of any additions or alterations you would like to make. Althea and I will make the required alterations, and our new and improved transportation will be ready for everyone to travel comfortably together."

We all climb aboard and wander freely, but carefully, around the ship. I do my best to watch where everyone walks, and try to fix broken boards and such as I see them so nobody gets hurt, especially Noni. Everyone begins to shout their ideas across the ship to me and Melanomie. It soon becomes a chaotic mess of noise.

I hold up my hand and shout with a laugh, "Stop! Wait! This is not working." Everyone stops what they are doing and comes over to me beside the sand stairway. I wait until they are all close enough to hear before continuing. "We cannot understand what everyone is saying like this, and there is no way we are going to remember everything that we hear. You are each going to have to remember what it is you would like to add or change and write it down for us inside the castle. This could give us all some time to meditate on what we want in further detail before making a final decision as well."

"I think that is a great idea," Mel agrees. "Once we have everyone's ideas we can put them all together and come up with our final design before we apply it to the ship." She gestures toward the steps and says, "Let's all go back inside, work on our ideas, and bring them all with you to lunch. Nedra, Nanoaj, you may share your ideas if you wish as well, and someone will draw them for you. Notyal, would you go first and make sure everyone receives something to draw or write their ideas on? "

"Yes, My Lady," Not says with a bow before taking his leave down the sandy stairs. We all follow behind in a single file after giving Not enough time to get a good head start.

As soon as the last of us is inside the castle and the door is shut, Not informs Mel that everyone will have all the proper supplies delivered to his or her room. Mel thanks him and dismisses everyone.

I decide to join Mel in her room as we work on our own ideas together, but I ask Nedra and Not to help me keep an eye on Apuri. He seems to be okay right now, maybe a bit tired, but I have no idea how to know when one of the headaches is going to come on.

Mel and I are waiting at the end of the hall to the guest rooms for everyone to come out. We decided we would all have lunch in the throne room today and work on combining our ideas for the ship together to save time. She says that she has an idea to help everyone's ideas come to life before having to actually do the work. I am excited to see what it is.

Mel is the first one inside the throne room. As soon as she enters, she waves her hand over the floor in front of her. Before we are all inside, a table comes up in the middle of the room surrounded by enough chairs for each of us. Not long after we are all seated a mer with blue scaly skin and gills walks in to take our lunch orders.

Mel and I go ahead and collect the papers from everyone. I am glad we decided to let them help in the designing. Most of this I would never have even thought of.

Apuri has suggested we add a lot of windows around the hull of the ship, mostly in the lower half where everyone can see under the water while inside the ship. He also suggested we make a pool in the ship which has been seconded by Notyal on paper. It looks like they may have worked together.

In addition to the pool, Notyal has requested we add a lounging area above deck for a relaxing ride. The food arrives and is passed out to everyone. Mel and I continue looking through everyone's sketches while eating. Mel still has not explained how we are going to display everything. We wait and let her lead the meeting when she is ready. I guess she wants to get a good look at everyone's sketches and ideas before moving forward.

Noni wants a play area where she will never get bored. I think we can come up with something fun for her. I will make sure to add some nature and sky magic elements as well. Hmm... We could even connect the play area to one end of the pool and have the lounging area on the other. It will have to be a long pool.

Lady Nell has drawn rooms on her paper. She wishes us each to have our own comfortable private quarters. That should be doable below deck. We will let her help with the design aspects. Tsar's kind of surprised me. He wants us to add as many plants to the ship as possible. Perhaps he is growing weary of sea life. I think we can work that in nicely with Noni's playground theme and just add a little here and there throughout the rest of the ship.

Aspen has drawn a beautiful crow's nest that actually looks like a nest of twigs, grass, and flowers with comfy pillows thrown in. I will have to ask her while we work out the design if she wishes this to be bird size or human size.

Nanoaj and Nedra both asked if there is going to be

enough room for them to land and ride on the ship so they do not have to fly the whole time. I already planned on that. Nedra also wants a few crystal decorations if it is not too much. I assured him when he told me that it is no problem at all.

Mel wants to make all of the floors and inner walls marble and pearl. I imagine she does not get to travel away from her castle often. This is probably a way for her to take a bit of home with her while we are gone. For the first time, I think about the fact that Mel is leaving her entire kingdom to help us with this mission.

I wish I could do something to show her how much her help and friendship means to me. I will just have to make sure I do not fail and she can return to her kingdom safely. Now, we have made it through everyone's ideas. Mine is the last in the stack. I decided to design the figurehead. I am glad nobody else thought of it. I figured it should be specific to our mission, so I actually made a large protruding model of a rainbow colored circle and triangle intertwined, the mark of magic. I decorated it with intricate vines which appear to be holding it onto the ship.

I glance down at the mark on my wrist. The once white mark remains black surrounded by swirling colors. Seeing it there, the proof of my recklessness, makes me angry at myself all over again. Images of the melted chairs and Apuri in pain flash through my mind. I feel myself sinking into an abyss just like Neoinas. Before it goes any further, Mel places her hand on my shoulder and pulls me out of my mind.

I thank her with a smile which she returns before standing and walking away from the table with the stack of ideas. "We will start with what we already have and add as we go," she says as she continues walking. She goes until she gets to a large clear area and stops to set the papers on the floor. She turns toward the table and smiles like she is about to start a game. "Althea, do you want to help?"

"Sure," I reply and walk over to join her.

She points at the sandy floor and says, "It is similar to

your art magic except we are using what exists, building from it. We need to make it small enough to stay inside this room, but big enough to give us all an idea of what the actual ship will look like. Just lean down and touch the sand like this, then drag it whichever way you want. It is like drawing with the sand." She leans down, touches the sand, and swipes her finger up in a curve bringing a line of sand with it into an arch.

I hear Noni gasp behind us and laugh at her excitement. She has been building sand sculptures everyday by hand. I bet seeing this is like a new level in a game to her. Mel and I quickly go to work to recreate our ship with all the newly added details. It does not take us long to get everything worked out. We get to our last spot, the crow's nest, and I call Aspen over to elaborate on details and size. She smiles and with a flash of color changes into her bird form. This is the first time I have seen her use her bird form since the Pyramid! She flies in a circle over our heads and says, "This size!" Then, she swoops down and transforms back right beside us.

I throw my arms around her in a hug as I fight back happy tears. "I was able to successfully shift at V's after all her help, but I was not sure how long I could hold it. When I could not think of anything to add to the ship last night, I went for a walk on the beach. With everything going on, I have not really had time to shift, so I thought I would try. It was effortless and exhilarating! I actually flew to the top of the castle and stayed in bird form for a while. That is, until I got uncomfortable. That was when I knew what I wanted to add to the ship."

I smile and hug her again. "Oh, Aspen, that is wonderful! I am so happy for you!" I really am happy for Aspen, but seeing her completely healed also gives me hope for Apuri. I glance over to see him sitting at the table with his head in his hands. He still does not feel well. I take a deep breath and turn back to the ship to add Aspen's crow's nest. When we are finished, Mel calls for everyone to come take a look and let us know what they think.

Apuri quickly stands with the others and acts like

nothing is bothering him. They all come together and walk around the ship and up the steps we made on both sides to see the work inside the ship. Through all the gasps and ooo's and aahh's we interpret that they like what they see. Mel gives me a side hug, and while squeezing my arm, she squeals, "We did it!"

I laugh and look at her sideways as I correct, "Almost. This is not the actual ship yet."

She waves her hand and scoffs, "That will be nothing now that we have done this. Oh, she needs a name!"

"Majesty!" Noni shouts excitedly. It fits the vessel well. We laugh at her enthusiasm and Mel as the name to the side of our model.

As we stand admiring our handiwork, someone knocks on the doors. Mel quietly goes to speak to her guards. I continue watching our friends as Noni becomes the star of our miniature ship which is conveniently just the right size for her. We all laugh as she stands at the wheel and commands orders like a proper captain.

The doors open to the room and we all turn to look as Mel walks back in followed by Leslie, Dianna, Clementine, and Tilda! I stand shocked for a moment before taking off in a run to greet my friends.

"What are you doing here?" I shout as I hug Clementine then Tilda. "I thought only Leslie and Dianna were coming."

Clementine gives Tilda a sideways glance before answering, "We did not really plan to, Sweetie. It is just…" Tilda finishes the sentence, "At the last minute things kept getting worse and worse. We figured 'All hands on deck' or we are all doomed for sure."

"But what about Indri and Idona?" I glance around to be sure they did not come in behind the others unseen.

"They are staying safe at home," she places her cool hand on my forearm and continues, "Althea, things are getting worse up there. The glamour has been forced back into the Painted Forest by great lengths. The humans have figured out something is not right. Though, I doubt they are admitting the truth to themselves or others. They have all started locking themselves in their rooms and not coming out. Everything in Reverie is... tense," she finishes with a raised eyebrow.

"Come on," Mel leads Tilda by the arm, "look what we are working on. You are going to love it!"

We all walk back over to the small scale pirate ship sculpted of sand. Noni is still parading to and fro giving orders as she sees fit. We all share a laugh at the sight.

"It is much too small for anyone to actually ride on, I would think." Leslie looks at the vessel suspiciously.

I laugh then explain, "This is just a model. We have not altered the actual ship yet. We can go ahead and do that now." Mel nods in agreement, and we all work our way through the doors and toward the back of the castle with our drawings.

As we walk out of the castle and onto the beach where the ancient pirate ship rests, I hear a chorus of gasps. Even I cannot keep myself from looking at the vessel in awe and wonder. She truly is a gift!

Everyone walks around the ship a few times before meeting back as a group to figure out our game plan.

Clementine and I work on restoring the wooden hull of the ship while Tilda and Queen Melanomie create new ropes from vines of seaweed. Clementine suggests that we use yellow cedar for our wood because of its strength and resistance to rot. She tells me to just think of yellow cedar when I use my magic and it will know what to do. We each stand on either side of the bow and place our hands upon the old cracked and worn wood and let our magic flow to restore the vessel. We are also going to make sure the ship as a whole gets bigger as we replace the wood to ensure enough space for all of our travelers, especially the dragons.

My hands get warm and begin to tingle. I glance at my mark and make a conscious effort to ignore the black mark itself and look to see what color surrounds it. The clouded colors swirl into greens and golden browns. The wood changes one plank at a time down the side of the hull until the whole thing looks brand new. Once the outside of the ship is finished everyone gathers around to move to the inside of the ship to begin working on the details.

Before we enter, Clementine stands at the edge of the ship alone to work her magic. She does not say what she is doing, just that she is preparing our canvas. After a few flicks and waves of her wrists and arms she pulls both hands into fists then turns around and smiles. "I think I have it all outlined for you, but if something needs to be moved, just let me know."

Now that she has piqued our curiosity, we all scramble quickly up the steps to board the ship and see what she has done. Nedra and Nanoaj fly up to sit on and observe from the bow and stern.

I am shocked to find the inside of the ship has been cleaned out. There are steps leading down to the empty shell of the ship and nothing more. Clementine has used her magic not to create something from nature, but to remove what was already made. I try to keep my jaw shut as I turn to look at her. I know my face still shows my shock at what she has done. I did not know this was possible!

Clementine just smiles at me like a woman used to surprising others with her gifts.

"Will you teach me?" I ask with awe and excitement filling my voice.

She laughs and replies, "Of course I will, Sweetie!"

"Shall we begin?" Mel calls from behind me. Clementine and I walk over to join her and the others in the middle of the ship.

Not waiting for Mel or Tilda to say anything, I take charge. "Everybody should go ahead and pick where you want your private rooms to be. We need some way to mark boundaries."

Notyal eagerly steps forward, "Oh, I have these! They work great for drawing!" He hands me a bag full of tiny white shells. They look like the ones scattered on beaches and sandbars. I pull one out and look at it between my fingers. I gently rub it on the pad of my thumb, and it leaves a thin white line.

"Okay," I say, "but I think we should make them a little bigger or it will take a while to finish." I pass some to Queen Melanomie, to Clementine, and to Tilda while keeping a handful myself. This time we do not change anything about the material we are working with, we simply expand it to make it larger.

I watch quietly as everyone scrambles about the empty ship to find their perfect spots. Aspen is walking with Lady Nell and Noni who is currently bouncing around from side to side like a little monkey. Tsar follows quietly behind them. Apuri and Not are discussing the best placement for the pool and the easiest access points for their rooms. I laugh. I feel like I am moving into college all over again. Apuri is now drawing windows onto the walls with his shell chalk.

Once it looks like everyone has chosen a room, I find a nice spot and start drawing out my room.

When all of the rooms are drawn, I follow Clementine and watch her remove the wood where windows will be placed. She starts her lesson on teaching me how to remove something created at our first window. "When creating we send the magic from inside us out to our focus spot. But when removing you have to break the material down back to its basic magic form and absorb it back into yourself. It sounds more complicated than it really is. Here, watch me. I place my hand on the surface. It is easier if the designated area is drawn out or has a clear border. With your hand on the surface, picture the material returning back to its pure form of magic. Usually this is whatever magic feels like to you. It is different for everyone, but I am sure you know what I mean." The wood under her hand begins to fade into nothingness. As I step closer, I feel heat from the area around her hand.

"Now," Clementine continues, "you just have to close the magic in your hand to return it. It feels a bit weird at first, but you will get used to it. Eventually, you will actually feel a bit of rejuvenation from returning the magic." She closes her hand in a fist and the heat disappears. Where there once was just a drawn circle is now a hole in the wall. I poke my hand through the hole like a small child and turn it to and fro with a laugh.

We move on to the next window mark where Clementine insists that I try. I control my breathing and place my hand inside the drawn circle. I clear my mind and focus on the wood. I picture it disappearing beneath my hand. Nothing happens. I resist the urge to huff in frustration. I focus on my breathing and on the wood. I calm my mind again. My hand starts to tingle and the wood beneath it warms. I feel my magic. This is it! I watch closely, but instead of the wood vanishing, it grows thicker. "Ugh!" I grumble as I throw my hands up. Clearly this is not my forte. I cannot help but think this would be easier if I were on Zoar.

Clementine simply smiles a soft smile balancing between pity and encouragement and steps forward to fix the spot herself. "You'll get the hang of it with practice, Sweetie. Don't give up." I huff a sigh in response.

While everyone else is still working on the inner details of their rooms, we continue on to the next window. I had hoped I would get the hang of it quickly to help Clementine finish the job faster. Clementine steps up to the drawn circle and clears it out in a matter of minutes. A dark feeling of jealousy bubbles inside me. I have to remind myself that Clementine was born a faerie and has been doing this her whole life. I walk over to the next window and push my hand against it. I just want the wood gone! With that angry thought flowing through my head, I release my magic. There is no tingle this time; it is just hot. Burning hot, just like the anger and jealousy inside. My stomach pulls like riding on a rollercoaster and I fall forward, my hand goes through the newly made hole. I catch myself on the wall with my other hand and stand back to look at the wall.

I catch a glimpse of my wrist as I pull it back through the

hole. The swirling colors are fading back into a rainbow cloud, but what I saw before that worries me. There were no colors; everything was black. I quickly hide the still black mark inside the swirling colors with my other hand and look around. I do not think anyone saw what happened. Clementine is already three windows down from me still working hard.

Suddenly, I feel a presence in my mind. Nedra. My cheeks burn with shame. I turn to look at my friend sitting on the bow of the ship. He does not look angry as I expected. Instead he looks worried. "Nedra, I," I begin through our private link, but I do not know what to say, so I stop. I turn away from him and find something else to keep me busy. Leslie and Dianna are now growing thin crystals in the window spaces behind Clementine. They ask if I want to join them, but I have had enough of windows, so I walk back to my room area instead and begin growing walls and a door from the hull of the ship. We are going to make an upper deck so we are just leaving the ceilings off of the rooms for now. I go ahead and grow myself a bed, a side table, and a small dresser while I am at it.

The work is actually therapeutic, much like cleaning. My mind and my heart grow clearer as I move from one wall to the next. Still, I feel Nedra's watchful presence in my mind. Neither of us mention anything about what happened, though.

I go ahead and start making walls for the other rooms after I finish my own. I see that Clementine and the sky faeries are nearly done with the right side of the ship's windows. They will be moving on to the left side soon. I have decided if anyone wants windows in their doors, I will just grow them that way to begin with. Mel and Tilda are making mattresses from various mosses now while Notyal is putting something bioluminescent inside each room after I make the walls. Everyone else is helping move the mattresses into the rooms when they are finished.

I finish all of the rooms' walls and sit down in the now long hallway between them all. I did not realize how tired I have become until now. Apuri walks out of one of the rooms and sits down beside me. "You look as tired as I feel," he says. "Maybe it is time we call it a day."

The others find their way over to join us and we all agree that it is time for a lunch break. Even poor Noni is dragging as she exits the ship. Tsar carries her the rest of the way into the castle. After lunch we all decide to retire for a nap before working on the ship again. Queen Melanomie assures us it will not take as long to finish the upper deck.

I feel refreshed after my nap. Like all of my worries just melted away with sleep. Unfortunately, the same cannot be said for Apuri. He has another migraine. Aspen has left some herbs to help ease his pain. Nedra assures me he will keep a watch on him while we go back to work on the ship.

Mel was right; it does not take near as long to build the upper deck. We start with making the floor all the way across the ship. Queen Melanomie covered the floors in pearl and marble using her magic as was her wish. We also have a viewing deck at the bow and a large room at the stern for eating and meetings.

Next we begin to grow the masts, pool, playground, and Aspen's crow's nest. Instead of a simple pole with a bucket on top, we create a tall sequoia tree. The limbs at the top weave together to create the basket or nest.

We let Noni design the entire playground, complete with a slide that goes into the pool. Notyal seemed pretty excited about this as well. Tsar has been marking places he wants a variety of plants grown. Clementine says she will surprise him with some of her favorites.

The Mer, unlike water faeries, are able to create furs and skins of water animals such as polar bears and seals just like the animal faeries are able to create fur for clothes and blankets inside Inon. Queen Melanomie said she will provide all of the sails, pillows, and blankets when we are finished using these furs. I do not think I will ever tire of learning about all of the wonders of Reverie.

We finally finish all of the details on the *Majesty* and head back inside to work on the details of our journey to find Zoar.

Nedra informs me that Apuri is still sleeping. He woke and chewed the pain reliever as instructed by Nedra then went back to sleep. Aspen delivers him a tea to drink when he wakes. She says it should help dull the pain and energize him. We want him to be awake when it is time to board the ship and leave.

The rest of us meet in Queen Melanomie's throne room. Mel quickly starts the meeting. "We have successfully finished the *Majesty* thanks to great teamwork. I am really proud of you all. However, we still have a few items on our list to check off before we can set sail. First, there is the matter of food."

"We have that taken care of!" says Leslie excitedly. "We stopped by Sengsourya on the way here and gathered all of the cloud food that was ready for harvesting."

"We have bags in our room," finished Dianna.

Mel's shoulders visibly relax with the news. She must have been worried about having to bring enough food for everyone, especially not knowing exactly how long we will be traveling with the possibility of food spoiling. Noni's face lights up at the mention of cloud food. Lady Nell gives her a stern look that says she is not filling up on desserts.

"Now," Mel continues, "Althea and I will make a compass to guide us to the island. I think the only other matter to discuss is actually getting the ship topside. I already have that one planned, but I would like to share it with you before we actually leave. We are going to encompass the *Majesty* in a sort of air bubble and let it float at a steady pace to the surface of the sea. Once we reach the top, we will use the compass to reach our destination. From there on, Althea will be in charge." She nods to me in acknowledgement. I return the nod.

"Althea," Nedra contacts me through our private link, "Apuri is awake and has drank the tea Aspen left for him. He is on his way to the throne room now."

"Great!" I reply through our link. "The sooner we can leave the better!"

I inform everyone else that Apuri will be here shortly. We decide to wait for him before having our last non cloud food meal. After we eat, Queen Melanomie will bid her subjects a temporary farewell and then we will board the ship to Zoar.

Chapter Twenty-Eight ~ The Dream Within a Dream

We are sailing smoothly on the quiet sea. The sky faeries and I have used some wind magic to keep the sails pushed to the max. We waste no time getting to Zoar.

Nedra and Nanoaj are enjoying the sky again, though they were warned not to fly too high. Leslie and Dianna did not want to talk about it much, but it was clear that Sengsourya is now completely off limits for everyone. Something about the wild creatures. I remember the birds we fought from the tower in Sengsourya. I wish we could have stayed to help protect everyone there. But the only way to put a stop to wild magic and all of its effects on the world is to reach this island.

"Please help me know what to do when we get there," I whisper. I think again of my dream about the Creator in the beginning. I have heard of God my whole life growing up, but He was always someone I did not understand. This all powerful being in the sky just wants everyone to worship him or face his wrath. Why even give us "free will" to begin if it is not really free. That is like telling a child, "You are free to make your own choice in this situation, but if you do not make the choice I want you to make, you will be punished."

That did not feel like the God I saw in my dream. He was happy and loving. I just feel like there is more to the story that is not being said.

"Althea!" I am shaken from my thoughts by the shout of my name. I look up to see Tilda, Clementine, and Queen Melanomie staring at me. I immediately blush with embarrassment. "Sorry," I explain, "I was just…"

"Daydreaming?" Clementine finishes with a laugh.

"How's it working?" Mel asks, looking down at the compass we created from the chobudda scale.

I look down. I almost forgot I was holding it. We fashioned a typical compass to encase the magical scale. When we are headed toward Zoar, the compass gets really warm and tingles in my hands as well as emitting a magical glow. If we veer off course, it cools down, and becomes dull inside its casing. "We are still on course," I say as I hand the compass over to her. "I just wish it could also tell us how far away we are. I hate not knowing."

Tilda chuckles, "If I were you, I would pick something else to hate. 'Not knowing' is something that will happen all your life."

I give her a snide smirk in reply and walk toward Not and Apuri's lounging area by the pool. Noni is currently playing hide and seek with Not on her playground. She loves the challenge of finding him while he is camouflaged into his background. He usually gives himself away by laughing, though. I smile as I take a seat and watch the young girl search high and low.

Apuri swims up to the edge of the pool beside me. He looks better than he has the entire time since I lost control of my powers. I subconsciously cover my mark as he begins talking.

"Everything okay?" he asks.

"Yeah," I answer, "we are still on course, and the skies

look clear. Hopefully we keep this up and make it to Zoar within a few days tops."

"That is not what I meant," he says with a look that pierces through to my core.

I do not know how to respond, so I stay quiet. Apuri glances over to Tsar and Lady Nell. They stand at the side of the ship, watching the water for any sea life that may surface. I follow his gaze and watch the couple embrace each other as if they do not have a care in the world. He points toward the horizon and whispers something in her ear that makes her laugh.

Apuri pulls himself out of the pool and sits on the edge with one foot still dangling in the water. He leans close to my chair, looking at me the whole time. My cheeks begin to warm and I find it hard to swallow. "I think it is time we finish our conversation. Don't you?" he asks in barely a whisper.

Caught off guard, I am speechless. I look around the ship for fear someone is watching. I am not sure why that thought scares me, but I relax when I do not see anyone looking this way.

"Would you like to go somewhere else?" Apuri asks with fear written all over his face. He probably thinks I am saying no, or that I do not know what he is talking about. Of course, I know. Our conversation at Pilate's home before Apuri traveled through one of Sage's mirrors has been piercing my heart since it happened. He made it clear that we were just friends when I thought a real relationship was blooming.

Now, out of the blue, he has one good day after I hurt him, and he wants to go back to that conversation! I do not know what else to do, so I nod and get up from my seat. I start walking to the door that leads to our rooms below deck. I do not even look back to see if he follows. If he does not, I think the privacy of my room will do me some good right now.

I make my way down the stairs and into the hall of doors. I turn and head to the bow where my room is located. I figured it would be best to be as close to the front as possible so I would feel the island as we approached. As I walk down the hall, I hear footsteps behind me. He did follow. The lump returns to my throat. My heart begins to pound in my ears. I walk a little faster as I approach the end of the hall and the door to my room.

I open the door and walk inside. I leave the door ajar and stop in the middle of the room. I try to filter my thoughts, come up with something to say when he walks in, but my brain does not cooperate. I hear his steps and the door shut behind him. I turn around to look at him, to make sure he is serious.

He reaches for my hands; I let him hold them in his, but I still do not say anything. He wants to talk, so I will let him begin. I will listen and respond when he is finished.

"Althea," he begins in a calm tone, "I am sorry. I know that what I said back at Pilate's hurt you, and I should not have left that way. I was being selfish. I did not want to leave you to begin with." I let out a scoff which he ignores as he continues speaking. "But I knew it would be that much harder if I admitted how I felt about you. I had a duty to my family. If I told you the truth, if I told you how much I really care about you, I would have forsaken that duty and my people." He pauses, waiting for a response, but I know he is not finished, so I stay quiet.

He rubs his hand on top of his head and goes on, "When I saw you again in the Painted Forest, I wanted to say something, but it felt too soon. I did not want to mess up the flow we had together making that feast. To be honest, I am not sure when I actually planned to say anything to you. I guess I hoped you would just realize it and say something first." He raises an eyebrow as he smirks at me. I return the gesture and continue to wait silently.

He sighs before starting again, "No, that is not your style, is it?" he says with a laugh. "And then when we got to Ceres and you heard about Wild Magic and lost control of yourself, I thought you were going to die. I had to do something to save you, but I didn't know what. Thankfully, you were okay; well, as okay as you could be, I guess. Unfortunately, I seemed to have picked up a bit of the bad end of that wild magic. I am not blaming you, so don't think I am. And don't you go blaming yourself, either." He sighs again and squeezes my hands. "The point I am trying to make here is that I have had some time to think. And, I have already talked to Nedra. So, Althea Bruadar, will you officially be my partner?"

It takes me a minute to catch my thoughts. I am actually more surprised by the fact that he talked to Nedra than I am about the whole situation. Though, I guess Nedra has been the one watching over him lately. "Ahem," he coughs to bring me out of my thoughts.

"Um," I start like a nervous fool, "I... uh, yes. Yes! Apuri, I would love to be in an official relationship with you. I am glad you finally came to your senses, but what if something happens," I gesture toward the front of the ship, toward the island.

He pulls me closer by my hands and shakes his head while saying, "We will cross that bridge when we get there. *If* something happens." Then he leans down and kisses me on the forehead.

I close my eyes and let myself melt against him. My whole body feels warm, like the ice wall I built around my heart has melted for good. "Thank you, Nedra," I whisper through our link. I can hear him hum in reply.

As we turn to walk out of the room, I get the feeling this is all too good to be true. Our last adventure ended with me dying. What if that happens again? I look at Apuri. I take a calming breath and decide I have to make sure that does not happen.

To quickly change the subject of my thoughts, I blurt out the first thing I think of to Apuri. "Do you believe in God?" I quickly look down after asking. This is not a subject Apuri and I have talked about before, and I do not want it to be awkward.

"You mean, do I believe in a supreme being, an ultimate power, that created the universe and everything in it? Yeah.

How can you not?" It is not an accusation, but I feel the question touch something in me personally. He does have a point. After everything I have seen and done, why is it so hard for me to believe there is a God?

As I ponder on our way to the upper deck, I realize it is not that I do not believe in God. I do not doubt that someone made this world and started life on it. I do not believe we are all here by mere coincidence. No, it is not that I do not believe in God, it is that I do not know God. A small spark in my mind says, "That is it!" as if I opened a small door that has been locked for so long I forgot about it. I push the thought back to meditate on it more later.

As we climb the steps hand in hand, Apuri asks, "So, are you ready to announce the good news?" I squeeze his hand and let out a breath with a smile, "Why not?" We both laugh and emerge onto the upper deck. When we walk out, nobody really pays attention to us, so I wonder if we should just tell them later as we talk to them. Apuri has different plans. He whistles loudly, bringing everyone's attention to use, and then raises our held hands into the air triumphantly. I laugh and lower my face embarrassed.

Tsar and Lady Nell cheer and clap. Tilda, Clementine, and Mel laugh and congratulate us. Aspen flies down from her crow's nest to give us a hug and congratulations. Notyal and Noni come to give hugs as well, though I think Noni is just joining in the fun because everyone else is. Leslie and Dianna smile and congratulate us from their lounge chairs.

"Well, it is about time," Nell says with a wink as she and Tsar walk over to us. I laugh and hug her. "I am happy for you," she whispers in my ear. "Thank you," I whisper back as we both get an extra squeeze in our hug before letting go.

We all meet in the room at the back of the ship to eat lunch. Queen Melanomie and Notyal did go ahead and bring some already prepared food from the castle. "Just enough for the first meal, at least," Mel said. We waited to eat anything when we first got on the ocean to make sure nobody got sick. Thankfully, everyone seems to be doing okay. Though, I suspect Aspen may be having a little sea sickness. The only time she has come out of bird form is to eat and to congratulate Apuri and me. She has spent the rest of the time sitting in her crow's nest. It is nice to sit down and enjoy a meal together in the pleasant room. It is more personal than Mel's castle halls, but with an elegance we did not have in Inon or Velmae's house.

We spend the next few hours relaxing on the ship, enjoying a little peace and calm. I take a short nap in my lounge chair, while Apuri continues to take advantage of the pool. I think perhaps we should have just made the pool his room. Clementine joins me at the lounging area. "I am definitely glad Tsar asked for these little darlings," she says as she strokes one of the red flowered plants beside her, making it bloom and grow a little more. Not, Nell, and Noni join in on the pool fun.

The four are playing some kind of water game when Apuri abruptly stops what he is doing and clenches his head between both hands. Before I can say anything, Nedra swoops down. He gently picks Apuri up out of the water while hovering over the pool so he does not hurt anyone. He lays him down beside the door leading to the lower deck. I jump out of my chair, but Tsar and Aspen beat me to him. Together they carry him below deck and into his room.

Apuri and Notyal chose the two rooms closest to the door so they could be the first ones into the pool, but Apuri's choice of room location was beneficial for this emergency as well.

I sit on the floor of the hall with my head leaned back against the outside of Apuri's wall while Aspen assesses how bad it is. She ends up using a substance made of one of the mushrooms we collected back in the Painted Forest to help him fall asleep faster. She covers the windows and shuts the door to ensure no light will bother his sleep. "He will be alright," she says before climbing the steps. Her expression says she does not quite believe the words she speaks.

I sit alone in the quiet dark hallway for a while. Again, I find myself praying. I whisper under my breath, "If you are really out there and you are good, please help him. I did not mean to hurt him. He does not deserve to suffer like this."

I stay in the hall outside Apuri's room until everyone else comes down the steps and informs me that it is getting dark outside and we should all get some rest. I reluctantly retire to my own room. Nedra assures me he will keep watch over Apuri.

I lie still in my bed listening for the faintest of sounds that something might happen. Either Apuri gets better or worse, or we run into something at sea. I hold the compass in my hand so I will know if the ship changes direction.

I stare out my cabin window until sleep slowly takes me.

* * * * * * * * * *

I find myself standing alone inside the Domain. It is eerily quiet.

"Hello!" I call out. My voice echoes into the space until it is swallowed by the clouds leaving me in silence again.

This is strange. The spirits usually do not bring me here and then not say anything.

I try to wake up, but I cannot. I panic at first and run in one direction and then another looking for some way out.

I am trapped.

With nothing else to do, I sit down upon the clouded floor and wait, for what I am not sure.

If the spirits did not bring me here, who did?

I look around with no answer.

I sit like this until even my breath and pulse are quiet. I doubt you could even hear a pin drop.

Back home, this kind of silence would drive me insane, but right now, it is actually kind of calming.

Who brought me here? I wonder again as I lean back against one of the clouds.

"You did!" something whispers. Or at least I think it was a whisper. It actually felt more like it was coming from within my mind. Like it was a thought, but it was not mine.

"Who's there?" I ask as I sit up cautiously.

I can hear my pulse and my breathing again, but no strange voices.

I pull my knees to my chest and wrap my arms around them to stay more alert.

It does not help. I find myself drifting off again into the peaceful, comforting silence around me. I rest my head upon my knees and give in to blissful peace.

"Hello, Althea." A deep, smooth, and comforting voice wakes me. I look up to an ever changing surrounding. I feel like I am in a room surrounded by ever changing projections. The Domain becomes the ship which in turn changes into the Painted Forest. A blur of green and I am at my abandoned apartment. I turn around to see my college campus. Faster and faster the images change around me until only light remains.

I feel like I just watched my life flash before my eyes again. But this time it was different than in Neoinas. There, it was like torture. I did not want to watch anything again. Here, one scene disappeared before I could barely recognize it.

I bring my hand up to shield my eyes from the brightness. I try to look around, but see nothing.

Is this like a dream within a dream?

"Why am I here?" I shout in a panic.

"Because you want to be," the smooth voice replies. My panic immediately disappears. A smile forms on my face. I could listen to that voice forever. It is comforting in a paternal way.

"You asked to come here," the voice answers my unasked question. "Not aloud, but in your heart. You have been searching for a long time, Althea. Now, ask me what you will."

"I..." I find myself at a loss for words. Is this really who I

think it is?

"Yes, Althea. I am real. And I am here to answer your questions."

"Does this mean I am dead?"

"No," He laughs and the image of milk and honey fills my mind. I smile again.

"Am I going to die?" I ask, afraid of the answer.

"Yes," He says, "eventually. But everyone must die. It is the natural cycle, the order of things, if you will. I am sorry, I cannot say when."

I let out a held breath.

"Can anyone meet you like this or is it just because I am a Dreamer?"

"Anyone who seeks Me, will find me. Your gift, however, allows you to do more than some," he replies. "Gifts are good in that way. They are as unique as their owners."

"I do not think mine is very good anymore." I say and look down at the black mark on my wrist.

The voice chuckles, and I find it comfortingly similar to Nedra's. "Gifts are how we use them, my dear. Take a look at your friends: Tilda and Melanomie could use their gifts to drown and destroy endlessly. Do they? Nell could beguile and cause terror to spread like wildfire. Does she? Nedra could conquer and rule over man and faerie alike. Why is it, do you think, none of your friends have bad gifts?"

I smile thinking of my friends, "They are good. They do not hesitate to help, even if they put themselves in danger. It is their hearts, not their gifts, that make a difference."

I can feel the smile in the warm light around me as the voice replies, "And you think yourself different from your friends? You think your soul is dark, tarnished beyond saving?"

"I lost control. I hurt someone very close to me. He suffers daily and it is all my fault!"

The voice replies gently, "Did you lash out at Apuri directly with your magic intending to cause him pain?"

"No," I reply defensively as I wipe the tears from my face.

"You see, my dear, you are good. Why else would you be risking yourself to save the world?"

Zoar! *"Will you help me?"* I ask, but I feel the warmth subsiding. Before I can say anything else, I wake up in the Domain. It is still quiet.

"Just ask." The thought enters my mind, but it is not my own. I smile knowing He just answered me. Before I can do or say anything else, I wake up.

* * * * * * * * * *

I wake up and look around my front cabin on the ship. I sigh at the warm feeling inside me. I feel like I cannot smile big enough to show how happy my heart is. I feel a warm tingling in the nape of my neck too. I roll over and stand up out of my bed. Something clanks to the floor.

I look down to see the compass, brighter than ever, sitting by my feet. I lean down to pick it up and almost drop it because of the heat it emits.

Then it all clicks in my mind, we are almost there!

I rush out the door, down the hall, and up the stairs to the upper deck! I run to the bow and look across the horizon. My heart pounds inside my chest as my eyes behold a small island in the distance surrounded by a pink glow.

Zoar! I set the compass down and take a step back. Am I ready for this?

A blur of color flashes in my peripheral vision and I follow quickly to find Aspen flying out to sea ahead of the ship toward the island.

What is she doing? What if it is not safe? I turn quickly to examine the deck of the ship and see who is around. To my surprise, everyone is walking toward the bow of the ship as if enchanted under a spell. Even Apuri is up here.

"Are you guys okay?" I ask, but nobody responds. "What is going on?" I wave my arms in front of them, but they act like they do not see or hear me. I turn around to check on Aspen. She is halfway between us and the island now. There is no way she will hear me.

Everyone on deck begins pushing past me to get closer to the island. I have to do something or they are going to go overboard! As quickly as I can, I use my magic to extend one of the braided ropes made from seaweed and vines to wrap around everyone. That does not last long, though. They begin fighting against the rope. Clementine passes her hand over it and it quickly disappears.

Not sure what else to do, I shout, "Nedra!" I do not know if he is under the island's spell as well, but I hope with all I have that he is not. I feel a flood of relief at his voice through our link, "We are on our way down, Althea."

Sure enough, I look up to see two spots descending toward our ship. "Please hurry," I mutter under my breath. I am still not sure how we are going to wake everyone up, but I feel better with the dragons helping me. I am very grateful they are not bewitched. Nedra lands with a loud *thump* right in front of the crowd of our friends while Nanoaj flies out to sea after Aspen.

Nedra turns sideways to use his tail and full body to hold everyone back. I squeeze on the other side of him to watch Nanoaj. I catch my breath as she closes in on Aspen and grabs her with one clawed food. She immediately turns back toward the ship. I turn back to Nedra and say, "Why are they acting this way? And how do we stop it?"

He replies, "It is the magic from the island, Althea. It is too strong for them. I am not sure how to stop it, but we have to get them somewhere safe or they will kill themselves trying to get to it." He pushes against them and barely knocks them back a step.

"What if we lock them below deck?" I ask frantically as Nanoaj lands with Aspen still in her grasp. The icy blue dragon looks straight at me and nods.

"How will we get them to go downstairs?" Nedra asks,

struggling against them. The faeries and mer have started using their powers against him and he is barely holding up. I quickly glance at Tsar and pray he does not decide to use his powers against Nedra.

I look around the ship for anything to help us save our friends and ourselves when my gaze lands on Noni's playground. The slide! I use my magic to lift the slide from the playground and position it in the doorway to the lower deck. I push it as far down the steps as I can get it so nobody gets hurt. Even little Noni is fighting to get to the island.

"Okay you two," I shout to the dragons, "get them over here and we will at least be able to get them below deck. Then, we can seal the door shut. We will have to be quick about it though."

Nanoaj hovers over Nedra until he pushes everyone back enough for her to get behind him, still carefully holding a struggling and screeching Aspen in her claw. Together, they are able to herd them over to the slide where I am able to grab them one by one and put them on the slide. I cannot help but feel bad every time I push one of them down the slide. I do not want to hurt them, but I know this is the only way to ensure their safety.

We get the whole mob down the slide and Nanoaj quickly releases Aspen into the doorway. As soon as Nanoaj's out of the way, we slam the door shut and I seal it off with pearl and marble like Mel's floors. The two should be pretty impenetrable. Still, I need to find a way to prevent my friends from using their magic to escape. Nanoaj flies around the outside of the ship covering all of the windows in a thick layer of magical ice that nobody but she will be able to remove.

The dragons and I head back to the bow of the ship to figure something out when a strong wind comes out of nowhere and pushes us faster and faster toward Zoar. The increased speeds cause me to stumble back against the railing at the back of our viewing deck. Nedra and Nanoaj catch their footing as the boat bounces over the waves and the wind blows so hard in our faces we can hardly breathe.

We ride like this until we can see the island in full detail. The strong wind dies away and the ship comes to an abrupt stop throwing me against the front railing this time. I stand up and gasp at the beauty of the island sitting now only a few miles away. It is just like it was in my dreams, but somehow, it is... more! I am not sure how else to describe it.

A scream from below deck pulls my attention from the island. I quickly run to where the door is encased beneath the marble. "What is wrong? Is everyone okay?" I shout. I am scared to open the door and get flogged by them again, but I am worried about what is happening.

"Althea? Is that you?" Lady Nell calls out.

"Yes, Nell, it is me. What is going on? Are you okay?"

"I am not sure," she replies. "Our magic. Althea, nobody's magic is working. And why are we trapped down here? What are you doing?"

I turn to look at the island. Maybe normal magic will not work too close to it. That would mean they cannot overpower the dragons if I let them out.

"I think you are right, Althea," Nedra agrees. "I believe only wild magic and that akin works here. That seems to be why the three of us were the only ones unaffected by the spell further away."

I remove the block over the door and let them out.

"I am sorry we had to trap you guys in there, but it was for your own safety," I explain to my friends as they walk up the steps. I can tell when Apuri enters the light that his migraine has returned. He closes his eyes and holds his hands over his temples.

I reach out to help him, but he cowers away as if I hurt him. I fake a smile to hide that his actions hurt me before I turn back and go talk to the faeries at the bow of the ship. Apuri walks back into the darker lower deck.

"I will make sure he is okay," Nedra whispers through our link, sensing my feelings. "Thank you," I whisper back.

"I have never seen anything like it!"

"Seen? I have never felt anything like it!"

"All that power… It gives me chills."

"It is really something isn't it?" I say as I walk up behind Tilda, Mel, and Clementine, joining their conversation.

They nod and move over to let me stand beside them.

"Why can't we use our magic?" Clementine asks, looking at her hand. She flicks her wrist like she did at her home to grow the dandelions, but nothing happens. They look at me like I have all the answers. I shrug my shoulders to show them I do not.

Nedra chimes in through our link, "Althea, our magic is not inhibited. We would not be able to communicate if it was. Look at the mark on your wrist."

I glance down to see the clouded rainbow of colors swirling around the blackened mark. To test my magic, I quickly conjure a small water bubble above the palm of my hand. I watch as the colors shift to a variety of blues and greens with undertones of browns like the shallow side of a river. He is right. Our magic works.

I look at the faeries, all of which have shocked expressions.

Suddenly, we hear Lady Nell yell from the other side of the pool, "I remember! Althea, I remember my vision!"

I glance back at Zoar before going down the steps to Lady Nell and Aspen.

"Nell, what's wrong?"

"Remember the vision I had back at Ceres that didn't make sense? Well, I'm not sure why more wouldn't come, but we were just leaning over looking at the water and it was there, clear as day. I saw…" She looks at Aspen who looks away.

"You should gather everyone over," Lady Nell says, and we wave them over as we walk to the lounging area.

Nedra asks Apuri if he is able to come up. He is still not well enough to join us, so Lady Nell goes on without him.

"Althea," she begins with a shaky voice, "you only have

a slim chance of success. If any of us leave this ship, the island will not accept us, you have to go alone. I am sorry. But that is not all. I can't tell you anything else or it may interfere. We cannot risk that. Wild magic has progressed significantly out there." She looks up and over across the sea as if she can see Wild Magic destroying the land on the other side. "You have to hurry," she finishes looking at me with dread in her eyes.

I let out a slow, deep breath then rub the palms of my hands on my thighs and stand up. "Well, no time like the present!" I say with as much excitement as I can muster given the circumstances.

Nedra comes over and lies down on the floor so I can climb up onto his shoulders. "Thank you, my friend," I whisper through our link as I throw my leg over to the other side.

Aspen looks at me with concern, "Althea, are you sure? Do you even know what you are going to do?"

Nedra pushes off from the ship into the sky. I shout down for everyone to hear, "Ask for help!" remembering my dream. They all look at me confused. I simply smile back and urge Nedra on.

"Do you really think it will be that simple, Althea?" Nedra asks through our link as we fly toward the island. "The Creator has not had a personal conversation with anyone in a very long time. Well before the war at least."

"I have faith, Nedra. If you will, fly me to the top of that cliff. It seems to be the clearest high point on the island." I point to the cliff that tops the cave Louveri visited in her dreams to Zoar.

As we fly toward the cliff I glance down at the different parts of the island: the pink sandy beach lined with the tall golden grass, the orchard, my avocado tree flourishing in the middle, the taller, thicker trees on the other side of the orchard that mark the wooded slope of the mountain.

I feel the magic rippling from the island. Every inch of my body hums with its energy. This island may not have been created for me like I first thought, but we are definitely made of the same magic.

Nedra lands gracefully at the cliff top and crouches down for me to slide off. As soon as my feet touch the grass-carpeted ground, I feel a rush of magic. It is similar to when you stand up too fast and the room spins, only I think my insides are the only thing spinning right now.

I turn and stroke Nedra's mane and pat his smooth ivory scales. "Nedra, I need you to do me a favor. I need you to go back to the ship and help watch over the others."

A growl escapes his throat, revealing he is not happy with this decision. "I will not leave you again, Althea. I made that mistake once with the Pyramid, and look what happened!"

"This is something I need to do on my own, my friend. Besides, you heard Nell's vision. They are all worried sick back there, and they could use you to help them feel safe. I will be okay, I promise." I rest my forehead against his and stroke his mane. "Besides, we still have our link. If anything happens, you can come get me."

He huffs then lets out that chortle of a laugh I love so much. "I should have known you would be so stubborn. Perhaps that is why I was drawn to you in the cave that day." He nuzzles my cheek and says, "Be careful dear one."

He stands up and takes a couple of steps back before pushing himself up into the air. I wave at him as he turns and flies back to the ship. Once he is out of sight, I walk to the tip of the cliff's edge. I take a deep breath and try to calm the nervous butterflies in my stomach.

Chapter Twenty-Nine ~ Help from a Friend

"Okay, God, now what?" I call out to the sky. Nothing happens. I pace back and forth for a few minutes before yelling, "Help me!"

"Sit down," a calm, quiet voice whispers in my mind. It stops me in my tracks and I do as it said. I sit at the tip of the cliff, cross my legs and rest my hands on my knees. Before I can say anything else, the voice tells me to close my eyes and place my hands upon the earth beside me.

I do as I am told and feel the rush of magic run through my veins, up my arms and into the rest of my body.

"Now, create!" The voice says with a rush as the wind swirls around me. I calm my mind and let the magic flow through me and back into the island.

After several minutes I open my eyes to see the cliff has expanded several feet in front of me, and it is still going. I am doing it! I am creating a bridge from Zoar to the mainland!

Only, it is not just me; it is like my hands are a tool but there is a stronger force at work. I look up and smile. "Thanks for your help!" I shout with joy as the magic continues to flow.

As the land bridge grows, I feel the energy from each part of it personally. Every rock, the dark soil, the thick grass, each one builds on top of the other and becomes a living extension of the island itself.

I close my eyes again, and while I let the magic flow into the bridge I remember being in His presence. The warmth, the light, but most importantly the love that shone all around me. I let all that energy fill me from the inside out as I continue building the bridge.

As I drift into a state of meditation it dawns on me that God has been right in front of us the whole time. The magic of nature alone, not to mention everything within Reverie, is a reflection of the magic I felt when I was with Him. When the hegira left the sodocs and chose love over hate and revenge, they received their powers. Love is the direct correlation to magic. Even the faeries saw an increase in magic when they joined together after the sodocs' invasion into Reverie and did away with the segregation between their different elements.

The creation of the first Dreamer was also an example of love. The little faerie girl and the elf both sacrificed who they were to become the Dreamer for a chance to save everyone else.

Something is different! I open my eyes but see nothing has changed. I can feel it, though. It is wild magic. I must have reached the mainland. Fear overtakes me and I withdraw my hands. What if the wild creatures attack me when they get here? I will not be able to simply wake up.

"You could use your magic to fight them," Nedra says, startling me from my thoughts. I place my hand over my racing heart. "You have been practicing," he finishes.

"I know I have," I answer, "but I still do not think I would be able to take them all on at the same time."

"I understand your fear, Althea. But you cannot give up now. Ask the Creator if He can help you."

"I know, Nedra. Thank you for the help. I will ask."

It takes me a minute to calm down again. I fight back tears brought on by my fear and swallow the lump in my throat. I place my hands back on the ground and pray for help again. I feel a small warm sensation deep within. I relax a little and allow the magic to flow again through my hands and into the ground below. I wish I could just leave when the bridge was finished, but I must remove it when all the creatures are here or they will simply cross back over.

"Have faith, child." The thought forms in my mind, but it is not my own. I smile and feel the tears from earlier roll down my cheeks, not from fear this time, but from love and joy at the knowledge that He is still with me. I let that love spread within and replace the fear.

With calm steady breaths I finish the bridge and trust God to keep me safe as the creatures begin to cross. My whole body begins to tingle as the creatures get close to the island. I close my eyes and begin to mutter things to distract me from the creatures' crossing. "It will be okay. You said, have faith. I am sure they will just come onto the island and make themselves at home." I hear them right in front of me now, but resist the urge to look at them. "Maybe if I do not look at them, they will not realize I am here." The thought feels ridiculous as soon as I think it, but I still keep my eyes closed. I feel something brush past my left side, then my right. Again, and again the creatures walk past me without any problems.

I feel a hot wind in my face and force my eyes open. I bite my tongue quickly to keep from screaming. A land shark is right in front of me, sniffing all around. What if this is the one that attacked me in my dream? Maybe he recognizes my scent and has come back for more. My heart races and my hands begin to shake. "Okay, God," I say in my mind, "what now?"

I expect to hear a thought that is not my own, but nothing comes. Instead, the small warm sensation inside reminds me of my revelation of love. Hmm. Could it really be that simple?

How do I show love to something like a land shark? Okay, think, Althea, think! It is an animal so I could make it some food. No, land sharks probably only eat meat. What else?

I close my eyes and picture some of my moments with Nedra. He is an animal I love. I love talking to him, hugging him, and rubbing my hand down his neck and mane.

I open my eyes and look at the land shark. I carefully raise one hand and gently rest it on the land shark's forehead. Out of the corner of my eye I see the colors swirl around the mark on my other hand. I do not turn away from the land shark to see what colors are visible, but I know I am using the same magic an animal faerie would.

The land shark pushes against my hand, and I resist the urge to pull away. "Love, no fear," I whisper, and the land shark lies down right in front of me with his head still pressed against my hand. Slowly, I move my hand down an inch then place it back where it was. The land shark's hot breath repeatedly blows on my chest. I pet his head again and again until I no longer think about the motion, the rhythm matching his breath.

He rests his head in my lap. "Nedra!" I call through our private link, "I am petting a land shark! Me! And a land shark! I wonder if he has a name."

Nedra laughs his deep chortle and replies, "So I am told. Maybe you should give him a name."

Hmm. How about Paul? Yeah, I like the sound of that! There was once a bully at my school named Paul. Halfway through freshman year he had a sudden change of heart and became the nicest guy and friend to everyone. "Paul," I say calmly to the land shark. "I think that fits you well."

I look up and realize there are no more creatures crossing the bridge. They are all here! I stop petting Paul, and he lets out a low growl. So, I replace my hand and twist my legs to turn around and look at the island behind me now crawling with wild creatures of all shapes and sizes. They are settling in.

I look back at Paul and say, "How about we go find you a new home, Paul?" He raises his head to look at me. I take that as an affirmation and stand up. Paul stands up behind me. We may have added love to our relationship, but he still looks creepy.

I turn to examine where would be the best habitat for a land shark. I look at the pink and black beaches on either side of the cliff, but they just don't seem right. Paul makes a sound so I turn to look at him. He sniffs the air in the direction of the pink beach. He slowly begins walking that way and I follow behind.

As our terrain becomes rocky, I realize where he is headed – the ocean caves under the cliff. Louveri had mentioned them before. Why did I not think of that? It seems obvious now that I have realized it, sharks live in the ocean and wolves like caves. Oh well, Paul has found his home and that is all that matters. I follow him to the mouth of the cave where he turns around. He looks at me for a long moment as if to say goodbye, then he slinks off into the cave.

"Nedra," I whisper through our link, "I am ready."

He does not reply, but I know he is on his way to get me. I return to the cliff top to get rid of the bridge and meet Nedra. A few wild trees have already begun to grow on the way there. When I finally reach the top of the cliff, Nedra is already there waiting for me. I walk up beside him and stroke his silver mane.

"Thank you, my friend. I could not have done that without you."

"Althea, I did not do anything."

"Yes, you did. You showed me how to love."

Nedra nuzzles against my neck then steps back and looks at the land bridge. Without looking back at me he asks, "Are you sure you can do this?"

I cringe inwardly knowing he is referring to my incident on the ship. "Honestly, I do not know. But I have faith that my new friend will help if I cannot." I look up and smile, internally laughing at the fact that I just called God my friend.

I bend down on my knees and place my hands upon the ground in front of me. I do not think about my lessons from the ship. Instead, I think about what needs to be done and I give all that to God through prayer.

"Do not take away," the thought forms in my mind, "create negative space from what once was."

"Okay, but what do I do with the stuff that is already there?"

"Give it to me."

I concentrate on my magic and let it flow once more to every particle of the bridge. When I feel a good amount within my grip, I think of the empty space that was there before the bridge. Not sure what else to do, I think, "Take it, God."

I hear Nedra rumble with approval, and I know it worked. Next, I create a bigger section. Again, and again I work like this until the bridge is gone. When I am finished, Nedra sees how exhausted I am and lies down on the ground beside me so we can fly back to the ship.

As we fly away, I look at the island and all of its new inhabitants. I smile and whisper to myself, "We did it!"

Chapter Thirty ~ We did it!

I can still feel the rush of magic from Zoar. Its heated vibrations run through my veins. Even the sea spray from the observation deck at the ship's stern does not cool the fire within me.

After our return from the island, I decided to ride up here with Nedra for the rest of the voyage back to Reverie. When Nedra landed near the pool, everyone was gathered around to congratulate us. I saw it in Apuri's eyes before he even had time to approach. My magic changed on Zoar. With the help of God, it has grown. That is the only reason I was able to create the bridge for wild magic to make it to Zoar.

Unfortunately, that means it also affects Apuri more. Aspen assures me she will find a way to help him. I do not doubt her abilities. I know if she could do anything to heal his migraines, she would have already done so back in Ceres.

She said we will go see Velmae as soon as we get back to Reverie. Perhaps she will be able to help him. She did heal Aspen's wings, after all. Mel and Tilda said we should make it back to Reverie before the end of the day with them in control. Until then I will pray.

I figured Mel would return to her castle and her people

in Ceres after we finished at Zoar, but she insisted on seeing us back before taking the ship home. She also insists that the ship, as well as her kingdom, will always be welcome to us.

Our plan is to catch one of the rivers that run into Reverie and ride it all the way to meet with the advisors.

The rest of our crew has retired to the lower deck to get some rest. I could tell Aspen wanted me to rest as well, but to join them in the lower deck would be torture for Apuri. I rub my hands across my face. I am not tired; I still have energy from the magic. I am just frustrated. I hate not knowing what to do. Not being able to help. I glance down at the once again changed mark on my wrist. I think the magic on Zoar cleansed it. It is not black anymore. Only a shadow remains beneath the mark itself which has returned to white, making it appear to float above the swirling rainbow surrounding it.

"Here, Sweetie," Clementine pulls me out of my thoughts, joining me on the observation deck with a cup of tea. "I figured you could use this. Though you do not look tired, you could use a little pick-me-up. Something has your spirit troubled. Wanna talk about it?" She turns and rests her back and elbows against the sleek marble railing. Her bright green eyes look into mine with a friendly smile.

"I am not sure." I sigh as I mimic her and rest back against the railing. Its cool surface soothes the fire in my veins for a split second before it sparks back to full fury again. I look at Clementine then down at my hands. "I feel like I am going to explode with the power inside me. I want to embrace it, explore it! But..." I glance toward the lower deck door.

Clementine rests her smooth brown hand on my arm, small green leaves tickling my skin cause the hairs to stand on end. "We will figure it out, Sweetie. He will get better."

She gives my arm an encouraging squeeze, and I smile back.

Nedra nuzzles my cheek and whispers through our link, "She is right, Althea. You must not give up hope."

I stroke his strong ivory scales. "I won't, my friend. I

won't."

We are jolted at the sudden slowing of the ship. We turn to find we are approaching the wide mouth to a river veering to the left. I look back and see both Mel and Tilda with their hands raised in the air and eyes focused on the water. They are controlling the waters to move the ship!

I was too distracted by my own moping about Apuri to even realize it before. They both begin to turn their hands in counterclockwise motions. I look over the edge to see the waters churning in the same direction, turning the ship toward the wide mouth of the river.

Clementine and I grip the railing as the choppy waters cause the vessel to throw our balance.

Once we make it past the mixing of the waters, we regain our footing. I look back at the captain duo pushing the ship upstream with their magic. Leslie and Dianna come up from below and head up the steps to the helm. I ask Nedra, aloud so Clementine hears, if he can fly me back to join them at the helm. I figure if I fly there instead of walking across the ship, I will remain at an acceptable distance from Apuri to prevent worsening his migraine.

"Need any help?" I ask Mel and Tilda after Nedra drops me off and flies over to join Nanoaj for a nap in the warm sun.

"I will not turn it away," Tilda replies. "Or extra company," she adds with a smile as Clementine joins us.

"We are using the water to push the ship as the wind pushes the sails. You have actually come at a good time; we are going to be fighting against the current of the river now." Mel explains with a gleam of excitement in her eyes. She is up for the challenge.

I stand between them and raise my hands.

"Just focus on the water immediately surrounding the ship. Use it to push us as fast as you can."

"How far are we going?"

"It is still a good way, but you will know when we are there."

I do as Tilda instructed and immediately feel the connection with the water below. If I reach a little farther, I know I could feel all the life thriving within it. I pull the water toward the ship with one hand, push it forward with the other. We all lunge back a step with a force that causes us to lose footing and focus. Tilda, Mel, and Clementine look at me with wonder and shock.

"Well, I am impressed," says Mel, her bright, silver eyes blinking at me in the sun.

"Me too!" Leslie laughs.

"Residue from Zoar?" Dianna asks in a serious, inquisitive tone.

I shake my head, "No, not residue. More like a level-up."

Mel rubs her hands together and winks with amusement. "Now that we know what we are working with, shall we try again?"

I laugh as Tilda and I rejoin her with hands poised and ready.

"Brace yourselves!" Mel bellows out over the ship as a true sea captain might. "You, too," she says looking at me. "Even if we lose our footing again, if you stay steady, the ship will not stop. We will rejoin when we catch our balance."

I adjust my footing, pushing one foot slightly in front of the other. I keep my knees relaxed and ready, then nod to my companions. Again, I reconnect with the rolling waters below, but this time I tighten my grip. In the midst of the link between the water and my magic, I can sense Mel and Tilda's as well.

As one, we push the water against the ship. This time I start out more gently and build up speed as we go.

The rush of wind in my face causes my eyes to squint and water. Carefully, I pull back some of the speed of the water a bit until I am using only one hand to control it. I use my other hand to create a shield of wind around us, pushing back against the oncoming torrent. When I am certain the shield will stay, I reconnect with the water and push us faster.

It does not take long for the work to become second

nature, and the thrill of rushing upstream, of keeping up with the twists and turns of nature's whim, takes over. I have not felt anything quite like it. Even while riding on Nedra, I trust him completely to be in control and get us where we are going. There is a rush in not knowing what comes next but having to react. And using magic to do it just makes it that much better.

I have driven a boat with an outboard motor a few times back home, but it does not begin to compare to this. I am not just driving on top of the water; I am part of it. I move with it as I will it to move.

Not long after the thrill begins to turn into a soothing lull, I notice a slight change in our surroundings. The colors become brighter. The surface of the river calms and carries a brighter sparkle. The blue sky shifts to pinks and then the beautiful soothing lavender. My mind buzzes uncontrollably with the rush of magic from Reverie's waters. I release my grip on the river slowly to prevent us from falling and take a moment to just appreciate the magic.

It feels like coming home! A feeling I was not sure I would ever feel again after my sister died. A tear rolls down my cheek as my friends wrap around me with hugs from every direction. I quickly wipe it away and hug them back with a laugh. "We did it!"

Mel walks over to the side of the ship to look at the east bank. "Now we simply have to find a good spot to dock the ship that is not too far or too close to your sanctuaries. We do not want a long walk, but we also do not want the humans to spot this beauty." She runs her hand along the magnificent railing of the vessel.

Nedra and Nanoaj, awake from their nap, offer to fly up above the trees until they find the sanctuaries and report back an ideal location for us to dock.

Everyone except Apuri surfaces from the lower deck to see what is happening. Noni runs straight for the play area, dragging Not with her, while the others join us in the meeting room at the back of the ship. We update them on what is happening and whip up a quick snack until the dragons return.

"Althea! We have found the sanctuaries, but you have a more pressing matter. You need to push the ship as fast as you can. I will tell you when to stop. Then, you must deboard as quickly as you can. There is a child lost and alone." He pauses, and I can hear the panic in his breathing, "She is a human child, Althea."

And, our adventures continue...

Dear Reader

I cannot thank you enough for reading my books! I hope you have enjoyed them as much as I have enjoyed writing them. While my stories are purely fictional, the hope and love they convey is very real. It comes from the one true God. His Son, Jesus the Christ, came down from His kingdom in heaven to die as a sacrifice on the cross so we could be redeemed of our sins. Because He lives today, we each have the choice of eternal salvation. My personal prayer for you today, Dear Friend, is that you know Jesus on an intimate level, accept Him as your Savior, and live your life to honor Him in everything you do. Remember to share hope, love, and light wherever you go!

My recommended Scriptures:
John 3:16
Romans 10:13
Luke 1:37

Sincerely,

Camella Wade

About The Author

Camella Wade

Camella is an Armor-wearing, Fruit-bearing, Truth-sharing Jesus Freak! She began her author journey while in the trenches of grief and spiritual warfare, at a time when she turned away from God in anger and hurt. BUT GOD! God is so good, friends! He is always present and waiting with outstretched arms. Camella rekindled her relationship with God and rededicated her life, including her writing, to serving Him.

Reverie

Althea discovers she is the Dreamer sent to save the world and restore the balance between those living in Reverie and the non-magic realm. She discovers darkness, meets new friends, and learns more about herself than ever imagined.

Reverie

Althea's strange dreams lead her to a magical realm known as Reverie. While there she learns someone is destroying magic – which will lead to the world's end – and she may have the answers to saving it. She goes on a journey full of fantasy and self-discovery, facing challenges and learning truths that will change her life forever. With the help of her new dragon and faerie friends, will Althea find the answers she needs in time to save them all?

Zoar

Althea has saved magic and defeated the Sodocs, but her journey's not over yet. She must go back to Reverie for a new mission. With old friends and new challenges ahead, Althea will learn more about Reverie, magic, and herself than she could ever imagine.

Emeraze

Wild magic nearly destroyed the world. Althea and her friends have created a refuge inside Reverie and moved all of the wild magic creatures to the island, Zoar. As they search for a solution to clean up the devastation worldwide, new problems arise at every turn. Now, humans, fae, and hegira must learn to work together before they destroy each other. Will Althea and her friends be able to restore what wild magic destroyed while finding a balance between both magic and non-magic realms?

Books By This Author

The Painted Forest Chronicles

This spin-off series from the Reverie trilogy teaches about the armor of God in practical ways while delving into the stories of some of the most beloved supporting characters and their lives in the Painted Forest.

I'm A Creator, Too

We are all creative because we are all made in the image of THE CREATOR. Once you realize you have that common denominator, you can use it to dive deeper into your relationship with God. This interactive devotional, written by Camella and Robert Wade, helps you tap into your creativity while referencing scripture to help you build and grow your walk in the Spirit.

Ducky's Adventures

Author Camella Wade makes writing a family affair with this fun series. She illustrates these original stories told by her children using composite photography.

Made in United States
Orlando, FL
01 October 2024

52210287R00205